ON THE CLIFFS OF
FOXGLOVE MANOR

Books by Jaime Jo Wright

The House on Foster Hill

The Reckoning at Gossamer Pond

The Curse of Misty Wayfair

Echoes among the Stones

The Haunting at Bonaventure Circus

On the Cliffs of Foxglove Manor

ON THE
CLIFFS OF
FOXGLOVE
MANOR

JAIME JO WRIGHT

BETHANYHOUSE

a division of Baker Publishing Group
Minneapolis, Minnesota

Published by Bethany House Publishers
11400 Hampshire Avenue South
Bloomington, Minnesota 55438
www.bethanyhouse.com

Bethany House Publishers is a division of
Baker Publishing Group, Grand Rapids, Michigan

Printed in the United States of America

Library of Congress Cataloging-in-Publication Data
Names: Wright, Jaime Jo, author.
Title: On the cliffs of Foxglove Manor / Jaime Jo Wright.
Description: Minneapolis, Minnesota : Bethany House, [2021]
Identifiers: LCCN 2020052791 | ISBN 9780764233906 (trade paper) | ISBN
    9780764239212 (casebound) | ISBN 9781493431557 (ebook)
Subjects: GSAFD: Christian fiction.
Classification: LCC PS3623.R5388 O52 2021 | DDC 813/.6—dc23
LC record available at https://lccn.loc.gov/2020052791

Scripture quotations are from the King James Version of the Bible.

Cover design by Jennifer Parker
Cover image of woman on cliff by Magdalena Russocka / Trevillion Images

Author is represented by Books & Such Literary Agency.

21 22 23 24 25 26 27   7 6 5 4 3 2 1

CoCo,
You are the miracle that set my life in motion.
I will forever be grateful God blessed me with you.
You may be a daddy's-girl,
but you'll always be my Baby Girl.
Walk close to your Creator.
Grow in God's graciousness.
Be strong, my love, be strong.
In a world that is fierce, be a warrior.

1

ADRIA FONTAINE

FOXGLOVE MANOR
APRIL 1885

He had ruined death for her, and the hope of it. Thwarted death on all sides, until the possibility of escape was removed entirely, and she was left with breath, body, and the plaguing memories of many yesterdays. Memories she would never allow to rise to the surface again. Like a shipwreck beneath the brutal waves of the expanse of cold lake, so were the abuses she had endured. It would be a monumental task to raise them from their graves, to revive them, and to see them sail again. And who would want to? Shipwrecks were things to be forgotten. Memories were like shipwrecks.

Uncertain future loomed in the distance. The wheels of the carriage rolled over stones and rutted road. To the right lay a flat expanse that boasted brown grasses with small sprigs of spring's green, outcroppings, and, in the distance, deep blue-green fir trees. To the left, imitating the cadence of her pulsating heart, were the waves. The waves of the lake that pounded the shore, the rocky cliffs, and battered the walls of lake caves. They stretched into the distance until the waters kissed the gray skyline, void of sunlight, with a lone gull weaving its way through the winds.

Ahead loomed the cliff. High enough to boast a lighthouse, but barren of such a beacon. Instead, like a scar on a beautiful face, was a stone house. Two stories high, stick-straight long, and with a turreted tower rising highest of all. One a princess might be kept prisoner in if this were a fairy tale. Only it wasn't. It was her life. And the house was Foxglove Manor. The old estate of her father's business acquaintance. In which case, hardly even a friend—and even then, her father had insisted Mr. St. John was more of an enemy. But the two men kept up appearances for the sake of their own selfish needs, and, for the time being, that included Alexandria, who now stared at the stone manor with a solid weight in the pit of her stomach. It was all made even exponentially worse because Mr. St. John had died—leaving her father grieving only the lost secrets Mr. St. John took with him to his grave. Mr. St. John left behind his wife, who was apparently ignorant of the tenuous ties between the two men. In the end, Mr. Fontaine needed to be rid of Alexandria—among other pressing reasons—once and for all. She was a blot on their family name. On their fortune of which her father was immensely proud. No one would ever question his reasoning. His daughter had attempted the unforgivable. It was Providence she had lived, but it was shameful she had not died.

Alexandria—known by most as Adria—jostled in the carriage, gripping the edge of its worn-out padded seat with tense finger-tips. She was dressed in black from head to toe, like a widow who grieved her lover. Only Adria was unwed. She had lost only herself, and that loss she grieved monumentally.

The carriage rolled to a stop outside a waist-high stone wall. There was a patchy lawn, remarkably green for the season of early spring, with splotches of snow still harbored in the shadows, and long plates of smooth rock jutting out here and there. The rock was at war with the grass, and above it all rose the arching branches of

8

battered trees. Trees whose arms reached toward the stone house, many of which were barren of leaves and promising they would stay that way. They were dead trees. The bark worn smooth by wind and buffeted by rain and lake water. Even atop a cliff, the lake's coldness reached. Icy and unforgiving.

With the opening of the door, Adria stepped wordlessly from the carriage. The trip from the southernmost bottom of the state by train as far north as she could travel had been more comfortable. But then she had had to abide people. At least the carriage had been lonesome. She was accustomed to lonesome.

"Your bag, miss?"

Adria turned to the driver, who held out her carpetbag. Yes. Of course. He was rented, after all, and would want payment and to be off. She took her one bag from his hand, trusting he would deliver her trunk to the manor, and extended the payment in the envelope her father had rationed out.

"This is for travel only, Alexandria. You will not squander it."

It had not been a question, but a command. *You will not.*

The Ten Commandments were friendlier than those her father had bestowed on her.

Adria tilted her lips in a small smile with the vague urge of necessity. *Be off!* She would be glad to be free of the driver, but there was no rejoicing. For here, at the wall of Foxglove Manor, Adria stood on the cusp of a new prison. One of obligation that would haunt her.

She sensed him before she saw him. His form, a misty gray behind the fogged windowpanes on the upper story of the stone manor. He bore his stature like a beast of burden, weighted by the mere fact of his being alive.

Adria met brooding eyes, hooded with no hint of color—he was too far away. The waves of the lake crashed against the cliff, sending spray airborne and misting her face with a fine dusting. She wiped her cheek with the clothed fingertips of her hand. Her glove was damp when she pulled it back. Wind wove around the trunks of weathered trees that embraced the manor, their gray, scraggly branches protesting with creaks and moans.

He turned from the window and disappeared.

Adria reached out as though she could draw him back. Pull him from the prison depths of Foxglove Manor. Whoever he was. Another soul harboring at the manor for the sheer sake of obligation? Or maybe there was more. More to Foxglove Manor. To Mrs. Reginald St. John.

Tendrils of dark curls swept over her face as wind gusted again, arguing against her arrival with the vicious bite of its cold edges. Stiffening her shoulders, Adria dismissed the strange man from her mind, from her dreams. She had seen him before. Many times. In the darkness of her heart, in those moments when her mind went far away. He was there. Tall and strong. A Captain. A soldier. A hero.

Adria squeezed her eyes shut. She felt the length of her dark lashes and knew they hid her sapphire-blue eyes. Eyes that had seen many things, closed against many more, and refused to open when she discovered the places inside of herself where Adria could simply *be*. She forced them to open. Forced herself to swallow any anguish that threatened to sour in her throat. A glance at the upper-story window. Empty. Perhaps he had never actually been there. A figment of her imagination. A phantom she always wished looked after her but whose existence was very suspect.

The iron gate clanked as Adria lifted the unlocked latch. She pushed it open and stepped onto the grass that struggled to revive with April's kiss of warmth. A stone path, rugged, with uneven levels and surfaces, stretched toward the entrance of Foxglove Manor. On the bottom stone step, a splash of autumn orange mingled with the fur of a mangy fox. Her left ear was half chewed off, leaving a ragged flap of gray that lifted over the length of thin muzzle. A full tail curled around her haunches, and only the fur moved in the wind. Fur that was sparse. At Adria's approach, the fox started to its feet, eyed her with beady suspicion, then scurried into the shrubbery, its tail stretched behind it like a flag.

One at a time, Adria took the steps. There were only four, and then she reached the door with the rounded top, the iron hinges, and the massive ring that hung in its middle. A last tentative look at the lake and cliff behind her. One long sprint and she could stretch wide her arms, open them to the frigid spring wind as her body met the air. A flight over cold waters. It was a special sort of freedom, deceptive in its consequences . . .

Adria shook her head. Clearing her thoughts. She raised the door knocker, but before she clapped it down, the door opened. Heavy on its hinges. Protestations ground out, and a wrinkled face stared back at her. Knobby nose. Liver spots on the cheeks that were as whiskered and patchy as the renegade fox. His suit was too large, sagging over his shoulders, yet the old man stood with a sort of pride that one might mock. Mock because he had nothing on his person to inspire pride, and so it was empty. Empty of human purpose but thick with the need to be important.

"Miss Fontaine?" His growl was stern. No welcome. Just a tired expectation of her arrival.

She nodded.

He opened the door further, ignoring the heavy bag in her hand.

Adria cast one last desperate glance behind her. At the lake. At the gray-blue air that stretched into infinity. Foxglove Manor would be her home now. But it was not her refuge. She stepped inside, her foot coming to rest on the dull wood floor. Adria knew she was more than her father's cast-off daughter. She was also his pawn in a scheme that spanned the lakes, coming to rest here, beneath the roof of Foxglove Manor.

"Come." The growl interrupted her shaky calm.

Adria followed the old man in his saggy suit down a dark hallway. She would not close her eyes now. She would keep them wide open. She would let the day bleed away until, tonight, she could reassess her future. And maybe—somehow—she could find *him* again.

2

KAILEY GIBSON

FOXGLOVE MANOR
PRESENT DAY

No one had believed her twenty years ago. Twenty years ago when she went missing, and twenty years ago when she was returned.

Kailey Gibson.

Five years old.

Abducted May 3, 2001.

Height 3.5 feet, weight approximately 46 lbs.

Last seen walking toward Blueview Elementary. Wearing blue jeans, a silver-sequined pink T-shirt, and pink tennis shoes.

It was a missing-child poster that had never been made. She had been taken at 7:45 a.m. and returned one block away from her front yard at 3:40 p.m. A school day. Her teachers had noted her absence. Her parents had questioned her. No one believed her. She was a five-year-old little girl who frequently became lost in her own secret world built between herself and her brother, Jude. Between her imagination, Jude's autism, and her parents' own inability to function properly, Kailey's abduction went unnoticed by everyone except Jude. But Jude was a vault of secrets no one bothered to try to crack. Least of all, Kailey's parents. Kidnapped for eight hours had changed nothing for the world. Kidnapped for eight hours had changed everything for Kailey's world.

Her car rolled to a stop in the allotted parking space that was marked only by a granite boulder she had to gauge carefully to avoid ramming her front bumper into. She shifted the vehicle into park, drawing in a steadying breath, and glanced instinctively at the man beside her in the passenger seat.

Jude stared into the distance, and what others might interpret as a vacant expression, Kailey knew was one of memorization. Every nuance of the property before them was being committed to memory, compared with that memory, calculated, then filed away. She leaned over the console and lifted the corner of the blue bandanna tied around his neck. Dabbing the spit bubble at the corner of his mouth, she also wiped away the white-crusted saliva. Sometimes Jude would study sights so hard, he would forget to swallow. Their parents had always been averse to that habit. They'd claimed it made Jude look—well, Kailey refused to remember the word, let alone say it.

She glanced into the back seat at the cats, who curled on the gray padding like a yin and yang of felines. One with black short hair and one with white long hair.

"We're here, Edgar. Poe." Kailey addressed the cats instead of Jude. Sometimes it was better to leave her older brother in the depths of his mind. Conversing was stressful.

Poe didn't bother to open his blue eyes, but the tip of his fluffy white tail twitched in response. Edgar's yellow eyes slit with narrowed suspicion.

"Yes. I know." Kailey unbuckled her seat belt and reached into the back seat with a grunt. She scratched Edgar between the ears. The cat tilted his head back slightly, his one fang on the left side of his mouth exposed as his upper lip pulled upward in a catlike snarl. It was really his way of smiling. But no one believed that either.

She should have buckled her cats in for the car ride. Or rather, put them in a carrier and buckled the carrier in. But it stressed them out too much—stressed *Jude* out too much. The incessant meowing set him on edge, and even though Jude also drew comfort from them, he didn't handle nervous energy well. Which made her own struggle with nerves and anxiety a bit of a quandary on more than one occasion.

"Okay, okay," Kailey breathed, reaching back to tug out her elastic band and let her straight dark hair fall around her shoulders. She fluffed it, snapping down the visor to take a quick glance in the mirror. Her mascara was smudged. She fixed it, and as she did so, she saw the white cat in the back seat. Poe opened a blue eye and yawned, a tiny irritated squawk releasing from his throat.

"Fine." Kailey could take a hint. While Edgar tolerated Kailey's affection and reasonable self-confidence issues, Poe had no patience for it. He was the man in the foursome that was made up of Jude, the two cats, and herself. There was no insult to Jude to identify the white cat as such. Poe would take on Dwayne Johnson himself if he felt it was necessary, and then he'd hiss in the man's face and make his customary little *pffft* sound before sauntering away.

Kailey studied her brother for a long moment. Jude's head nodded in a methodical motion. His mouth moved as if he were whispering, but there wasn't any sound. She could make some of it out, though, just by reading his lips. Numbers. Letters. He was reciting his sequences again. Sequences that never made sense.

Knuckles rapping on her window startled Kailey and sent Edgar flying into the back windowsill. Poe arched in a hiss. Jude didn't appear to notice the sudden interruption.

"Hello?" The definitively male voice was questioning. Kailey leaned away from her car door even as she eyed the intruder through the glass.

He had a dark brown eyebrow the color of wet bark on a tree after a rainstorm, and it cocked upward into an inverted v, while his left eyebrow remained as straight as a caterpillar on a warm summer day. His eyes were gray and matched the tempestuous waves of Lake Superior behind him. They matched the gray sky. Everything here at Foxglove Manor was gray. Gray, stormy, and tumultuous. Exactly as Kailey remembered.

"Alive in there?" The man's voice was hoarse—naturally so. Like he'd been yelling at a rave concert and never quite regained full use. His mouth was bordered by a well-trimmed beard. He waved a hand. There was a ring on his right thumb. It was black. Black silicone.

"Kailey Gibson?" he tried again.

Kailey jumped, the sound of her name startling her from her mental observation. She'd never outgrown living in her head. She'd simply outgrown talking. A ramification of eight hours huddled in a dark van with a stranger. Eight hours she would never get back.

Kailey rolled down the window using the hand crank. It was an old car she drove. Their uncle Tim's. He'd willed it to her when he died last year of old age and a lack of things to do. At least that was how he described his death in his eulogy, which he wrote prior to actually "kicking the bucket."

"H-hello." Darn stutter. She didn't have a speech impediment. She was just nervous, more so because the guy at her window was hot—in a rugged, Upper Peninsula sort of way. Clean-cut but with an edge of lumberjack, softened with a side of teddy bear.

He jammed his hands into his gray pants pockets and remained tilted at the waist, a quizzical expression on his face and a slant to his lips. He waited.

"Y-yes." Dang it. Kailey tried again. "Yes, I'm Kailey Gibson."

A hand shot through the open window. The same hand with the black silicone thumb ring. "Axel Pavlov."

"Like Pavlov's dog?" The words escaped Kailey before she could stop them.

He smiled, and it broke his face into laugh lines that stretched from the corners of his eyes. "I guess. My great-grandfather was Russian, but he was a farmer." His eyes shifted to Jude, who remained fixated straight ahead, then back to Kailey.

"Mm." Kailey squeaked and made herself smile. "Okay." It was a paltry response that required action to deflect the attention away from her inability to make proper human conversation. Kailey made quick work of preparing to exit the car. She didn't reach for Jude but tempered her voice into a familiar tone meant only for him.

"Jude, you need to unbuckle your seat belt."

She could tell he'd heard and understood her.

Kailey waited, well aware of the presence of Axel Pavlov outside her window. He waited too.

"Jude," Kailey prompted again. While she could unbuckle Jude herself, if her fingers so much as grazed him, he might launch into an episode. Touch was not a friend to Jude.

Finally, Jude reached for the seat belt, without removing his gaze from the view outside the windshield. There was a click, then the belt retracted. Jude reached for the door handle and pulled it toward him. The passenger door opened.

Taking his action as acquiescence, Kailey did the same with her door, but not before casting a nervous glance toward the cats. Poe narrowed his blue eyes.

Yes, yes. I know, Poe. Chin up. Eyes forward.

Was she the only person in the world who talked via ESP with their pet?

Kailey shook her head to clear her mind and realized Axel Pavlov continued to watch her. There was an entertained humor in the depths of his eyes, yet the taciturn expression on his face gave away nothing.

She glanced beyond him. To the expanse of water that was as frigid as the wind felt. Lake Superior in all its chilled glory. The sandy beach. The piles of driftwood. The massive cliff overlooking it all, and the manor. Foxglove Manor. A familiar stone house with layers of unremembered memories held captive in its walls and in Kailey's mind. Goose bumps raised the flesh on her bare arms when another gust of wind blew strands of hair across her face and resulted in her hugging herself.

"Hope you brought a coat."

Kailey wasn't sure if Axel was asking her or merely making a statement. She chose to believe it was a question.

"I did."

"He'll need one too." Axel tilted his chin up toward Jude. Jude stood on the opposite side of the car, ramrod straight, staring at the manor.

Kailey continued to nod in assent to the direction.

The moment grew more awkward.

Axel tipped his head toward the car. "Might want to grab them."

"Oh!" Kailey laughed nervously. "Yeah. Yeah, good idea." She spun, rolling her eyes at Edgar, who had perched himself on top of the gray wool pea coat she'd bought in 2010. It'd fit her well at fourteen. It was an old, outdated friend. Kailey opened the car door, yanked it from beneath Edgar, sending him jumping to the floor. She snatched a red hoodie emblazoned with a faded and crackled *Dungeons & Dragons* screen print that Jude could throw over his T-shirt.

"Jude? Here, buddy." She slid the hoodie across the top of the car. Jude retrieved it wordlessly.

Shrugging into her coat, Kailey relished the sensation of its familiarity, even though the shoulders were a bit tight and she had gained several pounds since her early teens. She'd never been tall—or stocky—or even really anything but average. Four inches over five feet and a standard 135 pounds. Not light enough for the Superior winds to blow her off the cliff, but not so fluffy that her coat split at the seams.

"Why don't you guys come inside?" Axel motioned with his hand toward the manor. The wind whipped his dark hair in multiple directions. He seemed unaffected by it. "The residents are anxious to meet you, and Teri is probably going to accost you the minute you walk in."

Maybe she'd paled a little, but there was a hitch in Axel's step as he guided her up the stone path. "I didn't mean that literally," he assured her, studying her.

Kailey offered a squashed smile.

Teri Breckley was the person whom Kailey had been coordinating with. She was the director of the Foxglove Manor home, also the head nurse, and had been the one to interview Kailey over the phone for the position of a home aide.

Yes, Kailey understood she wasn't remarkably qualified for the position.

Yes, Kailey recognized her high school diploma and an associate degree didn't lend itself to home health care.

No, she didn't have a problem serving as an elderly person's companion or helper.

No, she had no qualms assisting with meals, changing linens, helping groom or bathe a resident.

Yes, she understood it was unorthodox to request to bring her brother and expect him to receive free room and board.

Yes, it was okay to take fifty percent of her earned wages back to offset their accommodations for Jude.

No, she didn't expect them to help with her autistic brother.

And so forth. Details. All of which Teri had been cordial enough to arrange and make accommodations for, but Kailey had to assume that she was hired as an aide simply because few people had applied for the position. A position that included room and board in the remarkably old stone manor. What Teri Breckley didn't know was that Kailey had come to Foxglove Manor when she was five. It had been a summer rental then, and her family had been trying to discover respite here on the cliffs of Lake Superior. Kailey's mom had ruined that option and it had only been the beginning of a horrible nightmare.

They followed Axel past a tilting and tumbling stone fence. Jude remained a solid eleven paces behind. Eleven, because Kailey's feet would take up the twelfth pace, making the distance between them even and mathematically geometric in Jude's mind. That he didn't account for his own feet, therefore leaving only ten paces between them, didn't bother Kailey. So long as it made sense to Jude, that was what mattered most.

The familiar heavy wood door with its arched entry greeted Kailey as Axel opened it. He held it open with his left arm and stepped aside for Kailey to enter first. She was met with the smell of chicken gravy, most likely from lunch, and a whiff of peppermint. But more than that, she was greeted by a draft of cold air that curled around her ankles, crawled up her torso, and settled just under her skin. Even with her old pea coat on, Kailey shivered.

"Still cold?" Axel raised a brow, stepping in behind her and shutting the door.

Kailey scanned the entryway, its shadowed corners, its heavy wood trim, and its Gothic darkness that saturated every bare crevice. She nodded in response. "I'm always cold." And she was. She had been cold since the day she had been taken when she was five years old. She had been freezing since the day she asked her brother Jude to tell her why their parents had died. And she'd been frigid since the moment Foxglove Manor's door had closed behind them, the last time they'd taken exit of its dismal rooms, and the last time she had seen her mother cry.

3

ADRIA

"Fleur Cartier died in this room." Light from the candle made the shadows deeper. "The records of Foxglove Manor state she died of consumption. But rumor has it she was strangled in her sleep. By her husband, jealous of her secret love affair with an Iroquoian-speaking Indian. He was the one who built this manor, you know, before many white men inhabited the area and before Dr. Archibald Miranda resided here."

Adria didn't blink. Those stories hadn't the power to assault her sensibilities. She was more troubled by the candle, the lack of a proper lamp or even gaslights. She followed the willowy frame of an older woman—in her seventies, no doubt—who had inserted herself into the guarded welcome of the man, the butler or whoever was the owner of the grouchy expression.

Mrs. St. John's white hair swept upward in a proper roll. Her dress was black, starched, with a high collar, minimal puffs to her sleeves, and a wide brocade of purple lace—so darkly purple it appeared black—covering the silk of her shirtwaist. She rested the candle on an intricately carved table, ignoring the droplet of wax that fell on the tea-stained doily. Adria was mesmerized for a moment, by the slow cooling of the wax, when Mrs. St. John's strident voice split through her consciousness.

"Breakfast is promptly at eight o' clock. If you are tardy, then so be it, and so goes your eggs as well. See to it that you do not attempt to make an appearance in your housecoat and slippers. You may bear the ills of a soul owned by devilish thoughts, but I must not be forced to bear them along with you." Mrs. St. John turned, spearing Adria with a hollow-eyed expression made worse by the candlelight. "Is that understood?"

Adria nodded. Wordless.

Mrs. St. John tilted her sharp chin upward, her gaze skimming the length of her nose. She studied Adria for a long moment, considering, and then her lips pressed together, making the delicate wrinkles around them deepen.

"We exist by keeping a responsible schedule here at Foxglove Manor. We are nothing if not with a purpose. That is to heal the soul, for your mind, I see, is quite well."

Adria swallowed and noted her throat felt a tad sore.

Mrs. St. John's left eyebrow winged upward. "I do no favors to your father, Miss Fontaine. Foxglove Manor is not a charity, nor is it an institution. I merely fulfill a long-standing obligation between my husband—God rest his soul—and Mr. Fontaine."

Adria waited.

The candlelight flickered and cast its shadow long across the ceiling. The room was plain, really, and nothing opulent or notable. Only its furnishings seemed to reflect wealth of any sort, the woodwork all beautifully carved, and the four-post bed knobs turned to appear like the heads of lions. Outside, Adria could hear the rising crash of the waves, not as distant as she had thought they might sound. A storm was roiling them, awakening the waters from their restless slumber.

Mrs. St. John made no pretense to prepare the bed for Adria. Night had fallen quickly on Adria's arrival, and already Adria could see the last fading glimmer of daylight swallowed by the pitch-black of the great lake's throat.

"Tomorrow, we will spend our morning in the book of Job. One

21

must meet mourning with mourning and tribulation with tribulation if one is to learn how to rise from such." Mrs. St. John's eyes narrowed. "Or wither away, if you're of that mind-set."

"I'm not," Adria responded, feeling that if she didn't, her soul would somehow be judged—not that it hadn't been already.

Mrs. St. John gave a clipped nod. "Well then, good night, Miss Fontaine. I will see you in the morning. Tomorrow, I will make sure there are extra candles brought here for you should you need them." At Adria's undisguised wince at the idea of candles as the only source of light, Mrs. St. John continued, "It is impossible to have gaslights here on the cliff of Superior. Kerosene is rationed also. In the winter, shipments stall considerably as the lake freezes. Candles have served Foxglove Manor quite well since the time it was built in 1842."

And the brief history lesson was followed by the sort of look that made Adria certain she was allowed no more questions—or facial expressions.

Someone brushed her cheek with their fingertips. Light and feathery. A wispy tickle that startled Adria awake. She blinked several times, attempting to clear sleep from her eyes and accustom her vision to the dark room. Filmy curtains swooped off the canopy, and with it a chill that enveloped her, causing prickles to rise on her skin.

Adria pulled the covers closer, the nighttime shadows playing tricks on her imagination. A shadow brushed past the window to the right of her. A large window that spanned from just a foot above the floor to a few inches from the ceiling. Its glass was paned into four sections, two long and rectangular at the bottom, the others short and squat at the top. Like eyes with a split gaping mouth. Only light from a half-moon shone through the lace curtains. The shadow had dissipated as quickly as it had come. So quickly that Adria thought she might have dreamt it.

The cold had not left the room when she glanced toward the fireplace set in the far wall at the end of the bed. Coals smoldered on the grate. Orange and blue, flickering colors at the base of the wood that had been sacrificed for warmth. A rustling sound in the corner caused Adria to sit bolt upright in bed. Her hair fell over her shoulders and tangled with her fingers as she clutched the sheet and blanket to her breast. She leaned right, attempting to see around the post at the end of the bed that was swathed in gauzy canopy and tied back with a red, twisted cord. The lace at the window moved, as though a subtle breeze had instigated its wave. Only there was no breeze.

"Hello?" Adria dared to speak, dared to interact with the emptiness that had awakened her. A part of her warred with a persistent nagging of horror even as her curiosity initiated her words. "Is anyone there?"

Silence.

A coal snapped and shot orange sparks into the firebox.

Adria clutched the covers tighter, a flimsy shield against her nightgown, guarding her soul against the imagined spirits that teased her sensibilities and made Foxglove Manor far less friendly than the unfriendly it had already deigned itself on Adria's arrival.

A thud above her ceiling sent Adria diving into her pillows. The blankets and sheet were over her head before she could summon her senses and attempt to react with more maturity. Footsteps. Three, four, then five. They paused, directly over her canopy bed. Adria braved a look, teasing the sheet to just below her nose and staring up through the canopy's gauze. A blurry view of a ceiling depressed into itself as it vaulted inward, with scrolled trim and white chipped paint. In the night's hues, it appeared bluer gray in tone. The sort of color one would associate with a cold room set in a stone house on a stone cliff above a pounding lake filled with more stones.

If God was real, and Adria believed that He was, she was certain even He might pause for a moment to consider the secrets that ushered about the room with an elusive trait like that of a ghost. But God wasn't one to be deterred by secrets, nor by ghosts—did God even believe in ghosts, or were they a part of His creation? It was a theological conundrum that was not inviting to Adria. She had experienced enough frightful happenings as a very alive human being. She had no desire to explore the mysteries of the afterlife and God's provident hand on the souls of the departed—at least not at this time of night.

The footsteps ceased altogether now. Her curtains were still. The coals still alternated their colors but didn't spark back with any further conversation. All rustling had ceased. Oddly, Adria was warmer too. Perhaps because the covers were pulled up around her ears, or perhaps because . . .

Adria heard her sister's voice in her mind. A not-so-friendly one. A voice that taunted her thoughts more often than she preferred.

"All spirits leave a chill in their wake. No matter how you wish to escape them, they follow you and attach themselves to your insides. Like a leech in a murky bog, you must pry them from yourself, and they'll only leave of their own accord."

Margot had seemed to take perverse delight in terrorizing her little sister, and as Adria curled deeper into her pillows, she tried not to remember the green light in Margot's eyes or the little laugh attached to her whisper. A laugh that meant she enjoyed seeing the flicker of fear in Adria's eyes. Like their father, Margot's delight in another's discomfort was difficult to escape.

Adria had hoped she'd found her way out when Foxglove Manor became an option. But regardless of any ghosts that may live behind these stone walls, those of Adria's family would prove Margot's words to be true. They did latch on to her soul—on to her memories—and even closed eyes against the darkness could not shut the door on one's memories.

4

KAILEY

"It's such a relief to have you here." Teri tapped a finger on the chipped Formica counter in the dated kitchen. Water dripped from the faucet and splashed off the iron-stained porcelain sink. The smell of meatloaf lingered in the air, tainted with the scent of burnt coffee. Teri's face mirrored the same expression Kailey had noted on another nurse she'd passed in the hallway. Weariness. The pitfalls of being short-staffed. It wasn't new to senior health care, Kailey was well aware, but she was growing concerned she wouldn't be much help, in spite of any previous self-confidence.

"I don't have very many nursing skills," she admitted as she nibbled on the complimentary oatmeal-raisin cookie Teri offered her on their arrival into the damp room located somewhere in the middle of the stone manor. Glancing at Jude, she noted he was content eating his cookie as well, crumbs collecting on the bandanna at his neck.

"I already knew that!" Teri muffled a laugh and waved off Kailey's protest with a hand that boasted a ring on every finger, including her thumb. A streak of brilliant blue striped through her chin-length black hair. She wore scrubs emblazoned with emojis. Reaching for the faucet, Teri cranked on the handle. "Need to get

Axel in here to fix that washer. This thing drips like a soaked sponge after a hurricane!" She gave up and wiped her hands on her hips, her brown eyes twinkling. "There are days here at Foxglove I swear the stories are true and that sneaky child does tamper with stuff just to keep us on our toes."

"Sneaky child?" Kailey drew back.

Teri moved past her and beckoned for Kailey to follow her from the musty kitchen. Her tennis shoes were silent on the wood floors that were scuffed and dull from age. Kailey hesitated, and Teri noted it. "Oh, you probably wouldn't have heard yet. Foxglove Manor has our own resident ghost. A little girl. I've never personally seen her, but apparently she's lived here for over a hundred years and makes an appearance now and then to haunt and taunt. Rumor has it, she's not a friendly ghost."

"Huh." Kailey had nothing intelligent to add. How was one supposed to respond to a story that sounded like a children's bedtime tale meets the darker elements of the Brothers Grimm? Not to mention it stirred up the memories far sooner than she preferred, though she was stupid and knew eventually she would have to face them.

Teri shot a look over Kailey's shoulder, her expression hesitant. "Will—he be okay there?"

Kailey assessed her brother. Jude had settled on a chair at the wooden kitchen table. It must have been used as a cutting board substitute because it was marked with multiple scars from knives, and Jude was counting each one. Kailey met Teri's eyes. "He'll be fine." And he would be. Jude was always, if not responsible. He knew to stay in the room in which he'd been left by Kailey until she returned. The only thing that might upset him was if someone tried to convince him otherwise.

"All right then." Teri gave a quick nod and escorted Kailey from the kitchen. They went around a corner toward a flight of curving stairs that led to the second floor. "Be forewarned, your brother may see our ghost girl. She tends to be seen by the residents here, not the staff." Teri laughed again. "*See* her being the relative term."

"You don't believe in ghosts?" Kailey reached for the handrail as she followed Teri up the stairs. She wasn't sure if Teri was implying that Jude and the elderly residents were more susceptible to imagining things and thus insulting them, or if Teri was making a simple observation with no intentional undertones.

"Honey, I believe in *me*," Teri laughed as the stairs creaked beneath her feet. "It's the only thing I can predict, and even then I've been known to surprise myself."

It was quiet then between them. A comfortable silence as Teri led Kailey into a small room at the far end of the second floor of the house. She twisted the tarnished doorknob and pushed open the door, its hinges squeaking with a slow *errrrrr* that reminded Kailey of a horror movie right before the hollow-eyed poltergeist swept toward her with a dagger.

There was a window directly across from the doorway, its frame bare, its length opening the room to daylight and a vivid view of the yard as it stretched toward the cliff's edge on which Foxglove Manor perched. A line of trees on either side of an opening framed Lake Superior perfectly. Had she been able to see all the way across the massive lake, Kailey knew she'd have seen Canada.

But her attention was gripped by the room in which she stood, uneasiness prickling her skin. Teri didn't seem to notice Kailey's reticence. She pointed to the twin-sized bed with its blue coverlet and crisp white sheets.

"Nothing fancy."

No. No, it wasn't. When she was a little girl vacationing here in the rented manor, this room had housed a full-sized canopy bed. An antique, Kailey's mother had stated. At that time, there was only the frame left, the canopy long since disposed of. But that one vacation as a child, Kailey had imagined she could see shadows twining around the frame like a vine until they floated out the window and dissipated into the moisture-laden night air. She was supposed to have slept in this room, as a child, alone. But after seeing shadows, Kailey had snuck into Jude's room and slipped under the covers at the end of his bed. No one understood how smart he was—how strong he was. No one but Kailey.

A lump lodged in her throat, and she squeezed her eyes tight to block out the fond memories of Jude, and the deep sentiment and loyalty that still bound them together.

"Are you all right?" Teri was eyeing her with the concerned assessment of a nurse.

Kailey didn't realize she had reached for the doorknob and was hanging on to the door as if her own legs wouldn't hold her weight.

"I'm fine." Kailey managed a wobbly smile. "Just tired."

Teri didn't respond for a moment, then she nodded. "I know, it's a long drive here. There's literally nothing much to see after you leave Minocqua. Just woods, and shoreline, and black bears." Teri opened the doors to a basic Shaker-style wardrobe, its straight lines doing nothing to celebrate the Gothic elements that thrived in every original corner of Foxglove Manor. Instead, the room was hodgepodge, put together with oddities that were functional. A straight-backed chair. A Berber carpet runner of gray tones, probably purchased at Target and tossed on the wood floor so one's feet didn't freeze in the morning.

"I'll have Axel bring up an air mattress. You *did* state you preferred Jude room with you, and we can accommodate that. Although, like I said in our prior conversations, we don't have room for an actual bed."

Kailey nodded. An air mattress was no surprise, and it wasn't something that Jude wouldn't adapt to.

Teri smiled, an element of relief in her eyes. "Good. There's sheets and blankets in the wardrobe on the upper shelf. So, feel free to get yourself settled here tonight. Oh yes, and Axel said you brought your two cats?"

Kailey nodded.

Teri tilted her head toward the window. "Just be sure you keep them inside. If they get out, you'll never see them again. And, maybe keep them off the air mattress so their claws don't pop it." The director of the home chuckled and padded back toward the doorway. She'd been more than accommodating so far, and Kailey appreciated it. Now Teri paused and gave Kailey a look that Kailey couldn't interpret. A squinting look that made Kailey feel like Teri wanted to say more but didn't.

Teri opened her mouth, then shut it, then opened it again to speak. "The residents will like having cats."

All six of them—residents, that is, Kailey reminded herself. Six elderly residents, one home director slash head nurse, an additional nurse who swapped shifts, a cook who prepared meals and commuted from a nearby small town, and Kailey. Kailey the aide. Kailey the one who was here to keep the old people company and out of trouble. To help the nurses bathe them, clothe them, feed them, and anything else they might need. To help the night nurse on duty in case of an emergency. To exist as if she were important when she was as replaceable as one of the residents themselves. Someone who had come and would eventually go and probably leave behind extraordinarily little to be remembered by.

Kailey hoped it would be that way. For Jude's sake.

The bedroom door shut softly, leaving Kailey to her square room and her lone window. She needed to get back downstairs to Jude and show him the way back to the room. A tour would be necessary to familiarize him with the house in case for some reason he didn't recall it from their younger years. She was nervous the residents would be a problem. If they weren't respectful of Jude's boundaries . . . well, Kailey took a moment to collect herself as she stared out at the lake, its waves a never-ceasing cadence of foam, icy gray waters, and thunderous pounding on the rocky shore. The lake washed away so many memories. Memories of people who had come and gone through Foxglove Manor. Lives that were vapors now, mere wisps of voices that echoed in the hallways of the two-story stone house.

It was a cold place to vacation as a child. It was a frigid place to be banished to as an unwanted elderly person. And the people who worked here every day? Perhaps they had lives. Maybe even good ones. But Kailey knew the truth of it. The truth that Foxglove Manor would twist its way into your soul until one day it owned you, and it called to you, and it didn't cease haunting you until you returned.

"We're back," Kailey whispered to the air. To the ghosts. To whoever might hear and whoever would disregard.

Kailey watched a sea gull dip across the sandy yard with its patches of grass and overhanging, unpruned cedar trees.

A figure emerged.

Axel.

He stood with his back toward her, facing the great lake. In front of him, not far from the edge of the cliff, sat an old woman in a wheelchair. The wind whipped her red scarf westward. Kailey could make out nothing of the woman's features. She could only focus on Axel, whose shoulders were stiff and whose hands clutched the bars of the chair so tight it seemed his mind was at war with every instinct of his body. Every instinct that insinuated with one push he could send the old lady and her chair over the edge, smashing onto the rocks below. Diving into a watery grave. Swallowed by the lake, by the giant cold monster that it was.

She had seen it happen before. In her dreams, certainly, but her imagination as a child had always been vivid. Colorful. Irrevocably nightmarish at times. She couldn't forget the way she'd stared at the cliff's edge. Though a mere five years of age, it was as if she saw a vision of someone slipping over and falling to their death. A vision, an imagined scene—whatever it might have been, Kailey never wanted to see it again. It was one of the reasons it had taken her twenty years to come back. Back to Foxglove Manor, to the stories, to the memories, and worst of all, to the unanswered questions that taunted Kailey like a heckling sociopath who took joy in the suffering of others.

"What would you do if a bullfrog jumped onto your lap and started yakking at you?"

Kailey caught the question as she entered the main-level front room, Jude beside her, his hands curling and uncurling at his sides. Most people thought it was a nervous tic of his, but Kailey knew it meant he was relaxed. Too bad she wasn't.

"A bullfrog wouldn't have the gumption to jump on my lap. I'd yank his hind legs off him and feed them to the dog."

It was a violent answer. Either the elderly woman in the wheel-chair—the one with the red scarf whom Kailey had imagined Axel pushing over the edge—was sadistic in nature, or she merely despised frogs. Either way, the gentleman opposite her, in his own chair, cackled in response. He slapped a knobby hand on his knee, completely ignoring Kailey and Jude's presence in the doorway.

"We don't have a dog here, Maddie. Gonna have to come up with a new idear."

"Idea." Maddie corrected his grammar. Her lips tightened, then relaxed and she smiled just a little—just enough to soften the harsh edges around her eyes. "We don't have bullfrogs here either, Robert, so you know this is a ridiculous conversation."

A troubled scowl, so brief and so fleeting, brushed across the man's face. "Raymond." His muttered correction to his name went unheard by Maddie, who fumbled with a page in the book that rested on her lap.

Kailey ventured into the room, hesitant but knowing she needed to interrupt the little conversation that was so inconsequential she was certain the world would keep spinning. Jude followed, this time three paces behind that would equal—in his reasoning—an even four with Kailey's feet included.

Raymond lifted his blue eyes that were touched at the irises with an extra band of white indicating he had sight issues. He squinted, which deepened the wrinkles in his forehead. His nose was a bit large for his face, and the pores on the ends of it were quite notice-able. He had flecks of dry skin on his shoulders and chest, and she could see it flaking off his temples.

"Who're you?" he barked. His gaze shifted to Jude, then back to Kailey.

Kailey cleared her throat and wished she'd brought Edgar with her. The cat might have been a better segue than a *Hi! I'm the new aide!*

She tried it anyway.

"I'm Kailey. The new aide. This is my brother, Jude."

A chuckle was Raymond's response. He looked her up and down and then winked with the audacity of a ninety-year-old man with nothing to lose. "Cute as a button." Raymond gave a wobbly salute with his hand toward Jude. "How-do?"

Jude didn't respond. He looked past Raymond, and the old man furrowed his brow.

Maddie turned her head to look at Kailey. The red scarf draped around her like a small blanket, and her cardigan was as bulky and cozy as a fisherman's cable-knit sweater. Her brown hair was faded into a dishwater-gray, streaked primarily with white, and was pulled back into a knot at the nape of her neck. Her large brown eyes made no disguise in assessing Kailey.

"Why do we need an aide?" Maddie's question was to the point. Almost as though she didn't have enough time left on earth to ban-ter about niceties. But then she didn't seem stern or bitter either. Maddie seemed—lost.

Kailey couldn't quite put a finger on it. She chose to answer instead. "Well, let's just say I needed a job." Better to make them feel like they were helping her instead of her being hired to babysit them in their ancient years.

Maddie frowned, confusion evident in her demeanor. "I thought we just hired an aide. Fawn. Wasn't her name Fawn?" She cast a semi-desperate look to Raymond, who pushed on his wheels to get his chair to roll forward. A rescuer on wheels, an old-fashioned knight in shining armor.

"Dawn. Her name was Dawn." Raymond reached out and patted Maddie's hand. "And we always need an aide. Think of it, Maddie. Who's gonna read that to you?" His gnarled index finger with the top knuckle bent at an angle indicative of an old break and now arthritis pointed at the book in Maddie's lap.

Maddie frowned, obviously trying to calculate Raymond's words. She smoothed the page in the book with her hand. "Oh this? This was my son's book."

Raymond shot Kailey a look that was very telling. Say nothing. Do nothing. He was in charge. "No, it was Dawn's book. Our old aide. Remember, she got herself married last month?"

Maddie blinked several times and then awareness—or at least the pretending of awareness—settled into her disposition. "Ohhh, yes. Dawn. I always thought she should marry Axel. That boy is far too ruggedly handsome for his own good." Maddie swung her attention to Kailey. "Are you married?"

Kailey coughed to cover a nervous laugh. "Um, no. No, I'm not."

"There's hope for Axel yet." Maddie shut her book with a thud, the hardcover beneath her palms displaying the title of *Ivanhoe* in cursive, inset script.

"Don't go pestering that boy!" Raymond inserted with a snort.

"I have to have one last hurrah before I lose my mind, don't I?" Maddie quipped back.

Raymond rolled his eyes. "That's a kamikaze mission, Maddie. Axel ain't never gonna get married and you know it."

Maddie waved her counterpart off and leveled her chocolate-brown gaze on Kailey. "I am losing my mind, and Raymond wants to take all the fun out of it." She smiled then, and it touched her eyes. Kailey had the impression that in her younger years Maddie had been fits of fun and bursts of impulsive energy matched with a thick underlying source of honesty. Now she tapped her finger on the book's cover and gave a short nod. "Dementia is a stinker of a diagnosis, but I may as well roll with it until I'm so far gone, you all play with my marbles since I'll have totally lost them all."

She was at a loss for words. Kailey shot Raymond a look of nervousness, and he smirked, knowing full well the effect Maddie was having on Kailey.

"You have Alzheimer's, Maddie," Raymond chided.

"Same thing," Maddie retorted.

"Welllllll—"

"Shush." Maddie waved him off. "I never listened to my husband, bless the old man, why would I listen to you?" She chose to engage her remaining energy with a shove of her wheelchair, and she rolled it across the wood floor that was scuffed from years of use and a bit warped from Lake Superior moisture.

Raymond cleared his throat, drawing Kailey's attention. When she looked him in the eyes, she saw a sadness there.

"Maddie lost her husband over thirty years ago, or so I've been told."

Kailey offered a neutral smile. One that wouldn't be interpreted as offensive no matter how or what angle you looked at it. "She seems very—nice."

It was a polite statement.

Raymond snorted and rammed his thick plastic-lensed glasses up his nose. "Don't let her fool you. She can bite you when you least expect it. Never used to be that way, not even six months ago . . ." He looked around the room, into the high corners with the carved molding, the dark walls with built-in bookshelves, and finally toward a set of windows that overlooked the west side of the manor. A short expanse of patchy yard. Some cedar trees. A wheelbarrow filled with sticks. "Anyway, what's with him?" Raymond waved a hand toward Jude.

Jude had lifted his face toward the ceiling and appeared to be studying the crown molding. He seemed clueless that the conversation had switched to center around him. Kailey knew differently.

"He likes architecture," Kailey explained, skirting the intention of Raymond's question. She hated having to explain Jude's autism.

Not because she was embarrassed by it, but because she didn't want it to be how others defined him.

Raymond assessed Jude for a moment, then scrunched his mouth into a smirk. "Never did understand architecture myself. I was more of a grease-and-motors sorta man."

Jude's eyes darted toward Raymond, then back to the ceiling. Kailey wasn't sure if Raymond noted it, but she bit back a smile. Jude liked Raymond.

The old man brought his gaze swinging back to Kailey, his eyes sharp as they drilled into hers. "I get why Jude is interested in this house, though. Something about this place . . . gets under your skin, you know? An energy. Gives me prickles sometimes. Like it wants to come back from the dead and tell us something." Raymond settled his focus on Maddie, who thumbed through *Ivanhoe* while humming to herself. Humming a random tune that went into a higher measure before diving into a minor key that sent a shiver through Kailey.

She knew what Raymond meant. Kailey was no stranger to Foxglove Manor. It had haunted her when she was barely out of her toddler years. It had spooked her through memories that fogged her mind. It had called to her as recent as last week. An unknown voice. A cry. Maybe even a whisper that floated across the waves, drifted through her window, and brushed her face while she slept.

Come find me, the voice of the manor seemed to wail. *Come.*

And so she had.

5

ADRIA

She had known that Mrs. St. John had a daughter. Adria had not expected to be met in the front room by a portrait so large it hung a mere foot below the molded ceiling and almost touched the top of a side table that was only four feet above the floor. Adria stood in the doorway of the room, her intention to come and borrow a book from one of its shelves now thwarted as she met the silent stare of Theodora St. John.

The young woman could have been no older than Adria herself in the painting, only her dress aged her enough to make her in her early forties were she still alive. Blue eyes were painted to sparkle, yet Adria could see through the artist's ploy to the dull-ness in Theodora's expression. She sat prim in a chair, her dress falling in filmy folds around her slippered feet. Her hair was curled in ringlets, she wore a scooped neckline adorned with a pearl choker, and her skin was pale. There was no smile on her lips, and the only real oddity about the portrait was the fox that sat at her feet, nose tilted upward like nobility, its bushy tail wrapped around its body.

"My husband commissioned her portrait." Mrs. St. John's voice caused Adria to startle, and she jumped to the side as Mrs. St. John came up from behind her. She was staring at her dead daughter's image while her right hand held the hollow of her neck as if she were contemplating strangling herself. "Theodora was eighteen. She had just become betrothed."

"How lovely." A paltry response, but Adria could think of no other.

Mrs. St. John leveled a censorious gaze on Adria. "Lovely? Hardly lovely, my dear. Theodora plummeted to her death the day after this portrait was finished. We found her at the bottom of the stairs, her neck broken and her fox at her feet as if he had pushed her himself."

Adria listened to a clock ticking as silence lay heavy between them.

Mrs. St. John dropped her hand from her neck and cleared her throat. Her lips tightened. "I believe that Theodora stumbled over the wretched animal and he was the cause of her death. I had my staff put the creature down that very day. It never should have been allowed in the house." She spread her arm and swept it in front of her, all while staying expressionless. "The irony that later I would live in a home titled Foxglove is more than I suppose most mothers could bear." Mrs. St. John looked down her nose at Adria. "I am not most mothers," she declared.

"Foxglove is a flower, isn't it?" Adria attempted to steer away from the unsettling conversation. The way in which Mrs. St. John spoke of her deceased daughter was as detached as a doctor might speak of a corpse.

Mrs. St. John nodded. She moved into the room and proceeded to tie back a heavy lilac-colored drape with a gold cord. "Rose-pink or purple. Tubular little flowers with green foliage. It grows wild in various parts of the Peninsula. It isn't as prevalent here in the Upper Peninsula, but in the lower . . ." Her voice trailed as if she were weary of the science lesson. She turned from the window and eyed Adria. "We must talk."

Yes. Yes, they must. There was a purpose for Adria to have come to Foxglove. Not only because she was more than willing to find escape from her father when he himself offered it to her, but for other reasons as well. Ones that hung over her head and made sure she didn't forget where she had come from. However, that would not be Mrs. St. John's reasoning. Not at all.

"Be seated." She waved at a chair whose velvet seat bragged of wealthier days, its golden fibers now looking frayed, tempting Adria to question how well off Mrs. St. John truly was. But her pondering was thwarted as Mrs. St. John declared, "We must first discuss the ghost girl of Foxglove Manor."

Adria shuddered and drew her shawl tighter around her, but the flimsy silk sheath provided little warmth. Had there been a morning fire in the fireplace? Adria stared emptily into it, examining the coals for a glowing hue that would indicate there had been. But the room was cold—so cold now—that even embers would be of little help.

"Also," Mrs. St. John seemed to add before moving on to the topic of ghosts, "if you should see a fox—any fox—you must inform me immediately. They are not allowed here."

"No . . . foxes?" Adria couldn't help the squeak of disbelief at the end of her inquiry, because she clearly remembered seeing a mangy one on her arrival.

"Does that surprise you?" Mrs. St. John's fingernails drummed the arm of her chair. Her head was piled high with white hair in an ostentatious pompadour that only needed powdered and she might be reminiscent of a thin-nosed lady of nobility from the previous century. Though she was facing Adria, her neck was turned to allow her to peer out the broad, paned window at the lake beyond. "Nothing surprises me anymore. Not since Theodora. But yes." Mrs. St. John turned back to Adria. "Yes. I have the caretaker rid us of any of the awful creatures. A bad omen. That is what they are. And you will come to recognize that as well. When you see a fox, more often than not, you'll see *her* shortly thereafter."

"The ghost girl," Adria responded with understanding, knowing the answer but not bothering to ask its required question.

Eyes sparked. Admiration made Mrs. St. John's narrow eyebrow raise. "You're intelligent."

Adria offered a small, appropriate smile.

Mrs. St. John cleared her throat quietly. "I didn't mean that to be a compliment."

Adria twisted her fingers in her hands.

"Regardless," Mrs. St. John continued, waving a hand that boasted a sapphire ring, "we have a ghost here, at Foxglove. Inherited, of course; she didn't follow me, and it's not Theodora."

"Of course not." Adria entertained the idea that if she were Mrs. St. John's deceased daughter, the thought of returning to haunt her mother might be the most delicious prank. Ruffling the stiff-backed mother with midnight moaning. "Who is she, then? The ghost?" Adria inquired so as to rein in her thoughts.

Mrs. St. John drew in a heavy breath and, to Adria's surprise, rose from her chair, her deep blue dress rustling around her toes as she moved to the window. Her right arm rested around her waist, her left raised to cup her chin. "The waves are calm today." Her voice was distant.

Adria remained seated but looked beyond Mrs. St. John. It was a strange thing to state, considering the waves were rolling to shore with a persistent roar. The cliff on which the manor sat hid the shoreline, but Adria knew if she were to make her way down to it, she would more likely than not be sprayed with the icy waters of Superior.

"The ghost?" Adria prodded, more curious than she should have been.

"All I will say, Alexandria, is that you must make it your priority to avoid her." Mrs. St. John's voice bounced off the glass of the window. "She is young and impetuous. Timid but very, very savvy. She will suck you in with her innocence, and then she will stab you deeply with her evil."

Adria waited.

Mrs. St. John faced her, drilling Adria to her chair with a stern eye. "You will report any sightings to me immediately."

"And where is she—the ghost—seen most often?" Adria ventured.

Mrs. St. John coughed. "It doesn't matter *where*; it just matters that she *is*. The house rules are quite simple. You are here to be my companion and nothing else. Which means you will do as I say. Report to me if you see the ghost girl, tell me if you spy a fox on the grounds, and keep to your rooms and the ones I frequent. There's no need to be nosy and snoop in places you're not welcome."

"Such as the turret and its rooms?" Adria offered boldly, remembering the glimpse of a man in the window. A glimpse she questioned now had even been real.

Mrs. St. John's lips tightened. She reached for a locket watch that hung from a chain around her neck. Opening it, she observed its innards, then snapped it shut. "It's time for breakfast, Alexandria." She started for the door and then paused and spoke over her shoulder. "The fact of the matter is, Foxglove Manor is a lonely place." Mrs. St. John twisted at her waist so she could look at Adria full on. "If your father believes your mind and soul will find healing here, then he is sorely mistaken. There are many days I ponder throwing *myself* off the cliffs. And I—unlike you—have the morality to leave my days numbered by God and not myself. Beware, Alexandria Fontaine, or our manor's ghost will toy with your senses. So, if you think my worry is that you will explore the turret, then you are greatly underestimating my warnings."

6

"Whars you goin', girlie?"

The gravelly voice came from the old man's throat—the man who had met her at the door the day before when she'd arrived. Now that she observed him longer, Adria noted he was knobby all over, from his nose to his knuckles to his knees. Leaning against a smooth driftwood pole, his cap was pulled over his forehead, and shaggy white hair stuck out like bunches of toothpicks from beneath the wool. In his free hand, he held what appeared to be a cold meat pie wrapped in brown paper. He was no longer wearing a baggy suit, but instead wool trousers, a plaid shirt, and a buttoned-up wool coat.

Adria adjusted the hood of her cape, hiding her hands and arms inside its warmth. The ground beneath her feet was sporadic with grass and sand, and the cliff was tempting. Too tempting. A part of her wondered if it would be wiser to return to the manor, to the indoors. The other part was curious. Curious to know what it would be like to stand with her toes hanging over the edge, staring down at the debris-strewn beach below. Nothing warm or inviting. Only sand littered with driftwood and basalt rock and the spray of freshwater, cold as if it were just melted ice.

"I asked ya's a question."

Adria tore her gaze from the cliff's edge and scanned the lake that stretched for miles until it kissed the skyline far in the Canadian distance. She knew her eyes would reflect a sort of absence.

It was moments such as these that she tried to escape the world. Hide, just for long enough, until she could straighten her mask, renew herself by drawing strength from something inspiring, and relock the doors on memories that refused to stay stored away.

"I'm sorry," she apologized appropriately. It was ingrained in her to do so. If her father didn't backhand her for being rude, her sister would point out that it was the silence of the mouth that bespoke the mischief of the mind. In a way, she was right. Before Adria had considered her own personal exit from the world, there were brief and horrific moments when she imagined what it would be like if she were vicious enough to drop a bit of arsenic in Margot's tea. She hadn't, of course. Instead, Adria concentrated on being appropriate. Cause as little ripples as possible, while her insides churned like the waves of Lake Superior.

"Cat got your tongue?" the old man barked again and poked the end of his stick toward her.

Adria stepped back, careful to be sure it was also away from the edge of the cliff. A gust of wind wrapped her cloak around her legs. "The last I checked, cats don't capture tongues. I'm unsure where that phrase ever originated from."

A crack of laughter escaped him, and Adria noted the white stubble on his chin was a bit long for whiskers but not long enough to be called a beard. He pointed a finger that bent thirty degrees to the north with arthritis. "You've got spunk." He waggled the finger. "I like that."

They exchanged smiles. Adria found comfort that she had not been set to right as being sassy. A little piece of her warmed toward the curious man.

"Diggery Brahms be my name." His crooked smile revealed a missing eyetooth. "I be the caretaker for Foxglove Manor since before the war. Came here not long after Monsieur Cartier built this here house."

"A pleasure to meet you." Adria went on to admit her name to the old man, and he seemed to roll it around on his tongue as if trying it out.

"Aaaaay-dreeee-uh, eh? Curious name."

"My proper name is Alexandria," she added.

He shook his head in bewilderment and furrowed eyebrows that rivaled his hair for bushiness. "Proper names be a blasted waste of time. If you called me by mine, I'd be Deitrich Von Brahms. S'why I goes by Diggery and got rid of the *Von*. Too stuffy. Like them Southern gents what own plantations down yonder."

Adria tilted her head in question and studied Diggery. It was an odd comment. This far north, not many referenced the other world that was the South. Especially since the war. It might have been twenty years ago, and even though Adria had been born shortly after, it had touched her as well. Her father had never been the same man—or so her mother had sworn. Shortly before Margot found her hanging in the cellar. And folks wondered why Adria was such a temperamental child . . .

"Nope. Cat's got your tongue, for sure." Diggery ran a stubby finger under his nose and sniffed. "You talk less than a mute squirrel."

She didn't know what to say to that, so her silence reinforced Diggery's unorthodox description of her. "Why're you here anyway? At Foxglove Manor? Ain't no place for a young lady."

Adria pushed a strand of hair that blew out from under her hood, wispy in the wind. "I've been sent here to be Mrs. St. John's companion." It was the truth. Not in its entirety.

Diggery seemed to conclude that. His eyebrow rose up under the brim of his cap. "And?"

Adria shifted her weight onto her other foot and cast a glance at the waters. The waves rolled in persistence and were growing in height and strength. "And because my father felt it was best for me."

Still not the truth in whole, but this time Diggery accepted it with a nod. But a mutter followed, and Adria heard it well. "Seems like we all have our lies we hold on to."

Adria met the old man's searching gaze. It was introspective. One that burrowed into her soul, and for a moment she almost wished to confide in him. To tell him everything. Past, present, and the future that loomed so precariously unknown.

"See that there?" Diggery's gnarled finger attempted to point at an animal in the far corner of the yard. It was tucked beneath shrubbery, its long nose tilted into the air. Mangy fur was a mottled orange and gray. A tail that should have been fluffy was ratlike with patches of long fur hanging from the cartilage. Diggery continued, "That's one of the foxes of Foxglove Manor. She had kits a few years ago, but no more of late. Maybe this spring. We'll see."

Adria eyed the fox that looked as if she had died once, been buried, and then her partially decomposed corpse brought back to life. "I thought Mrs. St. John required that you rid the place of all foxes."

"She does." Diggery chuckled a throaty chuckle that reminded Adria of a man with too much phlegm in his esophagus. "I don't do her biddin'. I'm my own man and I'm from these parts longer than her. I tell the creature to stay out of sight and she does."

"The fox listens to you?" Adria was surprised.

Beady eyes clouded with age settled on her. Diggery's mouth twitched before he answered. "Everyone listens to me."

"Does *he* listen to you?" Adria lifted her eyes to the turret. She pointed to where she believed she'd seen the shadowed silhouette of a man when she'd arrived. Asking Mrs. St. John seemed daunting, but Diggery, for all his oddity, felt more approachable.

"He?" Diggery's voice raised a notch. He adjusted his cap, causing his gray hair to stick out farther over his ears. "*He*? Who's *he*?"

"The man in the turret window." Adria waited, knowing she had tenuously baited Diggery and feeling a bit guilty about it.

Diggery cleared his throat. "Don't know about a man in the window."

"I thought I saw someone there when I arrived here."

Diggery scrunched his face as though confused and shook his head. "Nope. No one in the window."

"We all have our lies to hold on to," Adria mumbled. Not brave

44

enough to repeat the old man's words in audacious fashion to his face, but unable to stifle them altogether.

Diggery snorted and kicked a piece of driftwood that had somehow made its way from the beach below to the cliffside above. "Cat don't got your tongue no more."

And with that, Diggery began to shuffle back the way he'd come, skirting the border of the lawn where it met with scrappy hemlock and cedars with a white poplar jutting out from between them.

He was perceptive. Adria realized she would need extra caution when around Diggery Brahms. Not only had she given him half-truths earlier during his questioning, but the full truth might endanger him. She didn't trust her father. He had driven her to try to cheat life in the way her mother had. Now he had sent her here, with *his* purpose in mind, not her restoration. She wasn't sure about Diggery—if she could trust the old man. Yet she was no stranger to determining someone's mental instabilities. Diggery was odd, quirky, and a bit pithy. But he was nothing compared to Adria's father.

Lewis Fontaine had lost his mind since the war, and with it he'd sworn he'd lost even more. For some, the war of the rebellion had been for just or righteous causes, causes of national rights, or human rights. For others, like Lewis Fontaine, it had been opportunity. Opportunity to smuggle. To scavenge. And, Adria had been planted at Foxglove Manor for one primary purpose—and it wasn't her own healing. She would never regain her position in the family, and she would be destitute and thrown to the streets unless she could recover treasures another war pirate had scavenged from Lewis. While men had given their lives, other men became land buccaneers. Their flag was neither Dixie, nor Stars and Stripes, nor did it boast a skull and bones. It was anonymous, nonexistent, but far more ruthless and deadly than any bayonet on the end of a rifle. It was the kind of poisonous evil inspired by greed. It had killed her mother. It had almost killed Adria.

Now she returned toward the lake, toward the distant horizon. It might kill her still.

⁓

There was a steamer on the vista. Adria could spy the billowing puffs from the stacks as they collided with the blue sky. She held her hand to her forehead to shade her eyes. The ship remained a safe distance from the rocky shoreline. Her captain must know the dangers harbored along the lake's coast. A lake that had lighthouses dotting its borders to warn of impending doom and danger. Seclusion was second only to the hollow purpose in her heart as Adria allowed her feet to carry her back toward Foxglove Manor.

"Thirty minutes. You may have thirty minutes to yourself at one o'clock every weekday afternoon," Mrs. St. John had instructed. Now Adria must return to being a companion. Sitting beside the narrow-faced old woman and listening to her breathing, occasionally uttering a complaint against the creaking framework of the old house or against the cold its stone did nothing to keep out.

Adria entered the manor quietly, pondering Diggery, dwelling on the feelings his words had stirred in her. She didn't like it being insinuated that she was a liar. That was her father's forte, not hers. Even now, her father seemed to lord over her, huddling in the back of her mind like a monster crouched and ready to pounce. There were so many memories she wanted to forget. He was not a kind man.

Mrs. St. John was nowhere to be seen when Adria entered the front parlor. In fact, there was a part of Adria that was almost certain the only occupant in the room since they'd sat there this morning was a daddy longlegs that hung off the corner of the fireplace mantel like a trapeze artist she had seen once at the circus. Leaving it to its peace, Adria determined if Mrs. St. John wasn't where she'd said she'd be, then it was no fault of Adria's if she vacated the parlor altogether. With her father's instructions to make her stay at Foxglove Manor worth more than just the supposed reestablishment of her mental health and their personal reputation, he'd left her only a little to go on to search Foxglove Manor for his missing, bootlegged war treasure. A few clues such as, Mr. St. John was behind her father's missing stolen treasures—the irony in that only enhancing the severity of the mission—and some mention of secret smuggling Mr. St. John had been involved in. There was nothing her father could lend her that would give Adria a starting point as to where to look for the treasure. Coins, jewels, even some bonds, her father had stated. Perhaps Mr. St. John had a safe. Or worse, he'd smuggled the Fontaines' bounty from Foxglove Manor through whatever resources he seemed to have. Just look for it, Adria's father had instructed. And don't stop looking.

But the quicker she could find something—*anything*—that might help her father, Lewis Fontaine, the Great Lakes smuggler, the sooner she could be rid of any obligation to him. He might be her father, but there was nothing about him that endeared him to her, and while Foxglove Manor was no respite from his storm, freedom did tempt her as almost within her grasp.

7

KAILEY

"Snooping?"

Axel's voice was tinged with humor and teasing, but still Kailey jumped and knocked her head against the doorframe of the second-floor bedroom.

"Sorry." Axel winced.

"No, I was looking for the storage room. Teri said there were some old books there that my brother might enjoy." Kailey reached up to rub the sore spot. It was minor. The room beyond her was Maddie's room. One of the six bedrooms on the second floor of the manor. An elevator had been installed since she had last been here, and while it made Foxglove a bit friendlier toward the special needs of its occupants, it still struck her as a bit odd that Foxglove had been made into a retirement home at all.

"Ahh, that room is downstairs. And yeah, there's quite a few books in it." Axel extended his hand. In it was a plastic grocery bag with cans of cat food inside. "Teri said your cats ate chicken pâté?"

"Or tuna." Kailey took the bag gratefully. It had been remiss of her to forget most of her cat food when she'd loaded her belongings, Jude, Edgar, and Poe into the car. The boys—albeit not including Jude—would be thrilled to be fed something other than dry cat food. "Sorry to make you drive all that way for it."

The manor was at least thirty miles from the nearest town, with *town* being a subjective word for a mix of necessary businesses posted along a harbor.

Axel shrugged, and his smile stretched off his beard and reached his eyes. His chocolate-brown hair was combed back off a broad forehead. Kailey tried to convince herself he was just a guy, with a beard, in a green flannel shirt, with a kind face.

Kailey wasn't accustomed to kind faces.

Axel gave her a wink that implied he'd caught her staring at him and he was okay with that. "The folks here will enjoy having cats again. We used to have a tortoiseshell female. She was great with the residents."

"She died?" Kailey edged past Axel in an attempt to put distance between herself, Axel, and Maddie's room. She wasn't sure what it was about the old woman that drew her curiosity.

"Yep. Cancer. That was a trip to town I could've done without taking."

He was sensitive under that Upper Peninsula backwoods-ness. She couldn't help but like that—like *him*. The feeling made her uncomfortable. Attraction was not a part of the equation in coming to Foxglove Manor. In an effort to get away, Kailey started toward the stairs, bypassing the elevator used only for residents. Axel followed her. Having him behind her made her stomach curl a bit. She'd never liked feeling exposed or vulnerable.

"Want me to show you around?"

"I need to get back to my brother."

Axel was still on her heels. "Sure. Yeah. I get that." Still, he kept up his congenial conversation. "I know you've been here for a couple of days, but Teri said you mostly hang out with the residents—and your brother?"

"That's what I was hired to do, and she understood Jude would be with me," Kailey responded before she realized her words could be taken as sharp or defensive.

"Sorry. I wasn't questioning your brother—just—no one expects

49

you to be with the residents twenty-four seven either. You can take breaks or . . . walk slower." His voice was weighted with teasing and seriousness at the same time.

Kailey didn't know how to respond. Besides, she had reached the bottom of the stairs, which opened into the front hall, so slowing down was natural anyway. Wood floors, scuffed but polished, smelled of lemon scent and sanitizer. A potted cedar bush was posted on either side of the front door. Edgar jogged across her path and gave her a quick *meow* as he headed off to some other section of the manor. The cats had adapted quickly. Even Jude had. Kailey had not.

Axel was still on her heels as she headed for the kitchen. "Have you been down to the beach yet?"

Kailey had to stifle a slight laugh at the irony. The beach. It sounded so lovely. Like warm white sand, tropical skies, and blue waters a person usually only dreamt about. This beach? Superior's beach? Its sand was mixed with the accumulation of freshwater whisking together debris and soil and lake weed. Its waters smelled like fish and fresh, crisp air. The shoreline was littered with rocks and driftwood. It was cold. So very, very cold.

Axel was waiting for her answer.

Kailey bent and put the cans of cat food in the small cupboard Teri had designated for Kailey to keep cat supplies in.

"No?" Axel finally supplied Kailey's answer. "Let me take you down to the water."

Down to the water.

It sounded so . . . doomed. Like inevitable drowning was mere moments away. Kailey squeezed her eyes shut as she stacked the cans, her back to Axel. "I-I'm not a big fan of the lake—and I shouldn't leave Jude too long . . ." Although she knew he was perfectly fine. He had a sudoku book, a pencil, and his ridiculously intelligent brain that required Kailey get him the *advanced* sudoku books.

She could almost feel Axel's contemplation on her back. When he didn't respond, she stacked another can of chicken pâté on top of the others. "I'm not a huge fan of water."

"C'mon!" Axel's encouragement bounced off her back. "Not a huge fan of water? Who says that and means it?"

"I do!" Kailey spun from her crouch. She couldn't help the irritation this time.

Her reaction made Axel draw back a bit, and he held up his hands. "Sorry."

Kailey tempered her breathing and released it carefully. "No. I'm sorry. I—" It was probably best to provide him with a little, so he didn't ask for more. "When I was a kid, we went on a vacation near a beach." Axel didn't need to know it had been here, at Foxglove. "My brother and I played along the edges—just wading. One day Jude fell, and it scared us both."

Axel looked as though he was trying desperately to relate. He crossed his arms over his chest and tilted his head. "Did he almost drown or something?"

That would have been hard to believe. The lake wasn't deep until one waded out yards from the shoreline, and even though Axel didn't know it had happened here, Kailey imagined various ocean beaches weren't much different.

"No. He just . . ." Kailey bit back a sigh. "Sudden accidents like that can upset Jude."

"His autism, right?" Gentleness entered Axel's eyes.

Kailey looked away and out the window at the trees that swayed in the same wind that tossed the waves in the lake. "Yeah." She waited for either the litany of questions to follow or the awkwardness that implied they wanted to give her their condolences for having a brother with special needs and yet knew how inappropriate that would be.

"I have a cousin with autism. He played Mozart when he was three. He's a genius."

Kailey looked up at Axel, searched his face, and noted he was serious. "Thanks."

He gave a quick nod at her gratefulness for his quick acceptance of Jude. "It's gotta be a bit unnerving to go to the water, then. All the memories of when you were kids?"

Kailey nodded, remembering quite vividly the day in the cold Lake Superior waves, Jude's screams, and the empty windows of Foxglove Manor that stared down at them with no life inside its walls that cared enough to help. "All the memories. Yeah. You could say that."

"Well then. There's no time like the present." Axel held out his hand. Callused palm up toward her, his fingers waved just a little as if to welcome her grip.

"No time like the present for what?" she asked, ignoring his hand. Ignoring the curls in her stomach that surprised her. Made her want to believe that if she reached out and took it, everything would be okay. It was the silliest feeling, really. It was based on nothing.

"Face your fears." Axel provided his simple explanation. His soft gray eyes were understanding, but there was also an underlying edge of confidence in them. "Face your memories."

He didn't know she'd been to Foxglove so many years before. Did he? No. Impossible. But she could tell Axel read her anxiety far more clearly than most people did.

"I don't want to. Not right now." Kailey offered an apologetic smile and expected the matter to be concluded. Instead, Axel took her hand, his skin rough against hers, and tugged.

"Which is exactly why now is the right time."

⁓

Her feet sank into the sand, and it had a suction-like grip around the sole of her shoes that gave some resistance before releasing her to take another step. Axel had long since let go of her hand. The platonic grip had meant nothing more than to encourage her, and yet Kailey still couldn't shake the feeling of it. She wanted to search for his hand with hers, retake it, and gather courage from it. Kailey resisted and instead allowed the memory to wash over her. She remembered this beach. She remembered wanting to hold a different hand—Jude's hand. He was older by ten years. He was brave and strong, and through her five-year-old eyes he had no disabilities other than their parents. A mother who was distant and always carried a thermos with her. Kailey never drank from it. The water tasted funny. She'd tried it once when not only the taste but a quick slap from her mom had kept her from ever trying it again. Dad? He had just been there. Somewhere in the mix. Holding it together financially, but always tired, always staring at Jude as if Jude were a huge weight on his shoulders.

So it'd just been the two of them, and that one family vacation to Foxglove Manor had been a family therapist's way of trying to unite them. In retrospect, Kailey assumed the therapist thought Mom had successfully gotten through her stint in rehab, and Dad probably had enough hours banked at the factory for a decent short vacation. It was hypothetically a good idea. But it hadn't worked.

Kailey paused beside Axel, the sand having turned darker beneath her feet as it was packed down by dampness. The water wasn't roaring today, and the waves weren't attacking the shore. They were gentler. More rhythmic than temperamental, and they seemed to understand that for now—just this moment—Kailey needed them to be that way.

"Do you know much about the lake?" Axel asked, his question so nicely dull that Kailey felt like engaging in conversation.

"No. Not really." She had been only five, but her vivid memories weren't of Lake Superior's ecosystem or its history.

"You had to have read *Hiawatha*."

"Hiya-what?"

"*The Song of Hiawatha* by Longfellow?" Axel continued, even though she hadn't answered. "Longfellow wrote a poem about this lake. On the shores of Gitche Gumee."

Kailey wrapped her arms around her pea coat as the wind picked up. A patch of ice floated into a basalt outcropping in the water. "Is that what they really call Lake Superior?"

Axel shot her a sideways smile. "It was Longfellow's interpretation of the Native name for it. It means 'Big Sea' or 'Huge Water,' but the Ojibwe people usually meant it for Superior."

It was nice, Kailey admitted to herself, recollecting the history of the lake and shoving aside the turbulent memories.

"You want to know what's really interesting about this lake?" Axel wasn't wearing a coat. He seemed immune to the cold wind as he stuffed his hands into the pockets of his Carhartt pants. He'd at least rolled his shirtsleeves down, but the air plastered the flannel against his midriff. He was fit. That much was noticeable.

"Sure." Kailey averted her eyes from his abdomen, shifting her focus to a sea gull that swooped to the water and then up again.

"They *say* the Great Lakes are burial grounds to over six thousand shipwrecks." Axel bent and picked up a smooth round stone. He flipped it through his fingers as if he'd done so a thousand times before. "You wouldn't think it"—a jerk of his arm and he skipped the stone twice on the water before a wave swallowed it—"but Superior alone has at least five hundred of them. Some ships may have even been used to haul armaments for the war. The Civil War."

"Seriously?" Kailey finally looked directly at Axel, and he met her gaze with a twinkle of intrigue in his eyes.

"Yup. They would smuggle them over the waters, various channels, to help fight in the war."

"Why smuggle them if they're already in the North?"

Axel shrugged. "I don't know. But it makes for a good story." He skipped another stone, then wiped his hand on his pant leg. "This lake has a thousand secrets. You just don't hear many of them about the Civil War."

"They probably prefer to stay buried." Her statement was telling, if Axel was only listening, but Kailey knew he wasn't. There was no real reason for him to read between the lines of her words. Axel knew nothing of Kailey herself. Of the fact that she understood why no one spoke of long-ago secrets on the shores of Gitche Gumee. Sometimes when history died, everything must die with it. She'd wanted to bury her history. To put an end to it. Reviving it—exploring it—was not on her list of things to do. But she had to. For Jude. For his incessant habit of mumbling numerical and alphabetical sequences. For his peace of mind. For the fact that late at night, when all should be quiet, she kept vigil by Jude's bed, watching him toss with unspoken nightmares. Listening to him mumble one of the rare sentences he ever spoke.

She's dead at Foxglove.

She's dead at Foxglove.

8

Kailey stood by the front window and held up her phone as if somehow, magically, the network would fight its way over the lake, through the trees, and pierce through the glass to her device.

"Might as well put that thing away." Maddie rolled up beside her. Her hair had been combed that morning, pulled into a neat little bun on her head. She had silver earrings in her wrinkled earlobes. A blush of matte lipstick on her lips. She had on a garish-colored pair of leggings that might look better on a middle schooler, but her long black tunic covered much of the yellow-flowered leggings and made them more subtle. In her right arm, Maddie cradled a stuffed lion. It was old and worn, its brown nose had loose threads, and its green eyes looked sad. Downright sad.

Kailey pocketed her phone. She hadn't wanted to call anyone. She'd wanted enough data to run another search. Another Google query to find out more about Foxglove Manor—there had to be something—that would bring closure to Jude as well as herself. Foxglove Manor might be far out on the peninsula, secluded in woods near the Porcupine Mountains, but it felt as though the demons that had followed them as children could follow them anywhere. They'd found them once at Foxglove, and who was to say it wouldn't happen again? They'd threatened her with promises, however empty, that they'd find her again someday. It was an effective threat for a small child. That she still couldn't answer their questions made their words more terrifying. For months—years—she'd looked over her shoulder, afraid they would return. But the questions drilled into her by kidnappers at the age of five had their answers embedded in the mind of Jude, the boy with autism. And now Jude was the man with autism, whom too many looked on as *less than* instead of what he was—a veritable genius.

"This is Bruno." Maddie lifted the stuffed lion for Kailey to see. "I'm a fan of these creatures." She settled it back in her arm and waited for a response. Kailey remembered the myriad stuffed animals in Maddie's room. "They all have names," Maddie went on. "Names and stories. My son gave me Bruno years ago. For Mother's Day. I never go far without Bruno."

Her son. Kailey had seen a few photographs in Maddie's room. None of them had a boy in them—or even a grown man. It might very well be that Maddie's failing mind was inserting a son where a son didn't exist.

"Why did you come here?"

Kailey stared down at Maddie, who returned the gaze with frank, open curiosity. She smiled a tad, wrinkling her already wrinkled cheeks further. "I don't mean to be rude, but you're a young thing, and pretty ones like you don't move to be with old ladies like me because they want to."

"Well, I enjoy—"

Maddie waved off Kailey's polite explanation and leaned forward in her wheelchair. "I might be losing my mind, but I'm not stupid. Not yet anyway." She laughed with a spirit that indicated in her younger years, Maddie was probably one to break out into uninhibited dance while frying eggs in the kitchen—or something to that effect. "Did you run off from college?"

"No," Kailey answered obediently.

"A jilted lover?"

"No." Kailey smirked. Maddie's insistence was good-natured and a bit funny.

"Ahhhh, then family. You don't want to be around your family."

"Jude and I don't have much family. Our parents died years ago.

We grew up primarily with my aunt, but we've never been very close. No, I'm not running from family. I'm . . ." She really didn't have a clear answer that was appropriate to tell an old lady with Alzheimer's. She was here because Foxglove Manor had woven its way through Jude's mind and not released him. Because the same memories he held captive in his mind were the ones she herself could remember only snippets of. Maybe she should simply say that she had brought Jude here with her to find a quiet place of peace and serenity, when in actuality she'd brought him here to reconcile them both with the past and try to bring about closure to the heavy fog that had settled over them.

Maddie's gray brow rose at Kailey's long silence. "Hmm . . ." She tipped her head toward stuffed Bruno. "What's that, Bruno?"

She talked to stuffed animals too? Kailey filed that away for future reference with regard to Maddie's reliability.

"Ahh, good question." Maddie patted Bruno's head, and the orange animal seemed to smile. Kailey shifted nervously, weirded out that she'd even had that observation. Maddie continued, "What is it you're afraid of?"

The air was sucked from the room with that one insightful question. Maddie's eyes were particularly lucid, and though there was warmth in them, there was also a strange mix of savvy and awareness. Maybe she'd underestimated the old woman.

Maddie waited for a moment, then smiled. A knowing one that accepted Kailey wouldn't offer her an answer—not a truthful one anyway. "It's all right. I understand. Sometimes the past is too difficult to rectify with the present."

"Mm-hmm." It was the only safe thing Kailey felt she could say.

Maddie laughed, and the wrinkles at her eyes stretched down her soft blushed cheeks to meet with the ones that edged from her lips. "You know, I can't recall your name, and it's not like I have much hope of recollecting it in the future. It pains me to accept that I won't always remember you. You're such a pretty thing. Nice also. But with such pain in your body and eyes." Maddie's expression turned stern, and she raised her left eyebrow with the swift expertise of someone who had long ago incorporated it into her repertoire of looks. "I'd like to smack whoever did that to you. One cheek and then the other, and then level a swift kick to their groin. It was a man. I can tell. While I don't validate villainizing the male species entirely, I do believe in the full dismembering of the ones who hurt women."

Kailey's legs gave out, and she slumped onto a chair that was gratefully not far away. Maddie was a conundrum of nice, intelligent, warm, grandmotherly, a little crazy, and a whole lot of hidden inner violence. She both liked Maddie and feared her a little bit. All at the same time.

Maddie reached over and curled her fingers around Kailey's hand. Her skin was soft, papery thin, and just slightly warm. "It's all right. You're safe here."

Safe here. Kailey didn't feel safe. But then she had never felt safe.

"Do you have my notebook?" Maddie's voice had altered. It was shaky, lost, and she looked around the room as though looking for something. "I seem to have lost my notebook."

Relieved by the diversion, Kailey pushed to her feet. She recalled Maddie scribbling on a notepad the day before. Spotting it across the room, Kailey patted Maddie's arm in reassurance. "Just a sec."

Kailey crossed the room and bent to retrieve the lined-paper notepad bound with a wire spiral top. She absently flipped it open as she walked back toward Maddie, who stared out the window in front of her. There was a page of sketches—googly-eyed animals with cute smiles and bow ties. Kailey flipped the pages as she neared the back of Maddie's wheelchair. The old woman faced away from her, and she was still stroking Bruno's head as if he were alive.

The letters on the page stood out in bold black. They had been written over many times, so that the ink bled through the page onto the one behind. Kailey froze and stared at the string of randomness.

Gnqgy jgq vvnlcsx

It was written repeatedly. Over and over down the entire page. Kailey turned to the next and then the next. No more googly-eyed adorable sketches. Just row upon row of the nonsensical letters. Kailey fumbled with the notebook, and it fell in a flutter of bent paper and scratching as the wire binding hit the wood flooring.

Maddie startled and shot a surprised look over her shoulder. Her brown eyes took in the notebook now lying up with its bold inscriptions screaming to be seen. She lifted her dark gaze to Kailey, and their eyes locked. A smile fluttered across Maddie's face and then dissipated, replaced by an expression of consternation.

"You see it too?" Maddie maneuvered her chair around so she could look more directly at Kailey. "She told me about them. I didn't believe her. But she's told you too?"

Kailey didn't know who "she" was. All she recognized was how similar—if not identical—the gibberish was to what Jude sketched on everything—every piece of paper, on the wall in permanent marker, and on her hand with gel pen—after the day they'd left Foxglove Manor. Kailey recalled the man in the van.

"Tell them to me!" he'd demanded.

Letters. He'd wanted letters. Numbers. He'd demanded them from Kailey, a five-year-old girl who barely knew the alphabet. G, she had said, and 12. It was all her little mind had remembered. She had even looked at her hand to see if the gel-pen ink would magically reappear after being washed off days before. But it hadn't. He'd yelled at her. Threatened Jude. Threatened her parents. In the end, her little five-year-old self had walked home. Trembling. Terrified. Her mother had scoffed at her and opened a new bottle of vodka. Only Jude had believed her. She knew this. Because he had written the letters and numbers again the moment she asked him. But after he did, this time he ripped the paper to shreds and took a permanent marker to every place he had written them, crossing them out, covering them with black ink until they were unreadable. He did it all while shaking his head and moaning.

"No. No. No. No."

The sequence had been a no-no to Kailey ever since.

"I'll get it." The knock on the solid arched door echoed in the front hall and bounced off what seemed to be every stone in the manor. Teri left the now-empty tray of medicine cups by Kailey.

There were four residents in the front room. Two remained in their units, napping or otherwise sticking to themselves and the friendship of their daytime soaps. Raymond had positioned himself beside Maddie, who was contentedly stroking Bruno's ragged fur as if he were her lap cat. The other two residents Kailey had been a tad slower getting to know. Opposite Raymond and Maddie were Stella and Judy. They were peppy older women, both of whom used walkers and sported a flirtatious glimmer in their eyes, who seemed intent on staying under the maturity level of an eighteen-year-old. Kailey had pegged them from the start as the fun-loving ones of the group. They eyed Raymond, but for the most part left him alone. Even Kailey knew after a few short days that his heart was loyal to Maddie.

Teri's voice filtered into the room. "I don't believe so, no, Officer." There was a bit of worry tingeing her voice. Kailey straightened in her chair and exchanged looks with Raymond, who appeared every bit as sharp as a man thirty years his junior. "No, we haven't seen anyone unusual about. I mean, out here? No one comes here unless they have a purpose to."

Words were muffled by the wall. Raymond tipped his head toward the doorway in a quick direction. Kailey took his cue and rose from her chair, tiptoeing to the doorway to eavesdrop. She glanced across the room toward Jude. Her brother had hunched his thirty-five-year-old shoulders over as he stared intently into a picture book about NASA and space.

"Axel around?" the man's voice inquired, drawing Kailey's attention back to eavesdropping.

"He should be," Teri replied. "I think he's out in the back shed prepping the mower and tiller for spring. I told him we'd like a small vegetable garden this year. Something some of the residents can invest in and tend to."

"Sure." He was clearly not interested. "Back shed, eh? If you don't mind, I'll drop in on Axel, see if he's ran across anyone unfamiliar."

Kailey's elbow knocked a framed photograph on the table by her hip. It fell over with a *plop* as the man—a police officer—stepped further into view. His gaze latched on to Kailey.

"How-do?" He gave her a nod.

"Hello."

"New to the area?" the officer inquired with a glance at Teri. Teri stepped between them, positioning a smile on her face that was both honest and reassuring.

"Kailey Gibson. She's our new aide—and her brother, Jude, is our latest resident." Kailey noted how Teri didn't attempt to explain why Jude with special needs had been incorporated into a home for the retired and elderly. Teri continued, "What a blessing she's been already—for me especially. What with only one other nurse on staff, being both RN and home director gets a bit raunchy with the amount of time it steals."

"Gibson, eh? All righty then. Just want to verify, ya know?" The officer flipped open a notepad. He was middle-aged. Had one too many doughnuts at some point in his repertoire as a police officer, and he had the vernacular of someone who was a full-on Yooper but had married a Canadian, only to birth a child from Wisconsin. Kailey almost laughed at her thoughts. No one would understand them unless they were from the area. The people were a breed unto their own.

Kailey determined to appease any suspicion. For it appeared the officer was searching for someone—something—and while it unsettled her, she knew it would be better were she up-front about it. She had nothing to hide. Hide *from* maybe. But hide? No.

"We're from Stevens Point," she supplied.

He smiled congenially. "I've got a cousin down there. You ever been here before?"

Kailey shot a look at Teri, who waited expectantly. She shifted her weight onto her other foot. "I—um—yes. Once, but it was years ago."

"You never told me that!" Teri's reaction was a mixture of pleasant surprise and confusion.

The officer wasn't finished with his inquiry. "You've got relatives up here?"

Kailey swallowed nervously. She really didn't want Teri to know—not because there was anything to hide necessarily, but because it complicated things. It made her taking the aide position and bringing Jude with her more personal than just being the doting guardian in need of employment. Teri would want to know why she was tied to Foxglove Manor—and Kailey had no idea how to answer that.

"No relatives. We vacationed here once. When I was five. My parents were Ron and Samantha."

"Gotcha. Yeah, I recall this place being a vacation spot years back. But, I can't say as I would know any of ya. But then I've been on the force only ten years now, and *uff-da*! Even my own mother didn't think I'd make it this long." His laugh was good-natured.

"Faith of a parent, it's inspiring, isn't it?" Kailey quipped back in small talk and humor, deflecting the question on Teri's face with a smile as though it was all no big deal.

"You betcha it is!" He flipped his notebook shut and jammed it into the back pocket of his uniform pants. He extended a meaty hand. "Detective Chad Ericksson. Nice to meet ya, Kailey."

She took it, relieved to see the lines on his face relax. He was clean-shaven, in his mid-forties, with gray in his dark sideburns and peppered throughout his eyebrows.

"Sorry to ask all the questions, but we're looking for anyone new in the area. Anyone who may've seen something suspicious that may be of help."

"That's pretty broad, Chad." Teri appeared to be on a first-name basis with him. "Suspicious of what?"

Officer Ericksson shrugged. "I'm not trying to alarm anyone, but there's been some—strange stuff goin' on in town."

"Strange?" Teri leaned against the wall, crossing her arms over her chest, genuine concern and curiosity emanating from her scrubs-clad body.

The officer looked between them and scratched his nose as he sniffed. He directed his attention toward Teri. "You know that Bascom kid?"

"Riley? She's, what, ten?"

"Uh-huh. Yup. That's her." Officer Ericksson shook his head. "Kid didn't show up for school yesterday. Teachers called her parents, and long story short, Riley showed up back at her home. But late. Nine o'clock in the evening. They'd called us, but it hadn't been twenty-four hours yet. 'Course as usually happens, she showed back up, but the gal swears she didn't play hooky or run away."

Kailey tensed. His look settled on her. "Says some stranger kidnapped her, then let her go. Weirdest story I ever heard a kid come up with."

She could hear a rushing in her ears. Like the distant sound of the pounding waves of the frigid lake, only more constant.

"Ope, looks like she's goin' down!" Officer Ericksson launched forward and caught Kailey by the arms before her knees gave out.

Teri yelped and hurried to grab a chair, pushing the wooden four-legged seat behind Kailey. Officer Ericksson settled her onto it, and Teri's hand rubbed Kailey's back.

"Put your head between your knees, honey. That's it. I can see some color in your cheeks."

The rushing began to diminish, and the cold clamminess that had washed over her skin began to fade. So much for subtle and flying under the radar. One mention of a story all too like her own memories and she'd collapsed like Scarlett O'Hara the day Rhett Butler left her without giving a—

"Miss Gibson?" Officer Ericksson's voice interrupted her scattered thoughts.

Kailey managed to side-eye him from where her head rested in her palms as she bent over her knees.

"Something about Riley's story set you off. What was it?"

Teri murmured something soft.

Officer Ericksson responded, equally as quiet.

Kailey could tell that Teri was simply trying to bargain for space for Kailey. But she was fine. Really. And, if she could help Riley Bascom get someone to believe her story, well then at least the little ten-year-old girl wouldn't have to suffer with the stigma of being a storytelling little liar her entire life.

"What if she's telling the truth?" Kailey managed to get out.

"Say what?" Officer Ericksson's eyes widened.

"I mean—what if Riley was kidnapped?"

"For less than fifteen hours?" Officer Ericksson clicked his tongue. "Doesn't make a whole lot of sense."

"But you're still checking into it? Leads and all that, right?" Teri interjected.

Officer Ericksson offered her a smile, and this time Kailey caught the shyness in it. A small spark of interest he was trying hard to hide. Wonderful. If anything, he was using this as a foundation to catapult a conversation with Teri rather than a sincere effort to validate the Bascom girl's experience.

"Did she describe her abductors?" Kailey sat up slowly. Teri's hand was still on her back, and Kailey sensed the woman's study of her.

The detective's expression shuttered. "Mebbe."

"*Maybe* you should listen to her. Maybe she's telling the truth."

"Well, that *is* why I'm here, Miss Gibson." Officer Ericksson stiffened. He was offended. So was she. Kailey wanted to rail against him to do his job. Why were children and women so easily cast aside as crazy? Just because a story didn't measure up with some preconceived concept of a logical sequence of events. Crime was rarely logical anyway. It had patterns, but no rules.

"Of course." Teri patted the detective on his arm. They exchanged a look, but now Officer Ericksson appeared sterner. He stared down his nose at Kailey, and she kept her head bent to avoid his eyes.

"You sure you're telling me everything, Miss Gibson?"

His voice echoed off the wood floor.

Kailey heard Jude cough in the room behind her. The squeak of a wheelchair as it rolled across the floor.

"Miss Gibson?" The tone in the detective's voice made Kailey lift her head.

"Yes, sir," she answered.

He studied her face before nodding. "Okay then. If you think of anything—or remember anything—I'll expect a call."

A business card was pushed toward her. Kailey took it. Think of anything? All she could think of was the dark van. The smell of damp vehicle carpet. The man interrogating her until she thought she would wet herself. If this girl—this Riley Bascom—had experienced the same . . . she should say something. But what? That she was kidnapped in a similar fashion twenty years ago? There couldn't be a connection—yet there was. Foxglove Manor. The lake. The region. It was too similar to be a coincidence, but too coincidental to make sense.

For now, she thumbed Officer Ericksson's card as Teri walked him to the door. If she remembered anything? She ran her finger over the black block letters of his name. Kailey knew there were things she should remember but didn't, about their last family vacation here at Foxglove Manor. They were the secrets she'd locked away the day Dad left the rental key on the counter and yelled at them to get in the car. They were the mysteries that lurked behind Jude's eyes and the tales in the string of letters and numbers he wrote incessantly until the day she was taken.

9

ADRIA

"Shutter the windows!" Mrs. St. John's cry from the hallway shattered the night. Adria launched from her bed, bare feet connecting with the cold wooden floor. How she had slept through the howling wind was beyond her comprehension, but Adria flew to the windows to close the shutters. She froze, mesmerized by the power outside Foxglove Manor.

The wind whipped not only the trees until their tops drew circles against the night sky, but it also pushed the whitecap waves into giant monsters. Broiling and frenetic, Superior boasted its name as the waters rose high and seemingly in different directions. Like a freshwater ocean in the precursor of a hurricane, the cliff on which the manor stood seemed more like a small mound in the storm. Barely a foundation on which they could be assured of their safety.

Adria's attention was yanked from the scene as a crash sounded on the floor above her. She grabbed at the shutters and slammed them into place over the window. Bolting across the floor, Adria was hardly aware of her thin cotton nightdress or the way her hair tangled about her shoulders. She opened her bedroom door and almost collided with Mrs. St. John, who glowed eerily by the light cascading from the candle in her hand. Her narrow nose appeared longer, her eyes deeper set and hollow.

"What are you doing, Miss Fontaine? Go back to your room!"

She hadn't expected the venomous confrontation from the older woman. "Is it a tornado?" Adria asked, breathless, unsure if she was more frightened by the storm's vehemence or Mrs. St. John.

"We don't get tornados here," Mrs. St. John spat. Whether it was truthful or not, Adria had no desire to press the issue. "It's a fearsome storm, that is all."

"I heard a crash. Shouldn't we check? It could be a broken window in the turret."

"Diggery will check in the morning." Mrs. St. John shooed Adria back into the bedroom. Adria retreated a few steps until she was fully embraced by the shadows of her room. "You can service me by remaining here as I've requested."

"But—"

A black glare speared Adria. "As your father would demand of you."

The bedroom door was shut in her face, a swoop of wind from the motion sending a strand of Adria's hair to brush her nose.

Waters roared, a pounding cadence like a line of soldiers on the battlefield, the drums preceding them in their march. Her room was cast into a nighttime darkness as teal tones washed over her white bedding, glistened off the polished floors, and reflected on her gown.

Another crash sent Adria flying to her bed. She launched into the middle of the mattress, her feet tangling in the covers. Lightning must have sparked across the sky. Adria saw flashes through the gaps in the shutters, followed by a rumble and then a sharp *crack* as thunder broke the sky with its terrific bass. It shook the room. The gauzy tapestries hanging from her canopy blew as though the wind had pushed through the stone walls to breathe its frigidity on Adria.

A man shouted. It was distant but strong, and filled with urgency. Adria stiffened in the bed.

It was unintelligible.

Again. Not unlike the cry of a man charging into battle, thrusting his bayonet into the midsection of his enemy.

"Cease!" It was Mrs. St. John. Her voice carried through the floor vent, the iron scrolling vibrating against its frame.

Footsteps. Running.

"That's it, that's it." That voice had to be Diggery. Soothing but laced with a nervous energy that catapulted Adria from her position in the bed.

She jammed her feet into her slippers and reached for the bedroom door. Opening it a crack, she peeked out, both directions. The hallway was long and dark, its floor uncarpeted, its walls unadorned, and it included three doors to other bedrooms. A strange hallway with little purpose other than the function of getting somewhere. It wasn't a gallery of portraits, nor were there any potted ferns on stands in the corners. The lamps in their sconces were dark, unlit, and served no real purpose.

Adria knew to go right meant to eventually find the stairs that led to the first floor. To go left was to explore areas of the manor she'd not bothered with before. She questioned the vision she'd had of the man in the turret window. She remembered Diggery's denial that he existed. She heard Mrs. St. John denying any concern that Adria explore the manor. It had not been lofted as any great mystery. No orders of avoidance had been issued. It was simply . . . well, it was the attic. The turret's room. A floor where, were Mrs. St. John in a larger metropolis, service staff would most likely lodge. Instead, here in the remote north of the Upper Peninsula, it was only Mrs. St. John, Diggery, and a housemaid whom Adria had yet to formally meet—not that one ever formally met a servant.

Her weight made the floor creak beneath her footsteps. Adria's fingers trailed along the plaster wall, moving over small bumps and bruises in its old finishing. She should have thought to light a candle. She should have thought to wear a wrapper. All the should-haves pounded in her head in echo to another pounding clap of thunder and another bit-off cry from Mrs. St. John.

The hallway twisted to the left, and Adria followed it. At the end, a door was open, and beyond it a steep flight of narrow stairs. They were enclosed stairs with wood paneling on either side. They were shadowed and dark, but Adria could hear the voice now, even louder and more intense.

"Hold! Hold!" Diggery commanded.

"I'll get a strip of linen!" was Mrs. St. John's response.

Adria's foot positioned on the bottom step, and she peered up into the darkness that embraced the soft glow of lamplight. She continued to climb, hesitation clawing at her ankles, feeling weighted. Something cursed at her from inside her mind, telling her she should obey Mrs. St. John. Reminding Adria of her worthlessness and how she had no business snooping into Foxglove Manor's business.

She was almost to the top of the stairwell. Light stretched and touched her bare toes as she landed her right foot at the top of the stairs.

"Why are you here!" The voice came out of the darkness and assaulted her. A large frame, dark with rigor and intensity.

Adria's eyes widened. A scream caught in her throat.

His eyes were blazing with fury. Empty, cold eyes that fisted her face with aggression. She knew she shouldn't have come. She cursed her curiosity. She cursed this place. Adria felt her footing slip as she fell backward, gravity pulling her down the steps like a demon clawing at a soul to pull it into the lake of fire.

"A curse is yours, along with the others here who lay among the dead . . ."

Words that sliced her dreams as consciousness wasted away into the thunderous depths of blackness.

⁓

"Hold steady, miss." A hand pressed against Adria as she struggled to rise. Opening her eyes meant increasing the throbbing headache, and the bright sunlight cascading through her bedroom window was enough to blind a person.

"Where is he?" Adria couldn't help but struggle against the hand.

"Who, miss?"

Adria squeezed her eyes shut and then opened them, willing the blurry film to dissipate from her eyes and for the form of the woman beside her to come into view. It wasn't Mrs. St. John—this must be the nameless housemaid of Foxglove Manor. Lifting her hand to her pounding head, Adria squinted.

Brown eyes.

Brown hair.

Fine features.

Petite.

The maid couldn't be over fifteen years of age.

"Where is he?" Adria asked again.

The woman—girl, really—gave a firmer push against Adria's shoulder. "Sit back, miss. You'll be the death of yourself and then me too, for certain, once Mrs. St. John catches wind that you passed on. Then where will I be but walking the shores of Gitche Gumee and waiting for the lake mermaids to curse me further."

Adria was intrigued. "There are lake mermaids?"

"More like a manitou," the girl mumbled under her breath. "A great spirit who rules the lake and protects his people."

"From what?" Adria breathed, somehow captivated by the story in the fogginess of the moment.

The girl's dark eyes lifted. "From the demons. Lake demons."

"I've never heard of a manitou before," Adria admitted.

"And you've never seen one of the people either." There was an edge to the girl's voice that distracted Adria. Nervousness, maybe. Shifty. Or perhaps she was purposely diverting Adria's attention. Regardless, Adria pushed against the mattress so she could sit up further. The girl wasted no time in plumping a pillow behind her back.

"You rolled down the stairs like a marble on a holiday."

The memory came back in a rush. His deep face and eyes. The bulk of the man looming over her.

"Who is he?" Adria asked, glancing at the side table for a glass of water.

The girl must have read her thoughts, for she moved from the bed to the bureau and tipped a pitcher adorned with hand-painted purple roses. Water made its sloshing sound as it hit the glass. "Who's who, miss?"

"The man. At the top of the stairs."

The girl chuckled and returned the pitcher to a ceramic platter that caught excess drips. "What man at the top of the stairs?"

Adria frowned as she took the offered glass of water. "I'm not losing my mind." She didn't state it forcefully. In fact, doubts rushed in fast enough to make her question herself.

You're a silly, stupid one. Margot had always made sure her younger sister was well aware of her inadequacies.

Adria shivered and drank the cold water. She watched the housemaid over the rim of the glass. "I know there was a man. I saw him with my own eyes. I heard him crashing and shouting during the storm."

"Perhaps, miss, you heard Diggery running into the ladder upstairs. My room is up there, and I did find a mouse nest on the top shelf of the wardrobe. He brought the ladder yesterday afternoon to clean it out. Ran into the ladder last night in the dark as he was trying to take it back downstairs."

"During a wicked thunderstorm that had Mrs. St. John shouting for the shutters to be closed?" Adria challenged.

The housemaid's eyes flickered, and her shoulders straightened. "Could be you took a greater knock to the head with that fall than you think?"

"Doubtful."

"Likely."

They were at a standoff. There was no part of Adria that wished to argue with the persnickety housemaid. She knew what she'd seen, and yet . . . even Diggery denied there had been a man upstairs.

"I'm Lula." The maid straightened the blankets at the end of Adria's bed. "I've lived here since I was ten. Mrs. St. John took me in and here I be."

The age of ten? A child couldn't have been of much assistance to Mrs. St. John, yet Mrs. St. John hardly seemed one prone to charity without some reciprocating benefit.

Lula didn't bother to wait for Adria to ask more questions. She was chatty—mouthy, really—and was juxtaposed to any of the etiquette Adria had been accustomed to from her father's staff.

"Mrs. St. John came here a bit over six years ago. Just before the calendar flipped the page into the eighties. Before that, Dr. Miranda lived here. Strange man, they say. 'Course, I never knew him. And before that, it was Captain Cartier, who built Foxglove Manor. Mrs. St. John's daughter had just passed on when she arrived."

"How did you both meet?" Adria watched Lula hang Adria's dress from the day before in the wardrobe. A shadow fluttered across Lula's face.

"I was an orphan. Sent me to the poorhouse, they did, over near Harbor Towne. Mrs. St. John needed maid service, and I was sitting on a bench there when she came in all haughty-like asking if any of the 'decrepit women' were capable of housework and were above 'ill repute.' 'Course, I stood up and offered myself at her service." Lula paused to half curtsy, half bow. Her brown eyes twinkled. "Mrs. St. John just stared at me, and I took that as a yes and hiked myself out to her carriage." At Adria's stunned silence, Lula added, "It tough up here, in the Peninsula. Copper mines, and before that fur trading . . . that's about all you've got outside of the railway and shipping. Home services are hard to come by, so a lady's gotta jump at the chance when she can."

"But you were only a child!" Adria shoved away the recollections from when she was of younger age.

Lula looked surprised as she tucked a tendril of dark brown hair behind her ear. "I was almost eleven. Old enough to do the dishes, dust a mantel, and spit-shine a floor. Better than starving in the poorhouse with no ma or pa to look after me."

Adria didn't counter Lula's argument with her own. That having no father would have been a blessing. That being independent and headstrong enough to escape by your own wits and an older lady's compunction to deal with the impertinence . . . well, it was better than other circumstances. Ones that made dying seem like a fairy-tale ending, and where the weight of a parent's threats didn't make your shoulders bend so low it was as if your wrists were shackled to the floor.

10

"Her husband owes me, and she knows it."

Even in her sleep, Adria could not escape the voice of her father. His bushy sideburns puffed from a face that was probably handsome in his younger years. She wanted to cry for her mother—as she had when she was little. And Mama had come. Adria could not forget the dark looks Mama gave her father, or how Mama had scooped up Adria and cuddled her to bed. Her only protector in a world that became far too large and frightening after Mama passed.

"St. John made no error when he purchased Miranda's manor. Too bad he died before he returned what was mine."

What was his. In her dream, Adria walked across the carpet, her bare feet padding soft on the muted tones of burgundy and brown wool. She stopped before a fireplace. She was in the study of Foxglove Manor. She'd been there earlier, to retrieve something for Mrs. St. John. Now she relived her visit there in her dream.

"Try to shame the family, Alexandria, and you've earned yourself passage to Foxglove Manor. Find it and I will forfeit all claim to you."

A threat to many a child, their fathers disowning them—turning them out into the world on their own. Especially as a woman. But for Adria, it was freedom.

The room was blurry on its edges, unfocused, and Adria's eyes strained to see what was above the fireplace. Her hair hung in dirty strands over her face, and she tried to push them away. But like the sins of generations past, they returned, stroking her cheeks and leaving trails of dirt behind. She lifted her face, squinting at the pieces above the fireplace.

She remembered now. Two sabers were mounted there. Long, pointed blades, crossed midway with their hilts a shining brass patina, and the grips corded leather with a wire wrap. They were unfamiliar. Not reminiscent of any sabers she'd seen before, and with the war over only twenty years, Adria had seen plenty of Union weaponry. Her father boasted of some of his scores when he pirated the lakes. A set of pistols were his favorite bounty, one he claimed he had not stolen but had been gifted by a returning Union general of some clout.

She walked over to the mantel, her feet seeming not to touch the floor anymore. Adria lifted her hand to touch the hilt of a saber, but its hot metal caused her to snatch her hand back. The tips of her fingers were reddened, as if she'd forgotten to use a hot pad to pull a pan from the oven. Tilting her head, Adria leaned toward the sabers, her vision caressing them almost as though they were something far more precious than weapons crafted to claim lives.

Adria gripped the edge of the wood mantel and then drew back, dropping her gaze to the scrolls carved into the wood. They were tiny scrolls, and her tender fingers ran across them. Like a blind man reading braille, Adria fingered the artistry in the wood until she was sure the scrolls spelled something. That they weren't just scrolls, but a letter. Two letters.

G. N.

Nonsensical gibberish.

Without caution, Adria's hand moved once more, back to the hilt, the brass, the saber . . . The fireplace burst into flames, hot flames that branded the inside of the firebox with creosote. She leapt backward as the flames followed, licking the edge of her night-dress, scorching her skin with blisters.

Adria screamed.

Her eyes locked with those in the face that began to form within the flames. A grotesque face, marred with scars and pock-marks, eyes glowing and squinted in fury. Then it transitioned, the eyes turning bulbous as the flames married with a green smoke that did not match the science of fire. It slithered around Adria's ankles as the flames crept up her legs. She felt no pain, only a sucking, sickening sensation that made nausea rise in her throat. The face elongated and then shifted until the eyes Adria stared into were no longer a stranger's. No longer someone she did not recognize. But her father. Staring at her from the flames and emerald smoke, until the windows shattered into the room with a force propelled by a wave from the lake, blistering in its cold. It doused the flames that encircled Adria's body, but as her father's image washed away, the sabers came undone and aimed toward her heart. They would kill her. Pierce her very soul. Yet the only thing Adria could do was grapple for the beautifully carved mantel as if it were a lifeline. The one thing that could save her. The unexplained purpose to parallel her horrors. But, as it had always been in life, and in her dreams too, purpose remained desperately out of reach.

~

"Where are you going, miss?" Lula dogged Adria's heels as Adria hurried down the long hallway with its dark, empty walls. Adria looked down at her fingertips. They were reddened, as if she'd touched something hot, only she'd just awakened. Awakened from the rest Mrs. St. John had insisted she continue to take after her tumble down the third-floor stairs.

"Where is the study?" Adria got turned around in this manor with its twisty halls and corners. But she had to see it. To reassure herself it was merely a dream. That the vision of her father's face—and even the stranger's face—was merely a figment of her dream and nothing more.

"On the first floor, miss. Around the left corner, beyond the parlor. Don't you remember?"

Ahh, yes. She remembered it now.

Adria hurried down the broad stairway that led from the second-floor bedrooms to the more inhabitable first floor. Here were signs of life. Signs that could potentially be interpreted as warm, if one avoided looking out the windows and seeing the expanse of the lake and its persistent, thrumming waves.

"What's to see in the study, miss?" Lula, for some reason, had not left Adria's trail. It was as if positions had shifted so that instead of Adria being Mrs. St. John's companion, Lula had become her companion.

Adria didn't answer, but instead she twisted the knob on the closed study door and flung it open. She stilled. Frozen. Staring straight ahead. A fireplace, cold with no recent embers or ash. Above it, a beautifully carved walnut mantel, and positioned in the center of the wall hung two sabers. Just as she had dreamt—or subconsciously recalled.

"Impossible," she mumbled under her breath, absently running her thumb over her fingertips. They were sore. She hurried to the mantel and ran her hand across the scrollwork. She released a sigh of relief. They were merely scrolls, like a snail's shell, curving around each other, some leaving a trail in the wood as if it were ribbon. Adria closed her eyes, to be sure her dream was simply that. Nonsense. Her fingers rubbed against the scrollwork. A curve, a loop, a ribbon . . . Adria snatched her hand back, her eyes snapping open.

G. N.

You wouldn't have seen them if you hadn't felt them. Of that, Adria was sure. But now she took a step back and eyed the scrollwork, noting how subtly two of the scrolls were carved into making the two letters. Or perhaps it was merely an artistic happenstance. The letters meant absolutely nothing anyway, yet there was no explanation for why they would have shown up in her dreams. She hadn't seen the letters before, not that she recalled. Never bothered with running her hand over the mantel to find them. Yet here she was, a perfect case of recollection, minus the roaring and violent fire. She glanced at the windows. They were in place, not shattered, the panes cloudy from not having been recently washed.

"Whose study is this?" Adria hurried to the desk in the corner. A massive desk, manly in its structure. An inkwell sat on its top. A pile of closed books. A ledger of some sort, closed, with a coating of dust on it.

"Dr. Miranda's, miss."

"Whose?"

Lula's brown eyes widened. "Don'tcha remember? He owned Foxglove Manor before Mrs. St. John moved here. He lived at Foxglove since he bought the place from Captain Cartier in 1859, just before the war started."

It was unimportant. With one exception. Adria's interest piqued even as her father's warm breath hissed with an imagined insistence in her ear. Find it. Find his missing goods.

"Captain Cartier. He sailed the lakes?" Adria inquired.

Lula shrugged scrawny shoulders. "How's I supposed to know?"

Adria opened the ledger, but Lula rushed forward and slapped it shut. Her palm remained planted on its top as she leaned over the opposite side of the desk and stared at Adria. "Do not snoop, Miss Fontaine."

Adria pulled back, surprised at Lula's vehemence. "I merely want to know who Captain Cartier was. What he did. Why he built this place, and why he sold it."

Lula opened her mouth to speak, then snapped it shut.

"He sold it because his wife, Fleur, passed away." Mrs. St. John's strident voice broke through the stale air of the study. Her skirts swished as she walked into the room.

Lula removed her hand from the ledger and wiped it on her apron. Adria remained positioned behind the desk.

Mrs. St. John continued as though she'd never paused. "There is not much point in remaining in one's home after those who kept it alive have moved on."

There was a distance in Mrs. St. John's voice that made Adria stare at her a little longer and deeper than before. A bit of pain etched in the woman's wrinkles, making her more human, more of a mother who'd lost her daughter through a horrible accident.

"Captain Cartier worked the Great Lakes, of course. Why else would he have been here, and why else would he have the title of captain?"

Adria denied herself the luxury of sinking into the leather chair. "What did he ship?" she ventured. *Goods?* Her father's smuggling and pirating on the lakes? But the timing didn't fit. Not really. If Captain Cartier had sold Foxglove Manor to the Mirandas before the war had begun, then the captain would have been gone before Adria's father started his running on the lakes.

Mrs. St. John waved her hand at Lula, and the girl scampered from the room without a backward glance. "Awkward little chit." Mrs. St. John rolled her eyes as she sighed through her nose. "What do you *think* the captain shipped, Alexandria? Copper. It is what everyone ships out of these harbors. The mines produce, the mills prepare, and the ships take the wares off to ports unknown to the small man here in the Peninsula."

"Was Mr. St. John in shipping?" Adria dared to ask. She had to make the connection somehow. It was difficult to determine how to go about finding even the slightest clue as to the whereabouts of her father's stolen goods—that he had stolen himself. The irony was not lost on her.

Mrs. St. John's lips pursed, and she stared down her nose at Adria. The high lace collar of her white shirtwaist was buttoned at the top with a navy-blue button and it looked too tight. Strangulation from one's shirtwaist would be an awful way to die. Adria bit her cheek to temper her smile. She thought of the worst things in the most inappropriate times. There were many ways one could die—one could *make* themselves die—but they shouldn't ask Adria for insight. She was a dismal failure at the taking of her own life. Perhaps it was because there was still a tiny seedling of hope that purpose could be found still. In spite of the nightmares. In spite of her father and of her sister.

"My husband was in shipping, yes. But it is a dull preoccupation to dwell on, Alexandria." Mrs. St. John folded her hands in front of her. There was scrutiny in her eyes. "I find myself of a mind to be read to. Something substantial. I've a volume on the French Revolution. I do believe it would behoove us both to fill our minds with something worthwhile rather than fiddling about an old room belonging to a long-dead Dr. Miranda, and now littered with my dead husband's toys and trinkets."

The woman spun and headed for the doorway. She stopped and looked over her shoulder, her gaze sharp. "Are you coming, Alexandria?"

Adria nodded but didn't follow. Instead, she glanced toward the mantel. She scanned the sabers mounted like souvenirs of something much larger than could be explained by the glistening metal. If there were clues or answers here, nothing stood out to Adria that made even the tiniest sense. Accepting it for the moment and shoving away the all-too-real memories of her chaotic dream, Adria followed Mrs. St. John.

"She'll come back." Lula's hiss from the corner of the entryway startled Adria. Adria clutched her throat, sucking in a gasp. Lula's eyes seemed larger than before. Deep-set and brown. Frightened, really. A part of her confidence seemed to have washed away and been replaced by fear. "When she comes back, Mrs. St. John will lose her mind, you know? Foxglove Manor ain't no friend to females."

Adria took a step toward the housemaid. "What are you speaking of?"

A thin smile stretched across Lula's face. Dull and resigned. It made little bumps rise on the skin of Adria's arms.

"I'm speaking of *her*, miss. The spirit that roams these halls. She always does when one asks too many questions. And it's always the females what's ask the questions. The men? They just up and leave. Like any rational soul would. Smart, they is. Men. Pretend to be brave, but they run like cowards. Only . . ." Lula blinked, her eyes almost glassy. "Only, there's a smartness in being a coward. A person stays alive when they run."

11

KAILEY

Poe opened an eye and observed Kailey for a long moment before closing it again and adjusting himself beneath the stroking hand of Raymond. He had found his person, and the fact that Poe had ceased sleeping at the foot of her bed in exchange for Raymond's made it more than apparent that loyalty was not particularly prevalent in the cat's repertoire. In another time, Kailey might have even found herself a bit jealous. Poe had, after all, been her first cat, followed a year later by Edgar. But Poe had always been moody—not unlike his namesake—and under the tender caress of Raymond, he actually had a contented cat-smile on his face. And he was purring. Heaven help her, if Raymond wasn't practically purring as well.

Maddie wasn't too far away. She seemed to find comfort in Raymond's steadying presence. Kailey approached her with a thermos of water with a plastic straw sticking out of it.

"Teri said you need to be hydrated today, Maddie."

Maddie batted at the water bottle, her eyes snapping. "Add some coffee grounds to that and I might consider it." She hesitated and looked to Raymond. "I like coffee, don't I?"

Raymond's look of exasperation gave Kailey a rare opportunity to smile. "Like a rabid fiend, Maddie, like a fiend."

"I thought so." Maddie *harrumph*ed and folded her hands in rebellion against the life-giving liquid.

Kailey bent and caught Maddie's attention. "Maddie, water is necessary. Please don't get me into trouble with Teri."

Maddie tipped her head and looked down her nose at Kailey, a little smirk puckering her burgundy-lipsticked lips. "Teri couldn't hurt a peacock."

"A fly, Maddie, it's a fly," Raymond inserted.

She waved him off. "A fly then, if you want to be picky. But I'm sure she couldn't snap a peacock's neck if she wanted to either."

Snap a peacock's neck?

"And *you've* snapped a peacock's neck before?" Raymond jousted verbally with the woman he so ardently also admired.

Maddie straightened her lime-green-sweater-clad shoulders and smirked. "Maaayyyyyybe."

"Pshaw!" Raymond's outburst caused Poe's ear to twitch.

"I used to butcher rabbits with my daddy when I was a little girl." Kailey blanched.

Raymond seemed unfazed. "Well, that's what you do on a rabbit farm. But, sure as shootin', you didn't have peacocks to butcher."

"You wouldn't know. We didn't grow up together."

"You lived on a rabbit farm?" Judy, with her permed gray hair distinctively flat in the back where she'd lain on it, hiked her way over and inserted herself into the conversation.

Kailey found it quite humorous the way she side-eyed eighty-seven-year-old Raymond when it was apparent he was smitten, besotted, and completely loyal to Maddie.

Maddie didn't bother looking at Judy, and Kailey wondered for a fleeting second if Maddie might not have been a bit of a mean girl in her younger school years.

"I did." At least she answered Judy. "At one point, my daddy had one hundred and eighty-two rabbits."

"What on earth would a person do with that many rabbits?"

Judy giggled and gave Raymond's shoulder a compatriot sort of shove with her arthritic hands.

"Eat them."

Kailey snorted then. She couldn't help it. Maddie's matter-of-fact response made Judy visibly gag. Raymond ducked his head under pretense of whispering in Poe's uninterested ear. Maddie exchanged looks with Kailey as Judy meandered away from the horrid concept of butchering rabbits for a living.

"She can't handle gore. Doubt she ever watched a horror movie in her life." Maddie chuckled.

"Did you *really* butcher rabbits?" Kailey couldn't help but ask.

"Of course. I did have a pet one too—I named him Hogan. He was even trained on a leash. Although . . ." Maddie squinted, trying to recall. "I do believe I got bored with him, and we ate him at Easter, but I'm not sure."

"You're the Ed Gein to the rabbit world, Maddie," Raymond sputtered. His thinning hair practically stood on end, and while he stared incredulously at his girl, there was humor in his eyes.

"Well, we can't all have the luxury of packing pets in pink-sequined purses and parading ourselves along Hollywood Boulevard, can we? Life happens." Maddie winked at Kailey. "My aunt used to say something entirely different, but my mama would wash my mouth out with soap and make me repeat 'Life happens' over and over again until I forgot the bad word."

"Did it work?" Raymond grumbled. "No. No, it didn't," he answered for Maddie. "And to think that slogan got so popular in later years, they put it on coffee mugs!"

"My son always said . . ." Maddie paused as confusion passed over her face. She drummed her fingers on the arm of her wheelchair. "Well, he used to . . ." She waved off the comment. "It's no matter."

Kailey and Raymond exchanged looks. It seemed whenever Maddie brought up her nonexistent son, the sharpness would ebb from her eyes. She became lost in a struggle to identify her vacant memories. Her spirit waned, and someone more insecure took its place.

Judy snapped a newspaper from a few seats away, glancing over its top to see if Raymond noticed. "Fancy that," she drawled, leaving her thought unfinished to invite someone to question her.

Kailey took pity on Judy since Raymond had diverted his attention once again to Poe, who was licking his front paw as if he'd just partaken in the rabbit butchering.

"What is it?" Kailey settled the water bottle on the metal TV tray by Maddie and moved over to sit beside Judy. A waft of sweet perfume from an outdated Avon bottle touched her nose. She'd seen it on Judy's dresser. Probably from the 1980s, the glass having yellowed with age.

Judy pointed at the insides of the *Harbor Herald*. "Little girl went missing for less than a day and swears she was kidnapped. Police have followed up, but with absolutely no leads." Judy tapped her finger on the column. "See? Right here. Someone best get that girl some help. She's making up stories left and right and going to get someone in trouble for it."

"What if she's not making it up?" Kailey snapped, immediately regretting her tone.

"Why would anyone take a little girl for just a few hours?" Judy's question was honest. Her eyelashes batted, this time out of curiosity rather than flirtation. She had ice-blue eyes, and yet Kailey could see evidence of cataracts in them.

"There's all sorts of reasons someone might take a little girl," Raymond muttered, not bothering to expound further.

Judy jumped at the opportunity to converse with him. "When I was working at the factory in Detroit, there was a little white girl who went missing. Everyone blamed her black neighbor, but it ended up being her brother who killed her and then hid the body."

Shifting uncomfortably, Kailey couldn't remain silent. "Stereotyping at its worst."

Judy's confused look reminded Kailey just how different generations could be. How what seemed normal to one was so desperately wrong to another. She would never dare to compare her experiences with those of minorities or other races, but Kailey understood what it was to be misjudged and accused of something you simply did not do. She'd also seen the avoidance from some people as they eyed Jude. His made-up language with Kailey only increased the element of "weirdness" surrounding Jude. Grunts, a few intelligible words, sign language, and even a few bars hummed from a song. She'd always understood her brother. Her beloved, big older brother whose depth ran deeper than any soul who could communicate clearly. Stereotyping and ostracizing because of differences were the worst sorts of cruelty.

"She's okay." Maddie's voice broke through Kailey's thoughts.

"What's that, Madeline?" Judy responded. It was apparent she hadn't earned the right to use Maddie's nickname.

Maddie pulled a different stuffed animal from where it had been tucked between her hip and the arm of the wheelchair. It was a green turtle. She stroked its back as if drawing some sort of comfort from it. "She's okay."

"Who's okay?" Judy's pencil-thin brows furrowed.

"The girl." Maddie barely concealed an eye roll.

Kailey was going to intervene, yet Judy was too quick. "How do you know Riley Bascom?"

Maddie frowned, her confusion evident. She began to claw at the turtle's back. Her intake of breath was shakier, and she tossed her head back and forth. "No, no. Not that girl."

Kailey pressed her hand on Judy's knee as Judy opened her mouth to speak again. Judy met her eyes, and Kailey gave her a warning shake of her head. Thankfully, Judy caught the hint and snapped her mouth shut. Rising, Kailey returned to Maddie, who was now blinking rapidly. Squinting. Looking left and right, as if trying to find someone in the room who simply had not yet spoken. Her eyes widened, and an expression of relief passed over her face.

"Oh, thank God," she breathed.

Kailey knelt in front of the woman. "Maddie?" She rested her hands on Maddie's knees, noting from the corner of her eye Raymond leaning forward. "Maddie, what is it?"

Maddie continued to stare into the corner. Kailey shot a glance at it. It was empty, save for a wooden plant stand and an overabundant fern.

"Maddie?" Kailey pressed again.

This time, Maddie responded, a small bit of awareness of the present returning to her expression. She dropped her gaze back to Kailey.

"Last night I saw her, and she was quite all right."

"Saw Riley Bascom?" Raymond inserted.

Kailey shot him a warning look to be silent.

Maddie shook her head. "No, no. I don't have the slightest idea who you're talking about. I'm talking about *her*. Lucy."

Kailey shot Raymond a quizzical look to see if he recognized the name. He shrugged. "Maddie, who is Lucy?"

Maddie's smile was soft, but her fingernails caught on the stuffed turtle's green fuzz. She was still agitated, deep inside.

"Dr. Miranda's daughter. Lucy."

"Lucy?" Raymond barked.

"Lucy Miranda?" Judy's response was a high-pitched inquiry of astonishment.

"Who is Lucy?" Kailey begged. She locked eyes with Raymond.

When Maddie didn't answer, Raymond drew in a breath that was deep and heavy. He rubbed his whiskery chin and then shook his head in a resigned sort of way.

"Who is Lucy Miranda?" Kailey insisted.

"She's the ghost of Foxglove Manor." Judy's strident voice brushed over Raymond's shoulder.

"No one ever sees her, not really," Raymond added quickly.

"Except for Maddie?" Kailey redirected her attention to the older woman whose face had gone vacant again.

"She sees things." Judy waved it off. "Besides, that ghost story has been around since before the world wars."

Kailey couldn't help but put her hand over Maddie's. The elderly woman shifted and then looked directly into Kailey's eyes.

No one believes me, she seemed to cry silently.

Kailey's hand squeezed Maddie's, and the woman adjusted so hers returned Kailey's gesture. She didn't know how, or why, or what sort of explanation there might be for this ghostly girl Maddie had referred to. But Kailey did know what it was like not to be believed.

It had been a full three weeks since they'd arrived at Foxglove Manor, and though Kailey slipped right into the routine, she'd been restless. Jude had become even more quiet. She missed his grunts, his periodic words. With her elderly friends all tucked in and content with some pastime or another, Kailey squeezed Maddie's shoulder as she moved toward the far end of the room. The look on Maddie's face was vacant now. The vibrant part of her had dissipated into a confused version, one that seemed to express grief in not being believed. Kailey wanted to reassure the old woman that she believed her—but that would mean admitting ghosts existed—and that thought was terrifying for a reason Kailey couldn't put her finger on. It was personal. Personal and too real, yet there was nothing to indicate to her why she would feel that way.

As Kailey approached Jude, she retrieved her mustard-yellow cardigan she'd thrown haphazardly over the back of a chair next to her brother. He lifted green eyes to her, his whiskers a three-day shadow, and half grunted, half spoke.

"Kay-Kay." He pointed to the book in front of him. It had glossy pictures of sharks and underwater sea life. His eyes sparkled, and he rocked ever so slightly back and forth in his chair.

"Great white shark?" Kailey identified it, but she figured he was excited about something she couldn't see.

Jude gave her a crooked smile. The kind of smile that corrected her and made him very much an older brother tolerating the ignorance of his little sister. He shook his head. Sticking his index finger on the page, he traced the dorsal fin on the shark, then the back fin, then lifted his finger and began to trace over every underwater object that was triangular.

"Tee . . ."

"Triangle? Okay, yes?" Kailey leaned over his shoulder to watch. A triangle in the coral, a triangle in a minuscule pattern on the tail of another small fish.

Jude turned the book so he could grab the corner of the page. He folded it in, creasing it. Anyone else and Kailey would have scolded them, but she waited expectantly. He saw something, and as usual she was curious to see the hidden treasure revealed. Jude bent the corner page until it touched the tip of the dorsal fin. Then he bent the edge in a straight fold as though he were going to create origami. He ran his thumbnail along the crease until it was razor-thin.

"Fah—new fah." He added a grunt and then hummed a few bars from the *Jaws* theme song.

Kailey saw it then. By folding the page in a triangle, he'd pulled part of the picture on the back side and folded it against the front-side photograph. The second fold created an illusion of lines, and suddenly the great white on the original page merged into part of a shark on the back page. And with the folds, it created an entirely new fish made up primarily of triangular sections.

"Jude. You're a genius. Yes, it's a new fish. You're so right. A new species. We'll call it the Jude Fish."

He laughed. It was deep and sounded so male, so adult, so . . .

Kailey stopped her thoughts. For every time she started to wish he wasn't immersed in his own special world, she remembered how desperately she needed him. Needed him to be Jude. Her brother. The one who protected her and loved her and brought her what little joy she truly had in life. God had created Jude, and there were no mistakes in him.

"C'mon, Jude. Why don't you take a walk with me? You need some exercise." For the umpteenth time, Kailey was grateful Teri had allowed her to bring Jude. Not that she would have come had she been unable to. Foxglove Manor was as much, if not more, in Jude's soul as it was in hers. Together, they would resolve it. Once and for all.

Kailey tugged a rubber band from her wrist and pulled her dark hair up into a messy bun, then exited the room, Jude on her heels, leaving Raymond to cat-sit Poe and watch over Maddie simultaneously. Judy had preoccupied herself with a puzzle, and as they left the room, Jude almost collided with Stella, Judy's sidekick. Stella reared back, her brilliantly dyed red hair a bit reminiscent of Lucille Ball. Her green eyes sparkled.

"Oh honey, you need to slow down. I'm half your size!" Stella looked between the two, but Jude's attention was leveled somewhere on the molding over the front door.

Kailey squeezed the elderly woman's forearm. "Do you need help with anything?"

"Nope. Just going to do a puzzle with Judy and vie for Raymond's attention."

At least Stella was honest. "Good luck with that." Kailey sincerely hoped the old women knew Raymond's heart was already long past gone over Maddie.

Stella smiled and nodded. "I would need it. It isn't going to happen, but it sure is a fine thing to muddle with Judy's senses."

Kailey offered Stella a cooperative laugh. The lady had spunk, and any other time, Kailey might wish to exchange banter.

Stella had moved past them while Kailey motioned for Jude to follow her. Instinct would have made her tug his blue shirtsleeve, but that instinct had been squelched in childhood. Instead, she glanced over her shoulder toward the front room and its occupants, even as Jude followed her without question. Three weeks at Foxglove and she'd immersed herself into its residents. Jude had found his place beside them—along with his pile of glossy picture books.

She'd avoided Axel, mostly because of the time on the beach when he had gotten too close to her personal story than she wished any stranger to. Teri had become a friend, as had Tracee, the other nurse who worked alternating day and night shifts. They were two happy individuals who tested Kailey's ability to stay melancholy. There were times in the past three weeks when she'd wanted desperately to believe life wasn't going to shift on its axis. But that was a falsity that her spirit knew she had to avoid falling for. Jude. He had been so unsettled, more so than normal.

Kailey thought of the day two months ago. The phone call. Their aunt who'd raised them, and the argument. Of course she could care for her own brother! Kailey's insistence had been loud, and she knew Jude had overheard it, she just hadn't banked on him comprehending the threats. That there were places where he could have 24/7 care and some independence, maybe even get employment that would suit his abilities. He could learn skills, and then Kailey would be free to go to college, to make something of herself. To be more than her mother had been. And there it was. That ever-present reminder of their alcoholic, depressed mom. And then it always led back to Foxglove Manor. A brief blip in what should have been an insignificant memory. But it had changed the course of all their lives. Jude had spiraled deeper into himself. Kailey had been abducted, then accused of lying and ignored for the better part of the rest of her parents' lives. And then . . . it was all over. Mom and Dad were dead. A car accident? Kailey suspected more now that she was older. Vodka maybe? Medications? Something had brought the car and the tree together in a mad collision that sent Kailey and Jude catapulting forward. Enter their aunt, and then Jude became her project, and Kailey was the little leech attached to Jude who somehow was blamed for who he was. All the while, Jude's fascination with patterns and sequences grew obsessive. Foxglove Manor had become their escape together, but it had also brought them back to some of the worst moments of their lives. Kailey would prove to her aunt she could not only care for Jude alone, but that she could help him reconcile what haunted him. To heck with what haunted her. No one believed Kailey anyway. They never had. Her abduction and its subsequent ties to Foxglove were nothing more than the extreme story of a girl who wanted attention.

Kailey ducked into a room she'd yet to enter, Jude following without question, and she shut the heavy wood door behind them. No. They weren't stories and clamoring for attention. Kailey could still feel the rough hands shoving her into the van. Feel the painful squeeze of his hands on her arms as he shook her.

"Tell me the sequence."

She'd no idea what he wanted it for. Why it even mattered. But even at five, Kailey knew it existed. Jude wrote it everywhere. Yes. Foxglove Manor was alive. It had eyes in the walls and a soul in the floorboards. Kailey could sense it—*feel* it—and so had Jude.

The room they'd entered was musty and unused. Even though it was on the first floor, it didn't appear to serve much of a purpose other than storage. Some old furniture had been pushed against a far wall and covered with sheets.

"If that's not the proverbial creepy old mansion scene out of a movie," Kailey muttered. Several boxes were piled in an opposite corner, taped shut with packing tape. There were medical supplies beside them. Extra cases of adult diapers, boxes of TP, bottles of hydrogen peroxide, and a case of Band-Aids. Some plastic, recyclable bedpans were nested into each other and set on a chair.

Windows were almost floor to ceiling to her left. Outside, Kailey could see the yard, the cedar and poplar trees that bordered it, and the old iron fence just before it met the cliffside. The expanse of Lake Superior was calm today—well, as calm as Lake Superior ever was. Kailey shifted her attention back to the room. There was a fireplace with a thick wood mantel. Jude stood in front of it, studying the curling scrolls in the wood. Above it was a broad expanse of a wall, empty except for some remnants of hangers indicating something had once been mounted and displayed there.

The door clicked open behind her. A face peeked in with wide hazel eyes. "What's brought you in here?"

It was Tracee, the other nurse. She was closer in age to Kailey's twenty-five. Probably in her early thirties. She stepped into the room but held on to the door as if she were intruding. "Did you find our resident ghost?" Her expression was teasing.

Kailey mustered a smile. "No. No ghost. I was just—" What *was* she doing? Had she expected by exploring the old manor she'd somehow stumble on Lucy Miranda's spirit? An explanation to the *feeling* she had? The sudden onset of memories she'd stifled deep inside?

She didn't know. She hadn't a good explanation. Kailey tugged the sleeves of her sweater down over her hands until only her fingers peeked out. "What—what *is* the story of the ghost?"

Tracee waggled her brows, still hanging on to the door as if she had only a moment to spare. "Oh, there're several versions. Which one do you want to hear?"

Kailey shrugged. "Whatever is most accurate."

Jude had moved from the fireplace to the far wall, where he ran his hand over the inset bookshelves, void of tomes but bearing the mark of a craftsman in the geometric shapes carved into the walnut.

Tracee laughed and stole back Kailey's attention. "Sure. An accurate ghost story. That makes sense. I personally prefer the story where Lucy Miranda is the little girl who guards the missing treasure of an old pirate."

"A pirate?" Kailey's eyebrows winged upward. "Like Blackbeard? Aren't they in the Bahamas or something?"

Tracee shook her head. "Not if you know the stories of North America's inland seas. The lakes are full of old pirate tales. Maybe not Blackbeard-worthy, but definitely pirates."

Kailey nodded. "What was the treasure?"

Tracee snorted. "If we knew that, it wouldn't be a mystery."

"What do you mean?"

Tracee opened the door further and leaned on it, her scrubs a bright blue against the dark wood. "Okay. So, I grew up in Harbor Towne, which you know is about thirty minutes from here. There was stuff smuggled through its harbor other than just the honest trade of copper. Supposedly, during the Civil War, there was a great amount of loot stolen from one of the lake's pirates—or smugglers—and hidden somewhere here at Foxglove Manor. No one's ever found it."

"Civil War loot?" Kailey scowled in confusion.

Tracee returned Kailey's look with her own widened eyes. "I dunno. That's the mystery. And supposedly, people over the years see a little girl—dressed in white, of course, 'cause all ghosts are—and she's warned people away from this place. She guards the treasure and doesn't want anyone near it."

Kailey remembered Maddie's insistence that the little Miranda girl was all right. As though she'd been hurt herself. "How did the little girl die?"

"No clue." Tracee pushed off the door and tapped her watch. "Time for afternoon meds." She turned, then paused and looked over her shoulder at Kailey. "But for real, Kailey, it's all just a story. Every old house has a ghost story." She studied Kailey for a moment, a concerned expression on her face. "I don't believe any of it's true."

Kailey nodded, and Tracee took that as confirmation Kailey accepted her explanation. The nurse disappeared to hand out medications. Kailey breathed in deep through her nose, sucking the musty air into her lungs and resting her hand on the mantel. She eyed the faded outline on the wall. It seemed to be in the shape of an X. Funny. X marks the spot. Pirate treasure. Maybe if she busted through the wall, she'd find Civil War relics.

A crash across the room made Kailey jump. An unintelligible shout escaped from Jude. She whirled from the fireplace in the direction of the noise, even as her brother launched himself across the room and in front of her.

A windowpane had shattered, glass shards spread across the floor in dangerously wicked spears. A gust of wind blew its cold breath across Kailey's skin.

"Jude. Jude, let me past you." Kailey reached to move her brother but restrained from touching him. Jude shook his head. He was taller than she was, broader, and he held his arm out and behind him as if to hold her back and shield her from something—or someone. Kailey peeked around him. Nothing had broken through the window. There was no rock on the floor that someone might have thrown to break the pane. Her shoes crunched on the glass as Kailey edged around Jude.

"Kay-Kay!" He was insistent and moved in front of her, blocking the way.

"Jude, I'm all right. It's okay."

"Kay," he said again. He hummed a few bars from the movie *Pyscho*. That felt oddly appropriate to the moment, which admittedly was ominous at best.

"Jude. Shush. It's all right." This time, her brother let her pass, and Kailey neared the hole in the window. She crouched to peer through it, mentally chiding herself that she'd be better off to back away in case of a repeat that would leave her face shredded. Instead, she stared through the broken pane as she noticed movement at the far edge of the cliff. A fox. A mangy red fox sat there, still, staring back at her. Its fur was illuminated by the lake. Its black eyes were difficult to make out in the distance.

The wind howled through the broken window, and Kailey felt her breaths come shorter, stronger, as though someone were sitting on her chest. It was a powerful sensation, and there, in the back of her mind, she heard Jude whisper. But it wasn't a whisper from today, or this moment. His lips remained closed. It was a whisper from memories past. A buried recollection.

"Hide, Kay-Kay, hide."

The fox slunk away into the trees.

Kailey reached down to pick up a shard of glass, and it sliced her finger. A drop of red stained its edge. Her blood. And for some reason, it felt portentous and telling. Blood had been shed here once. Here, at Foxglove Manor. She had known it as a child—her family had known it—*Jude* had testified to it. But it was all in the past, all in a tale that shouldn't have been told. A tale that must be forgotten. So forget she had.

Wiping the droplet of blood from the glass, Kailey brushed it off on her jeans. But she was remembering a little more every day. She was no stranger to Lucy Miranda's mystery. Jude had warned her of it—so long ago.

"Stay away, Kay-Kay," he'd instructed. Then he'd given her the sign for *danger* and slapped his leg. Perhaps she should have listened. But she hadn't. Twenty years later, Kailey had come back, and she'd brought her vulnerable brother with her.

12

"You didn't see anything come through the window?" Axel swept broken glass into a large dustpan and dumped the pieces into a five-gallon plastic pail.

"No." Kailey hugged herself. She was thankful that the situation hadn't been more upsetting for Jude. Thankful that he'd willingly returned to the front room, to his picture book of the deep sea, and to the company of Raymond and his posse of women admirers.

"Strange." Axel rested the broom against the wall and squatted to peer through the broken windowpane. "It's gusty out there, so I could see if a branch broke the window, but there's nothing there."

Kailey waited. Axel reached out and tugged at a piece of glass still clinging to the window frame. The piece came loose without much effort. He checked both sides of it as if somehow the cause of the window shattering had been captured in the glass. With no answers, Axel tossed it into the bucket and stood.

"Guess some things are unexplained." He pinched the bridge of his nose as if to contemplate that very thing. The unexplained.

Kailey shuddered and squeezed her eyes tight for a long three seconds, allowing them to burn. When she was anxious, she forgot to blink—or at least it felt that way—that her eyes were fixed in an open stare, fearful she'd miss whatever ghoul waited to leap out and claw at her memories with crusty, sharp-nailed fingers.

Axel rested his hands at his waist, Peter Pan–style, with legs apart and elbows sticking out. His jeans bunched at the top of his work boots. His gray Henley shirtsleeves were pushed up to his elbows, and a navy-blue T-shirt peeked out from under it at his neckline.

"You okay? You didn't get sliced, did you?"

"No. I'm fine." Kailey mustered a smile, hiding her cut finger behind her. She glanced at the empty spot above the fireplace, then at the mantel, then the firebox. Looking anywhere but at Axel would be the best right now. He was focused on her with his deep-set eyes. It was just a broken window. He didn't need to glower. But he wasn't glowering. He was studying her, which was worse.

"It's just a broken window, Kailey." Axel's words echoed her thoughts. "No one blames you for it."

She averted her eyes. Otherwise she knew he could see inside her, the memories pounding at her subconscious and wanting to explode like a movie on a massive drive-in theater screen. Re-play and replay. That night . . . her mother had screamed. No child should ever hear such a thing—terror threaded through the voice of their mother. Kailey squeezed her eyes shut again, irritated at the assault of the unwelcome memory.

"Kailey?"

She whipped her head up to look at Axel.

"Kailey, are you okay?"

"Yeah." Kailey rubbed her eyes. "Sure. Yeah, I'm fine. It just scared me is all."

Axel hesitated, a frown settling between his eyes. "What brought you in here anyway? No one ever uses this room."

Kailey shrugged, at a loss as to how to answer. "I don't know. Exploring?"

Axel's mouth slanted in a crooked smile a bit disguised behind his beard. He gave a small laugh. "Welcome to the storage room. Need a bedpan?"

Kailey matched his laugh, only his had been genuine, while hers was forced. She could tell he knew it too. "Nope. No diapers either."

A shadow flickered across Axel's face.

Kailey winced. "Sorry. I wasn't trying to be insensitive."

Axel waved her off and nudged the bucket of broken glass with his boot. "Nah, don't worry about it. It's a fact of life—getting old. I just remembered my grandpa hiding diapers between folded towels in his bathroom, so no one knew he had to wear them."

Kailey noticed a flicker on the floor, and she bent to retrieve a shard of glass that had missed Axel's cleaning efforts. "I don't remember my grandparents." It was something anyway. She could offer him something of herself—of Jude—of who they were.

Axel held out his hand for the glass. Kailey reached out to place it in his palm. His skin on her fingertips was warm and she tugged her hand away. As he flipped the glass into the bucket, it was obvious Axel hadn't been affected by the contact.

"That's too bad." The glass clanked as it fell on top of its mates. "Grandparents are cool to have around."

"If they're good ones," Kailey mumbled.

He shot her a quick look. "Yeah." Reaching for the metal handle on the bucket, Axel lifted it. "You have any other siblings?"

"Besides Jude?" Kailey suddenly didn't know what to do with her hands. Her arms. She crossed them. Then uncrossed them. "No," she answered as she rammed her hands into the pockets of her jeans.

Axel crossed the room, brushing past her. She felt him—his entire presence—even though he'd never touched her. Setting down the bucket by the open door, he retrieved a scrap piece of board he'd propped against the wall, then snagged a hammer from a separate tool bucket that also boasted a myriad of wrenches, screwdrivers, and other assorted tools. Axel pulled a few nails from a box inside the bucket and put them between his teeth, the pointed ends sticking out.

"My dad and mom got a divorce when I was theven," he mumbled around the nails.

"Seven?" Kailey clarified.

He nodded, striding back toward the broken window. "Unreconthilable differethes."

Unreconcilable differences. Got it.

Axel removed one nail from his clenched teeth and tipped his head toward the window. "Help?"

Kailey didn't know what she could do, but obligation moved her forward. It wasn't as if she was directly responsible for the window breaking, but a huge part of her felt as though she was.

"Hold thith." Axel lifted the board and held it over the broken window. It spanned the width of it. Kailey did as she was told. Axel held the nail over one of the board's corners and then brought the hammer down on its head.

Kailey jumped.

Axel shifted for a better position. His shoulder brushed hers. She smelled juniper, or cedar, or some sort of pine scent lingering on his shirt.

"One more." He pulled another nail from his teeth and pounded it in another corner. Gray eyes met Kailey's. There was nothing in them but sheer platonic kindness. Still, her insides twisted. "Switch spoths."

They switched spots, and Axel pulled the third nail, pounded it in and finally removed the fourth nail from his teeth. He waggled it toward Kailey. "And my mama told me never to chew nails. This was my dad's bad habit."

"Your mom was smart." Kailey smiled.

Axel met her eyes, and she melted just a little bit more than she thought was humanly possible. "Choking on a nail isn't how I plan to go out. I tell her that too, every week on the phone, but she doesn't believe me."

Kailey laughed then. She needed to laugh. Even if it was little. If it was shy. If it was foreign.

A knock on the door's frame snagged both of their attention. Teri stood there, her face pale and her eyes rimmed in red. It was the sort of expression Kailey was familiar with. The hesitant *I have bad news* look that was premonition to tragedy.

"What's up?" Axel lowered his hammer. There was gravity in

his voice. Kailey took a step nearer to him, realizing she had only after her arm brushed his.

Teri cleared her throat, dabbing at the corners of her eyes. "I'm sorry to bother you both. I—I just got a call from Officer Ericksson."

"More news about Riley?" Axel asked. "I thought she was home safe."

Teri nodded at his reference to Riley Bascom, whose abduction story still sent ripples of uneasiness through Kailey. "She's fine. But they just found her father. It looks like a suicide, but they're still investigating."

Kailey went cold.

"You're kidding." Axel's voice was low, and it echoed in Kailey's ears.

"It's just awful." Teri shook her head and sniffed. "What are we going to do?" She waved her hand in the air, and Kailey noted she was clenching a tissue. "No, no. That's selfish of me to even ask at a time like this."

"Why?" Kailey looked between Teri and Axel. Axel's chest was lifting in a heavy sigh. "Were you close to Mr. Bascom?" She couldn't make the connection as to why Teri and Axel would be so affected, other than simply having human empathy for the second traumatic event in the Bascom family and the nearby small town.

Teri's mouth twisted with emotion. "Oh, that's right. You probably don't even know." She made an obvious attempt to swallow back tears. "Mr. Bascom is—*was*—the owner of Foxglove Manor."

Kailey searched her recollection, attempting to piece it together. The owner of the retirement home? Foxglove Manor? She'd not heard of him before, she was sure of it. No, she'd interviewed and passed everything through Teri. She'd never stopped to consider there had to be an investor or owner behind the home for the elderly here at Foxglove.

Teri was still explaining. "Mr. Bascom used to have Foxglove Manor as a vacation rental. Then he and his wife turned it into this home. This place of respite. They are older themselves—in their fifties—and Riley was their surprise child and—oh, my word . . ." Teri clapped her hand over her mouth, and Axel moved to embrace the director and nurse. Teri sobbed into Axel's shoulder.

Mr. Bascom's death meant little to Kailey, but she began to shiver anyway. Not with suppressed emotion, or even shock, but because Mr. Bascom had owned Foxglove Manor. Owned it when she'd vacationed here twenty years before. When she'd heard her mother's scream echo down the hall. Heard the crashing waves against the cliffs as their car door slammed, her father half shoving them in so they could get away from Foxglove. It was Mr. Bascom's ten-year-old daughter who had just been pseudo-kidnapped—like she had been shortly after her first and last visit to Foxglove. They were all tied to this place. This awful, accursed place.

13

ADRIA

"Roses don't grow here," Diggery explained. Adria trailed behind him, out for a brief respite. She glanced up at the stone manor's turret and at the window. It was dark, with no signs of a man, alive or spirit. "I suppose one could try," Diggery continued, "but I don't have much of a mind to."

He motioned toward a pile of smooth rocks, some as large as his foot, piled in miniature towers. "I prefer to make cairns. Stacking them atop each other ain't no easy task."

Neither could it be easy to haul them from the shoreline below the cliff to the garden where they stood in rows. It was a curious hobby.

"They're beautiful," Adria responded truthfully, because they were unique in their own ways. Stones the color of a rusted bucket, gray like the tops of the lake's waves, blue like the blown-glass swan on her mother's desk back home, and even white. "What inspired you to create them?"

Diggery scratched the back of his neck as he stood over his creations. "Wellllll, not sure I have a good answer for it. Lots of folks use them as markers on trails. My mum said they were memorials for loved ones passed away when she was a lass. And I know the Israelites used them to mark a momentous occasion—if you're familiar with the Old Testament stories. Me? I just think they're nice, I guess."

Nice. If only life were as simple as a pile of water-smoothed stones. Yet to become so smooth and restful, one had to be tossed and turned and washed over with the turbulence of time and of life. Maybe one day, she would be smooth.

Adria couldn't help but let her eyes lift to the turret window again. Certainly, it had been confirmed several times there was no man in the attic. But she couldn't deny her suspicions were watered and fed by the vision on the day of her arrival and the recollection of a dark hulking form on the stairs. Now the window was dark. Its arched glass was split into panes, and the stones around it matched the gray of the stones in Diggery's cairns.

"I wonder if . . ." Adria stilled. Her conversation trailed away. She latched on to Diggery's arm. "Diggery! There!" She pointed to the window. "A man!"

Diggery stiffened and shot a startled glance toward the turret. "There's no man, miss."

There had been. The window was dark again. But Adria was certain she'd seen a flash. A flash of a face, the outline of shoulders, shaggy hair.

"See? No one's there." Diggery chuckled, his laugh throaty but also a bit nervous.

Adria gave him a look of doubt. "Diggery. Speak the truth."

"I *am!*" He jerked away and glared at her, though his scowl was more like the stern perusal of a puppy dog. "Now leave it alone."

It was possible Diggery was lying. Mrs. St. John and Lula too. Why, Adria had no fathomable reason. Unless . . .

"You'll look for anything—anything—*that might give us an idea of the whereabouts of my goods."* Her father's voice ripped through Adria's subconscious. *"St. John knew where it is hid. He was a lofty, idiot of a man who thought himself guardian and protector of it. But it's mine. It will be mine. You will make it mine again, Adria. You owe me this."*

Everyone owed her father, or so it seemed. Her, most of all. But maybe so did Mrs. St. John and Diggery. Maybe Foxglove Manor was no more a beacon of potential freedom from her father than the ocean was no more powerful than the lake itself. And the man in the attic? Perhaps it was he they were hiding.

———

She would be wise to wait until all were asleep. Everything in Adria resisted prolonging her exploration of the third floor and the turret, but she knew if she attempted it in daylight, Mrs. St. John would intervene. Or Lula would act oddly, insist that the ghost of Foxglove Manor would haunt Adria, or simply become arrogant in her explanation of the rules.

"You don't visit the third floor. Ain't nothin' to be seen there and it's my quarters." She'd already instructed Adria the past two mornings, without prompting, reading intent where Adria had not dwelled on it. Had Lula remained quiet, Adria might have accepted the explanation of the other night. But not now.

Adria pushed the lace curtain away from her unshuttered bedroom window. The moon was clear in the sky. A half-moon, its wakeful eye glowing on the tops of the waves as they ate the shoreline with persistence. In the far distance, Adria thought she might see the outline of a steamer, but it was difficult to make out. A boatful of copper ore bound for Canada or perhaps merely starting its journey to alternate ports, where they would disperse the goods throughout the lakes. She let the curtain fall back into place and slid her feet into her slippers. Tying the yellow ribbon at the neck of her housecoat, Adria pulled her waist-long wavy hair back into a tie. Margot called her hair "dog-hair brown," and from her earliest memory, Adria had disliked its color. Her mother had corrected Margot and said that Adria's hair was the color of acorns, but it was too late. The image of a scraggly dog was firmly implanted in Adria's image of herself.

She ignored the candle that practically begged to be lit. Adria coveted light as she opened her door, wincing when its hinges squeaked. She peeked up and down the hallway. Emptiness greeted her. It was after eleven at night. She knew Mrs. St. John retired at nine every evening, but Adria wasn't sure about Lula. And Lula would be the biggest of her worries, considering she roomed on the turret floor. Adria wasn't sure if she would have to pass Lula's quarters or even if the girl would be asleep. She prayed it was so, even as her slipper-clad foot landed on the bottom step.

A week ago, Adria had climbed these steps only to catapult backward and spend a day in bed after seeing the looming, crazed form of a man. Perhaps she should rethink this action of snooping after daylight. If he did exist, and if she had been told lies, then he could be dangerous. The step beneath her foot creaked. It was loud and protested her weight with its strong declaration. Adria froze. She heard herself breathing.

In.

Out.

In.

Out.

Silence met her. No one seemed to have been disturbed by the stair's outburst. Adria dared another, palming the wall on her left to balance her climb. The top stair was mere feet away. She could almost feel her eyes dilate, trying to see through the darkness. There was nothing but blackness at the top of the narrow, walled stairs.

Finally, she was at the top. Adria's feet planted on the third floor, and she peered into the blue-black shadows. It wasn't a large landing. It appeared the turret floor was a mere pittance in footage compared to the first and second floors. She could make out the dark outline of a door to her right. There was a lone window next to it, shedding a bit of the moonlight across the floor. A tiny glass vase hung from a hook next to the door. A sprig of wilted foxglove flowers decorated it. A sign that the occupant was female—for what man would bore himself with putting flowers outside his door? Adria made a quick deduction that it was Lula's room. She could see the quirky, snippety, and whimsical girl doing just that. Lula would declare herself the third-floor princess if she could, of that Adria had no doubt.

To the left, the landing stretched a ways before the roofline began to dip lower. At the end of it was another door. This one's latch was made of iron, as were the hinges. More fitting for a man's room. Adria questioned the validity of her sketchy logic, even as she tiptoed toward the door. Her slipper caught on a sliver poking up from a floorboard. She paused to unhook it, chiding the snag in the satin that couldn't be helped.

The floor creaked again, only this time Adria was standing still. She froze, inches from the door. She could see the indentations on the black iron hinges. Hand-forged most likely, dents from the hammer when the iron had been orange-hot and pliable. Adria waited, but nothing more was heard. She hovered her hand over the latch. If she opened it, and if there wasn't a man, then she would be able to look out the mysterious window once and for all, correcting her visions as simply that. Imagined sightings of a shadow man. But if she opened it and there was a man . . .

Adria dropped her hand. It was foolhardy, what she was about to do. In spite of the insistence from the other occupants of Foxglove Manor, Adria hadn't believed them. Which meant, if she were correct, there *would* be a man behind this door, and why did she want to come face-to-face with someone hidden and locked away for all sakes and purposes in a turret like some male Rapunzel in a Brothers Grimm tale?

"I'll be rid of you for good if you find what belongs to me."

She could hear her father's whisper and feel his hot breath against her ear. His hands holding her upper arms as he stood behind her, tugging her firmly against him. His fingertips bruised her.

"You're poison to this house like that which you drank. If you're so anxious to be free of us, then so be it, but you will serve one final purpose in penance for the shame you've brought on my good name."

Yes. Her father's good name. Lewis Fontaine. A respected shipping baron with ships on Superior ports, Lake Michigan ports, and even some connections in the other Great Lakes. She'd heard that people as far away as Lake Erie knew of Fontaine—though not his smuggling practices during the war. He would recover from the scandal of a daughter's attempt to free herself of him by drinking large doses of medicines. He would not recover if she were free of him without repaying the debt she apparently owed him for no reason other than being born his child.

"Your debt is to me," she whispered beneath her breath. The moments when he took his anger out on her or her mother, leaving bruises behind. Margot miraculously escaped his attentions. She was pliant. She was manipulative. She was like him. Adria was defiant, always defiant, and though she suffered quietly, she had done so with her chin lofted. The day she'd drank from the bottle of poison, she had prayed it would leave him forever scarred in her wake. Her failure to succeed had now brought her here. Before this very door. Questioning if the man inside—*if* there were a man inside—had anything to do with her father's stolen loot.

She abruptly placed her hand on the latch and pushed the door open. She had nothing to lose anyway.

14

The turret window was directly across from the door. Adria stared out of it and saw the trees, the lake beyond, and most of all, the half-moon. The room was cast in violet hues of night. A small bed—more of a cot, really—lay empty. The covers had been skillfully placed and tucked, the pillow fluffed and undented from anyone having lain on it. She dared a step into the room. A tall wardrobe stood to the right of her, and skirting that was a desk with a straight-backed chair. Adria narrowed her eyes, trying to see through the darkness to the top of the desk. There were a few envelopes on it. Letters. An inkwell. An ink pen on its dish. There also appeared to be a pocket watch with a long chain dangling over the side of the desk. But it was difficult to see.

Intrigued, Adria walked over to the desk. She peered down without touching anything. Yes. It was an open pocket watch, and if she was making out the hands clearly, they had stopped turning at two o'clock. Morning or night, she couldn't know. Reaching out, Adria moved to pick up the watch.

"Don't."

She squealed, snatching her hand away as she whirled toward the direction of the voice. The door to the room slammed shut, and behind it was the tall form of a man.

Adria's breaths came in short, frightened gasps. She clutched at her housecoat, pulling it around herself as though he had caught her alone in her own bedroom. Only he hadn't. She had caught him alone in his. Adria backed up, her behind hitting the desk.

The man took a step toward her. It was wobbly, unsteady. The moonlight illuminated strands of long, straight hair that fell over his face. Deep-set eyes came into view, but their color was hidden by the night. He wasn't as tall as her father, but close to it. His shirt was untucked and hung over dark trousers. His hand was wrapped around the neck of a crystal decanter, a whiskey-colored liquor sloshing inside it.

"Who are you?" Adria managed to squeeze out the words, even as an all-too-familiar feeling of dread made her rigid and rooted where she was.

He gave a quiet bark of laughter. "Who am I? *Who* am I?" He veered in his steps, and his head dipped, then righted. His right index finger danced in the air as he waved his arm toward her. "You may call me Mr. Crayne."

"Crayne?"

"*Mr.* Crayne."

Adria nodded. "Yes. All right then." She'd learned, even through her defiance, that to be stubborn with a man sloshed with liquor was to invite needless trouble.

"And you. Who are you, oh, disturber of my peace?" Mr. Crayne stepped forward, and this time she could make out glazed blue eyes. Whiskers on his face were unshaven and coarse. His shirt was unbuttoned at the neck down to the middle of his bare chest.

Adria averted her eyes.

"Well?" he demanded and lifted his arm with the decanter. Liquid splashed onto the floor. "No name? Nothing? You're a ghost, then. I must assume you're a grown-up Lucy sent to torment me further."

"Who?" Adria frowned.

"'Who' is right." Mr. Crayne spun toward the window and stumbled over to it. He slapped the windowpane with his palm. "See that lake out there? It's deep. Dead ships lie at its bottom and mock the living above. Do you feel mocked, Lucy?" He turned, spearing her with a black look.

"I-I'm not Lucy," Adria sputtered. Everything in her made her want to flee, but it was as though someone had glued her feet to the floor. She was unable to move under his stare.

In a few strides, his long legs swallowed the distance between them. Lowering his face to hers, a strand of his dark hair brushed her cheek. She could smell whiskey on his breath.

"You're *not* Lucy. No. You are Alexandria Fontaine."

Goose bumps rose on her arms.

He ran a finger down the length of her jaw, his skin cold against hers. "Aren't you afraid of me? A drunken man with whiskey his best friend?" Pulling back, Mr. Crayne glared down at her. "I suppose they told you I didn't exist. Like so much at Foxglove Manor does not *exist*." He lifted the decanter to his mouth and took a swig, then wiped his lips with the back of his hand. "Iiii . . ." Mr. Crayne drug out the word as though searching for the next one. "I never *was* a man. I was only a boy. Just a boy. Then *bang!*" he shouted, his voice deep and baritone.

Adria yelped, and her backside bumped the desk, sending the pocket watch to the floor in a clatter of metal chain.

Mr. Crayne reached around her until she was trapped between him and the desk. He slammed the decanter down on the desktop with vehemence. His face was inches from Adria's.

"War does that, Miss Fontaine. Takes a boy and ruins him for manhood. Yes?" He tugged at his shirt, and Adria's eyes widened as the drunken Mr. Crayne lifted it up and pulled it over his head. "See?" he demanded, turning so that now she was nose to his bare back. A scarred back. Long, puckered white scars scored him.

Horrified, she didn't move.

"See?" he repeated, arching his neck to look over his shoulder at her. "Touch them! *Feel* them, I say! That is *war*, Miss Fontaine. And she says I am shameful. Blast it all, woman, why won't you touch them?"

Mr. Crayne cursed and grappled for Adria's hand. She resisted, pulled against his fingers as they wrapped around her hand, squeezing them together. He raised her fingers, and in compliance to avoid worse, Adria finished the movement and touched one of the scars. It was warm—hot, really—and thick. She ran her fingers down the length of it, then dropped her hand. Mr. Crayne turned back to her, his bare chest white against the night. "You see, Miss Fontaine? There is no forgiveness when a man loses his mind to battle. There is no understanding that the outward scars are merely a glimpse at what lies inside." He reached for the decanter, and his chest brushed the front of her housecoat. Stepping back, Mr. Crayne took another drag from the decanter.

Adria dared not move. She remained still. Silent. Old instincts rose and quashed her courage, her curiosity.

They stood there, nose to chest, until Adria managed the wits to raise her head and look up at the lean man with muscled arms and chest.

"My name is Adria." She wasn't sure why she whispered. She wasn't sure why she gave him her informal name. But she was completely unprepared when he lost his balance and fell into her. Without thought, her arms came up beneath his.

"Help me," he whispered desperately in her ear. "This must end."

Mr. Crayne collapsed, his weight too heavy for Adria to hold. They fell to the floor in a tumble of nightdress and trouser-clad legs and were splashed with the pungent amber of whiskey. The decanter had also fallen with a crash, the neck breaking from its body.

The bedroom door flew open.

Lula stood in the doorway. She took in the sight. Mr. Crayne and his naked chest. The whiskey. Adria in a housedress. The two of them entangled on the floor, with Mr. Crayne showing no evidence of remedying it any moment soon.

"Ohhhhh, Miss Fontaine!" Lula's hand covered her mouth in a gasp. "Now what have you done?"

15

KAILEY

A lone church bell pealed while a foghorn sounded in the distance. It was gray outside, with the withering air floating around their ankles like ghosts hovering just out of reach. She didn't know why she had come, why she'd accepted Axel's suggestion to attend Mr. Bascom's funeral with him. She hadn't known the man, and the last funeral she'd been to had been her parents'. Teri offered for Jude to stay behind at Foxglove. Kailey had jumped at the chance to get out, but she felt guilty leaving Jude behind.

Kailey stuffed her hands into the pockets of her coat and stood beside Axel as they waited by the car. A line of mourners moved toward the open grave in the cemetery. She could see Mrs. Bascom, now a widow, and beside her, clutching her hand, was a younger girl with strawberry-blond hair pulled into a braid. Her dress was navy-blue, and she had a cable-knit sweater pulled over it.

"That's Riley," Axel whispered in her ear. "Poor kid. She's been through a lot."

Kailey swallowed the lump in her throat and followed Axel as he joined the group. They cluttered around the gravesite with the man's casket hovering over the opening like a New Year's ball waiting to drop. Only, there was no celebration here. Mrs. Bascom's weeping was not quiet. It was a strangled wailing, and she leaned against another woman who was holding her up as best she could. The reverend wore a collar, the only patch of white in the lake of black. He opened the graveside ceremony with the typical "Though I walk through the valley of the shadow of death, I will fear no evil" speech. Which had never made sense to Kailey. Not really. How did one not fear evil? It was so real, so active, that not fearing it seemed foolish.

Axel glanced down at her and gave her a sad smile. She startled as his fingers brushed hers, then took hold of her hand. Platonic. She was sure of it, but she didn't pull away.

Some mousy-looking woman began to warble the old hymn "How Great Thou Art." Kailey willed away burning tears and stuffed down the intensity rising inside her. How great was God? How paltry He was, more like it. Or was she really that unbelieving? Kailey looked away from the woman, but the strains still echoed through her soul. No. She'd believed in God all her life. As a little girl, He was the only thing close enough to a hero to convince Kailey there was hope. But as life proceeded and only grew more dismal, God became more mythical. A fable. Inactive in righting any wrongs. Yet here they were, at the graveside of a man whose death was under investigation, listening to a minister of God who insisted they should fear no evil. Was this place not proof that evil had won? And if God allowed such things to happen, then how was He a hero? And if God was no longer a hero, then what purpose was left?

"Kailey." Axel's elbow nudged hers.

She reached for the tissue he extended to her and dabbed at the tears.

The song ended, and people began to disperse. Kailey observed Riley, standing off to the side of her mother and brother. She stared at the casket with an expression that knifed at Kailey.

"Yes, little one. I know exactly how you feel."

Their families' well-being was placed on their shoulders during those wicked hours they'd been taken. If it was the same people, then Riley had been told similar things.

"We know who your family is. Things can happen to them. Speak up now."

What had they demanded of Riley? The same questions they'd plied five-year-old Kailey with? And Riley was older. Ten, if Kailey remembered correctly. She had to have been more helpful than Kailey had been. Perhaps Riley knew what Jude knew—the secrets locked in his mind and elusive to Kailey's memory. They'd all been connected to Foxglove Manor. Perhaps Riley had told the abductors what they needed to know, and they'd released her because of it. Unlike Kailey, who'd been so young, so petrified, she couldn't have answered their questions even if she had actually known the answers. Riley's father's death *could* be merely a suicide. Not that it was any better than murder, but it had removed other ill-will intent from the equation. If Riley had—

"Kailey!" Axel's sharp voice was an echo in her ears.

She had to speak with Riley. She had to find out what had happened. If the police didn't believe Riley, and if Riley hadn't given the abductors the information they needed, then they were still out there. Returned, for some reason, after twenty years, this time targeting another little girl.

Kailey broke her grip with Axel, ignoring his questioning look, and wove around a couple and ducked between two men. There she was. Inches away. Kailey could smell fresh earth. Damp air. She could also smell a sugary-sweet scent from the girl. Like a strawberry lip gloss mixed with a scratch-and-sniff sticker.

"Riley?" Kailey hadn't removed her hands from her coat pockets. Her hair was pulled back in a low ponytail, and she hoped the expression on her face was kind. Understanding. Nonthreatening.

Riley's eyes were brown. Large. An element of confidence warred with a flash of fear.

Kailey took a small step backward so she didn't intimidate the

116

girl. "Riley, I—my name is Kailey Gibson. I'm so sorry about your dad." It was pithy. "So sorry." Words that were empty.

Riley nodded and glanced toward her mom, who had buried her face in some man's shoulder.

"Riley, do you mind if I ask you a question?" Kailey tried not to wince at her own audacity. But she had to know. She needed to know.

Riley shrugged.

"Did they ask you about the treasure of Foxglove Manor?"

Riley's eyes widened, fear visible by the way her cheeks flushed red and her eyes dilated. "I don't know what you're talking about." She shook her head.

"Riley . . ." Kailey offered the girl a smile of comradeship and sad understanding. "I know not everyone believes you—but I do. I know you were kidnapped and I—"

"What is the meaning of this!" a man's voice roared, interrupting Kailey's attempt to communicate with the girl. Riley flung her arms around the man and buried her face in his coat. "Why in the name of all that's holy are you asking my niece questions like that at her *father's grave*?"

"Kailey." It was Axel. He had come up beside her, and now his hand touched her elbow.

Kailey stiffened. "You believe her, don't you?" she asked the man. "You believe her when she says she was abducted?"

"Kailey." Axel's voice hardened with warning. He turned toward Riley's protector. "Jason, I'm sorry, man."

Jason only frowned. "Get her out of here, Axel. I don't know who she is, but keep her away from Riley."

Kailey wasn't going to be deterred. "Riley, what did they ask you? Did you tell them? Did they let you go 'cause you told them what they needed?"

Riley pressed into the man further.

Axel now gripped her elbow and pulled. "Kailey, knock it off. Leave Riley alone with her uncle. Come on."

She shook him off. "I need to know. *We* need to know! Jason? Jason, is it? Do you believe Riley? Or are you all telling her she's making up stories?" Kailey felt tears filling her eyes. "'Cause she needs you to believe her. This isn't a game, Jason! Please don't brush her off."

"Axel, I swear . . ." Jason's tone was grave.

Axel took hold of Kailey much more forcefully this time. Attendees of the funeral were beginning to stare.

"Axel." Kailey tried to explain herself to him. He needed to understand she wasn't some nutso stalking a little girl with insensitive questions. It was critical—*critical*—that they listened to Riley. "We need to know! If Riley withheld anything, they may not leave her alone."

"Come on, Kailey." Axel began pulling her toward their car.

"No." Kailey wrestled against his firm grip. "They may be why Mr. Bascom is dead."

"Oh, my word!" Mrs. Bascom wailed loudly as she clued into Kailey's protests.

"I'll call the cops, Axel. Get her outta here." Jason had urged Riley into the arms of another woman and was striding toward Axel.

Axel held up a hand. "I've got her, Jason. I'm sorry." He leaned into Kailey, his fingers tight enough on her arm that she whimpered at his grip. "Kailey, we're going to leave now. You're causing a scene. You're hurting Riley. We're going to get in my car. Then we're going to drive away. Then we're going to take a long walk and you're going to tell me what in the devil has you so messed up."

Kailey looked desperately over her shoulder. She'd lost sight of Riley. All she could see was the furious eyes of Jason, Riley's uncle. Hear the wailing of Mrs. Bascom. See the horrified and astonished faces of some of the guests.

She wouldn't admit Axel was right. Irritation at the situation, at Jason, at herself, at Riley, and mostly at the ones who had set these calamities in motion, roiled in her gut.

"Fine," she ground out between her teeth. But her cheeks burned, and her eyes stung with tears of urgency and extreme shame. Deflecting Axel's grip, Kailey covered her emotions with a snap. "Don't. Touch. Me."

She hurried to his car, head down, tears racing down her cheeks with the speed of Sonic the Hedgehog. It hadn't gone well. Her impulse had backfired horribly. She had made a spectacle of herself. Wounded Riley further, most likely. And now, God forbid, Axel was going to dig for the truth. The truth that even she hadn't been able to piece together since she was five years old.

Axel's "walk" meant a hiking trail through the state park. They had left Lake Superior in the distance and driven until his SUV wove through the Porcupine Mountains and miles and miles of forest. Parking, Axel led Kailey to a trail, glanced at her feet, and winced. Yes. She had ballet flats on. She glanced at his feet. Hiking boots. Figured.

Wet leaves and patches of snow blanketed the forest floor. A squirrel chattered in the leafless trees above them. The breeze had a touch of warmth to it.

"We won't go far," he said with a sideways glance.

Kailey was rehearsing what she could say to describe her irrational urgency at the graveyard. Something akin to the same sort of panic she'd felt as a child had familiarized itself with her all over again. The needing to know, to understand, and then that undefinable sense of needing to run, escape, and forget. Now, without thinking, she'd half accosted the ten-year-old Riley Bascom at the graveside of her dead father. A shiver rattled through Kailey from the inside out. Dead parents. Only another commonality between her and the younger version of herself. Foxglove Manor was only the starting point.

She followed Axel along the trail, but her feet felt like weights were strapped to her ankles. For the most part, it was a paved trail leading up a heavily wooded hill. They reached some steps—stone—probably constructed in the 1930s when parks were being established. She fixated on Axel's heels as he hiked ahead of her, a bit frantic to come up with a satisfactory explanation that would assuage his need to reconcile the situation but also protect her own privacy. Her own past. Her own sanity.

The path began to open into a flat, granite surface. It plateaued at the top of the hill and in a few moments, the trees grew sparse, and instead the range spread before her in an endless stretch of treetops below them and blue sky in the distance. It was a different sort of lake, this forest, and the drop-off was deep and cavernous. While the range wasn't of Rocky Mountain status, its hills were still impressive, and the miles upon miles of woods made Kailey pause to catch her breath. In the middle was another lake, significantly smaller and more in line with what she pictured an average lake might be. The view was stunning. It was diminishing. She felt small. Small and stupid.

"They call this place the Lake of the Clouds." Axel's words floated over her shoulder as he came up behind her. His breath warmed her neck, reminding her she wasn't wearing a scarf and that he was a very solid confidant in comparison to the range before her that made her a bit dizzy. The breadth of the place was almost overwhelming. Not unlike the pieces inside her that created a valley so deep and so vast that she feared if she were to venture back inside, she'd get lost forever.

"It's beautiful," she murmured.

Axel's hand trailed across the small of her back as if he wished to reassure her as he rounded her. That alone made her shiver again. Kailey wrapped her arms protectively around herself, watching as Axel approached the edge like a comfortably experienced outdoorsman. He perched his boot-clad foot on a rock.

"Sometimes the clouds settle over the trees and the lake, and standing here you almost float above them. It's like being lofted over everything you can no longer see and make sense of, and yet knowing that if you stand here, you're on a solid rock."

Kailey tightened her arms in a self-embrace and not because she was cold. "Solid rock is . . . nice," she said.

"It is. It's unmovable."

There were spiritual undertones in his observation. They seemed purposefully put there. She didn't pursue it.

Axel cleared his throat and pivoted on the rock so that he faced her. Kailey wanted to shrink under his scrutiny. Eyes that didn't know her at all but insisted they knew everything.

"Want to talk about it?"

Why did he have to be so nice? Kailey toed a crevice in the rock floor. No, she didn't *want* to talk about it. She knew, deep in her heart, that Axel hadn't brought her to Lake of the Clouds to simply enjoy the view. She appreciated he wasn't hog-tying her and making her talk. But she also had a strong feeling he would keep them here until she gave him enough of an explanation to appease Riley Bascom's uncle Jason, who, truth be told, had every right to be irate with Kailey.

The wind picked up and blew strands of hair across her face. Kailey uncurled her arms from hugging herself to brush them away. Her eyes met Axel's. He had a kind face. Weathered. Bearded. Soft and yet strong simultaneously. She didn't have experience with strong men. Only weak ones—her father included—or masked ones who threw little girls into the back of a van and interrogated them for hours with questions they couldn't answer.

"Jude is the only strong one I know." She spoke without realizing it.

"What's that?" Axel's hands were shoved into the pockets of his sherpa-lined denim jacket.

Kailey ducked her head. "I was just thinking . . ." She let her words drain away. Thinking. That was a pastime she'd avoided for years. Caring for Jude, now that was her focus. Finding him peace, that was her goal.

Axel bent to pick up a pebble. He flicked it over the edge. "So for his sake, what happened back there at the cemetery?"

For Jude's sake? What did he have to do with it? Kailey opened her mouth to snap at Axel, but then she clamped her lips shut. No. No, Axel was right. Everything she did was motivated by her fierce concern for Jude. Images of his lined notebooks, filled with the same sequences of gibberish that had only increased in regularity lately, flooded her mind.

Kailey made pretense of avoiding eye contact by fumbling with a stick of gum she found stuffed in the depths of her coat pocket. "I know it wasn't wise of me." She unwrapped the wrapper, crinkling it in her palm. "But it's so important they don't dismiss Riley's experience. Her kidnapping." She put the gum in her mouth and chewed. "And her father dying seems so coincidental with the timing of it—" *Carrrrrrrrreful*, Kailey warned herself and bit down on the gum—and her tongue. "Just—it's important to take kids seriously."

"Jason loves his niece very much, and her mother loves Riley too. I believe they wouldn't dismiss Riley as easily as you're suggesting they do," Axel said.

Kailey looked away from Axel's piercing stare. He was digging.

What happened to you to make you think Riley would receive disbelieving treatment?

It was the unspoken question plastered across Axel's face and etched into the worry lines at the corners of his eyes.

"What if Mr. Bascom was murdered?" Deflect. Always deflect. Kailey was good at that.

"It was suicide," Axel supplied.

"Was it?" Kailey challenged.

"The coroner stated he died of asphyxiation—in his garage."

Kailey hadn't heard that detail.

Axel continued. "Classic circumstances."

"Still," Kailey insisted, swallowing her frustration and ignoring the way she felt her cheeks flame with emotion. "Riley deserves to be taken seriously. Mr. Bascom's death should be—well, it all should be taken seriously."

Axel crouched and then adjusted his position so he was sitting on the ledge. He was about four feet from the edge. He patted the rock next to him. "Sit down."

Kailey shook her head. "I'm fine here."

"I wasn't asking." For all his gentle smiles and congenial mannerisms, there was steel in Axel Pavlov's voice. Still, he reached out an arm, wiggling his fingers. She obeyed. Resisting internally while biting her tongue and instinctively reaching for his hand. He tugged her down beside him. Their knees bumped as she curled into a cross-legged position. Kailey caught a whiff of his cologne or deodorant or whatever it was. It was piney. Like Christmas meets a log cabin with evergreen boughs and cinnamon sticks.

"Why did you come to Foxglove, Kailey? Really. Be honest."

Kailey chewed on her gum with such intensity her jaw would probably be sore later. "I told you. I needed employment that complemented my also caring for Jude. He can't be without me, and I wasn't going to farm him out to some care facility. Foxglove Manor would be good for us." She knew many care facilities were fabulous, but the idea of leaving Jude . . .

Axel wrapped his arms around his knees and looked out over the lake and the clouds. "Good for you," he repeated. "Why?"

"Huh?" Kailey lifted her head.

"Why would Foxglove Manor be good for you?"

"The people," she inserted quickly. Falsely. "You know, relationships are stimulating for Jude, and important for his continuous development. And, I love old people. They're—calming and caring."

"So, you came here for old people and Jude?"

"Yep." She could tell Axel wasn't buying into her lies. Kailey sucked in a breath. "Listen, I—shouldn't have pushed Riley at her dad's funeral. I just don't believe people should dismiss her story. That's it. It's that simple."

Axel tossed another stone over the edge. Kailey watched it plummet toward the blanket of treetops below them. "Kailey, it's not quantum physics to figure out that the momentum of your coming to Foxglove, bringing your brother, and being so invested in Riley Bascom's story lends to something you're not telling me. Something that's still very much in play in your life."

Kailey choked on her gum. She coughed.

Axel patted her back. "I get you don't want to tell me, and I respect that. But I need to know you're going to leave the Bascoms alone. We can't have you unsettling Riley, and—I don't know exactly what's going to happen with the manor now that Mr. Bascom is gone. So, we don't want to jeopardize the future for Raymond, or Maddie, or Stella, or any of the others."

"I know." Kailey nodded, pushing the gum into the gap between her teeth and cheek for safekeeping. "Just—can you make sure Riley's uncle is aware? That the man who took her didn't—that he doesn't come back?"

"How do you know it was a man?"

"Aren't most abductors men?" Kailey disputed.

"Are they?" Axel countered.

"It's not hard to come to that conclusion."

"At least he's gone now." Axel gave her a sideways glance.

"Is he?" Kailey followed his leading statement.

"Sure. The police say if Riley's story is true, they're long gone now."

"*If* Riley's story is true? See, that's my concern, right there," Kailey mumbled, moving the well-chewed gum in her mouth to the other side of her teeth.

"Police said Riley played hooky more likely than not and concocted the story."

"She didn't." Kailey gritted her teeth.

"How do you know?"

"Because I know." Kailey clenched her jaw.

"But how?" Axel pressed.

"Because I *know!*" Kailey scrambled to her feet and stood over him. Her voice echoed over the trees. A vulture soared below them, circling something dead on the forest floor. A flock of birds alighted from a tree near them and took to the air in a flurry due to Kailey's fast motion.

She met Axel's upturned face, and her body went cold. He had figured her out. Too quickly. Too easily. She was a pathetic liar.

"Did someone hurt you as a child, Kailey?" Axel's realization was quiet. "Take you away from your parents or something?"

Kailey's chin trembled. She tasted tears. "I'm going back to the car."

"Kailey, wait."

She waved him off and hurried back toward the path. Toward the forest. Toward the darkness of the canopy of trees that would envelop her and hide her away from the exposed position on top of the clouds.

16

"Help me . . ."

A whisper floated through her subconscious, waking her. The sheets were twisted around Kailey's legs, her T-shirt stuck to her chest with sweat, and the purple shorts she'd worn to bed were tugged up over her hips. Her bedroom was cold. Kailey opened her eyes, her breaths coming in fast, short gasps. Someone had spoken, and as they had spoken, they'd touched her. Ran fingers down the side of her face, under her chin, skimmed her neck . . .

She shot up in the bed, untangling her legs and grabbing her phone off the nightstand. Kailey tapped it. 3:38 a.m. A quick glance toward the window showed the lake illuminated beneath the moon. Waves rolling in with their persistent attack on the shore. The cedar and poplar trees swayed, but there was no major storm, no gusts of wind, no thunder or lightning. But her face tingled. Tingled from the feeling of a whisper touch trailing her skin, ominous and threatening.

There was enough moonlight in her room to make out the shapes of the antique wardrobe, the dresser, the wing-back chair in the corner, a bookshelf, and her pile of discarded shoes by the bedroom door. The air mattress on the floor beside her bed held the mature, male form of her brother. Jude was curled in the fetal position, his light-brown hair tousled, his chin covered in whiskers. In his hand, he still held a pencil, and on the floor beside him lay a sketch pad with a half-drawn image of a fireplace on it. The fireplace from the downstairs study, along with its intricately carved mantel.

She glanced toward the in-room phone. The intercom light blinked red. She wasn't typically on call during the night, but she was reachable if needed.

Kailey swung herself out of the bed and padded across the floor. She hit the intercom button for the main nurse's room.

"Tracee?" Kailey called softly into the intercom.

She was met with a white noise of empty response. Either Tracee was asleep or she was assisting a resident and wasn't in her room.

Kailey tugged her shorts over her hips, then wrapped her arms around herself as she peered about the dark room. She eyed the light switch but resisted flicking it on so she didn't awaken Jude.

Help me.

She'd heard the voice so clearly. Like a little girl pleading to be carried. A little girl whose legs were weary, whose body was tired. Kailey looked at her bedroom door and stilled. It was opened a crack. Two inches at the most. She ran her fingers through her messy hair and tentatively approached the door as though it were going to turn into a monster and leap out to scream in her face. It didn't. She palmed the doorknob and pulled it open. The hallway beyond was empty and long. Two hall lights with very dim bulbs were lighting the path. She had the brief recollection of there being a carpet runner down this hall when she was five. She remembered it because it'd been warm under her bare feet when she'd snuck to the room where Jude had slept. Snuck there to sleep where she felt safe.

"Help me." The voice dropped to a whisper, but the breath of it seemed to lift a tendril of hair by Kailey's ear. She slapped at it like one would a mosquito and spun, staring back into her bedroom. Empty. Her heart punched her chest from the inside out, and Kailey took short breaths, blowing them out through open lips.

"Hello?" she called quietly. Her voice echoed down the hallway.

Eerie with its power to sound loud when really she'd barely raised her voice above a whisper.

With no answer from the hallway, Kailey pulled back into her room and tiptoed to the wardrobe, flinging open the doors. Her clothes hung there like limp, lifeless bodies. All in a row.

Edgar.

Poe.

Kailey swiveled her head left and right, searching the room for her cats. Both were missing. Edgar, who normally curled beside her legs, was nowhere to be seen. Poe . . . maybe he'd been the one to slip through the doorway in search of his buddy Raymond. Only . . . Kailey squeezed the bridge of her nose. Poe couldn't open a door. He was a cat. And unless the door hadn't been latched tight, the idea of a fluffy white cat turning a doorknob was ludicrous.

The hallway floor creaked under the weight of a footstep. Kailey hurried back to the doorway.

"Tracee, is that—?" The empty hallway met her vision.

She'd heard the footstep. She'd heard the child's voice.

Kailey stepped into the hall. The doors to the other rooms were all shut. Closed and harboring sleeping residents. She tiptoed past them, noting that her own weight made the floorboards complain. They were cold beneath her bare feet.

In her peripheral vision, a flash of white at the end of the hall snagged Kailey's attention.

"Hello?" She snuck toward it, reticent to explore, but an unseen force—call it curiosity?—tugged her forward. "Hello?" Kailey hissed, wanting to avoid waking the residents. She reached the end of the hall and looked around the corner, toward the turret-floor stairs. When she was five, she'd ventured there. An unsuspecting little girl climbing creepy old steps to an empty set of rooms in a round, turreted space. She'd not returned, not then, and not since she'd arrived back at Foxglove Manor.

"Hellllllp me."

With the whisper came a brush of chill, caressing Kailey's face like the breath of the dead. She froze. At the base of the stairs was a girl. Her blond hair almost white, hanging over her face. Her skin was translucent, her dress hung to just above her ankles. Or nightgown. Yes, that was it. It was a nightgown. Gray in the darkness, with long sleeves that hugged her wrists.

The little girl stepped onto the bottom step as though she were going to ascend to the turret, but instead of her feet balancing on the stair, she hovered just above it. The girl's bare feet were pointed like ballet toes. She raised herself onto them, then lowered herself to her heels, then back up to her tiptoes again.

Kailey wanted to shout—to scream—but her voice was strangled as she was pulled into the little girl's eyes. Black eyes. Shrouded in violet hues as if someone had beat her with fists. Her face was sunken, the skin around her mouth puckered—wrinkled—the sure sign of death and partial decay.

Kailey couldn't move as her hand clutched the corner of the wall. Her body trembled, terror racing through her like a roller coaster out of control.

The little girl moved up another stair but remained facing Kailey.

She opened her mouth, dark and cavernous, as if to utter another plea for help. Instead, from the pit of it a moth fluttered, carrying itself out of the girl's mouth and up the stairs, disappearing into the dark.

"Help me, Kailey." The girl's whisper was a pleading whine. "Hellllllllp me . . ."

"Kailey."

A hand lightly slapped her face.

"Kailey."

She could feel herself being pulled, sand scraping the bare skin of her back. Her body was shivering. Her legs were in water. A cold wave rolled over her, soaking her, spraying onto her chest and bared arms.

"Kailey. C'mon, Kailey, wake up." The hand was stinging now. She squeezed her eyes tight, against the cold, the pain.

Groaning, she rolled to her side and coughed, trying to curl into the sand as if it would somehow provide an insulated warmth.

Voices murmured around her. A warm hand pushed wet hair off her face. Two arms wriggled under her, jostling her, pinching her skin unintentionally. She was lifted—hoisted, really—with an awkward stumble.

"Let's get her to the manor," a woman said. "Jude is frantic."

Yes. Jude.

Kailey bounced against a man's torso, her head hitting his shoulder bone. There was nothing comfortable about being carried. Kailey moaned, trying to open her arms, but she was cold. The cold seeped into the marrow of her bones, and she realized the clicking she heard was her teeth.

A door must have been kicked open because it slammed into a wall.

"You found her!" Raymond's voice—relieved—in the distance.

"God bless you." Teri's words drifted into Kailey's conscious mind, and somehow she knew whoever Teri was thanking was the person carrying her.

"Take her into the infirmary." *Tracee.* She was giving orders in her short, no-nonsense way.

"N-no," Kailey whimpered. She tried to open her eyes, but they were heavy. "Jude."

"Put her on the bed," Tracee directed.

"I'll get some heat pads." A whiff of frankincense followed Teri from the room.

Kailey was lowered, her body meeting the softness of the mattress. A vague recollection came to her. She was in the infirmary. The only downstairs room that had a bed in it in case a resident was sick enough to need special care.

"I need to go. Jude—he needs me—"

"Shh, Kailey," Tracee interrupted her protest, running her palm over Kailey's forehead. Kailey finally got her eyelids to cooperate. She opened them. Tracee was worried. It was etched in her face, even though she was tending to business. Axel was shaking out a blanket from its folded square. He laid it over her as Tracee ran a thermometer across Kailey's forehead.

"She's just under ninety-six degrees. She's verging on hypothermia. Start rubbing her feet, Axel." Tracee took the heat pads Teri had returned with. They were wrapped in orange plastic. She ripped them open and started shaking them. "I'll put these on pressure points around her body, but we've got to get her out of her clothes."

"Maddie is coloring with Jude," Teri's voice assured them all from the distance. "She has him calmed now."

The blanket Axel had laid across her was tugged off. Kailey tried to clutch at it and pull it back on.

"No, Kailey." Tracee pressed her arms back down gently. "Shh. Just hold on."

Kailey was aware of her wet shorts being tugged off. She had a fleeting, out-of-body question as to whether Axel was still in the room. Her T-shirt was next. Then blessed warm compresses met her skin. A heating pad was laid over her chest. The blanket was returned. Someone was rubbing her feet between warm palms. She opened her eyes just a slit. It was Axel, fixated on her feet as if he could will his personal warmth into hers. She supposed it wasn't all that bad if he'd seen her in her underwear, not if he was helping her get warm.

She wondered if Axel had ever had a girlfriend. Maybe he'd never seen a woman in her wet pajamas before? Or without them, like she was now, beneath the blanket.

Kailey's mind wavered from its senseless rumination. Her skin tingled as warmth began to return.

Teri's arm slipped under her neck. Kailey met the nurse's eyes. "Hey, sweetie. Sip this water. It's warm, with some lavender. Let's get some heat in you."

Kailey did so, the liquid soothing her tongue and throat.

Tracee skirted by Teri and placed a blood-pressure cuff around Kailey's arm. "This will squeeze a little. I'm sorry." She pumped, the band tightened, pinched her bare skin, held, then released. "It's high." Tracee tugged at the cuff, and the Velcro made a ripping sound.

"Eesh," Teri muttered.

"She's going to be okay, isn't she?" Axel asked, his hands not pausing in their rubbing of her feet.

"She is now. She's not full-blown hypothermia, thank the Lord," Teri replied. "But much longer in that water and we'd be calling 911."

"And you know how quick they'd make it here." Tracee gave a sarcastic snort of doom. She leaned over Kailey and held a light up to her eyes as her fingers gently lifted Kailey's eyelids. "Pupils responding normally. I don't see signs of a fall or a concussion."

"How on earth did she end up at the bottom of the cliff in the water?" Teri mused, clicking her tongue as she urged Kailey to sip again. "Sip, sweetie."

Kailey did so. Coughed. She had to speak. Had to explain . . . A vision entered her memory. The little girl on the stairs. She'd seen her disappear up the stairs, begging Kailey to help her, and then . . . then there was nothing. Only blackness. Now she was here, in the infirmary. She could hear voices in the hall. Raymond. Stella. Whispering loudly so their hearing aids could pick up each other's voices.

"She's been missing since bedtime last night!" Stella said.

"I saw her head to the restroom at eleven," Raymond responded. Yes, Kailey remembered peeking into his open door and waving at him on her way to the bathroom just before she went to bed.

"Something's not right," Stella inserted.

"Darn tootin' something's not right!" Raymond snorted.

Their voices cut off as the infirmary door was shut. Tracee blew a breath from her mouth, and her hair lifted off her forehead. "Our local snoops are concerned about you," she said, then gave Kailey a smile.

Axel's hands on Kailey's feet had slowed to a stop. Teri was slipping warm socks over them. Axel stood and stared down at her, helplessness on his face.

"Kailey?" Tracee eased herself onto the bed next to Kailey. "Can you tell us what happened?" She pushed wet hair away from Kailey's face.

Kailey swallowed, the aftertaste of lavender on her tongue. She drew in a shuddering breath. Her mind was becoming clearer, her memories more vivid, but she still couldn't process logic enough to filter her words.

"The little girl . . ." Kailey squeezed her eyes shut and then opened them again. She locked gazes with Axel. His expression encouraged her even though she read confusion on his face. "She—she's in the turret."

"What little girl?" Teri tucked the blanket around Kailey's feet.

Kailey frowned. "She's—white. White hair and nightgown."

Tracee exchanged looks with Teri and then lifted her head to give Axel a meaningful glance.

"What?" Kailey looked among the three of her caregivers.

Tracee's hazel eyes were sharp and searching. "Kailey, how did you get on the shore at the bottom of the cliff?"

Kailey ached to remember. Ached to recall. She searched her memory, but all she could see was the little girl's dark eyes. She could hear the pleading in her voice.

"She—she wanted me to help her." Kailey ignored the way the others in the room stilled. "She's younger than Riley. Maybe as young as I am. We're so little. Too little." She could see for some reason her words confused them. A thought spiked through Kailey, and she struggled to sit up. Tracee pushed her back onto the pillow. Kailey swiped at her arm, an urgency rising in her throat. "No, let me up. Please."

"Kailey," Axel intervened. He crouched by the bed and caught her hands. "Lie down. You need to get warm."

Kailey shook her head. "Riley. The little girl last night—Axel, they need to be heard. *We* need to be heard!"

133

"Shh," Tracee soothed behind Axel.

Teri tapped Tracee's shoulder, and Tracee nodded, moving out of the way.

Axel reached for Kailey's forehead and rested his palm on it. "We'll listen, Kailey." He glanced at Teri, then back to her. "But you need to get some rest first. Okay? Just rest."

"I don't want to rest." Kailey struggled, but Teri was leaning over her now.

"She's going out," Kailey heard Teri observe.

"Is she okay?" A worried question from Axel.

Kailey heard them talking, but it was a distant echo. She focused on Axel's eyes. So gray. Like the lake. Like the girl's nightgown.

The steadiness of Axel's expression reassured Kailey. Her eyes were heavy. So heavy. It reminded her of when she was five. The darkness. The weight of the air in the van.

Help me.

Hellllp me.

Her eyes flew open. Axel was staring back.

"Don't let him take me!" she begged, grappling for Axel's hand. "Please."

"I won't." His grip tightened even as his profile started to lose focus.

Kailey closed her eyes, then tried to reopen them, only to have her lids win the battle and shut again. "I won't," she heard once more, just as she slipped away into sleep.

17

ADRIA

The switch to the back of her legs was as surprising as Mrs. St. John's crazed shriek as she came upon Adria at the bottom of the stairs.

"How dare you!"

The switch stung Adria's skin. She screamed, curling against the wall as Mrs. St. John reached around her and brought the switch down in another fluid motion. Mrs. St. John's eyes were sharp in the light that glowed from a lamp.

"You're a meddling, wretched girl!" She raised her arm again, but Adria held out her hands.

"Stop, *please!*"

Mrs. St. John hesitated, the switch raised in the air.

"I heard noises. I thought maybe Lula was ill and needed assistance!" It was a lie. A horrible untruth, but Adria had long learned that lies often became saviors in the face of violence or threat.

Lula appeared at the bottom of the steps. She cast a desperate glance toward Adria and then nodded vehemently. "Yes, yes, ma'am. I was coughing up a storm and Miss Fontaine, ma'am, she only was tryin' to help. You know that Mr. Crayne does what he wants, and I couldn't keep him hidden if I locked him in his own room myself!"

Mrs. St. John's arm lowered, taking the switch with it. She glared between the two of them, weighing their words and appearing to doubt them, evidenced by the fine lines deepening between her eyes.

"My daughter, Theodora, would never have been so shameless. Going upstairs in your nightdress. Prodding into the business of others. You were not to go to the third floor, Alexandria."

Adria nodded, even though internally she argued that Mrs. St. John had never said not to. Probably to throw off any curiosity by showing a lack of concern. It hadn't worked. Neither had their lies that no man lived on the third floor.

"I'm so sorry." Adria offered the appeasing apology while cringing inside. She'd promised herself, the day the carriage pulled away from her childhood home, that she would never grovel again. Never allow another to touch her. The throbbing welts on the backs of her legs proved that vow to be wrong. Oh, so very wrong.

"You will return to your room, Alexandria. Nothing more will be said about tonight. When the morning dawns, you will go about your business as before. Mr. Crayne is nothing but a story, and one you will not tell."

Adria ached to ask why. Why must this Mr. Crayne be kept a secret? So utterly drunken, he was a walking mess of worthlessness defined by scars. Hardly worth hiding, considering Foxglove Manor was already remote as it was.

"Alexandria?"

The sharp edge to Mrs. St. John's voice reminded Adria of the swift sting of the switch in the old woman's hand. She couldn't speak. She was withdrawing. Going to the secret places inside herself she fled to when the tension was too high, the threat too real, the—

"Leave the girl alone." Mr. Crayne's baritone and slurring voice echoed down the stairs. There was a thud, and then a thump, and then he stumbled his way to the halfway point of the stairwell, bent, and peered down at them. His dark hair was wild, dropping in straight strands over his eyes like an unshorn mutt's. "She's no threat, and you're an idiot if you think otherwise."

Adria's face grew cold as she paled. The audacity of his words! She exchanged looks with Lula, who stood primly off to the side, hands clasped in front of her and eyes wide.

"Mr. Crayne, I must insist—" Mrs. St. John sputtered.

He waved her off with a hand that gripped the neck of a brown bottle. "I said *leave her alone*. So do it."

A drunken hero was not on Adria's list of hopes and dreams, but for the moment, she was grateful that Mr. Crayne was willing to insert himself between her and this wicked side of Mrs. St. John.

Mrs. St. John raised her chin at the man, staring down her nose at him like a general headed into battle. "*I* am the mistress of Foxglove Manor, Mr. Crayne. Your orders mean little to me."

His eyes darkened. He lifted the bottle to his mouth, hesitated, then thought better of it and lowered it back to his side. Mr. Crayne's challenging stare never left the widow's face. "*I* am the guardian of Foxglove Manor. *You* mean little to me."

Mrs. St. John blanched, her face paling in the lamplight. She tucked the switch under her elbow and, with a snort of derision, stalked away down the hall until she disappeared around the corner.

Silence pervaded.

Lula had yet to move.

Adria was frightened, intimidated, and oh so very relieved Mrs. St. John had been chased away.

"Well then!" Mr. Crayne broke the tension, hoisting his whiskey bottle into the air as if in celebration. "As the dead man once said, 'War, at the best, is terrible'!" He took a swig and wiped his whiskered mouth with the back of his hand. "But I won this battle. Now off to bed. Both of you. Do your duty and leave me alone."

Mr. Crayne staggered back up the stairs. Lula and Adria remained rooted in stunned silence. The door to his room thudded shut.

"That man," Lula finally whispered with a dismissive roll of her eyes and a shake of her head. "Quotes the old President Lincoln like he was God hisself, eh? And him bein' a—" She cut off her sentence.

Adria frowned. "A what?"

"Never mind." Lula waved her off and issued an exaggerated yawn. "I've no intention of not following orders, and neither should you. He may have risen to the challenge against the missus tonight, but you never know what you're going to get from Mr. Crayne."

"Who *is* Mr. Crayne?" Adria asked.

Lula eyed Adria with a look of caution. "He's Mr. Crayne, that's who he is."

"What did he mean he was the guardian of Foxglove Manor?" Adria pressed, sensing her tenaciousness returning slowly, a force in her bloodstream now uninhibited by Mrs. St. John's condemnatory presence.

Lula yawned again, waggling her fingers in the air. "The man fancies himself to be a lot of things, Miss Fontaine. But level-headed and someone to believe ain't one of them!" Lula hurried up the stairs in the direction of Mr. Crayne.

Adria remained still at the bottom of the stairwell. She heard Lula's door close. She heard the faint sound of a rattle, like a chain lock being slid over and into place. Was Lula afraid of Mr. Crayne? Or perhaps Mrs. St. John?

Or maybe, Adria reminded herself, being afraid just came with the territory of living in Foxglove Manor.

"You lied to me." Adria hurried after Diggery, her shoes sinking into the sandy soil. He ignored her, hiking ahead with a shovel in his left hand. He used the spade against the earth to balance himself as he walked.

"Diggery!" Adria lifted her dress above her ankles with her right hand and hopped over a waterworn log that had somehow made it from the shore below the cliff to the yard of Foxglove Manor. Diggery's mangy fox skirted them by dodging the shadows in the tree line. Her tail brushed the long stems of the tubular flowers, pink and barely blossomed in the early spring. Foxglove. It was a beautiful backdrop against the evergreen of the trees, if only the red fox was in health and had a beautiful coat.

Adria shifted her attention from the fox to Diggery, who stopped at the base of a large boulder. He leaned the shovel against it and braced his palm on the cold stone as he carefully lowered himself to a kneeling position.

"Diggery?" Adria attempted again to garner his attention.

"I've got flowers to plant." It was a grumble, dismissive in nature. Strangely, Adria didn't see any flowers, but from his wool coat pocket Diggery pulled a much smaller spade, and he began to work the soil at the boulder's base. "She likes flowers. I'll give her flowers," he muttered crossly.

"Why did you lie to me?" Adria pressed again.

Diggery's chin almost met his shoulder as he looked sideways at Adria. "I didn't lie to you," he snapped.

"You did," Adria insisted. She hiked to the boulder and placed her hand on it, looking down at Diggery. "You said there was no man on the third floor. But there is! Mr. Crayne. He's a drunkard and half out of his mind."

"Then you know why there's no *man* on the third floor!" Diggery slapped the earth with his gloved hand and began to spade the dirt again. "Not a full man, anyways."

"Who is Mr. Crayne?"

"He's none of your concern, that's who he is. Now, Mrs. St. John wants flowers. Pink ones. I aim to plant them here. She can see them from the side windows once they blossom. Her daughter's favorite color, and I'll be a blasted idiot if I don't make sure it happens for her." He gave a snort. "Not 'cause I care about the woman's feelin's, mind you, but 'cause I care about my own food and lodgin'."

"What happened to Mr. Crayne?" Adria skirted the inapplicable topic of Theodora St. John, who hadn't even died at Foxglove Manor, and tried to return the conversation to Mr. Crayne.

"'What happened to Mr. Crayne?'" Diggery mimicked her, chucked the spade into the ground, and sat back on his heels. He looked up at her from beneath his bushy eyebrows. "Child, you ever hear the story of the battle of Stone's River?"

Adria shook her head. "No." She caught a blur of orange as the fox darted into the trees, her paws soundless against the earth and patchy snow.

"Happened in Tennessee, during the war. Both sides went up against each other. Both sides lost a lot of men. Both sides sat back when it was done, and neither side had a winner. Out of every battle in the war, that one took the most men when you added up both sides."

Adria had heard of many battles, but most were her father's bragging of ships he looted on the lakes. Alcohol conquests, even timber, and then of course, the bounties of war that had been smuggled north only to be looted by him and then their ships scuttled.

Diggery coughed. Hacked, really. He reached into his pocket for a grimy handkerchief and wiped his mouth. "Point is, some battles are best never started. Too many casualties at the end of it, and if you just keep marching forward, eventually you'd just leave it behind. Peaceful-like."

Adria brushed wavy hair from her face as the breeze picked up. "I only asked what happened to Mr. Crayne."

"Aye." Diggery nodded, skewering her with a stern look. "That's what I'm tellin' ya. Leave the battle before you wage the war, child, and you won't have any casualties."

18

The missive was short. *Find it.*

Adria crumpled the telegram in her hand and dropped a coin onto the extended palm of the messenger who had carried the telegram miles from the nearby town. Her father's words were clear and undisguised, even though anyone else reading the two words wouldn't understand the brevity of them. They threatened her freedom, her physical well-being, and her mental state, which was no less fragile than two months ago when she'd decided meeting God face-to-face was a far more tolerable outcome than seeing her earthly father one more time.

For some reason, God had spared her. For obvious reasons, her father had not.

Adria shut the arched door of Foxglove Manor with a firm thud.

"Who was that?" Lula appeared out of nowhere, and Adria yelped, crunching the telegram further in her fist.

Adria collected herself. "It was a messenger. He had a telegram for me."

"Oh?" Lula's brows rose in the undisguised curiosity of a teenage girl.

"From my family," she said to appease the girl while images of her father's stern visage floated through her mind, followed by the echo of her sister Margot's superior aura. She always stood behind their father. She was his favorite, his eldest, and she shared his vicious ability to bid farewell to one's conscience and engage in the suffering of others.

Lula was waiting as though she expected Adria to continue. When Adria didn't, she lifted her duster, feathers shaking out some of the dust, and said, "Well, I'll leave you to it then."

Adria let the girl go on her way, even though she caught Lula's look over her shoulder as she fluffed the feathers across the hall tree. Of course, they didn't receive visitors at Foxglove Manor on a frequent basis. It was little wonder Lula was curious.

Ducking her head, Adria skirted Lula and her furtive glances and hurried up the stairs toward her room. She uncrumpled the telegram as she went, her thumb brushing the ominous two words.

Find it.

Find it.

It was like the peal of an alarm bell repeating itself over and over again. She'd never forget the moment he'd flipped a gold coin in her face and stated rather viciously that there were more where that came from. Smuggled northward by looters from the South and then taken by her father—a loyal Unionist, but truthfully, more loyal to himself. That her father believed Mr. St. John was responsible for its whereabouts, was obvious. Gold. Confederate treasure. It made Adria feel like a pirate's first mate answering the man's barking orders on pain of death.

What was it her father had said?

"Given St. John's own lack of integrity, he's too greedy to have pilfered the treasure or to have smuggled it away into Canada like everything else he touches."

That statement alone had indicated the gold was here—at Foxglove Manor—waiting for Adria to uncover. And then what? Contact her father, of course, but hide it from Mrs. St. John? Or perhaps the woman knew of it. She might hold the answers, and the placement of a simple, straightforward question was all that was required. Adria feared the switch that had left bruises on her legs. Not to mention, she'd never heard of anyone willingly giving up a treasure trove of gold—even if one hated and despised what it stood for—the South and its political ambitions and other morbid sins that should have been instinctually detestable to any man. But apparently had not been, could not be forced, and would potentially never be.

Gold.

War.

Adria considered Mr. Crayne and his scars. Recalled her father's words about Mr. St. John and smuggling and—

"Oompf!" The deep voice matched the force with which her head plowed into his chest. This time clothed in a fresh white shirt and fully buttoned. There was no naked skin to make her blush, but she did anyway.

Adria was stumbling back when Mr. Crayne's hand steadied her. She stared at him, incredulous. He was on the second floor. He'd not been on the second floor since she'd arrived. His eyes were red but clearer than the previous night. He'd slicked his black hair back, damp from being washed, which revealed a broad forehead and a vein that spanned it. She imagined it protruded when he was extremely angry. Adria made a note not to anger him beyond what she already had.

His gaze penetrated her. "Reading and walking is a definite recipe for an accident."

Adria crumbled her father's telegram in her hand.

Mr. Crayne offered no apology for the night before. They stood at an impasse in the same hallway where Mrs. St. John had taken a switch to the backs of her legs, staring at each other. He studied her as if curious to find out more about her. She knew her expression was that of a woman wishing to flee, yet something about the man kept her standing in the same spot he had steadied her. Almost as if he had pounded nails through her shoes to keep her there.

"Must we stand here all day or shall I pass?" Mr. Crayne was gruff, but there was a bit of humor in his voice.

Adria could only answer honestly, and it wasn't until the words were out of her mouth that she realized he might interpret them as sassy rather than compliant. "I'm quite small. I'm sure you can find your way around me."

Mr. Crayne rose to her challenge, but he didn't bother to step out and away from her. His chest brushed her arm as he slipped past. Pausing, he looked down at her. "I see no reason to be holed up in that blasted turret. Particularly now that you're aware of my existence. Perhaps you came to rescue me?"

Adria blinked.

He smiled. When he did so, it transformed his dark features into a much more pleasant version of himself. "No? Hmm. Well, I do wonder why *you've* come to Foxglove. No one comes here because they wish to."

Adria didn't answer. She couldn't rightly admit she had tried to meet the dear Lord in person. Nor was she about to spread the truth of her treasure hunt to anyone other than herself.

Mr. Crayne must have read something in her eyes. His narrowed and he quirked an eyebrow. "Be careful, Alexandria. Foxglove hides many secrets that aren't soothing to a woman's palate."

Adria nodded obediently.

His ominous words both irritated her and frightened her. Mr. Crayne eyed her for a long moment before moving toward the stairs leading to the first floor.

Adria hesitated, then whirled around to face him. "Why did you call me Lucy?"

He froze but continued to look away from her toward the other end of the hallway.

"Last night you called me Lucy," Adria explained. "Who is she to you?"

Mr. Crayne turned. His expression was unreadable, whether carefully crafted to be so or because this Lucy was as uninteresting as he made her out to be, Adria wasn't certain. "She's no one, Alexandria."

"A past love, perhaps?" Adria spoke before thinking. She bit her lip.

Mr. Crayne gave a shout of laughter. "Not even a little bit, my dear. In fact, I hope you are spared knowing Lucy." Mr. Crayne straightened his shoulders and rubbed the bridge of his nose between his bloodshot eyes. "If you ever meet her, it will not be a good omen."

―――――

Mrs. St. John pulled a needle with a long thread of silk through her embroidery. The silence between them was hardly companionship, and while Adria recognized this was, after all, her primary duty at Foxglove, she kept finding herself glancing at the door and out the window. For a glimpse of Mr. Crayne, she admitted to herself. He felt so familiar, so real. Yet he also felt dangerous and out of reach. A man who had shadowed her dreams like a hero who might swoop in one day to rescue her, only to find herself dismissing that image in place of the real Mr. Crayne. The drunk Mr. Crayne. The man who was unattractive, disturbing, and in truth, unacceptable. She chided herself for being even a little bit entranced by him. Most men, after all, were simply wicked at heart. Yet there was a hint toward gentleness in Mr. Crayne that told another potential story.

"My Theodora used to love to embroider." Mrs. St. John's voice broke into Adria's musing. She glanced down at her own embroidery. It was crooked and uneven. She was not fond of it.

"Theodora would embroider the most beautiful of linens. Always with that horrible fox at her feet."

Adria didn't know how to reply.

Mrs. St. John continued. "When Theodora was little, she was fascinated by threads. Her favorite color was gold." A shadow fluttered across the woman's pinched face. "Ironic," she mumbled.

Adria didn't miss the inference, nor was she unaware of the way Mrs. St. John pressed her thin lips together as if commanding herself to be silent.

"Gold is a beautiful color," Adria replied, feigning interest in her embroidery while stealing looks at the woman for clues, hints, or anything that might be of help.

"Yes," Mrs. St. John agreed but said no more.

"And did Mr. St. John prefer that color as well?" Adria ventured. She was met with silence, and as it drew on, Adria dared to lift her head and meet Mrs. St. John's sharp look.

"Why on earth would you ask that?" Mrs. St. John's gray eyebrow winged sharply over her left eye.

"Because often a little girl idolizes her father," Adria supplied quickly and without personal experience, recalling Mrs. St. John when pushed into temper. She didn't see a switch, but Adria had no doubt the woman could find other tools with which to inflict physical pain.

Mrs. St. John eyed her for a second, then seemed to view Adria's question as harmless. "Yes. My husband did fancy the color gold as well. He had me sew gold buttons onto his coats." She pulled her needle through the material, adjusting her grip on her embroidery hoop. "My husband was a captain for the Union. It is difficult to fathom that twenty years have passed. So much has changed and yet . . . so little."

"He was against slavery?" Adria admired him if for only that.

Mrs. St. John gave her a pointed look. "He was for success, Alexandria."

Of course. Adria had often heard that from her father. Less so the concern for human lives and more so the concern for the proper political positioning.

"Not everything is about the slave," Mrs. St. John murmured.

"And, obviously, not everyone values human life." Mr. Crayne's baritone flooded the room, silencing them both. He filled the doorway with his imposing figure. "Nor do all men remain faithful to a cause."

Startled, Mrs. St. John poked her finger with her needle, and she immediately raised it to her lips to suck at the droplet of blood.

Adria fell silent.

"I've no wish to debate with you," Mrs. St. John muttered around her finger.

Mr. Crayne lifted his eyes to the portrait of Theodora, which hung on the wall behind Adria. He leveled his gaze there for a long moment but said nothing.

"You should be grateful." Mrs. St. John's cryptic comment caused Mr. Crayne to stiffen.

"Should I?" he countered.

Narrowing her eyes, Mrs. St. John lowered her hand and reached for a handkerchief to wrap about her sore finger. "You're alive, aren't you?"

"Am I?" Mr. Crayne's response was so cryptic, Adria found herself holding her breath.

Mrs. St. John ogled him for a moment, then pointed at him with her index finger. "They could have done far worse to you."

"Yes." Mr. Crayne's expression deepened. "They could have shot me instead of locking me in this godforsaken place like a madman."

"You *are* a madman," Mrs. St. John snapped.

"I am a *prisoner*." Mr. Crayne's voice rose. "I have been a prisoner for twenty years."

"No one ever said you couldn't leave Foxglove." Mrs. St. John lifted her chin haughtily. There was a look on her face that made Adria wonder if Mrs. St. John hoped Mr. Crayne *would* leave.

He glanced again to the portrait and then dropped his gaze to Adria before addressing the benefactress who sat before them like a begrudging, bitter woman.

"We both know better." Mr. Crayne's mouth straightened into a tight line. "I will never be free of this place."

"We all have our duties," Mrs. St. John responded.

"And what is yours?" Mr. Crayne's address to Adria made her tongue-tied. She stared at him. He lifted his eyes again to the portrait, then back to her. It was as if he were trying to tell her something but could not vocalize it.

"I have no duty," Adria finally answered.

Mr. Crayne nodded. "Of course." But it was more than obvious from his expression that he didn't believe her in the slightest.

19

KAILEY

She sat on the cliff, her knees pulled to her chin and her arms wrapped around her legs. Staring out over the lake was hypnotic, and even though the wind bit through her cable-knit fisherman's sweater, Kailey remained. Her headache was dull but throbbed with a beat that opposed the rhythm of the waves.

In the distance, Kailey could make out the form of a yacht. A fisherman's yacht maybe, or perhaps one of those excursion boats that took divers out to explore the shipwrecks that littered the bottom of Lake Superior like a disregarded burial ground. She vaguely recalled her dad having gone out on one when they'd vacationed here. He had tried on his diving suit in the house, and she had watched him, silent from her perch on the bed. For a moment, her father had almost seemed . . . normal. He hadn't smiled at her or really given her the time of day, but Kailey was used to that. Neither she nor Jude had been on her parents' life list of greatest wishes. Instead of a Dr. Seuss Thing One and Thing Two, her mom sarcastically used to say they were "Accident One and Accident Two." Looking back, Kailey figured if they'd had living grandparents, it would have been likely that she and Jude would have been put under their guardianship. As it was, her parents did just enough to slip under CPS's watchful eye, and the time or two Social Services had been called on them, they'd been able to cover for their lack of attentiveness. Abused? Not physically. But being all but ignored left its own set of scars.

"Can I sit here?"

Kailey glanced at Axel, who lowered himself beside her, not waiting for an answer. Yesterday she'd spent in bed, recovering, Jude not far from her side. Today her body was warm enough, while her mind—her soul—was the sort of deeply troubled that was making it incredibly difficult to fake normal. She didn't say anything to him. His rugged profile was accompanied by broad shoulders encased in a Carhartt work coat. There was nothing stylish and everything comforting about him.

"I'll be straight up with you. You have us worried, Kailey." Axel wasn't one to beat around the bush either. He palmed the back of his neck as though he regretted being so blunt but also found it necessary. "You scared the tar out of Jude. He was almost inconsolable. If it weren't for Maddie taking him under her wing . . . Their mutual interest in numbers and letters is weird, but it served its purpose."

Kailey didn't know how to answer him. What *had* happened? She knew she'd had the worst nightmare of her life—or was it real?—and then she awakened freezing cold, half submerged in Lake Superior. A ghost girl perched at the bottom of the turret steps, a moth flying from her mouth—it was the stuff of horror movies. She couldn't shake the echoing sound of the girl crying for help. That mournful, childlike voice had wormed into Kailey's subconscious. She'd found it hard to concentrate on her job, on Jude, on the residents . . . So here she was. Perched on the cliff overlooking Lake Superior.

"I don't know what you want me to say." She stated.

"Good." Axel gave a slight laugh. "I prefer that you don't make something up. Just tell me the truth."

The truth? That was asking a lot, and like the iceberg that doomed the *Titanic*, Axel was chugging straight toward it. Kailey rested her chin on her knees and stared at the yacht that moved on the horizon. She needed to appease his curiosity enough to keep him from digging. He already guessed too much—*knew* too much.

"I don't know how I got in the lake. One moment I was in bed, and then . . ." She hesitated. She could either launch into a complete family history and out her parents as pathetic excuses for adults, or she could focus on the here and now. That might answer the deeper questions. Unlock the memories that sat just out of reach.

"You know how people joke about there being a ghost at Foxglove Manor? The one Maddie claims to have seen?"

"Lucy?" Axel asked, his expression carefully passive.

Kailey nodded. "I saw her."

He didn't say anything.

She was glad.

Kailey pushed a tendril of hair from in front of her eyes as the wind blew a gust through the trees and ruffled the tips of the waves on the lake. "I must have been dreaming. I never believed in ghosts before. But it was—*she* was—super creepy."

Axel seemed to accept her explanation. "From what I've heard, Lucy doesn't normally talk. When you were coming out of your cold, you mentioned she'd spoken to you. I've never heard of Lucy doing that—in any of the stories."

"So, it was a dream?" Kailey grasped at the straw of hope.

Axel's mouth thinned in a smile. "Well, that'd be my guess. It still doesn't explain why you ended up on the beach."

"I swear, I wasn't trying to drown myself."

"I believe you."

"You do?" Kailey lifted her head sharply.

Axel nudged her with his shoulder as if teasing. "Yeah. Why wouldn't I?"

For a million reasons. The first being, he'd be the first person besides Jude who ever had. She took courage in the white flag of peace he figuratively waved, and she felt guilty for the recent events he'd been witness to—especially seeing her shivering in her underwear.

Embarrassing. Offering him a morsel of her past wouldn't hurt—couldn't hurt—worse than the other rare times she'd opened to someone and they'd looked at her like she'd lost her mind.

"You're right. I *was* abducted when I was little." Kailey couldn't look at Axel now. She charged on before she lost confidence. "It was so similar to Riley and—it was shortly after my family had returned home from vacation. We'd vacationed here. At Foxglove Manor. When it was a rental."

"I didn't know that." Axel's response was a mixture of surprise and question.

"You wouldn't have reason to." Kailey focused on a sea gull swooping down over the waves. "Anyway"—she brushed off his confusion—"like Riley, people thought I'd just played hooky, but what five-year-old plays hooky? The only person who believed me was Jude. I explained everything to him, just like I had the police. He believed me. They didn't."

"What about your parents?"

Kailey shook her head. "My dad was absent most of the time. He had learned to drink so well he could function normally. He just didn't really have an interest in me, or especially Jude. My mom . . . she was always depressed. I found out a few years ago from some records I uncovered that she was bipolar and refused treatments after she was diagnosed. She treated herself with her own concoction of opiates and vodka." Kailey gave a *tsk* of laugher. "Funny, huh? I have quite the dysfunctional family. When things would get tense, Jude would always tell me to hide. 'Hide, Kay-Kay,' he'd say."

"What inspired a family vacation to Foxglove?"

Kailey appreciated the way Axel inquired but didn't judge with his tone. Also, she was grateful he seemed fixated on the yacht on the lake almost as intently as she was.

"My mom's therapist. Apparently, the theory goes that family vacations in remote places force them to talk to one another. Like quarantining during a pandemic." She gave a healthy snort. "That's a lot of fun."

They shared mutual laughter surrounding their past experience with historic events.

"Did it help?" Axel asked.

Kailey swallowed, the sudden lump of tears making her throat sore. "It signed my mom's death warrant." She swallowed again. The waves rolled onto the sand, then withdrew, then rolled back again. "After we got home, not long after I went missing for a day, Mom was driving Dad home from work and decided it was time, I guess. She tried to end it and succeeded. Apparently, she didn't want to die alone, so she drove Dad into the tree as well."

A gull chortled as it dived past them.

A piece of driftwood bobbed in the water, around it a long green patch of lakeweed draped like a woman's hair.

"I'm sorry." Axel's response was appropriate. Unemotional.

"It's not your fault," Kailey snapped, then bit her tongue, squeezing her eyes shut, then opening them. "Sorry. I just—"

"No, I get it. I mean, I don't, but I get it's got to suck to remember all that."

Kailey sniffed. "We ended up in foster care. Jude was fifteen and special needs, so they separated us for a while. Then my aunt came out of the woodwork, and they assigned her guardianship. She wasn't all that bad growing up. She was single. She did her best." Kailey breathed in deeply of the cool lake-water air. "She put me in therapy when I was in my early teens."

"Did she believe what had happened to you?"

Kailey shrugged. "I dunno. By then I wasn't even sure I believed it anymore. But Jude—he never stopped. He always insisted—in our secret language, of course—that I needed to be careful. But nothing more happened except, Jude, he's gotten more agitated lately, or maybe focused is the more accurate word. Ever since I was little, he wrote this gibberish all over. After I was kidnapped, he quit. Until recently. Now that's all he seems to do, that and look for patterns in everything, and I thought maybe if we came here—" she let her thoughts trail as the wind picked up and whipped stray ends of hair across her face; Kailey pushed them away—"maybe I could remember why they're important. Figure out why I was taken. What is it about Foxglove Manor and what happened here that made someone take a little girl, interrogate her, then leave her on her home street as though nothing had happened?" Kailey met Axel's gaze. "And why would they repeat that twenty years later with another girl?"

Axel held up a hand. "This is where it disconnects for me. Who are *they*? What do you and Riley Bascom have in common?"

"We have Foxglove Manor in common. Apparently, Mr. Bascom owned it when I vacationed here as a kid, and he still owns it. Owned it, I guess you'd say."

"So, you were kidnapped as a kid because you vacationed at Foxglove?"

While it wasn't a question of her sincerity, Kailey could definitely make out the confused resonance behind his question. She tugged the cuffs of her sweater over her hands, her arms still wrapped around her knees.

"I was kidnapped as a kid because of what I *saw* at Foxglove Manor. What my brother saw, more specifically. I'm willing to bet that Riley saw the same thing."

"What did you all see?"

It was a natural question to ask, yet Kailey made careful pretense to avoid Axel's inquiring look. She cleared her throat. "I don't remember."

"You don't remember." It was a statement of disbelief. She'd expected it.

"I didn't remember when I was five, and I don't remember now. Only Jude remembered."

"Why didn't they take Jude?" Axel touched her knee with his fingertips and added quickly, "Not that I'm saying it would have been better if they had. But he was older. It would've made more sense."

"No, it wouldn't have." Kailey shook her head vehemently and finally accepted Axel's direct gaze. The cliff beneath them was solid, but the wind was picking up and the waves followed suit, as did her heartbeat. "Jude has autism. We—*I* was the only person who could communicate with him. It was a language we made up. Words, sign language, different sounds. You know he can't put his thoughts into words like we can, and he can't communicate in a way that anyone is willing to stop and learn."

"But why would they have chosen to take you if Jude was the one who remembered whatever it was they wanted?"

Tears burned, and she looked away, wiping her eyes with her sweater sleeve. "I was five, Axel. Five years old with a secret language I shared with an autistic older brother who couldn't communicate and who the world pretty much wrote off as stupid." She didn't even try to hide the bitterness in her voice. "But he is brilliant. I knew that. I knew it every day of my life. But he wouldn't be able to tell them anything, so I was their next best hope. What was the gibberish? What had we seen at Foxglove? I couldn't answer them—I was afraid, I was little." Kailey sensed an urgency welling up in her. The sort of anxiety that made her stomach curl with fear. She felt Axel take her hand and she didn't fight it. Grounded. She needed something—someone—to ground her. "I don't remember. I see snippets of nightmares. I hear my mom scream. But . . . but I don't know, and I could've stayed that way if Jude hadn't started writing the numbers and letters again. Over and over. He even wrote them on his bedrail at home—in permanent marker. I just need it to all go away—to be over. I need to believe they won't come back for me, and now that they won't come back for Riley. It's been twenty years and they're still out there? Still haunting little girls? It's a different motivation for a predator, but it's very real, Axel, very real!"

The wind blew between them for a long moment. Axel gave a big sigh and ran his tongue along the inside of his cheek as if he were searching for missing popcorn hulls from an earlier afternoon snack with the residents.

Kailey swiped at her eyes with her free hand, brushing away the wetness that had formed. Axel hadn't released her hand, but he hadn't acknowledged her blubbering confession either.

"Say it."

"Say what?" He gave her a surprised look.

"Say that it's the most outrageous story you've ever heard."

"Well, it is, but that doesn't make it untrue." He gave her hand a reassuring squeeze. "What *do* you remember? About Foxglove Manor? About whatever it was Jude saw, or you experienced, or what Riley might have seen?"

Kailey looked down at their clasped hands. She would have been mortified if Axel could have read her thoughts in that moment. The wish that his handhold wasn't platonic, but that it meant something. A yearning inside of her awakened. To be wanted. Cared for. To be held.

Kailey drew her attention back to the question. "All I remember is there was something about a hidden treasure. My kidnapper kept asking me where it was. Over and over again. He asked me what letters and numbers we'd discovered. Like, did I know the alphabet? But worse." She drew in a shaky breath, ignoring the taste of lake on her tongue, the mist from the waves, and the way Axel's eyes darkened momentarily when she bit her lower lip. "All I remember is my mom. Her scream. And tears, lots of tears. And . . ." The dream that had compelled Kailey to the water's edge two nights before haunted her again. It was what had brought her to the cliff today to begin with. That memory. The girl. The plea. It was familiar—vaguely, but it was familiar.

"I think—I *know* it has something to do with ghost girl too."

His eyes flickered in response. "She's only a dream." Reassuring only went so far when faced with the spirit world and the heavy question of its existence, and if it did exist, what was its power over a human soul?

"Are you sure?" Kailey posed the darkest question in her heart. There was no answer.

20

She might be unsure whether she believed in ghosts, but Kailey knew that her brother did. Firmly. Lifting his sketchbook, Kailey eyed the sequence of letters and numbers. They were written in tiny elfish print, forming the curved outline of a child's form. Holding the page away, one might not even notice the lines were actually made up of a repetitive order. They curled around the soft jaw of a young girl, created the fine strands in her long, unbound hair, flowed with the nightgown that pooled around her bare toes. Jude was a genius the way he applied his propensity for patterns into art. He was also terrifyingly accurate. The only thing missing from the image was the ghost girl's gaping mouth with a moth fluttering from its cavern like a bad omen before the demon followed.

Kailey dropped the sketchbook onto her bed, fixing a stiff smile on her face as she addressed Jude. He waited, expectant, his body straddling a wooden chair, a pencil clutched in his left hand.

"It's very nice." And it was. Kailey had no qualms that she communicated any deceit to her brother, because she didn't. Whether she liked the ghost girl herself captured on paper was beside the point.

A branch scratched at the bedroom window. Kailey jumped and shot it a glare.

"Kay-Kay?" Jude asked, concern etched into his brow.

Kailey rounded the bed and bent a bit so she could see her brother at eye level. "I'm all right."

Jude grunted and shook his head. He made some signs with his hands and fingers. Ones that no one but Kailey could decipher. He finished by slapping the back of the chair, pointing at the sketchbook, and giving a guttural "No." He started to sway back and forth in his seat.

Kailey retrieved the sketchbook. "I really *do* like it," she assured him, Jude's doubt about her authenticity well communicated. "But . . ." She glanced at the window. Stupid branch was scratching again. She'd not heard it before. Or maybe she had. Perhaps that was the sound at night she'd attributed to the ghost girl and her dreams, but instead it could be logically explained. She drew in a deep breath, turning the sketch toward him. "Jude, have you seen her?"

He rocked his upper body again as if he were seated in a rocking chair. His eyes fixated on the sketch of the ghost girl.

"Jude?" Kailey coaxed.

"Giiih, giih!" He rammed his finger into the girl's penciled face.

"Yes?" Kailey nodded to confirm his reaction.

"Giih!" Jude was more insistent this time, and she understood he wasn't saying yes or no.

"Girl? What about the girl?" Kailey squatted lower, her knees cracking.

Jude's rocking intensified.

She waited. Giving him time. Too much stimulation conversationally would upset him enough to make any communication confusing at best.

Jude jerked his head to the left and looked at the offensive branch that slapped at the window as the wind gusted. His sudden movement startled Kailey as he leapt from the chair and launched himself toward the window.

"Jude!" Kailey stumbled to a standing position as Jude's palms slapped against the windowpane. Once, twice, then a third time.

"Ma. Ma. Ma." With every slap, he uttered the word.

Instinct made Kailey want to reach for him. To pull Jude's hands from the window and help calm him. But touch would only tailspin the situation. She moderated the tone in her voice, careful not to convey any emotion.

"Jude, let's sit down."

"Ma." Another slap of the palms against glass.

"Buddy, let's—"

Jude spun around, his blue eyes wide and his mouth open. A small bubble of saliva beaded at the corner of his mouth. He snatched his sketchbook from Kailey's hand.

"Ma. Giih." Jude traced the girl's lined face with his finger. "Kay-Kay, see?"

"I see, Jude, I see." She did. She saw the ghost girl. She heard her brother calling for their dead mother. She comprehended that he was trapped inside a body that refused to cooperate with his intelligent mind, so unique and so undefinably beautiful.

Jude shook his head vehemently and slammed the book onto the desk. He retrieved the pencil that had fallen to the floor when he'd leapt from his chair. With left-handed precision, he began to write across the face of the ghost girl.

Gnqgy . . .

Desperation flooded Kailey as she watched him drift away into his somewhat catatonic state. Just him and his sketchbook. His sequences. It was episodes like these—the barely averted meltdowns—that had been the final motivation for Kailey to bring her brother back to Foxglove Manor after all these years.

That he believed Lucy the ghost girl to be real seemed obvious to Kailey. But what the letters and corresponding numbers had to do with anything, she couldn't say. Even worse, she couldn't define why, after twenty years, Jude had started calling for their mother.

"Ma," he muttered under his breath. "Ma."

Ma is dead, Kailey wanted to say. To remind him. It seemed horrid and somewhat pitiful that anyone needed to be reminded that their mother was dead. Dead wasn't something one usually forgot, unless the ghosts of the one lost made you believe they were still alive.

—⁓—

Finding out more about Lucy Miranda seemed to be the ticket to finding a semblance of peace of mind. Things pointed back to her, whether she was a delusion, a legend, or really a ghost. Still unclear how Riley Bascom's recent one-day abduction fit into it, and now even more disturbed with Jude's sketch of the ghost girl, Kailey was loath to agree with Axel's observation.

"The police aren't ghost hunters, and for them Riley's abduction is a random act of youthful hooky." Axel's conclusion had been delivered with a cautionary brow-raise. To which Kailey bit her tongue. She'd made the choice to come to Foxglove after all. She had been the one to bring Jude and herself closer. Closer to the shadow memories, to the ones that clung to the back of her mind.

"If we need to find out more about this Lucy ghost, we should probably track down the history of Foxglove Manor. If I recall, Lucy was a Miranda, and that family owned it prior to the Bascoms." They'd entered the kitchen after settling Jude safely in the sitting room next to Maddie and under the cooperative and watchful eye of Tracee.

"Go." She'd waved them off. "Have a date over coffee."

The twinkle in Tracee's eye boasted of her lack of tact. Axel hadn't responded. Kailey knew she was blushing, and all in all it didn't make sense. They weren't on a date—or dating—or even remotely close to any declared attraction. Axel was taking a break from yardwork, while she was . . .

Kailey followed him into the kitchen, questioning her intent behind following him into the kitchen. It probably wasn't wise to pursue his help. To trust him. With anything. But here she was. Sitting at the table, and Axel was placing a kettle on the stove to steam water for pour-over coffee.

He leaned against the counter and crossed his arms over his chest. Kailey fidgeted with a paper napkin.

"I should ask Maddie," she mused.

"Maddie?" Axel drew back. "What would she know?"

"Well, she's seen Lucy the ghost, and she has this notebook . . ." Her words trailed as she recalled the random letters and numbers. She folded the napkin along its crease. "Jude has a sketchbook with the same markings in it."

Thankfully, Axel didn't press her but instead gave her the benefit of the doubt. "We can ask her. But she has Alzheimer's, so we'd have to be careful with anything she tells us. She thinks she has a son, for Pete's sake."

"And we know she doesn't?" Kailey had found Maddie's memories of her supposed son to be quite convincing.

Axel sagged his head to the left and raised an eyebrow. "Teri would know if she did, and she doesn't."

Raymond insisted Maddie didn't have a son either. Kailey considered that as she folded the square napkin in half. She heard the water starting to simmer on the stove. "How do Raymond and Maddie know each other so well? He's pretty protective of her."

Axel chuckled. "Yeahhhhh. He's a good guy, Raymond. I don't think they know each other outside of being residents together at Foxglove. I've worked here as the handyman for, oh, I'd say about six years now? Raymond came about two years after, and Maddie is more recent. She's only lived here about a year."

"So, he just adopted her then," Kailey concluded.

"When there's attraction and commonality, love can be a wild-fire." Axel's comment was low. Direct.

Kailey focused on folding the napkin lengthwise, but she noticed her fingers shaking.

Axel noticed too. He cleared his throat. "Anyway, back to Lucy Miranda."

"Yeah." Kailey nodded.

"Okay." Axel breathed deeply through his nose. He turned to

the stove as the kettle started to scream and snatched it from the burner. Busying himself with the pour-over, he spoke over his shoulder. "There's a book in the study with some of the history of Foxglove Manor in it. I've never looked at it, but Teri has. You could chat with her too. And—" He cut off his words.

Kailey paused while folding the napkin into the wing of an origami crane. She looked over at Axel, who slowly poured a stream of hot water over the coffee grounds in the pour-over's funnel. "And what?"

Axel shook his head. "I was gonna say, you could talk to the Bascoms, but that's not a good idea."

"No." Kailey mentally chided herself for being a stupid idiot. Who approached a ten-year-old child about her kidnapping anyway? She'd burned any potential bridges that might be there. Or . . . "What if you asked Jason?"

"Jason Bascom?" Axel shot her an incredulous look. "Riley's uncle? Oh sure. I'm sure he'd be totally cooperative." The sarcasm was thick, and maybe he was trying to be funny, but it eased the blush from her face and replaced it with that old familiar sting of being criticized.

Kailey bit back a sassy retort. Instead, she folded the second origami wing. "Well, you'd think he'd want to know what happened to Riley. What *really* happened to her. And, if Foxglove Manor was part of the motivation behind the kidnapping, then he might know something that Riley's dad knew. Before he killed himself." She hesitated. "*If* he killed himself."

The kettle dropped onto the burner with a *clang*, and Axel turned. "If?"

"You already know I have doubts." Kailey bit her tongue. She'd said too much already. Opened up, splayed out some of her past, and now she was word-vomiting her suspicions like a kid who'd had too much sugar. She was intoxicated with being able to talk without being shut down. Intoxication was dangerous.

Axel ignored the pour-over and took a step toward her, his head tipped, studying her. "Okay. I'm willing to listen." He tugged out a chair and sat down. His knee brushed hers.

Kailey bent her leg back beneath her chair and determined to stay very, very focused on her napkin origami.

Axel rapped his knuckles on the table. "What's your theory?"

Kailey shook her head, suddenly mute, and if she were honest, a bit afraid. Afraid that he would, for sure, determine she was either losing her mind or a conspiracy theorist who saw ghosts. Either scenario sounded loopy.

"Kailey." Axel's hand came down over hers, effectively flattening the crane. "Kailey?"

She lifted her eyes.

He watched her.

The smell of coffee permeated the air like the essence of peace.

"Okay, fine," Kailey breathed.

"All right." Axel drew his hand away but didn't move from his straddle of the chair, his arms crisscrossing its back.

"Can I have some of that coffee first?" Kailey was tempted by its tantalizing fragrance, and the idea of distracting Axel from his confident study of her face.

"Only after you tell me what you're thinking."

"My conspiracy theory?"

"If you think that's what I've labeled your ideas as, you make me out to be a judgmental monster. You've no idea what's really going through my head."

"What *is* going through your head?" Kailey countered.

His voice lowered. It was gravelly. Sexy. Insinuating. Terrifying. "Do you really wanna know?"

Suddenly, her flattened crane was very interesting again.

Axel pushed himself off the chair. "Fine. I'll get you coffee and then you tell me your suspicions."

As he poured the coffee, Kailey struggled to find the words. There were none. As Axel set the mug of coffee in front of her, the steam rose to her nose and she inhaled.

"See? Magic-talking potion. Speak, woman." Axel straddled the chair again.

Kailey managed a smile. Perhaps it was time to be more than honest. What was the worst that could happen? Axel would conclude she was exaggerating, lying, concocting ideas based on images that were formed as a child? She tapped her mug with a fingernail.

Axel's hand closed gently around her wrist, forcing Kailey to lift her eyes. She met his gray ones and was reminded of the lake's waves in the early morning as sunrise drifted across them. Flecks of yellow dancing over the blue-gray waters. Warm. Friendly. Fierce underneath.

"I get the feeling it's been just you and Jude for most of your life. But, Kailey, some of us are more than willing to come alongside you. Teri, Tracee, me. Heck, even Raymond—although he might have an ulterior motive 'cause he really wants Poe to be his fluffy white cat and not yours."

Kailey snorted a soft laugh. She eyed his hand. His thumb absently stroked the sensitive skin on the underside of her wrist. She had a feeling he didn't even know he was doing it.

"You get along with your mom?" she asked suddenly.

His eyes softened. "Yeah. She's great."

Kailey sniffed and lifted the coffee mug to her lips, forcing Axel to release her. "I think Jude misses our mom."

"She doted on him?" Axel furrowed his brow as if searching his memory for any references Kailey had made toward the emotional connection with their parents.

She shook her head. "No. No, he was Mom's first mistake—I was her second."

"Oh."

Kailey knew Axel understood then. In that one little "oh," he expressed an understanding as to why Kailey resisted being open. Resisted friendship. Resisted . . . trust.

Another sip of coffee.

Axel waited.

He really wasn't going anywhere.

Again, what was there to lose? She'd just end up where she'd been a couple of weeks before Foxglove Manor. Her and Jude. Together.

"Okay." Kailey blew out a long breath. She adjusted her position on the chair and curled her hands around the warm mug to draw strength from it. Coffee equaled strength, right? It was a mathematical equation that made sense to a creative soul.

"My theory is simple really," Kailey began, then launched into sharing her thoughts before she could stop herself. "There's a treasure here—at Foxglove Manor—and it's been around for a long time. Whoever took me as a kid knew—somehow—that Jude had stumbled onto it, or at least knew how to find it. They banked on the fact Jude had told me, but I was too little to be of any help. I'm guessing they've been looking—all these years. Treasure hunters do that, you know? They're relentless. It's why they kidnapped Riley, since her father owned Foxglove Manor, and she must have given them the impression she knew something. And maybe she does. Maybe she's hiding it? Who knows? But regardless, someone wants to find a treasure, and Foxglove Manor is the epicenter. Jude knows something, and now probably Riley too. Maybe she told her dad—or maybe they went after her dad—but now he's dead. That can't be a coincidence."

She took a deep breath. Her ramble had been fast and furious. Kailey took escape by sipping her coffee. Axel seemed to be contemplating, his lips twisted into a thinking expression.

"Yeah, it's farfetched. But let's go with it. So then how is the ghost of Lucy Miranda important?"

It was a good question. "She keeps coming up? I saw her. Maddie saw her. People *see* her supposedly enough to build a little ghost story here. Who is she? Is she part of the treasure of Foxglove Manor?"

"There's no specific legend of a treasure, though. Lake pirates and smugglers, but a treasure here at Foxglove?" Axel frowned.

"Oh, but there is!" Teri's voice in the doorway startled them both. Coffee sloshed from Kailey's mug onto the table. Teri noticed and retrieved a washrag. "Sorry, I didn't mean to scare you. I was coming in to start measuring out late-afternoon meds for the residents."

"It's okay." Axel waved her off.

"You've heard of a treasure?" Kailey ignored the explanation.

Teri wiped the coffee from the table. Her brown eyes were round and earnest. "Oh sure. The ghost story is talked of more because—well, a ghost is a ghost. But where there's a ghost, a lake, and pirates, there's sure to be a treasure, right?"

Axel looked perplexed. "How come I've never heard of this *treasure*?"

Teri snapped the washrag at him. "Because you're too busy tinkering around with stuff. You're not a history nerd." She smiled and tossed the rag into the sink. "I'm not either, so all I know is, supposedly, years ago—around the time of the Civil War—there were rumors of Civil War gold. My own dad is related to plantation owners in Virginia who supposedly hid most of their wealth when the war broke out. Afterward? Their plantations went bust, their gold was never recovered, and they pretty much fell off the radar of wealthy Southerners."

"Where'd their gold go?" Kailey ignored her coffee that was growing cold rather fast.

Teri chuckled and looked between them. "Well, that's the mystery, hon. No one knows. It happened a lot during the Civil War. Gold and Southern investments disappeared or were absconded with by the Union. Not sure I blame them. There's enough ethical and moral issues behind that war as it is—don't get me started."

"So, you're saying the lake smugglers were part of this missing gold?" Axel concluded.

Teri nodded, then shrugged. "Well, not necessarily *my* ancestors' missing gold, but yeah. Civil War gold. And some like to tease that Lucy Miranda—your ghost girl—guards it."

21

ADRIA

"She's dead! Lord, help us!" The shriek filled the hallway in an echoing wail.

Adria sprung from bed and threw open the bedroom door. Lula rushed down the hallway, her eyes frantic, the whites of them larger than the color, reminding Adria of a spooked horse. Arms waving wildly, Lula stumbled to a halt and reached for Adria's arms, clasping them so tight her fingernails dug into Adria's skin.

"She's *dead*, Miss Fontaine! Dead as a *doornail*!"

"Who?"

"The missus!" Lula's fingers dug deeper. "Mrs. St. John. I took her bedtime tea to her and there she was, lyin' on her bed, her mouth hangin' open like a puppet's!"

Thumping sounded from the direction of the turret room. Mr. Crayne's shadow appeared at the opposite end of the hallway. "What's the meaning of this?" He didn't sway tonight, no slurring either.

Adria was relieved.

Lula released her and spun to direct the force of her panic at Mr. Crayne. "Mrs. St. John is dead, sir. I tell ya, she's *dead*!"

Mr. Crayne pushed past Lula and stormed in the direction of

Mrs. St. John's bedroom. He disappeared around the corner, and Adria exchanged glances with Lula before they both hurried after him. Mrs. St. John's room had a faint glow coming from it, casting onto the carpet runner that spanned the length of her wing. Adria and Lula burst into the bedroom, Lula wringing her hands and mumbling, "Sweet Jesus, Mother Mary . . ." repeatedly until Adria had the sudden and inexplicable urge to slap the girl into silence. She buried her hands in her nightdress instead.

Mr. Crayne cradled Mrs. St. John's limp wrist in his hand, fingers pressed to her skin. The older woman was truly, as Lula had described, sprawled across her bed. She wore the same dress she'd worn at dinner, but her white hair was loose, its wiry curls splaying from her head like Medusa's crown. Her face was white, her eyes closed, her mouth hanging open.

"She's dead, ain't she?" Lula didn't even attempt to speak reverently in the presence of the deceased.

Mr. Crayne looked beyond Lula to Adria. "Come here." His direction brooked no refusal, so Adria brushed by Lula and neared him. There was graveness in his eyes, and he lowered his voice so Lula would have had to strain to hear him.

"Mrs. St. John is *not* dead. Yet. Fetch Diggery. Have him go for a doctor."

"A doctor?" Lula had come up behind them, and her panicked voice was thick with unshed tears. "Mr. Crayne, you've had too much to drink, sir! The doctor is miles away, and Diggery can't see in the dark!"

"Blasted prison, this is!" Mr. Crayne's growl shushed Lula into silence, even as he recognized the truth of her words.

Adria eyed Mrs. St. John. She saw her chest rise ever so slightly and then fall. She narrowed her eyes and leaned toward the woman's prostrate body on the bed. "Mr. Crayne"—she pointed—"what's wrong with her neck?"

He followed the line of her gaze and frowned. A dark red line spanned Mrs. St. John's neck. It was fast turning blue.

"Oh, dear Father in heaven, St. Peter, and throw in a St. Paul, she's been *strangled*!" Lula shrieked.

"Get out of here, Lula!" Mr. Crayne shouted, and Adria jumped at the severity of his voice. "You're of no help wailing like a banshee. Go and get Diggery."

"But what's he goin' to do?" Lula argued.

"Go!" Mr. Crayne's directive must have startled some life into Lula's otherwise immobile body. She ran from the room, her shoulder hitting the doorjamb as she went. She bounced back, rounded it, and disappeared.

Mr. Crayne lowered his head to Adria. His eyes drilled into hers. "It indeed appears as if someone has attempted to strangle Mrs. St. John. Her pulse is weak. Find some smelling salts. Some spirits. There's whiskey in my room. Fetch that as well."

"What will whiskey do?" Adria couldn't help but ask.

"It's not for her," he retorted.

Adria didn't bother to argue. Instead, she ran from the bedroom and fumbled her way in the nighttime darkness through the hallways and up the stairs to the turret room. Lula's bedroom door was open to the right, but Adria ignored it and hurried into Mr. Crayne's room. She was struck by the tangy smell of whiskey and cigar smoke. It was strong. It was something a man would embody. Power. She snatched the decanter of gold liquid she only hoped was whiskey and hurried from the room.

Smelling salts. Perhaps Lula would have them! Adria hurried across the landing and entered Lula's bedroom. It was a simple servant's quarters. The bed was still made. There was a dresser at the opposite end of the room with baubles and trinkets littering its top. Adria fingered them. A few stones from the lake. A necklace of tarnished chain with a little cross dangling from it. A wooden jewelry box. A glass vial. Adria reached for it and removed its stopper. She sniffed. The pungent, eye-watering smell assured Adria this was smelling salts.

Within seconds she was back in Mrs. St. John's room, handing the vial to Mr. Crayne, who immediately waved it beneath the woman's nose. At the shocking scent, Mrs. St. John's body convulsed, her eyelids fluttering.

"Mrs. St. John?" Adria crawled onto the bed beside her. She patted the older woman's cheek, noting the feathery softness of it. A softness that contradicted the bitterness of her heart. The woman moaned. Mr. Crayne waved the smelling salts beneath her nose again. This time, Mrs. St. John's eyes opened into narrow slits. She coughed, then grabbed at her throat.

"S-sore," she rasped.

"Should I get her water?" Adria shot Mr. Crayne a desperate look.

"No, no," he shook his head, pulling back from Mrs. St. John as awareness seemed to seep back into her face. "That won't help this type of sore throat."

"Wha . . . hap—?" Mrs. St. John coughed, squeezing her eyes shut and grappling for Adria's hand. Adria allowed her to take it and was a bit relieved when the woman squeezed her fingers with returning strength. She really hadn't wished the other day that Mrs. St. John would have died by her shirtwaist's strangulation. She really hadn't wished Mrs. St. John dead. Not at all.

Mr. Crayne interrupted Adria's harried thoughts. "We were hoping you could tell *us* what happened."

Mrs. St. John opened her eyes slightly. "Me?" Her voice sounded a bit stronger now. "I don't . . ." She swallowed, wincing. "So strong. They were—so strong."

"Who?" Mr. Crayne demanded.

Adria glanced up at him. His dark hair falling over his forehead, his brow drawn into a scowl, his dark eyes snapping. He seemed in control. In command. Utterly powerful and roguish and . . . Adria looked away as he reached for the crystal bottle that held the whiskey. He took a swig, wiping his mouth with the back of his hand.

"What?" he boldly questioned Adria, who stiffened.

"Nothing." She shook her head. She wasn't surprised, just . . . saddened.

He hoisted the bottle. "Cheers." He lifted it again toward Mrs. St. John, who was pushing herself up on the bed. "And cheers to you, madam, for your quick recovery from strangulation and attempted murder."

"Impudent wretch," Mrs. St. John spat.

Adria was tempted to agree with her.

Mr. Crayne eyed them both and took a step back. "Now that you're quite alive, I will go rescue Diggery from Lula's guaranteed exaggeration of the very lifeblood seeping from your body."

"I'm not bleeding," Mrs. St. John protested while casting a nervous sweep over her own body to verify her declaration.

"I've seen bloody corpses before. Piles of them. You, Mrs. St. John, are not one of them." He winked. A wink that indicated every ounce of disdain he held for the old woman. He strode toward the bedroom door.

A quick survey of Mrs. St. John told Adria she would be all right for the moment. She chased after Mr. Crayne, catching up to him in the hallway and surprising herself with the audacity to reach out and grab on to his elbow. He stopped and glowered down at her.

"You're really going to leave us? Alone? With a killer roaming the halls of Foxglove?"

Tongue in cheek, he stared at her for a long moment. Finally, he responded, "You truly believe I would have power of any sort to stop such a force?"

"Not with that, you wouldn't. It's not right." Adria pointed at the crystal decanter.

"Not right?" Mr. Crayne hugged it to his chest in an exaggerated motion. "This is what keeps a man alive, Miss Fontaine."

She shook her head in disbelief.

He leaned forward until his nose almost kissed hers and she could smell the whiskey on his breath. "You'll learn, Adria, that to survive, one must find their elixir. This is mine. What is yours, I wonder?"

"I don't . . . have one," she mumbled, disconcerted by his nearness.

"Oh, but you do." He stepped back and raked her with his dark gaze, from toe to head and back down until he stopped at her eyes. "You imbibe in cowardice. You imbibe in self-disdain. You imbibe by doing the will of others instead of your own. Tell me, Adria, which is worse? To be influenced by liquid gold or to always know what's right and instead ignore it? Wicked men bidding you to do their duty, and you just going along with it because . . . is it right? Perhaps. Or wrong? Maybe. And then there's the power the man holds over you. Now that is assuredly *not* right."

Somehow, she knew he spoke of her father. How he knew, she couldn't say. But suddenly it was apparent he knew her secrets. Or at least assumed them. Unfortunately, he was also very right. It was an altogether different sort of strangulation, his rightness.

"We all have a choice to do the *right thing*." Mr. Crayne took another long chug from the bottle. He tilted it back, his dark eyes burrowing into hers. "But most of us lack the gumption to make it. Look at me." Another arm toss with the bottle in his grip. "A pathetic excuse for a man, holed up in a place like this, with too much in here." The same hand that gripped the decanter now extended an index finger and jabbed at his temple. "Too much. It's disabling. And the *right thing* is right there. Taunting me. Liquor is a damning sort of thing." He tipped his head toward hers. "But"— his voice lowered to a hissing whisper—"so is the act of taking one's own life."

Adria paled.

Mr. Crayne spun on his heel and marched away, albeit this time more unsteady than when he'd first arrived.

~

"It be that Lucy Miranda, I tell ya." Diggery rammed his boot-clad foot onto the shovel, and it sliced into the dirt at the base of one of his carefully stacked cairns. "Comin' in the night. Doin' what she does."

"Ghosts can't strangle a folk," Lula protested. She sat on the ground beside him, eyeing the mangy fox that watched them from a safe distance under the shrubbery.

Adria stood a few paces away, hugging her shawl around her body, listening.

"Can they, Diggery?" Lula pressured the elderly man to respond with an answer that would appease her. He took another chuck at the earth beneath his shovel.

"Who else is around to strangle the missus? You?" he threw at Lula. She shook her head vehemently, eyes wide with fright. "You?" Diggery glanced at Adria. She merely watched him, and he turned away, letting the shovel drop to the ground. Bending, he picked up a rooted plant, green-leafed with pinkish-purple tubular flowers. Foxglove. Of course, it was fitting the wildflower profligate around its namesake, the manor. Fitting, also, that Diggery would care enough to plant them within view of Mrs. St. John's window. She continued to stay secluded in her bedroom, barring the door with a chair and yelling at Adria and Lula to stay away lest they try to murder her once again. It was all so exaggerated that Adria would have laughed had she not seen the bruising around the woman's papery-skinned neck. Someone, indeed, had tried to stifle the breath from the woman's body. Why and who? One certainly couldn't blame the ghost of a little girl. Could one?

"I don't believe it." Adria finally found her voice. Lula looked up at her and stopped picking blades of grass. Adria met her eyes. "I don't," she insisted. "If I did believe in spirits, I certainly wouldn't pin the attempted strangulation on a woeful ghost child."

"She has a point." Lula shifted her look to Diggery.

Diggery grumbled from where he stuffed the foxglove roots into the hole. "Then it was Mr. Crayne 'cause it sure as shootin' wharn't me."

"Mr. Crayne was upstairs in his room," Lula countered.

Diggery sat back on his heels, rather flexible for his age, and stared at them both. "Then we've either a ghost or an intruder who slips through the halls at night intent on death. Neither one suits me, and if Mr. Crayne won't do nothin' about it, then you won't see me inside that place if you paid me in Confederate gold and coin."

Adria sharpened. She eyed Diggery. He had returned to patting the dirt around the foxglove, his fingers getting dirt tucked under the nails. "Confederate gold?" she inquired as casually as she could, while at the same time her father's recent direction to find his loot rang heavily in her mind.

Diggery chuckled. He looked up at her. "That, and all the other nonsense them Rebels snuck around with on these lakes. Sneaky sons of—" He caught himself. "Sneaky, they were. Rumor has it, Dr. Miranda what owned Foxglove during the war, and Lucy's father was one of them."

"One of who? A Confederate?" Adria shifted her weight onto her other foot and tugged her shawl tighter. The waves of the lake behind her were calm today, but the air itself was chilly.

"The secret ring," Lula interjected with a thrilled shiver. "A society. Confederate sympathizers posing as Union loyalists. They lived on all the lakes. Dotted the harbor towns. Built mansions, secret tunnels, and all the like just to smuggle Southern wealth to safety."

"No one ever proved that, eh?" Diggory retorted.

"Wouldn't be secret if they had," Lula quipped back.

"So it's rumored?" Adria could envision it all in her mind. It fit perfectly with the story her father had painted for her. And, if he had intercepted Southern sympathizers, how much more glory would he have taken in pirating their booty? And then if they stole it back from Adria's very Union-bent father, it would have been salt in an open wound.

Diggery dismissed her with a wave. "Never you mind. Mrs. St. John'd have your hide if you ever said that aloud."

"I just did," Lula groused. "And my hide's still on me."

"Bug off." Diggery gave her a sideways glare.

Adria let them continue to verbally spar, but her attention turned and fixed on the fox under the bushes. Her nose twitched. Her beady eyes seemed to read Adria's mind.

Mr. St. John.

Her father.

Missing gold.

It all seemed to interconnect, even Dr. Miranda the prior owner and his dead ghost daughter, Lucy. Foxglove Manor seemed to be the center of it all, and after last night's horror with Mrs. St. John's attempted strangulation . . . Adria looked up at the turret window. Her eyes locked with Mr. Crayne's. He stared down at her. Silent. Brooding. Knowing.

It was becoming a strong possibility that she wasn't the only one looking for the missing treasure. But if it wasn't a ghost taking vengeance on the occupants of Foxglove Manor, then who among them had the savagery to kill?

22

These sorts of things were best done at night. Under cover of darkness. Stealthily and with catlike finesse. Adria knocked into the side table and grappled for the Chinese vase that tilted and tipped. She righted it, then strained to see through the darkness. Into the corners. The shadows. All of Foxglove was cloaked in midnight's caress, and aside from the waves outside that rumbled and roared, the only other sound was the ticking of the grandfather clock in the study.

Mrs. St. John had kept her busy all day. The last three days, to be precise, since refusing to leave her room to avoid certain death. Adria could hardly blame the woman. As it was, she had scarcely slept and had taken a strange sort of comfort from the thumping noises that had so frightened her the first night at Foxglove Manor. It meant Mr. Crayne was awake. And if a man was awake, perhaps there would be chance of saving if someone attempted to suffocate, strangle, slice, or disembowel.

The days had been just as long as the nights. Embroidering for a total of thirteen hours, playing seventeen games of whist, and sipping two goblets of wine under pretense that it tasted good when Adria considered wine to be just shy of horrific to her taste buds. But it was fitting, after all. Foxglove Manor was proving to be its own sort of horrific.

She tiptoed into the study and stood in the doorway, realizing the wine had made her tipsy. But she had procrastinated long enough. What was she hoping for? That the gold her father swore was his would simply appear in plain sight? Or perhaps Mrs. St. John would have a slip of the tongue and state its whereabouts?

You know, dear, your father's gold? Well, my husband stole it from him and hid it in the cellar. If you look behind the shelf of canned tomatoes, you're sure to find it.

If only it were that simple. That easy.

Adria stubbed her toe against the leg of a chair, and she grappled for the chair to stop herself from careening forward. She was not the epitome of stealth, this much was certain. A part of her wondered why her father didn't just come to Foxglove Manor and take what he believed to be his by force. Or by coercion. Blackmail? It was a bit of a puzzle why he was relying so heavily on the wits of a daughter who just recently saw fit to drink enough liquid poison that she should have been dead.

"I'm not particularly reliable, Father," Adria muttered into the silent study of Mr. St. John.

The moon was gracious enough to lend some light, illuminating the silver of the crossed sabers over the mantel. Adria hoped that Mrs. St. John was sentimental enough to have left it all as Mr. St. John had left it the day he died. A year prior, Lula had informed her when she'd asked.

"Mr. St. John moved here before the missus, as they'd owned the place since just after the war," Lula had educated Adria. "Mr. St. John—so Diggery says—was a grouch, and he believed Mrs. St. John sent him to Foxglove Manor while she stayed in Lansing, just for some peace. But after Theodora died, she couldn't take being in the same house where the young woman had tumbled to her death."

So, Mrs. St. John had followed her husband to the remote outpost of Foxglove, perched on a cliff, named after the very animal for which she blamed her daughter's death. The irony was mindboggling. But now, Adria considered whether Mrs. St. John's arrival to Foxglove hadn't thwarted her husband's secret smuggling. Assuming he was as covert as Adria was beginning to believe he was. And if what Diggery had implied was true, Mr. St. John was less of a Patriot and more of a Rebel. But then that made Adria's mind twist into confused fits.

She skirted the set of four comfortable chairs arranged in a semicircle facing the fireplace. Her toe was throbbing from stubbing it. She was not adept at spying, and Adria was well aware of this when she reached Mr. St. John's massive desk. Or at least the one he'd apparently adopted after Dr. Miranda had sold the property and moved on. Either way, she peered down at it, attempting to make out the objects that graced its top. An inkwell, a pen, a dish, and a small bronze statue of a horse. There was also a pipe stand with a very cold pipe resting in it, as if its owner would return at any moment, assign it fresh tobacco, and light its tangy innards with a flame. A few books were piled at the very end of the desk. Adria lifted them and held them just beyond her nose to read the titles.

System of Transcendental Idealism by F. W. J. Schelling

The Holy Bible

Uncle Tom's Cabin by Harriet Beecher Stowe

Curious, Adria opened the cover of the last book. The title page was marred with an ink pen.

Gnqgy . . .

Odd. She'd have expected Mr. St. John's signature to identify the book as his. The five letters were cryptic. Purposeless. It was a scarring, of sorts, as if disrespecting the book by scribbling on its pages. She had heard of this novel. Her father, in his own self-righteous way, had touted it as a "stain on the South's ethics."

She rubbed her finger over the handwritten letters. A long line had been crossed through *Uncle Tom* and another through the authoress's name. Even the nature one might assign to a crossed-out title sent a shiver through Adria, and she slammed the book shut. Mr. St. John was for the Union. He *had* to be, Adria reminded herself. He lived in the Union. He'd *fought* for the Union. The very north of the North. He couldn't get much more northern unless he crossed into Canada. But there was something ominous in the striking through of the name of a fictional slave. Something evil. Self-serving.

Adria tucked the book beneath the Bible as if the Scripture's power itself would wipe out any wicked intent. The room washed in darkness as clouds covered any slivers of light that had been afforded her. If only she had a lamp, searching the study for clues to her father's stolen bounty wouldn't feel so—

A creak outside the study door caused Adria to freeze, her hand resting on the Bible as if taking a holy vow. She strained to see through the room, which was empty outside of herself. Another creak, like a footstep, the weight of a man—or woman—outside the study in the hallway. Stealth was not on the side of whomever was coming toward the very room where Adria stood like a poised statue that had no concept of how to break free into its own movement. Knowing she should duck, perhaps hide under the desk, Adria instead maintained her frozen position. The study door was half open, but now the pale skin of a hand with thin fingers curled around it. With a strained groan, it began to swing open, the movement mesmerizing in its eeriness.

An arm appeared, then a shoulder, then the form of a girl entered the room. Adria blinked rapidly, attempting to clear her vision. She could see through the girl, a luminescent sort of vision. Like a cloud. Her bare feet padded across the floor, and she was oblivious to Adria. Her eyes were dark, almost bruised-looking, in a face that rivaled ice for its translucent whiteness. The girl was clothed in a white nightdress. It fell to her calves, and the collar was made of lace. Her hair was almost as white but with a tinge of gold to it. Adria realized she was seeing the girl very clearly for the room being so shrouded in darkness. She tried to move, to wrench herself out of her frigid stupor, but it was as though an unseen force rooted Adria to the ground, with the Bible beneath her hand, the copy of *Uncle Tom's Cabin* beneath that.

The ghost girl took deliberate steps toward the mantel, lifted her hand, and ran a finger over the scrollwork carved so beautifully into the wood. Her fingernail was black. She turned and, in that moment, noticed Adria. She could be no more than eight, yet her expression was stony. Frightful. With an emptiness in her eyes. Cracks ran along her cheeks like they were made of porcelain. Her lips were as pink as the foxglove Diggery had transplanted earlier that day.

Adria tried to speak. Tried to cry out. But her mouth was sealed, her teeth clenched.

The little girl turned and walked toward Adria, purpose in her steps.

"Help me," the ghost girl whispered, the words drifting through the stale air of the room like a haunting that planted seeds deep in Adria's soul.

"Help me." Eyes widening, the little girl startled and jerked to look over her shoulder. Every part of her cloudlike body seemed to tense. She swept her head around to skewer Adria with a hollow gaze of panic. "It's not right. They're here again. Help me!"

A moan ripped through her parched throat. Adria tossed her head to the right, and her cheek met the cool cotton of a pillowcase.

"She's awake!" Lula's voice pierced the air with the subtlety of a drunk announcing "drinks for all" in a saloon. Pounding on the floor indicated she was running from the room, and another more distant declaration made it obvious that Lula was in search of someone.

There was a moment of blessed silence when Adria kept her eyes closed, confused. She was in bed? But she had only just been in the study. Just seen the ghost girl with her luminous skin and horrible face. Heavy footsteps convinced Adria to open her eyes. It hurt to let the light in, but morning was here, the sun shining through the lace curtains, and outside, the consistent thrum of the waves of Lake Superior maintained their minute-by-minute rhythm.

A chair squeaked as weight settled onto it. Adria turned her head to the other side, her cheek once again finding the softness of pillow and cotton. Mr. Crayne settled on a chair, his features solemn. Sharp lines in his face made him seem more daunting, and even in her muddled state, Adria could tell his eyes were clear. He was sober. In control of his faculties. But there was a storm brewing in his expression.

"It's been two days," he announced without fanfare.

"Two?" Adria managed.

"We found you two mornings ago, collapsed in Mr. St. John's study with a Bible splayed over your chest like a shield."

"Maybe it was," she murmured, recalling the ghost girl's urgent cry. "Did they come?" Adria finished.

His face darkening, Mr. Crayne studied her. "Did *who* come?"

Adria looked away. She would sound like an addlepated ninny if she began to wax poetic about a little dead girl floating about Mr. St. John's office. It was one thing to hear the stories of the ghost of Foxglove Manor, but quite another entirely to have seen it. And she didn't believe in spirits—in ghosts. So where did this leave her now? A crisis of her own beliefs, perhaps, and not one she was anxious to decipher.

"Alexandria?" Mr. Crayne's sharp voice brought her back.

She looked up at him. "I don't know who. Never mind. It doesn't matter." She expected him to press the matter. Oddly, he didn't.

Leaning back in the chair, Mr. Crayne crossed his arms over his chest. His white shirt was simple, tailored, not elaborate and certainly nothing to notice. But Adria did. She noticed the cords in his neck. She noticed his chest that was broad and like the chest of the imaginary hero from her dreams. She had seen him before, and in them he had been strong, and his chest a place she would hide her face in. He would wrap those immensely strong arms about her and nothing evil would ever pass through again.

Adria squeezed her eyes shut again to block out the ridiculous nature of her thoughts. It was folly, that's what it was. Imagining such crazy ideas about a man who made whiskey his bedtime—and daytime—partner was irrational.

And she was irrational. Adria knew she was. In more ways than she wanted to speak aloud or recognize internally. The emotional jumble inside her that settled into the dark melancholy of hopeless dreams had caused her to take drastic measures before. Now? She could feel herself fast losing control of whatever little control she'd conjured herself into believing she had.

Mrs. St. John's strident voice drifted down the hallway, followed by the unending chatter of Lula. Mr. Crayne glanced at the door, and then in a swift motion he leaned forward and cupped Adria's face in his palms. He lowered her face until she could catch a whiff of last night's whiskey and a tinge of this morning's black coffee.

"Listen to me closely, Alexandria. Will you? Listen to me?"

She nodded, but mostly because of the pressure of his palms to her cheeks. It was too familiar. Controlling. That control a man held over a woman, and in the end she was only to hold still and allow him to wield his power.

The pressure of his hands disappeared as he yanked them back as though her cheeks were hot coals. There was wounding in his eyes, a sad understanding, and he tucked his hands away as a soldier might hide an offensive weapon in front of a lady.

"Please listen."

She nodded again.

"Say nothing to Mrs. St. John. Nothing to Lula. Nor to Diggery. What you saw, what you know, what you think. It must stay between us. Do you understand?"

He knew she'd seen Lucy? Or was it something else? Regardless, Adria nodded anyway. "Yes. But why?" she whispered.

"We found you on the floor, Adria. You didn't respond. Lula thought you were dead."

"She thought the same of Mrs. St. John," Adria argued softly.

Footsteps in the hall made Mr. Crayne send a surreptitious glance at the door once more. He nodded. "Yes. And one of these times, Lula may be right. There is more at play here at Foxglove Manor than you know, Adria. You must stay far from it. Out of sight, and silent. No more nighttime dalliances in Mr. St. John's study. No more asking questions of Diggery. About the Mirandas, or the St. Johns, or any of the stories of Foxglove."

"Why?" she asked again, even as Mrs. St. John began to open the bedroom door.

"Trust me," Mr. Crayne whispered. His eyes begged her.

Adria nodded. She didn't know what else to do. Between the girl in the study, Mrs. St. John's attempted strangulation, and Mr. Crayne's insistent orders . . . she simply did not know what else to do.

23

KAILEY

The wailing was the first indication that something was wrong. Maddie's wobbly cries drifted to Kailey's room, and she leapt from her bed, stuffing her feet into sheepskin moccasin slippers and running toward the door. She almost collided with Tracee as the nurse on duty rounded a corner, her purple scrubs black in the hallway's dim light. Kailey noted the resignation in Tracee's eyes, but also noted that Tracee didn't lessen her pace toward the elderly resident's room.

"She does this," Tracee tossed over her shoulder at Kailey. "Every now and then, Maddie has a night terror." Tracee shoved open Maddie's bedroom door. The woman's room was a small replica of a miniature living quarter. A lift recliner in forest-green, a dresser with family photos in a collage of frames, a twin-sized bed with rails, and a television. The lamp on the nightstand was on and cast the room in a soft, golden glow. The windows were shuttered, barring any view of the lake.

Maddie sat in the bed, her shoulders hunched forward, clutching her sheet and green blanket to her chest. Her eyes were wide but unfocused. Her mouth was open, wrinkled lips gray. Her hair was askew, frizzy and gray, pulled into a braid for sleeping but mussed from her tossing.

"Maddie, hon, it's Tracee." Tracee hurried to the woman's side and lowered the bedrail. She reached out and pressed her hand over Maddie's wrinkled one, which clutched the blanket so tightly her knuckles had turned white.

"Go away!" Maddie's voice quavered, shaking with tears and fright.

"Maddie. Maddie, wake up." Tracee lightly patted Maddie's cheek.

Maddie turned a desperate look to Tracee, not noticing Kailey, who hung back. "They're coming for it." Maddie dropped her voice to a frantic whisper. "Hide it. Hide it, Tracee!"

Tracee frowned and exchanged bewildered looks with Kailey.

Kailey waited only a moment before realizing Tracee was at a loss for what to say. She eased next to Tracee and received a welcoming nod from her. Settling her backside on the edge of the bed, Kailey leaned forward and pressed her hands onto Maddie's blanket-covered legs.

"Maddie? Who's coming?"

Tracee frowned. "Kailey." There was questioning in her statement. A sort of unspoken wonder of why Kailey was entertaining the woman's night terror. Kailey could only recall how awful it felt to be doubted, to be told everything was all right when it wasn't. She ignored Tracee.

"Maddie? Who's coming?" she repeated.

Maddie started trembling, her brown eyes lowering from Tracee's face to meet Kailey's. They widened. Hope rose in them. She leaned forward. "Yes. Yes, *you*. Help me, child? Help me?"

"Yes, yes, I'll help you." Kailey edged closer, and Maddie dropped the blanket to her waist and shifted her death grip on Kailey's hands. Her fingers were cold, her palms smooth, her hands shaking. Maddie sucked in a shuddering breath.

Kailey sensed Tracee moving away.

Maddie demanded Kailey's attention with a swift squeeze of her fingers around Kailey's hands. "They want it. They'll take it and make it theirs. Don't let them."

"What do they want?" Kailey urged.

Maddie's eyes widened in surprise, still glazed in a half sleep that was creepy and surreal simultaneously. "The gold. They want the gold."

A wild cry erupted from the old woman's lips, but it was one of pain and not fright. She clutched at her chest.

"Tracee!" Kailey yelled, realizing the nurse had disappeared. In a moment, Tracee rushed back into the room. She had some pills in cup and a glass of water. Urging Maddie through the motion, the old woman swallowed the pills. Tracee gently persuaded her to lie back on the pillows. She positioned her stethoscope to listen to Maddie's heart.

"Is she having a heart attack?" Kailey bit her lip in worry.

Tracee shook her head. "No, I don't think so." She seemed content with the heart rate and set to work wrapping a blood-pressure cuff around the woman's arm. Pumping, the cuff expanded, and Maddie moaned from the squeeze of it against her delicate skin. It held, Tracee read the gauge, and then the cuff began to deflate. Tracee removed the cuff.

"It's high, but not abnormally so. I think she'll be fine."

"You think?" Kailey frowned. "Are you sure?"

Tracee blew a breath through her lips as she assisted Maddie in taking another sip of water. She nodded as she did so. "This isn't the first time. These night terrors and then the stress, it causes a panic attack and she just needs some help sedating."

"The pills?" Kailey sought to understand.

Tracee pulled back from Maddie and set the cup of water on a nearby stand. Maddie was calming, her eyelids heavy. "They ease her anxiety and help her sleep. Poor Maddie." Tracee reached out and moved Maddie's braid over her shoulder. She straightened the blankets. "She's already managing through the psychological torture of knowing she's losing her memory and, in turn, her faculties. But to add night terrors to it? I'm actually surprised she didn't start calling for Jim."

"Jim?" Kailey thought the name sounded familiar but couldn't place it.

Tracee shot her a quick eye roll. "Her imaginary son. The one she swears she has but doesn't."

Kailey wanted to understand more. "Who admitted her to Foxglove Manor?"

Tracee smiled. "Her niece. She's a nice lady, but she lives quite a distance away. Ohio, I think. Anyway, she's in her fifties but just not set up to care for her aunt. She felt Foxglove would provide Maddie with that restful place."

"But it's so far out. It's . . ." Kailey paused. Come to think of it, if tonight *had* been an emergency, an ambulance would have almost been a joke. The nearest town was twenty minutes away. "Why have an old folks' home this far from a hospital?"

Tracee fingered Maddie's wrist, taking her pulse again. Her lips moved in a silent count and then she released it. "There's a doctor who lives within eight minutes of here. He's on call most of the time."

"But in an emergency? What if Maddie was having an actual heart attack?"

Tracee didn't seem bothered by the logical line of questions. "We do our best, Kailey. We call the doctor, and we have an emergency process already in place with the hospital. The fact is, here in the UP, nothing's going to be super quick. We're up north. Not a metropolis."

It was a nice thought, an assisted living home on a cliff overlooking Lake Superior. The country, the seclusion, the beauty of the place would be stimulating for someone shut in during their later years in life. Still, if she had someone she cared about, Kailey couldn't fathom placing them in a home that wasn't within minutes of good medical care.

"People do what they can, Kailey." Tracee read the doubt on Kailey's face.

"And the night terrors?" Kailey pressed, unable to shake the uneasiness in her bones. "Who is Maddie afraid of? And—and what *gold* is she talking about?"

Tracee waved her off. "It's a dream, Kailey. Nothing more."

"But—"

"Kailey." Tracee held up a hand to stop her. Her hazel eyes were kind—understanding even—but there was also a firmness in her tone. "Maddie has Alzheimer's. She thinks she remembers a son she never had. She—she isn't right in her mind anymore, and you can't put stock in what she says."

"I thought Alzheimer patients actually had decent long-term memory and it was short term that suffered," Kailey argued. "What if she's remembering things that we don't understand?"

"For some, yes. Yes, they do remember things from long ago. That's why you'll have an Alzheimer's patient calling for their mother when they're ninety-two years old and bedridden. They think they're five again and Mommy is just down the hall. But that doesn't mean they recall details. Heck, my own grandpa had it and he forgot who I was!" Tracee's eyes flooded with tears for a moment, and she turned away, sniffing. "It's an ugly disease, and there are few satisfying explanations. You just have to roll with it as best as you can."

"She said they were coming for the gold." Kailey dogged Axel's feet as he trudged across the yard toward the trees, pushing a wheelbarrow filled with branches and debris. "She said they were coming."

"And?" Axel reached a brush pile. He paused long enough to shoot a quizzical glance in her direction before manhandling an armful of branches and tossing them on top of the pile.

"What if . . . ?" Kailey waited. Axel was making too much noise to hear her. He turned and tugged off his leather work gloves.

"What if what?"

Kailey crossed her arms over her sweater-clad chest. "Well— Lucy Miranda."

"The ghost girl," Axel supplied. He waited. His eyes were completely unreadable, and that annoyed Kailey.

"What if there *is* a ghost? If the stories about Foxglove and hidden treasure are real, just like I said the other day? If Lucy's ghost guards the treasure, and the treasure is the gold Maddie was talking about?" She watched Axel bite the inside of his cheek in an attempt to stop his smile. "I'm serious," Kailey concluded.

It was noble of him to try so hard, but his scruffy cheeks broke into a quick grin that he quickly wiped from his face. "You realize that sounds like *National Treasure* collided with *The Sixth Sense*, don't you?"

"I never read either of them."

"Actually, they're movies."

"Still." Kailey shook her head. She looked beyond the cliff to the lake. It was calm today. Strangely calm. The waves were small and more subtle. She turned her attention back to Axel.

"You don't know about *The Sixth Sense*? How do you not know that movie?" Axel was sidetracked.

Kailey stared at him.

"Bruce Willis?"

She winced.

"'I see dead people'?"

Kailey frowned.

"Really?" Axel shook his head. "Man, we need to have a movie night."

"I'm serious, Axel. Please. You didn't laugh at me the other day when I brought up the idea of a treasure. Of my brother and Riley Bascom." She couldn't forget Maddie's panic from the night before. She couldn't just dismiss it as nothing—as a night terror or as some awful side effect of a disease.

Axel's expression grew serious. He tossed his gloves into the now-empty wheelbarrow and rested his hands on his hips. "*Do* you believe in ghosts? In spirits, Kailey?"

Did she? Kailey pressed her lips together and shrugged. "I don't know. I never have, but sometimes they seem to make sense. So many people have stories of things happening, sightings, doors closing. I watched a show once about a piano that would start playing in the middle of the night. And what about those gadgets they have that record other frequencies and you can hear someone speaking?"

"You've been more than curious about ghosts, I see," Axel observed.

"Do *you* believe in ghosts?" Kailey retorted.

Axel gave her a gentle smile. "I believe in God."

Kailey snorted but smiled back. "Duh." Okay, she sounded like a middle schooler.

Axel hooked his thumbs in his jeans pockets. "Whether or not ghosts exists, or spirits, or demons, or however you want to label it, I believe God is the one I'm going to spend my time focusing on. The others steal the attention otherwise, and really, He usurps them all. I mean, I'd pit God against a ghost any day."

Kailey laughed this time, yet it didn't quell the anxiousness inside her. "Well, let's just pretend that ghosts *do* exist . . ."

"Okay. Listen." Axel kicked at a stick. "If all of that is true—and I say, *if*—that doesn't explain why Maddie would know a thing about it. She doesn't fit into the puzzle, and it was apparent she was having a nightmare."

He was right. She was a resident of the manor, not a part of its history.

"But Jude—his scribbling and Maddie's—they're the same," Kailey argued.

Axel nodded. "Okay."

"That can't be a coincidence, because they're like—like a *code* or something. Random letters and numbers strung together? The same pattern?"

"I'll give you that." Axel ran his hand through his thick, wavy hair. "But it's gibberish." He opened his mouth to say something, then snapped it shut and diverted his attention to the brush pile.

"What?" Kailey pressed.

"Nothing." Axel bent and picked up some sticks that had fallen from the pile and threw them on the top.

"What were you going to say?" She didn't want to let him off the hook that easily.

Axel sighed and faced her. "What we *do* know is that you were taken as a little girl by someone who wanted something from you. You've pieced together it was something Jude told you. The rest is all conspiracy, Kailey." He stepped closer to her and reached out, but she stepped back. Something flickered in his eyes, and he dropped his hand to his side. "Until you remember more—until you remember what exactly they said to you and what happened here at Foxglove when you were a kid—it's all just speculation."

Kailey hated the way her chin quivered. Hated the way she felt her cheeks flush with emotion. Frustration. It was easy for Axel to blanket a lack of ghostly belief under the canopy of Christianity. It was easy to assume legend and lore was simply that, and that Maddie and even herself were just victims of bad dreams. But it felt awful. It was reminiscent of the feelings she'd suffered through.

"No, you couldn't have been kidnapped."

"Tell us the truth, where were you?"

Axel interpreted her silence as an invitation to try again. "I'm not saying you're not right. I'm not saying that there couldn't be hidden gold and delusional elderly women writing codes that your brother writes."

"And ghosts?" Kailey interrupted.

"Sure. Ghosts. I'm just saying, it's a lot of story with little to set our feet on. But I *want* to believe you, and I *do* believe that you were abducted."

She gave him points for that.

Axel must have seen something in her face that gave him the courage to reach out. His fingers took hers, and his skin was callused. Warm. Infused with a quiet, determined faith—the desire to help and the struggle not to dismiss realism along the way. "Kailey, you need to remember."

He tugged.

Kailey let him.

Axel's embrace was light, but the feeling of his arms around her, however unfamiliar, brought an undeniable sense of hope. She was not alone. Not in this moment anyway. And, if she was going to remember, Kailey would need someone to hold her. Remembering was critical, but it was also traumatic. She knew she needed to recall. She had known it all along. For twenty years, she had known it. In every therapy session, she had known it. When Jude had stopped writing his gibberish, she had known it, and when he'd begun again and started experiencing anxieties and traumas because of it, she had known. But remembering meant revisiting the worst moments of her life. That moment when she was stolen. That moment when she truly believed she would never see Jude again. That moment she knew she would never live a life without the tentacles of fear clinging to her like a leech that could not be removed.

24

Kailey gripped the steering wheel until her knuckles hurt. She glanced into the rearview mirror a fifth time since pulling out of the driveway of Foxglove Manor and turning the car toward Harbor Towne. Jude sat beside her in the passenger seat, a beautiful hardback book about Egyptian hieroglyphics in his lap. She gave it a sideways glance. It reminded her of the string of letters and numbers he was obsessed with. They weren't pictures, but they seemed like a language.

The car surged down the empty road, trees swelling up on either side until it was as if they were driving down a forested aisle. Kailey adjusted her fingers around the steering wheel, realizing she was clutching it in a death grip. It wouldn't sit well with Axel if he knew where she was going. He would try to stop her—and he should. She should stop herself. But something inside her convinced her that if she could only talk to Riley Bascom, it might help trigger the memories of her own seven-hour abduction. Kailey imagined the upcoming conversation after knocking on the front door of the Bascom home.

"Hi, I'm Kailey Gibson. I was wondering if you have a moment?"

Riley's mother would stare at her with suspicion, and Kailey couldn't blame her.

"What do you want?" A proper question from a guarded mother.

"I wanted to ask you some questions—perhaps your daughter as well. I know you're going through a very bad time with the passing of

your husband, but I can't skirt the story Riley told the police. About being abducted for a day? It's my story too, Mrs. Bascom. It happened to me twenty years ago."

"Get off my property." Mrs. Bascom would glare.

Kailey would engage the most pleading expression she could. "Please, Mrs. Bascom. Five minutes? Just five—"

"I'll call the cops." The tone would be one of warning. Dire. But behind Mrs. Bascom would be the big brown eyes of a ten-year-old girl.

"Mama?" Riley would break the tension.

Mrs. Bascom would turn to her daughter with sternness. "Riley, go back inside."

"I want to talk to her, Mama," Riley would argue, and in her expression would be an unspoken camaraderie that Kailey would be drawn to.

"I said go back inside," Mrs. Bascom would demand.

"Riley, I believe you," Kailey would interject. "I believe your story!"

Riley's face would light up with hope. A hope that hadn't been extended to Kailey when she was little—when no one would believe her.

Kailey jerked to attention as her phone beeped and the GPS gained a signal. "Turn right in five hundred feet." She did. Four miles. Another right. "Turn on Zaehr Road." Half a mile. Left on Platte Lane.

"Your destination is on the left." The GPS was set to a male's Australian accent. Sexy and robotic. Kailey rammed her finger against the end route button. Having a cell signal was great. Her phone pinged with notifications from unread emails and app alerts.

"Kay-Kay?" Jude broke into her silent sparring with herself.

"What?" Kailey forced her attention to Jude.

He smiled, his front teeth crooked. "Home? Fa ooo?" Jude lifted a finger and pointed at the Bascom house. "Ooo?" His voice rose in pitch.

"No, buddy. It's not a home for me." Her response stung her worse than it would Jude. Jude. Always looking out for her. Wanting her to be happy. Protected. Secure. "Our home is at Foxglove," she concluded.

His eyes narrowed, and he shook his head back and forth in a jerking motion. "No. No."

Kailey diverted his attention by singling out a photograph of King Tut in the open book on Jude's lap. "It's King Tut," she added blandly.

"Two one." He dragged his finger down the length of Tut's mask. Then crossed it. "Teen." He lifted five fingers.

"Twenty-one and fifteen?" Kailey leaned over to inspect the mask. She assumed he was correct, but for the heck of it, she snagged her phone and Googled it. A proud smile touched her lips. How her brother could know by eyeing a photograph that the mask of the pharaoh was twenty-one inches high and fifteen inches wide was beyond her. Not that the measurements weren't anything out of the ordinary, but the way Jude saw objects as numbers and measurements still bewildered her.

"Go." Jude waved at her, then lifted his book so close to his face his nose almost touched the spine.

Kailey reverted her attention back to the task at hand. Being outside the Bascom home was frightening, and a part of her wanted to stay sidetracked with the exploration of Egypt. Instead, she stared at the blue door. The gray siding that needed to be power-washed. A bicycle lay on its side in the front yard. Pink. Rusted wheel guards. The windows were dark. A red hummingbird stained-glass ornament hung in one of them. The front stoop had a flowerpot on it, but it was empty. No flowers. No one had apparently had the heart to spring garden. Not after a child claimed she'd been kidnapped, and her father had died just as suddenly.

Kailey's imagined conversation replayed in her head as she exited the car. She shut the door but leaned in through the open window.

"Hang here, okay?" she addressed Jude, but he ignored her. Entranced in his book. Thankful for the billionth time that Jude was a more stationary type of guy instead of wandering and need-ing continual supervision, Kailey started up the cracked, shifted sidewalk. She recalled Axel's observations that he'd pit God against a ghost anytime. But what about the truth? Would God win over the truth, or would the truth win and stay shrouded? She should pray. Kailey lifted her hand to knock on the front door. She should. Really. She should. But she brought her knuckles down on the door before she could whisper even a *help me*.

Well, this wasn't what she had planned on. Kailey met the fur-rowed brow of Jason Bascom, Riley's uncle and resident human guard dog.

"Aren't you—?" His eyes darkened. "I told you to stay away from my niece."

Kailey shifted her weight on her feet and nodded with an ear-nest indication that she meant nothing but respect. "Yes, sir. I understand. I—"

"You what?" His shoulders were squared, dressed in an Oxford shirt that hung loose over his jeans. He was well-groomed and even a bit upscale for the Bascom home surroundings. He'd look more like he fit in if he had on a baseball cap, a flannel shirt, and a pair of beat-up Carhartt pants.

Kailey drew in a steadying breath. "Your niece's story resonated with me, Mr. Bascom."

He was a handsome man really, if she cared to consider it. Which she didn't.

"I must apologize for my behavior at your brother's graveside ceremony," Kailey added swiftly.

Jason Bascom's face remained expressionless.

"If you would allow me a moment to explain, I'd—"

"There's nothing to explain." He started to close the door, and without thinking, Kailey slapped her palm against it.

"Please!"

"Get your hand off the door," he gritted out through clenched teeth.

Kailey was certain if looks could kill, she'd be dying a long and torturous death. She spit out the only thing she could think of. "What if your brother didn't kill himself? What if he was murdered?"

Bascom froze.

Kailey held her breath.

He looked over his shoulder into the house, then stepped toward her, effectively nudging her backward as he closed the door behind him. "What the heck do you think you're doing? What right do you have to make such a preposterous claim?"

"Not much. I don't have much right. Just a little," Kailey answered quickly.

"A little? Do justify that, please."

It was an official invite, however thick with sarcasm.

Kailey sucked in her hopes and fears and launched into an explanation. "When I was five, I vacationed at Foxglove Manor with my parents and my older brother. Long story short, something happened when we were there. Something my five-year-old mind blocked out, and my brother—who has autism—could remember but not communicate with anyone except me."

"I'm listening," Mr. Bascom stated. Maybe it was her reference to Foxglove Manor, the property his brother owned, that snagged his patience.

"When we returned home, I was taken—by a man. He put me in the back of a minivan. I don't remember how long we drove. I don't know what he looked like. He wore a ski mask. He tried to make me tell him what I knew about Foxglove Manor—what Jude, my brother, had told me. But I was only five. I was too scared, too afraid. So he released me. Sir, he held me for seven hours, and after I returned home, no one believed me when I told them what happened."

Kailey paused. Mr. Bascom appeared to be digesting her words.

She plunged ahead before she completely lost her nerve. "I relate to Riley's story. I don't think she's lying that she was abducted—or that she's making up stories. I believe she knows what my brother Jude knew—what I probably know but just can't remember because of the traumatizing events. And for your brother to pass away, so suddenly, right after?" She couldn't really explain the ghost of Lucy Miranda or Maddie's claim about gold. Maybe Jason Bascom didn't even know about the old stories circulating around his brother's property. So she opted for something more vague. "What if the same guy who took me when I was five took Riley? And what if your brother—maybe he stood in the way somehow, and they killed him?"

"My brother asphyxiated himself in the garage, Miss—Gibson, is it? Hardly murder. Your story is offensive and outright vulgar."

"I know it doesn't make any sense, but please listen to me. If there's an old treasure at Foxglove Manor, and if it's been kept hidden all these years, then—"

"Old treasure?" Mr. Bascom's frown deepened to facial valleys. "What the—you're nuts, lady." He turned quickly and opened the door in a retreat.

"Mr. Bascom!" Kailey surged after him. "Do you believe Riley?" she blurted out.

Mr. Bascom stopped, turned, the door half open behind him. He skewered her with a glare. "What did you say?" His voice dropped in tone.

Kailey cleared her throat. "I asked if you believe your niece."

"Of course I do."

"Then if you do, don't you think we need to compare stories? The police aren't getting anywhere. She wasn't even missing for twenty-four hours. It's a closed case, isn't it?"

He had no response but seemed to be contemplating. Weighing his options.

Kailey hurried on. "If you don't think your niece is a liar, then you have to know she isn't making it up. Did her father believe her?"

Jason Bascom clenched his jaw and gave a short nod.

"Was he doing anything about it?"

Bascom sucked in a shuddery sigh and gritted out, "He was—asking questions, yes."

"So why would he take his own life when he's in the middle of fighting for his daughter's?" It might have been an insensitive question to ask, but Kailey could see it fell hard and made its point fast. She studied the man's face before her, saw the shadow of grief pass through his eyes, the softening in his mouth, and the sag of his shoulders. "Please, Mr. Bascom. No one believes this story is more outlandish than I do. But I need answers. For myself. For my brother." She glanced over her shoulder at Jude, sitting in the car. "Riley needs answers, and—and your brother deserves to have his daughter protected. At all costs."

Bascom ran his hand over his eyes, rubbing them until he gripped his nose between his index finger and thumb. "Fine." He dropped his hand. "But you don't say a word to Riley about my brother's death. You don't bring him up. You can only ask her questions about what happened to her."

Relief coursed through Kailey. She closed her eyes for a moment, then opened them. "Thank you," she breathed.

He held a finger in front of her nose. "But your conspiracy theories? If this is all a big joke or a publicity stunt or some sick prank you're playing, I'll sue. I'll press charges. I'll file restraining orders and come after you with everything I have."

"I understand." Kailey nodded. She did, and to be honest, his threats made her tremble inside. She would have to prove her theories credible. And since when were stories of ghosts, gold, and modern-day kidnappings surrounding an old manor ever anything but a classic story written on the musty pages of forgotten books?

25

ΛDRIΛ

The note card fell from her shaking fingers and swept back and forth through the air before landing faceup on the wood floor at the base of her bed. Adria stared down at it and could see her father's sparking eyes in the words. She could hear his voice.

I've heard nothing from you.

It was filled with a million insinuations. The threat of him—*him*—was enough to make her shudder. Going home was threat enough, and yet a nagging intuition told her he'd meant more than that. Adria eyed the telegraph on the floor, then swept her gaze to the letter that had also been delivered that morning. Her first letter delivered through the postal service to the great Upper Peninsula. It had taken weeks to arrive, which meant her sister had to have written it not very long after Adria had been found, revived, and quickly whisked off to Foxglove Manor with mission and mystery.

Her fingers trembled as she reached for it, her thumb brushing the ink and her sister's flowery script. The envelope was stained as if it had encountered rain at some point. Adria prayed it was still legible, and at the same time she prayed it wasn't. Margot would have nothing good to say—she never did—but she also delighted in explaining their father's intentions like a lead weight held over

200

Adria's head. A defined threat was always delivered via Margot, whereas their father preferred vague insinuation. Adria was certain the vagueness drove her mad. The question of the undefined trauma that was sure to be delivered was far worse than being allowed to prepare oneself for what they knew was coming.

Ripping open the envelope, Adria tugged the letter from its innards. There was no smell to the paper, though she was certain when it was first penned, Margot's French perfume tinged with jasmine and vanilla tones would have saturated it. Still, Adria held it to her nose, not out of a sentimental hope that she could capture a scent of home but to remind herself of the poison that was Margot's taunting.

My dearest Alexandria . . .

The letter's salutation revived in Adria the nausea that came from her sister's patronizing. Margot wished to control Adria, to manipulate her emotions and to glory in the misery eventually administered by their father. It was her source of entertainment. Adria almost ripped the letter to shreds right then to cheat Margot of the satisfaction of such. But again, her need for definition of the threat was too great.

Father is quite beside himself, even though it has been mere days since your departure. Friends and business relations still inquire as to your sudden removal from society, and we are bothered by the pestilence that is having to explain your absence. I'm afraid rumors are spreading that you are with child and we have spirited you away. If you return to home, you no doubt will face many insinuations. However, we will address that when and if the time comes. Father said he wishes it were merely a child. They can be handled. But a daughter—a sister—attempting to end her own walk on this earth? That is damnation at its worst and an unforgivable sin. It is because of this that I write to you with our father's intentions. There is not much you can do to satisfy him. Should you retrieve what he has asked you to from the halls of Foxglove Manor and from Mr. St. John's dead possessions, I believe Father will show mercy and allow you a return, or allow you to stay at Foxglove Manor under the care of Mrs. St. John and away from here, as you seemed so bent on achieving. It would be your penance, fulfilling Father's will, and might redeem you into a purgatory of sorts, if not from hell itself. But Father is quite certain you are not of sound mind or character, and to be truthful, we are both afraid you put forth no effort in acquiescing to his requests. That being such, his patience already runs thin and will become more strained as time passes. He has indicated that an institution would probably be a better outcome for you, if Foxglove Manor does not give up its ghost and release to you what is rightfully ours. For assuredly your lack of initiative to cooperate with the business of our father, along with your previous fall from grace as you attempted to cease your own breath, proves that you are indeed mad. There are hospitals that can help you. That can make you see the error of such thinking, aid you in establishing a sound perception of things, and perhaps repair the dismal failure you have become to Father and to the family name.

Be that as it may, time runs swiftly, my dear sister. Mad or not, your duty is to the Fontaines, to our father, and in essence, to me. If you wish to continue running away from that which makes you a Fontaine, do be an angel and purchase your illusioned freedom once and for all by pleasing our father and doing his bidding. While I dismay that your alienation from the family home is not to your best interest, I also dislike the image of leaving you at an institution. They do so look like a prison, don't you think?

Many regards and prayers,
Margot Elizabeth (Fontaine)

Adria could not breathe. It was as though her life, her full nightmare, and the futility of living it rushed back to her like the demon it had always been. The little desperate glimpse of freedom she had tasted and hoped for by coming to Foxglove Manor dissipated into despair. Panic welled in her. Nasty, breath-catching panic. An institution? No. An *asylum*! That was the fate that awaited her if she didn't succeed—and quickly—in uncovering her father's stolen goods. Goods that never belonged to him in the first place! And they claimed *she* was mad? She'd been driven to it. Reminded of her worthlessness since the moment she could first recall a memory.

The darkness swept over her, that old familiar cloak of despair. Adria crumpled Margot's letter in her hand and chucked it across the room. It bounced off a lampshade and onto the floor by the window. No. No! She must destroy it. Destroying wouldn't make it go away, but it would be a release of sorts. And she needed a release.

A sob raked at her breath as Adria hurtled across the room toward the letter now balled and wrinkled. She retrieved it with a swipe of her hand even as she was distracted by the view outside the window. Dusk was settling after another fruitless and monotonous day with Mrs. St. John. They had avoided all talk of danger and schemes, pretended that nothing was amiss or abnormal, and Mrs. St. John had waxed poetic about her dead daughter and all that Theodora was in comparison to all that Adria wasn't. The yard and the trees were navy-blue and deep green, mournful colors that screamed of the inevitable curse that had attached itself to a soul once born. Living was a curse. It truly was. There was no hope for escape, and the illusion of freedom was simply that. If she even did find her father's goods—gold or whatever it might be—staying at Foxglove would only be entering another prison. It seemed the bars had already risen around her. Suffocating her, claustrophobic with its reality.

The lake was wild tonight. A storm was rolling in, and the clouds that stretched over the waters were rolling, gray and black, with violet clouds inserting themselves as if to mock the colorless death that lived in the sky. An imminent violence that pushed and shoved the water into raucous waves that beat along the shore, threatened any ships out on its depths, and dared any lighthouse to penetrate the blackness.

Life was the lake. It was wild, unpredictable, and yet it was guaranteed to take one's life if one tried to traverse it. Falling into it would be falling to bottomless depths, that deep floating in a free fall of brilliantly cold water sucking from anything living to give nothing back but proof to the earth of its power. Life had the power to ruin—she would not allow it to ruin her. One last action would be the power Adria had to control her destiny. To find freedom—be it heaven or hell—from her battered and bruised life. A soul that was never worth much value to begin with.

The cliff beckoned to her. Its flat outcropping like a ledge where one might determine which evil was worse. To live or to die? Perhaps they were of equal evil, only one was guaranteed to plague, where the other was deceptively final. There was a peace in finality—even if damnation landed at the other end of it.

⁓

She'd forgotten her shoes. The ground was icy cold beneath her bare skin, but Adria reveled in the pinpricks of pain. They heightened her senses even as she moved across the lawn. The sky was spitting rain, a misty dew that at first came down gently but now was more like needles being driven into her skin. The wind whipped her dress around her legs, and Adria hitched up her skirts until they rode above her bare knees. What was propriety in one's last moments anyway? Her breaths came in quick gasps, but even as she walked toward the cliff, Adria had the sensation that she watched herself. Her sister's whispers reverberated in her mind.

You are mad.

An institution . . .

There was no freedom, no purpose to be had, when one's life meant so little. A burden to her family, and Adria didn't even really care except that it only emphasized how unnecessary she was. Her hair broke free from its constraints as the wind beat against her. The roar of the waves was overpowering, and if she had screamed, if she had raised her voice to God and cried for salvation, He could not have heard her. The lake was victorious. Her father was victorious.

Darkness was quickly settling around her, and as Adria's feet connected with the smooth platform of black basalt rock cliff, she lifted her face anyway. Rain pelted against it, abusing her skin, a staccato of reassurance that yes, finality was a gift. A gift to her battered soul and a gift to those she left behind. She released them of their perceived burden while relieving herself of hers.

Adria paused at the edge and curled her almost-numb toes against the rock. She was wet, her dress plastered to her, her hands still clutching her skirts high up on her legs. Long strands of cold, damp hair blew in the wind, slapping against her neck and her face. The shoreline below was sand and rock and driftwood, but to the right several yards, the cliff jutted out farther until it plunged beneath the depths of the furious lake. Adria moved to it, the rock slippery beneath her feet. A thrumming from the waves beating against the cliff sent a vibration through Adria's body. Her breath caught in a sob, and she knew she was weeping, though she couldn't feel her tears from the rain that ran down her face.

Oh, that she was worth fighting for!

Oh, that there was purpose beyond Foxglove, beyond her father's greed, beyond the entrapping of life that centered around one's success only to be met with death regardless of whether you ushered it in yourself or waited for death to hunt you down like its prey.

Oh, that there was a God mighty enough to still the waves. That He could shout louder and stronger. That He could love with wild abandonment instead of lord over the earth with the judgment that was deserved and just. Even God seemed to doom her soul, and in that there was never freedom—here or in eternity. It was all for naught.

Adria lifted her arms, releasing her dress. She wanted to fly. The freedom of a bird, with the wind powering beneath its wings and lifting it over the storm. She ached to find the brilliant blue and the sunlight that hid somewhere beyond the clouds. To revel in the crystal clearness of a lake that didn't seek to kill but instead to lull one into a blissful peace.

Her body swayed. Adria closed her eyes. Such a dream was too beautiful to be possible. Too elegant to be true. Life was brutal. Death was violent.

Adria felt the mist rise from the waves as they crashed into the cliff. She embraced it, sucking in sobs as she did so. She didn't want to die. She didn't want to face whatever lay beyond. But there was nothing here either. It was all bleak. Bleakness. Emptiness. A free fall into oblivion—

She screamed as arms slammed around her body and dragged her from the cliff's edge. Fighting against the pull, Adria screamed again, kicking wildly as they pulled her back, lifting her much smaller body into the air.

"You will not do this!" Mr. Crayne's baritone filled her ear and overpowered the sound of the waves.

Adria struggled against his ironclad grip, raking her fingernails across his skin as he clutched her with a hold that hurt because of its ferocity. "No!" she cried. "Let me go. Let me fall!"

"Are you mad?" He sounded angry against her hair and face. She felt his mouth against her ear.

"Yes!" she screamed in response, her throat aching as the word scraped from the depths of her soul. "Yes, I am mad! I am mad, mad, and deserve the pit of hell!" Adria kicked at Mr. Crayne. Her foot connected with his shin, but it didn't even sway him.

Mr. Crayne pulled her farther away from the cliff until he stumbled backward, taking her with him to the ground. Stones and pebbles dug into her skin. Her legs were bare as her dress tangled with his body. He lay against the ground and she against his side, but his arms had not released her. Adria knew he understood she would run this time. Run to the cliff and take flight for a brief and glorious moment of freedom.

"We all deserve hell!" Mr. Crayne shouted into her ear as the rain came in torrents now. "You for your wicked thoughts of self-damnation, and me for my devotion to false causes and the bottle."

"Then let me go!" She struggled against him, and this time Mr. Crayne pulled her on top of him, her chest against his, her face inches from his. Adria could see the fury in his eyes. A protective sort of fury that throbbed with fervor and emotion.

He glared into her eyes. "We must fight the war, Alexandria!"

War. War of the soul, the mind, the heart, and perhaps even a physical war that left scars across a man's back. She recalled the feeling of his puckered skin, and her eyes widened.

"I can't fight anymore." She felt herself weaken in his grip.

Mr. Crayne released one arm and lifted it to push her hair from her face. "It is not your decision to cease fighting."

"Why not?" She dropped her forehead against his. The rain ran between their skin. "It's all for naught."

"Never." Mr. Crayne's gaze drilled into hers. "As long as you have breath, there is purpose. We must fight to find it."

"I've no strength left."

"Nor do I," Mr. Crayne mumbled, his lips moving against her cheek. "But it is out there. We must find it."

She collapsed into him then, and he held her, there on the cliffs of Foxglove Manor.

26

The carriage rolled to a stop in front of Foxglove Manor, the horses at its hitch tossing their heads. Mrs. St. John let the curtain she held back with a wrinkled hand fall into place, blocking her from view.

"Good. It's about time." She moved toward the front door, pausing long enough to address Adria with her snapping tone. "You're no longer needed. Go clean your face, you look like death."

If only Mrs. St. John knew. Adria's head pounded with a fierceness after last night's mortifying display on the cliff. Mr. Crayne had finally led her weeping form back to the manor, escorted her to her room, and summoned Lula, who had helped Adria prepare for bed. By the time she'd slipped beneath the warmth of the covers, her teeth were chattering yet her cheeks were flushed with the embarrassing warmth of shame. Twice. Twice now, she had toyed with the temptation of death, been thwarted, and awakened to shame that grew deep roots in her heart. Mr. Crayne's words, his admonitions, and even his empathy resonated with her, but also struck empty. A war to find their purpose was no war at all when the enemy was clear, while the side you were fighting for was murky and undefined.

She approached the sitting room door, following in Mrs. St. John's footsteps. Visitors at Foxglove Manor were rare at best. She couldn't help the curiosity that nagged at her. Adria hugged the wall, eavesdropping as Mrs. St. John's voice murmured and was met with the deep tones of a man.

". . . nothing to be done about it." Mrs. St. John's sentence floated to Adria's ear. She tilted her head toward the door, straining to interpret the visitor's response.

"They must be moved," the stranger insisted.

"No." Mrs. St. John's voice was sharp. A hesitation. She tempered her tone as if aware someone could be listening. "It is best to pause. There is no reason to unsettle things. You know what risk would be taken if we were to transfer it now."

"Your husband would not agree, madam."

"My husband is dead." Mrs. St. John's bluntness silenced the visitor and made Adria catch her breath. "He left me Foxglove Manor, but *you* left me Mr. Crayne. Now I must bear the burden of both, mind you, and I will not have more disturbances while I am under this roof."

"You aren't being asked." There was warning in the man's words. The kind that insinuated Mrs. St. John was not as superior or ma-triarchal as she wanted to be when it pertained to Foxglove Manor.

"It is too unpredictable. There's a young woman here now, and if it's seen, you could shatter it all," she argued.

"As I stated previously, this isn't a request."

"And as I have made clear, Foxglove Manor is my property. My husband left it to me. I have accommodated you and your Mr. Crayne, but I will not be cowed by threats. I have already lost my dear Theodora, so truly, I have nothing left you could take that would leave me more bereft than I already am. Your threats are empty."

Adria had to admit that Mrs. St. John was formidable in her own right. Her words were like a verbal switch, not unlike the one she'd taken to Adria's legs the night Adria had discovered Mr. Crayne.

"This isn't the end of it."

Mrs. St. John gave a delicate snort. "I would be foolish to as-sume that it was."

Their voices dimmed. They had moved to the door and out of Adria's hearing. She slipped from the room and snuck a sly inspection around the corner. The man's features were undefinable for the most part. He wore a derby hat, a wool suit that was neither indicative of wealth nor was it threadbare. A handlebar mustache was his primary feature, as it was a brilliant white. For a brief moment, he looked over Mrs. St. John's shoulder and noticed Adria. His eyes narrowed. She ducked behind the corner and held her breath. The front door closed. There was silence. Mrs. St. John had apparently exited the manor, along with her mysterious visitor.

———

"You shouldn't be here, miss." Lula met Adria at the top of the stairs. Adria met the girl's earnest concern with a fake confidence.

"I need to see him."

Lula's expression shifted, a shadow flitting over her face. "He's—not himself, miss."

Adria stifled a sigh. Fight the war? Find the strength together? He should have let her throw herself off the cliff last night. It was midafternoon and he had vanished. So much for unified resistance against the vices that held them together. Desperation choked her and she swallowed back the hot tears of abandonment. It was a familiar feeling, after all. She should not have been surprised.

"I understand." Adria nodded and turned to return downstairs.

"Wait." Mr. Crayne halted her. Adria was reticent to meet his gaze. Instead, she locked eyes with Lula, who seemed taken aback at his sudden appearance.

"Sir, I thought you were—ill." Lula hurried to explain the reason she'd refused Adria access to him.

It was apparent he was as disturbed as Adria. His shirt was unbuttoned at the neck and hung over his navy-blue trousers, loose and wrinkled. His dark hair was rumpled as though he'd ran his fingers through it repeatedly, agitated and bothered. The scruff around his jaw and mouth and lower cheeks was dark and unshaven. Red-rimmed eyes were either from lack of sleep or else he had taken comfort in his decanter after seeing Adria into Lula's care the night before.

"I'm not ill," he admonished the girl, but he didn't seem angry so much as firm.

Lula nodded. "Sorry, sir. I can run and get you some tea, if you'd like."

"Coffee," he grumbled. "Lots of coffee."

"Absolutely, sir." Lula looked between them then. Her face showed her awkward predicament. It wasn't proper to leave Adria just outside Mr. Crayne's bedroom door.

"Go, Lula," Mr. Crayne commanded.

She gave a sideways curtsy that was remarkably out of place and shuffled past Adria, hopping down the stairs speedily. Once she had disappeared, the two of them stared at each other for a long, poignant moment. Adria wanted to breathe, but she couldn't. Perhaps she would end herself this way. Lack of oxygen under the brooding gaze of a drunkard who apparently was fighting to find his sobriety.

"Come." He spun on his heel and reentered the turret room.

Adria hesitated. She had been inside only that one time, which had ended badly. Not only had he stripped to the waist and bared his scars, but Mrs. St. John had taken a switch to her. She'd no desire to repeat the experience.

Mr. Crayne poked his head out of the room. "I said *come.*"

So she did. Adria followed him and then yelped when he reached around her and shut the door firmly, locking it and giving the knob a quick shake to determine it had indeed locked.

"Mr. Crayne, we can't—"

"And where will the scandal be told, Alexandria? And to whom? You and me, alone in a room with a bed? Spread the word far and wide, it will never reach Canada, for there's no one to take it beyond the gates of Foxglove Manor. Besides, our intentions toward each other are far from carousing."

Adria felt herself blush. He was right, of course. His logic reigned, yet Adria couldn't help but notice how her stomach quivered in his presence. He was commanding and strong, while at the same time she noted his hands were trembling.

"You are ill," Adria stated before she could bite her tongue.

Mr. Crayne shot her a glance. "Ill? Not of the sort most would relate to." He waved a finger toward his full decanter. "Pour it out."

"Pardon?" Adria squeaked.

"You heard me. Pour it out before I guzzle it. I've not the strength to."

"But you said we must find the strength," Adria countered.

"You are mine, I will be yours. I spared your life last night. Now"—he shook his finger at the whiskey—"you save mine."

"But won't it . . . ?"

"Make me desperate? Miserable? An ogre who may throw *himself* off the cliff tonight? Very possibly. But do it anyway."

"But—"

"Do it!" Mr. Crayne roared.

Adria flew toward the crystal bottle and snatched it from the dresser. Hurrying to the window, she flung it open and removed the topper, tilting the bottle until the whiskey poured from its neck, falling to the yard below. She noticed Diggery's fox slinking along the tree line. It startled and froze, turning its mangy head toward the disturbance. Apparently, the fox found the whiskey to be of no threat, and she slipped into the underbrush, only the white tip of her tail waving in farewell.

"It's gone." Adria pulled her arm inside, the empty decanter with it. She moved to face him and caught her breath when she realized he'd come up behind her and stood very close now. Staring down, studying her face as if trying to read her thoughts.

"Why?" he asked.

She knew he was referring to the night previous. Why had she stood on the edge of the cliff, her arms outstretched? How did she explain? There was no feasible explanation to the desperation she felt. The emptiness. "I have no acceptable answer," she murmured.

Mr. Crayne rubbed his hand over the back of his neck. She could smell the faint scent of liquor mixed with a ginger spice. It was masculine. Tempting. She recalled the feeling of his arms holding her in the rain. There was strength in them. A strength she craved. Adria backed away a step.

"What weighs so heavily on you that you would sacrifice your life?" He was relentless and took a step toward her.

Adria cowered, clutching the decanter to her chest. She stepped back farther, but her backside met the wall, and her shoulders felt the breeze from the open window. "My father," she choked out. She could trust Mr. Crayne—or so she hoped. But she had little to lose since she'd been willing to lose it all last night. "He is . . . not a kind man." It was a ridiculous understatement. The dark shadow that flickered in Mr. Crayne's eyes verified he comprehended it as such.

"And your father holds control over you even while you're under Mrs. St. John's . . . shall we say, her cold and collected care?"

"My father releases control when he sees fit." Adria spoke the truth because she wasn't exactly sure how to lie to a man like Mr. Crayne.

"He threatened you?" His voice lowered.

"Since I was born," Adria muttered. Her fingers tightened around the bottle.

"He hurt you?"

"Since I was old enough to walk." Adria's eyes teared.

"You've tried it before, haven't you?" He referred to last night again.

Adria nodded.

"He is that brutal that you would face death before you face him?"

Adria swallowed. Her throat tightened with emotion. She gave a slight shrug. "I have meant nothing most of my life, therefore I am nothing. I have already failed, and I've no—"

"Failed at what?" Mr. Crayne crossed his arms over his chest. He hadn't backed away, and his presence so near her was intimidating.

Adria looked away. Failed at being whatever it was her father wanted her to be. Now she was failing at finding his elusive pirated war booty.

"Failed at what?" Mr. Crayne's hand gripped her chin and he turned her head, forcing her to face him.

Adria looked down at her shoes. At his shoes. At the floor. There was a scuff in the wood. A scratch. It should be polished.

"Alexandria?" His fingers were gentle, yet they still tightened on her chin.

Adria lifted her eyes. "My father's shipping company is merely a—portion of what he has excelled in."

"Shipping?" Mr. Crayne furrowed his brow and tilted his head. "He owns ships on the lakes?"

Adria nodded. "Since before I was born. He—used to intercept other ships. Loot them. He built his wealth on the backs of those he stole from."

There was little expression on Mr. Crayne's face now. His fingers trembled and he dropped his hand, hiding it in his pocket. "And you are here because . . ."

Adria bit the inside of her lip, debated with herself briefly, then threw caution to the wind. "During the war, my father had looted property off a ship. Shortly afterward, his own ship was raided and taken from him. He holds Mr. St. John accountable for its whereabouts, although I'm not sure how or if Mr. St. John is even connected to it."

"And he sent you here to recover them?"

Adria nodded.

Mr. Crayne sniffed in disbelief. "A lake pirate too cowardly to do his own hunt for his bounty. He sends his daughter."

"He had to." Adria dropped her gaze again. "I was his shame."

"He is his own shame." Mr. Crayne leaned into Adria. She could feel his eyes urging her to look at him. She did and was immediately held captive by him. "I warned you before, Alexandria, and it still holds true. There is much here at Foxglove that runs deep beneath the surface. It goes far beyond Mr. St. John, extends well into Dr. Miranda, who owned Foxglove during the war and whose daughter, Lucy, was a casualty of all that lies below Foxglove. Your father has sent you to find his bounty, but does he know what else you would be ensnared in if you did so? I think not." Mr. Crayne searched her face. "Or maybe he does." There was a question in his voice. But it wasn't one Adria could answer. "Do you know what it's like to be imprisoned, Alexandria?"

What an odd question, considering that very concept had sent her fleeing to the cliffs last night. Adria nodded, though somehow she felt she underestimated Mr. Crayne's own experiences. He ran a finger down her cheek. His touch burned Adria's skin. She shivered.

"Let me tell you more of what it is like, my dear. Let me tell you of the scars on my back. Once you know that, you will know why it is you who is giving me the will to be whole again. You who inspired me that some still need protecting and not that which I've been placed over. But you. The innocents. Victims of a lost war that I've come to despise with every ounce of my blood. But a war that is not yet over—may never be. So why fight?" He looked out the window as if his eyes could make out the whiskey that had soaked the ground below. "Drowning is a delightful way to assume ignorance, Alexandria. By liquor or by lake. But we must—" he grasped her shoulder and leaned in—"God help me . . ." Mr. Crayne's eyes squeezed shut as if fighting demons, or fighting her, or perhaps fighting the pull of her as Adria fought the pull of him. When he opened his eyes, he seemed more in control of himself. Mr. Crayne ran his finger down the length of her nose. "Plead ignorance, Adria. Ignore your father's quest of greed. Flee. Whatever you must do. But do not dig any deeper within the walls of this place. The ghost of Lucy Miranda the child will seem like a fairy tale with a pleasant ending compared to what else you will uncover if you don't."

27

KAILEY

Riley Bascom had a very direct gaze for a young girl. She watched Kailey but didn't say a word. Her uncle set a glass of water on the coffee table and eased onto the couch next to his niece and across from Kailey. He'd been gracious enough to invite Jude in, but after reassuring herself he was all right in the car, she declined. Jude didn't need to hear this. It would unsettle him. Besides, she could see him from where she sat, through the window. His head bent. Intent on the book in front of him.

"Riley's mother isn't here at the moment. I will be staying with Riley." It was obvious Jason Bascom was staking his authority over Riley, and Kailey nodded.

"Yes, Mr. Bascom."

"Jason," he supplied.

"Jason," Kailey acknowledged. She reached for the water glass and took a nervous sip before setting it back down, noting Jason pushing a coaster toward her. It was white ceramic with ladybugs painted on it. Kailey rested the glass with a *clink* against the coaster. She cleared her throat. Approaching Jason Bascom had been intimidating at best, so how she could be even more nervous now in front of Riley was a mystery.

"Riley, my name is Kailey Gibson."

Riley simply stared at her. She had the same unreadable expression as her uncle.

Kailey continued, "I was wondering if you could . . ." A glance at Jason garnered her a nod of encouragement. "If you could tell me about your experience of a few weeks ago."

A question flickered in Riley's eyes.

"When you were taken," Kailey clarified. There was no mistaking the quick look Riley cast her uncle. She dropped her gaze to her hands and nervously picked at her fingernails. Kailey edged forward on the couch. "Riley, I know this isn't easy. I know . . . I know it feels like no one believes you. But I do."

A fast exchange of looks.

Riley picked at her thumbnail.

"I believe you." Kailey studied Riley. Her blond hair was ombré in its tone and color. Her eyelashes were long. Her face was pale, but that was to be expected considering her recent experience and her father's sudden death. Kailey reached for her glass again, if only to make Riley more at ease with the natural, nonchalant movement. "How many people took you, Riley?"

The young girl stopped picking her nail. She looked up. "Two."

Kailey nodded. "Can you tell me more about them?"

Riley moved closer to her uncle, and Jason placed a reassuring hand on her knee. "They had masks on, so I don't know what they looked like." She reached for the end of her braid and sucked on it. Jason gently pulled it from her hand, and he tipped his head toward Kailey. "It's okay, kiddo. I want to hear this too."

The girl relaxed visibly and leaned into Jason, though her eyes rested on Kailey. "One of the guys was tall. The other guy was like—well, he was sorta small." Riley's voice caught.

Jason squeezed his niece's knee. "Do you think it was a woman?"

"I dunno." Riley shrugged.

"Tell me what happened that day, please?" Kailey urged.

Riley sniffed and wiped at her eye like she might be warding off tears. She shifted and pulled her legs onto the sofa. "I was walking to school. This van pulled up. The guy jumped out and pulled me inside, and they drove away. I was yelling and they told me to shut up." She stopped.

Jason gave Riley a reassuring smile. "It's okay, kiddo."

"I stopped 'cause they had a dog with them, and the guy who was in the back with me said if I screamed, he'd hurt the dog."

Classic child manipulation. Hoping Riley's memories would jog hers, she waited. Riley sniffed, coughed, and then shrugged.

"He asked me a whole bunch of questions. The van stopped out in the woods. They tried to get me to answer their questions." Riley shrugged again.

"What sort of questions, Riley?" Kailey asked. "What did they want to know?"

Riley widened her eyes. "Stuff about the manor. Stuff about—" She cut off her words and looked at Jason.

He leaned toward her. "What is it?"

Riley bit her lip, then twisted her mouth to the side as if trying to decide whether to answer honestly. "I told the police all this."

"I know you did," Jason said, "but your dad was with you, and I wasn't. I'd like to know too."

Riley drew in a heavy sigh. "They asked me stuff about Dad. Like where he kept stuff."

"Where he kept stuff?" Kailey could not relate to any of the conversation.

Riley nodded. "Yeah. Like . . . well, sometimes when he'd go out to Foxglove Manor, he'd bring things back. Once, he brought me a jewelry box he said he found in a room upstairs. And then there was an old book he brought home once too. All kinds of junk is stored upstairs."

"The turret room?" Jason inserted.

Riley nodded. "Yeah."

"What did you tell them?" Kailey asked.

Riley frowned. "I told them he kept stuff all over the place. Dad wasn't picky about it. Sometimes he sold it at the flea market in the summer."

"Were they looking for something specific?" So far, nothing Riley was saying was dredging up any familiar memories.

Riley hesitated. She looked at her uncle. "They asked me about my letter."

"Letter?" Kailey inquired.

Jason nodded. "Riley's class wrote letters to the local paper about historical stuff. They were studying it for their fourth-grade history class."

Intrigued, Kailey tapped her fingers against her jean-clad leg with pent-up energy. "What was in your letter, Riley?"

"The codes." Riley exchanged looks with Jason and then returned to picking at her fingernails.

"Codes?" Kailey prodded.

Riley nodded. "Yeah. Like the ones hidden at Foxglove Manor. Dad and I used to make a game of it to see if we could find them."

"I don't understand." Kailey looked helplessly to Bascom.

He rested a hand on Riley's knee. "They say back during the eighteen hundreds, a previous owner had renovations done to the place. He was a sympathizer for the Confederacy and apparently hid codes within the house. That's where the old legend about the ghost girl guarding secret treasure came from. It's all a lark."

"Did you find these codes?" Kailey addressed Riley, tamping down the excitement that curled in her stomach. Codes. Gibberish. The letters and numbers that made up lines of the ghost girl's face in Jude's sketchbook . . .

Riley shook her head. "No. It was just a game Dad and I played."

A sudden vision assaulted Kailey. It was foggy. She was lying on the rough carpet of the floor of a van. The man was asking her for the code—give them the code—remember the letters and numbers?—they wanted that.

"And you're sure it was a code?" Kailey pressed.

Riley shrugged. "That's what Dad called it. War ciphers."

Kailey reached for the glass of water, suddenly thirsty with a feeling of uneasiness she couldn't identify coursing through her body. "War ciphers?"

Riley nodded. "Civil War."

"Blue and the gray," Jason supplied. "Apparently, the Confederacy used ciphers a lot to disguise communications."

"I'm still confused about the Confederate thing," Kailey admitted. "We're in Michigan. The Upper Peninsula. We're practically in Canada."

Jason laughed. "You're not from Michigan, are you?"

Kailey shook her head. "No, I'm from Wisconsin."

Jason nodded. "Figures. Even if you were born and raised in the UP, you wouldn't claim that it's 'practically Canada.' We're very Michigan around here."

"Still . . ." Kailey was stumped. She took a nervous gulp of water and swallowed. "Wouldn't you mean Union ciphers?"

Riley interrupted. "Dad said they were Confederate. That there was other stuff at Foxglove Manor that was Confederate too. He found some swords once and said they were something like Robert E. Lee would've used. I don't know, but the guys who took me wanted to know if Dad and I had found the codes. They let me go after I told them what I could remember."

"You remembered these codes?" Kailey saw images of Jude's notes with gibberish. Maddie's notebook with letters and numbers in a sequence that matched Jude's.

Riley shook her head. "No. We never found any. Well, once Dad found like a wooden box that had two letters carved into it, but he said they were initials."

"What were they?" Bascom interjected.

Riley shrugged. "A *g*, I think? Maybe a *y* or a *c*? I told them that too. They said they didn't want to hurt a kid, but . . ." Her eyes filled and she swiped at them. "They said they were getting sick of hitting dead ends. The tall guy asked about Lucy." She lifted her index finger and bit at the nail.

"The ghost?" Jason rolled his eyes.

"Yeah." Riley nodded. "They wanted to know if I'd seen her."

"Have you?" Kailey didn't miss the surprised look Jason shot her.

Riley shook her head, her eyes growing wider than they already were. "Ghosts freak me out. No, I haven't seen her. I don't wanna see her! I don't know what they were talking about, but—" This time a sob caught Riley's words, and she cast her uncle a desperate look. "I'm sorry!" she whispered.

Concerned, Jason pulled the girl close to him. He stroked her hair as his eyes met Kailey's over the top of Riley's head.

"Sorry for what, Riley?" Empathy swelled in Kailey. It was so bewildering how, as a victim, one could feel somehow responsible. Like they had done something wrong. Shown a lack of judgment. Even asked for it, somehow.

Jason murmured something that Kailey didn't catch, but it made Riley pull away from him. Tears had soaked her cheeks and part of Jason's shirt. She stared up at him. "They—they said since I didn't know, they'd have to ask Dad."

His brows pulled together, and Jason frowned. "What do you mean, they'd ask your dad?"

Riley drew in a shuddering breath. "I don't know." A helpless look and Mr. Bascom tightened his comforting hold on his niece. "I was scared!" Riley whimpered. "The man was scary. He kept hitting the inside of the van with his hand like he wanted to kill someone."

A memory swept over Kailey in a rush.

A man's fist slamming into the inside wall of the van.

Her scream.

The words *"Maybe your parents know."* Her abductors had referred to her parents too. After they'd—

Kailey surged to her feet, her hand accidentally hitting the glass and sending water flying across the coffee table. Jason jerked back into the couch, pulling Riley with him.

"What the heck!" he snapped, glaring at her.

Kailey fumbled for some way to clean up the water, but she was flustered. "I'm sorry. I'm so sorry." She pulled a tissue from her jeans pocket to wipe up the pool of water, but it soaked through almost instantly.

Jason sent Riley on a mission to retrieve a towel. When the girl had left the room, he snatched the sopping wet tissue from her hand. Kailey froze and her eyes locked with Jason Bascom's. He was steely-eyed and stern. "You said you were abducted. What did Riley say that triggered you?"

He was perceptive. Kailey's breaths came short and fast. "It's just . . ." She didn't want to admit it out loud—not to Jason Bascom, not to anyone. It was too fresh, too startling, too awful. She hoped she was remembering wrong. She hoped the irrationality of it would wear off to a plausible explanation. But there *was* a plausible explanation. It was just one she didn't want to accept.

"What is it, Kailey?" Bascom pressed, releasing her arm.

Kailey realized she was shaking. She lifted her hand as it trembled and pushed the hair back from her face. "I-I remember. They threatened to talk to my parents too."

"So?"

Kailey's knees gave out and she sagged onto the chair. Looking up at Jason Bascom, she managed to drag in a deep breath before expelling it. "So, it was only a week or two after this that *my* parents were killed. In a car accident."

His face paled. "Like my brother died after Riley was taken?"

Kailey nodded. "My kidnapper made some comment about the ghost girl too, and that it was easier to get it out of a kid. But if they couldn't . . ."

Jason closed his eyes. "Then they went after the parents to fill in the missing blanks."

"Yeah." Kailey felt a tear trail down her cheek. "I couldn't recite the codes my brother wrote down. I didn't know until now that that's what they might even be."

"Your brother actually found some?" Doubt etched on the man's

222

face. She could tell Jason Bascom found the legends of treasure and ciphers to be farfetched.

Kailey shook her head. "I don't know. I-I think maybe he did!"

"Did your parents ever see them? See anything at the manor that would support this notion?" Jason asked.

Kailey met his eyes but didn't bother to answer. The vacation at Foxglove Manor was a shrouded memory she'd made herself forget. But now the high-pitched screams coming from her parents' room refreshed themselves in Kailey's memory. The shouts. The door slamming and the sound of shattering glass. Worst of all, she remembered her mother's incessant mumbling. Over and over. As a little girl, Kailey had seen it before. Her mother, the side effects of her addiction. But this time, Kailey's dad had pulled her from the window where she hung half in and half out, her arms bloodied from the broken glass. She'd kept repeating only one word. Over and over and over again. They'd packed and left the next morning, and in three weeks' time, both of Kailey's parents were dead.

Jude's scribbled gibberish.

Her mother's repetitive mumbling.

It all matched Riley's story—different yet very much the same. And all of it had one name in common. The one word Kailey's mom had never stopped muttering.

Lucy. Lucy. Lucy. Lucy.

28

She sensed him before she saw him. Twisting the shot glass between her thumb and forefinger, Kailey shrank into the bar as if
its glossy top would become a portal and she could dive into it.
The cranberry vodka sloshed over the edge of the high ball as Axel
slid onto the stool beside her. She felt his eyes studying her, but
all she could hear was country music over the speakers, smell the
cigarette smoke mixed with liquor, and see the bartender wiping
down the counter.

"How'd you find me?" Kailey ventured, still fingering the glass.
Neither hell nor high water would have her swigging it in front of
him. Axel had come too soon. She didn't even have one down yet.

"You mean, find you both?" He tilted his head toward Jude, who
sat at a corner table, a tall glass of soda in front of him along with
his glossy-paged Egypt book.

Kailey blushed.

"Is that your go-to?" He ignored her question and pointed at
the drink.

Kailey pushed it toward him. Shame? Maybe a little. Relief. Yes,
that too. "Not typically."

Axel took the glass and moved it to the side of him farthest away
from her. "I thought you'd try and pass it off as just juice." There
was teasing in his voice that gave her some relief.

Kailey drummed her fingers on the bar, now unsure of what to
do with her hands, with the pent-up nerves, with the consuming

memories that made her want to rail and scream and at the same time drink herself into oblivion so she could forget again.

The bartender approached. He had a big belly, a black T-shirt, blue jeans, and a full beard. But his eyes were kind. "Need anything?" he asked Axel.

Axel offered a grin. "Coke."

"Captain or Crown?"

"No, just the pop," Axel assured the bartender, who smiled and clicked his tongue.

"Ehhhh, I took you for a whiskey man." The bartender noticed Kailey's cocktail on the opposite side of Axel and winked at Kailey. "Your conscience arrived too soon, eh?"

Kailey mustered a wobbly smile.

The bartender looked between them. "One Coke comin' up. You want somethin' different, honey?"

Kailey nodded. "Water."

"On the rocks?" The bartender winked again.

She smiled. "Sure." He was a cheery poke of sunlight through the dark clouds gathering heavier over life. She'd left the Bascom home to escape, but she couldn't bring herself to return to Foxglove Manor.

A glass of ice water was set in front of her, a lemon perched on the lip. The bartender slid a tall Coke toward Axel and then pounded on the bar top with the palm of his hand and a knowing look in his eye. "Want a refill for your brother?"

Kailey looked over at Jude. His glass was half full. "Probably not. Too much sugar."

"Okay then," the bartender said. "I'll leave you two alone."

"Thanks." Axel nodded, then slipped the paper off his straw.

Kailey took a sip of the water, the chill of it reminding her of the water she'd spilled all over the Bascoms' coffee table.

"Wanna talk about it?" Axel ventured.

"No," she answered truthfully.

"But you came to a bar . . ." His statement felt a bit judgy, and Kailey stiffened.

"It's not like Harbor Towne has a McDonald's or even a coffee shop."

"True." Axel took another sip of his Coke. He glanced around the room. "But we do have three bars and a supper club from 1974."

Kailey gave a small snort.

Axel nudged her arm with his elbow. "I didn't mean you shouldn't have come here. I meant you came here instead of coming home."

Home. Was that what Foxglove Manor was supposed to be? Was it even a home for the residents there? Maddie, haunted by her delusional visits. Raymond, worshiping the losing-her-mind Maddie from afar. Stella and Judy and the other residents, typically holed up watching daytime television. None of them received visitors there. Tracee and Teri were more than their nurses; they were their only family, it seemed. Foxglove Manor was a lonely place. Cold. Empty of hope. Of purpose. And it had stolen far more than it had given. No. Foxglove Manor wasn't home.

"Home died when my parents did." Kailey chugged the last of the ice water and almost welcomed the brain freeze that followed. She squeezed her eyes shut and then slipped from her stool. Tugging a twenty-dollar bill out of her pocket, she set it on the bar. "Here you go." Kailey snagged the attention of the bartender.

He winced. "That's too much, honey."

"Keep the rest as a tip." Kailey didn't have money to throw around, but she didn't want to wait. Didn't want to give Axel time to dig and prod and poke into her business. She needed to get away. To get out. Weaving between the tables, she did just that, aiming for the door as Tim McGraw crooned in the background and the crack of balls displacing on the pool table met her ears.

"Kailey!"

She heard Axel's shout as she pushed the front door open. The evening was fast settling into dusk. Dang it. Jude. She spun on her heel to turn back to the bar and ran into Axel.

"Let me through, please." Kailey tried to sidestep him. Axel moved to block her. She cast him a look of desperation. "I need to get Jude."

"Jude is fine."

"I'm not leaving him alone."

"He's not alone. We're just right outside the door." Axel's expression was firm. Great. She was nose-to-nose with his serious and stern side.

"Running away isn't going to help anything," he stated.

"I know," Kailey muttered, hating that he was right.

"Where'd you go today?"

Like heck was she going to tell him that.

"You went to see Riley Bascom, didn't you?"

She focused on the bar behind him. The neon beer sign hanging in the window. "Maybe."

"You're lucky Jason didn't call the cops on you for harassment."

"I had his permission." She sidestepped Axel, shoved her hands in her coat pockets, and started back toward the bar.

"Did you find what you were looking for?" His words bounced off her back and were the last straw in her emotional weakness. Kailey spun.

"Do you think I'm cuckoo and you're just babysitting me?"

"Kailey." Axel seemed perplexed, as though he didn't understand why the verbal accusations were even flinging from her mouth. His actions had not proven anything but an attempt to support her. Maybe she was spewing out her worst fears and doubts about herself. Maybe it was what she always feared. Her family *had* been dysfunctional at best, and now the imagery of her mom's bloodied arms, leaning out the window like she was going to jump, and screaming the ghost girl's name . . . Yeah. Sane and normal didn't run in her family. To be honest, Jude and his struggle with autism was probably the most normal thing about them.

"Kailey." Axel touched her arm. It was a light touch. Nothing aggressive or even assertive. In fact, she might have been able to process that easier. It was the care in his touch and the expression in his eyes that slayed her. She paused but chose to let her head hang as she stared at the toes of her leather mules. He wasn't going to let her avoid him—avoid *it*. "What do you remember?"

It was a simple question, but it was like kicking an anthill and having them run up your pant legs. She wanted to dance and flail, strike out in anger, swat at the offense, and spare herself. But they would just keep coming. The memories, the fear, the trauma. Like a plague of Revelation proportions. Who needed end times and apocalypse stories when life itself was shrouded in enough pain to make living a questionable activity at best?

She pictured Edgar and Poe. Their furry bodies that she could bury her face in. Breathe in their unique scents. Edgar was sweet, while Poe smelled like firewood. But regardless, they wouldn't ask questions. They would just provide comfort and care and diversion. She needed diversion.

"I need my cats." The words slipped from Kailey's mouth like a random statement that had nothing to do with anything. She curled her lip to avoid the tears. She looked up to the sky and away from Foxglove Manor's handyman, whose worst problem in life was running out of his morning coffee.

"Santa Claus!" Kailey cried.

"What?"

"Santa Claus." Kailey pushed on his shoulder again, to shove him away, to get him to go. "It's my escape word. When a conversation is too much, I Santa-Claus it. My therapist said I could."

"Yeah, well, I think Santa Claus is a cop-out from the real thing." Axel's words dared her. Challenged her.

"No, he's not." It was a stupid argument. She crossed her arms.

"Really, he is. A nativity is more appropriate."

"Oh, well, I can't exactly yell 'Jesus Christ' as an escape word." Kailey sneered.

"Why not?" Axel crossed his own arms, his feet spread apart, ready to challenge her.

"'Cause it'll sound like I'm cursing." Kailey snorted. She wanted to ask if he was dumb. Stupid? But she knew he wasn't. He was manipulating her triggers to make her react, to keep her angst escalating so she would explode. So she would be forced to deal with the fallout of it all. Kailey hated Axel for that, and at the same time she had a strange sense of gratitude.

"Maybe people should yell His name more often," Axel went on. "Like a cry for help, you know?"

Kailey rolled her eyes and blew out a big breath. "I believe in God, if you're implying that I don't."

"I never said that."

"Well, I do," Kailey reaffirmed.

Axel nodded, his arms still crossed.

Kailey eyed him. "But *Jesus* doesn't exactly swoop down from the heavens to make everything okay. You know? And I get annoyed when people think that *praying* is going to help. That *Jesus* is going to just magically fix everything. It's ignorant and—and stupid—and people bring it up at the worst times."

She watched carefully for him to get annoyed. To react. But Axel didn't. Instead, he waited for a car to pass by as they stood outside the bar. When it did, he eyed her for a long moment. So long, the tension built between them. Thick. Wordless. Heavy with feeling. Finally, Axel responded. But Kailey wasn't prepared for it. She wasn't prepared for him to reach for her, nor was she adequately prepared for him to pull her stiff body against his. Her chin rested on his shoulder. He embraced her like she was everything to him— but she knew she wasn't. Axel Pavlov didn't know her that well. He didn't understand who she was. He hadn't seen her scars. The ones deep inside that were still tender and more infected than she wanted to admit. But he didn't whisper Bible verses. He didn't even pray. He didn't respond with an apologetical defense or even try to convince her that somehow God had a plan and it was all going to work out for her good. None of that rolled out of him.

In this moment, Axel just held her. Held her until she felt herself weaken against him. Felt a sob escape. And he held her as the first of many tears fell on his flannel shirt.

29

ADRIA

He was going to tell her. She knew that some sort of an answer to the mystery of who Mr. Crayne was had to be forthcoming. But Adria wasn't expecting the door to the turret room to burst open, Mrs. St. John in the doorway with Lula cowering behind the woman. Mrs. St. John's gaze landed on Adria, the telling key that had unlocked the door dangling from her finger.

"You're a little chit," she said through clenched teeth.

"Enough." Mr. Crayne stepped just in front of Adria, his shoulder shielding her.

"Enough?" Mrs. St. John's white eyebrows winged upward. "I've not even begun yet. You're nothing but a pestilence, Mr. Crayne, you know that already. But you, Miss Fontaine? You are as your father implied in his letter to me. A troubled girl, unstable and prone to very, *very* poor judgment. As evidenced by your presence here. Alone. With Mr. Crayne, in his bedroom, once *again*."

Mr. Crayne didn't move from in front of her. Instead, he held out his left arm as if to hold her behind him.

"Your implications of Alexandria's discretions are abhorrent."

"*Abhorrent?*" Mrs. St. John's eyes sparked. "*You* are abhorrent. You have been since the moment I arrived here at Foxglove Manor, before my husband passed, God rest his soul. A bane to inherit not only this godforsaken place but to inherit *you* as well."

"Then leave." Mr. Crayne's command sliced through the air.

Lula gasped.

Adria couldn't help but reach out and put her hand on Mr. Crayne's back, as if by doing so it might somehow protect him from Mrs. St. John.

"You know very well I cannot do that." Mrs. St. John's voice lowered, instead of the shrill fury that Adria expected.

"Then we are at an impasse. I will not tolerate your berating of Alexandria, nor taking a switch to her as if she were a wayward and deviant child. She is a woman. She shall be treated with respect, even if you are her benefactress."

"She *is* a woman," Mrs. St. John repeated. She tilted her chin upward. "And as such, she should not be in your room. I answer to her father, you know very well that I do."

"And you fear him?" Mr. Crayne raised a brow.

"Loathing does not equate to fear, my dear man."

"Then why take me in?" Adria could stand it no longer, and she stepped out from behind Mr. Crayne. "Why assist my father if you hate him so much?"

"I've never met your father," Mrs. St. John spat. She sniffed and blinked rapidly, aggravated by the direction the conversation was taking. "He was my husband's acquaintance."

"Still, you took me in?" Adria pressed.

Mrs. St. John pressed her lips together tightly, deepening the wrinkles around them. She eyed Adria for a moment before answering. "My husband was indebted to your father. Taking you in wipes free that obligation."

"You are obligated to many, are you not?" Mr. Crayne's question held a touch of ironic humor in it. Almost a taunting. The older woman straightened and elbowed Lula away, as the girl was crowding in too close.

"I am obligated to the memory of my dead husband and my

beloved daughter, Mr. Crayne. I will not besmirch their memories. And you, Mr. Crayne, are not free of obligation yourself. Tread cautiously with your arrogance and your drunkenness. You too are replaceable should they determine it to be necessary."

"Should who determine it?" Adria looked between them. "Who are you speaking of?"

Mr. Crayne stared sideways down his nose at her. His eyes narrowed. "Remember what I said earlier, Alexandria? Leave it be."

"Yes." Mrs. St. John sniffed in derision. "Leave it be." She mocked Mr. Crayne. "We wouldn't want to upset them, now, would we?" She spun on her heel and bumped into Lula. Pushing the girl aside, Mrs. St. John turned to add, "God only knows how appalling it could all become. We know our places, Mr. Crayne, and it is time you teach Miss Fontaine hers. Before it all comes to ruin."

A sweep of her dress and Mrs. St. John exited the turret room. Lula looked between them as if debating whom to follow, but finally she took her blossoming young figure after Mrs. St. John.

Adria could hear Mr. Crayne breathing. Controlled. Heavy. She saw him look in the direction of the empty decanter. He squeezed his eyes shut and rubbed his hand across them. A few beads of sweat had popped out on his forehead.

"I've caused you trouble," Adria ventured, apologizing with her tone if not her words.

Mr. Crayne opened his vivid blue eyes and stared at her. They bore into Adria with a brutal honesty of a man craving what he could not have. Liquor, she assumed. Adria took a hesitant step back. Yes, he wanted liquor.

Mr. Crayne reached up and unbuttoned his shirt. She stared at him, in shock and not a little wonder as he stripped it from his torso, just as he had the night she'd first met him. Only he was not drunk now, nor did she think he was attempting to seduce her. Although, it was all highly inappropriate, and for certain—

"You see?" He turned his back to her. Once again, Adria's eyes caressed the puckered scars. Not in a straight line, but one at his waist and the other spanning the length of his left shoulder to his waist. "This is the cost of war, Alexandria. The cost of pursuing causes that, in the end, are futile and wicked."

"W-what happened?" Adria refused to reach out and touch them. Refused to look away as well.

Mr. Crayne turned, the breadth of his chest exposed. He shrugged back into his shirt. "I was a prisoner of war." His announcement was muffled as he looked down to button his shirt. "Captured by the Union and dumped into hellish circumstances at a prison camp on Lake Erie."

"You fought for the Confederacy?" She couldn't help the squeak of surprise.

Mr. Crayne lifted his eyes momentarily before returning to the middle button on his shirt. "I did."

It was hard to fathom. Alcohol aside, he seemed to be a man of high standards. He didn't fit what she had always imagined a Rebel would be like. Men willing to enslave others. Men defying the nation to build their own. She also hadn't known there was a prison camp on Lake Erie. Her father had never mentioned it in his talk of war, of the Union, of sailing his ship and plundering others.

"I was only seventeen." Mr. Crayne dropped his hands from his shirt. "I didn't know anything other than it was my duty to fight. I spent the bulk of the war in the camp. Cruel. Vile." He pierced her with a stony gaze. "There is no *good* side in war, Alexandria, only the occasional good man. Of which I am not one of them."

"How did you come to be here? Why didn't you return home after the war ended?" Adria asked. She dared to take a step toward him now. His countenance had shifted a bit. He appeared more vulnerable. Lost in memories. Oh, how she knew what it was like to lose oneself in that which you wished you could forget.

Mr. Crayne's eyes darkened. "Returning home when debts are to be paid . . . there was no option given, and I couldn't ask my family to pay them on my behalf. Besides, they believed me to be dead. Resurrecting myself would have encumbered them in a nightmare."

"But how did you come to be at Foxglove Manor? What is it that you and even Mrs. St. John are bound to?"

Mr. Crayne met her step, and Adria drew in a quick breath as he shortened the distance between them. She looked up at him. He was older. By the age he'd indicated during the war, he was twenty years her senior. Yet in his eyes there was camaraderie. Understanding. Longing even, if she were honest.

He threaded his fingers through her hair. "Remember what I said, Alexandria. I would tell you what it was like to be imprisoned. I do that so you do not join me here. The war has not ended, my dear, sweet Alexandria." Mr. Crayne rubbed her skin lightly with his thumb.

She shivered at his touch. Their eyes were locked in a mutual hold fraught with lack of air, a heavy weight between them, drawing them closer until Adria realized she'd placed her palms on his chest. Could feel his warm skin through his shirt.

"It has not ended." Mr. Crayne leaned forward and mumbled against her temple.

Adria closed her eyes.

"And with it comes its many secrets. Secrets men will kill for." He pressed his lips to her forehead, then spoke against it, moving along her skin. "I would not let that happen to my family. I will not let that happen to you."

~

Diggery's fox slunk along the bushes, her patchy fur even more ragged-looking as it collected moisture from the dripping bushes and melted ice patches. Adria pulled her coat tighter around her, also tucking in the ends of the warm scarf that covered her head and neck. She glanced up at the turret window. Mr. Crayne was not to be seen, which was all the better. His cryptic warnings had impacted Adria greatly. Sent her into a frozen state of inactivity for two days before she realized such a decision would only expedite the threat in her sister's letter. Institution. Her father's mission for her. Either direction Adria moved, she was apparently in danger.

She braced herself against a tree for a moment as a wave of nausea swept over her, and something akin to a cold sweat, even though the air was frigid. Exhaustion was setting in and quickly. She'd not been sleeping well. Not since Mrs. St. John had been choked by some unknown assailant, not since she herself had the surreal vision of the dead girl, Lucy Miranda, and certainly she'd not caught up in the afternoons by napping. Mrs. St. John refused to be alone. At all. Even at night, she had taken to having Lula sleep on the settee in her bedroom. As if a teenaged girl would pose a deterrent to any intruder with murder on their mind.

Now, Adria took a few deep breaths and willed herself to stop spinning. She looked through the trees toward the lake, admiring its steely blue color as it reflected the cold, spring sky. She moved her attention toward the stacked stones of Diggery, the foxglove he'd transplanted, and she loosened her grip on the tree. A few questions. That's all she wanted to ask Diggery. And surely Diggery was safe and nonthreatening. She would still be well within the confines of Mr. Crayne's orders to leave things be, while perhaps finding information that might lead her to wherever Mr. St. John had hidden her father's treasure.

The old man with his stooped shoulders crouched several yards ahead of her. The fox nosed her way toward his outstretched hand, snatched the strip of jerky he held out, and scurried away with a beady-eyed glance in Adria's direction.

"He warned me you'd be pesterin' me." Diggery's voice cracked the air. Adria approached him as he staggered to his feet. Wiping his hands on his pants, Diggery eyed her, his cap crooked on his wiry hair. "I ain't got much time for chattin', girlie."

Adria couldn't help but smile at Diggery's attempt at being grouchy. He failed quite miserably, as she could see the hunger in his face for human interaction. He truly did live a solitary life, keeping to himself in the little shed out back of the house.

"How long have you lived here, Diggery?" she asked.

He drew back and mustered a scowl. "Goin' right for the kill, ain't ya? No niceties from you, I see."

Adria bit back another smile. She didn't want him to think she was laughing at him.

Diggery shuffled toward the foxgloves and a rake that lay in the lawn. "I've been here since way before you were born. Thought I told ya that already."

Adria nodded. "Yes, but I was wondering if you could tell me about Mr. St. John?"

Diggery looked honestly perplexed. "Mr. St. John? What's to know about him?"

Adria carefully chose her words. "Did he—well, what did he do for a living? Seeing as he lived this far north and all."

Diggery waved her off and bent to retrieve his rake. "Bah. What difference does that make to a gal like you?"

Adria braced herself against the chill of a gust of wind. "Did he own a ship?"

"Own a ship?" Diggery's voice rose in surprise. "What're you gettin' at?"

"I was just wondering if he was—in shipping. Like my father." She was treading on thin ice. Adria held her breath.

Diggery eyed her before turning his attention to the rake and attacking the dead leaves that had collected against the side of the manor. "Foxglove is on the lake, girlie. Everything up here is around shipping." It didn't answer her question. Not directly. Adria waited as Diggery pulled back a line of wet, brown leaves. He huffed for a second, then leaned on the rake to look at her. "Mr. St. John was a businessman. That's all I know 'bout that. I mind my own self and I do a good job at it. Seems like others need to learn that lesson."

Adria didn't miss his implication. "That gentleman who visited Mrs. St. John the other day. He knew her husband too."

"Sure," Diggery responded. "So's the reverend in Harbor Towne, and so's some congressman outta Lansing, and so forth. What're you gettin' at? That Mr. St. John *knew* people? Important people?"

She was bumbling the line of questioning. It was getting her nowhere with Diggery. How did she come right out and ask what she really wanted to know? Had Mr. St. John smuggled goods like her father? If so, where did he hide them? And assuming Diggery knew that, could he take her to them so she could tell her father she'd found them and be released from the imminent threat of him?

Diggery was watching her. He tipped his head to the side and clicked his tongue. "You remind me of Lucy."

"Lucy Miranda?" Startled, Adria heard the squeak in her voice.

"Aye." Diggery returned to raking but spoke over his shoulder. "'Course, she was a little thing compared to you. I was a lot younger then too. Twenty years ago. My sixties were a lot kinder than my eighties, what with this rheumatism and all."

Adria shifted her weight onto her other foot and waited. She'd not put the thought together that Diggery would have known the dead girl. It was common sense, really, just not something she'd paused to consider. "How did she die?" Adria asked instinctively.

Diggery stilled, his hands gripping the wooden handle on the rake. He stared at the ground and his voice lowered. "Ohhhh, you'd best not be askin' those sorts of questions. Dr. Miranda did all he could to save his girl, that's all you need to know."

"Is that why Dr. Miranda sold Foxglove Manor to Mr. St. John? Because Lucy had died?"

Diggery hefted a deep breath. "Miranda invested in this place. It was all run down when he got it. The man worked day in and day out, like a man obsessed, to restore it. Put in new molding, new floors and windows."

"Was he rich?" Adria asked.

Diggery gave her a sharp look. "What's it matter where the money came from? Fact is, this place was his world, and little Lucy was the princess of his castle. Nothin' mattered to the man after she passed on. It all was worthless. All of it."

"All of what?" Adria was afraid to ask for fear Diggery would stop speaking. But he rewarded her persistence with a sharp look.

"Foxglove Manor, the . . ." Diggery cleared his throat, and the tone of his voice shifted. "But that's all in the past now. War's over and done with. Nothin' left to remember there but a whole lotta heartbreak."

"For a place so far removed from where the battles actually took place, it feels like the war touched Foxglove Manor more than one would assume." Adria waited, hopeful her words were bait enough to get a further response from Diggery.

They were.

He laughed. A cackle really. Followed by a cough. Then he returned to raking the wet, moldy leaves. "You have no idea. It's a code that can't be cracked, this place, Foxglove Manor. But with Mr. Crayne guarding it all, it also won't be cracked. He won't let it. *Can't* let it."

"What do you mean?" She was breathless.

Diggery looked at her, a sternness in his eyes. "Truth is, you're asking about Mr. St. John when you should really want to know about Mr. Crayne. *He's* the guardian of Foxglove Manor, and he's the one to pass through if you ever want to know its secrets. Not me. Not Mrs. St. John. We're just pawns on a chessboard. But Mr. Crayne, he's been the knight since the day we arrived here. Guarding. Vigilant. Though he's a sorry excuse now. He started out with ambition—he knew he owed—well, a decade of drink can ruin the best of men."

"Who's the king?" Adria asked softly.

"The king of this chessboard?" Diggery clicked his tongue again. "Let's just say the Confederacy ain't dead, missy. Ain't dead, and ain't poor neither. But I'm keepin' my mouth shut. I already said more than I should, and you know me. I ain't one to talk."

30

A hand pressed against her skin. Cold. Raising the bumps on Adria's arms even before she opened her eyes. Her bedroom was dark, the windows shuttered because of the storm outside. She felt a weight on her chest, pressing down, and then the sensation of her blanket being pulled down her body. Slowly being removed. She watched it glide over her legs and fall to the floor. No one was there. Adria couldn't move. Terror seeped into her marrow, and she opened her mouth to scream, but there was no voice. The presence in the room had stolen that too.

A movement to her left made Adria shift her eyes toward it. A shadow fluttered past, then dissipated. Then, with no explanation, her bedroom door slowly began to open, bringing with it a complimentary drawn-out creak that chilled whatever warmth was left from Adria's body. She tried to move and found the weight had lifted. Petrified but drawn by something uncontrollable, Adria followed, her bare feet padding on the floor until she reached the doorway.

Lucy stood in the hall. Her cavernous eyes, gaunt face, and white skin pasty in the darkness.

"Help me," she whispered. A whisper that curdled Adria's insides. Adria shook her head, fighting to find her voice.

"L-lucy?"

The little girl turned suddenly. "Find the gold!"

Adria followed her stare and then looked back.

Lucy had vanished.

A sharp pain clutched at Adria's chest. She clawed at it as she lost her balance, her body careening to the floor. The pain spread down her arms, and she curled her knees up to her chest, moaning. Her foot connected with a side table that graced the hallway for decorative purposes, and a porcelain figurine fell from it, shattering when it hit the floor.

Pounding from the stairs vibrated on the floorboards. Within seconds, Adria heard Lula's shriek, Mrs. St. John's outraged yet concerned cry, and felt the arms of Mr. Crayne sweeping her from the floor. Desperate, Adria tried to open her arms. They were heavy, and it hurt to speak.

"Lucy."

"Shh," Mr. Crayne muttered.

"I saw her!" Adria cried.

Mr. Crayne laid her on her bed. Lula discovered the blanket on the floor, and as Mr. Crayne settled the sheet over Adria, Lula rearranged the cover.

"We must do something!" Lula cried, her voice watery.

"She'll be fine. She's delusional. Her father said this might happen," Mrs. St. John's vociferous tone interrupted.

Mr. Crayne leaned over Adria. She could smell the faint scent of whiskey on his breath. Perhaps he'd not been successful in tonight's battle. But she hardly cared. The pain in her chest eased, but the room spun. Circles. She grabbed for Mr. Crayne's hand, and when she found it, Adria refused to release it.

"The gold." Adria squeezed his hand and demanded his attention. He gave it to her. Adria felt some of her wits returning. "She said to find the gold."

Mr. Crayne looked confused as he shook his head. "I don't know what you're talking about."

"See? Nonsense. I will write to her father in the morning." Mrs. St. John hurried from the room.

Lula wrung her hands, yet Adria ignored the girl. "Lucy said to find the gold. I have to. I have to find it. I have to find what Mr. St. John stole from my father. I need to find . . . What is it?" She was rambling. She could hear herself but couldn't stop talking. "What are you guarding here at Foxglove that is so important?" She was crying. She could feel the tears on her face.

"Lula, go. Fetch some whiskey."

"Sir?"

"We need to calm Alexandria. It's the only way I know how."

"Yes, sir." Lula's feet pounded on the floor as she ran without grace from the room.

Mr. Crayne leaned over Adria. She could see his eyes. See the concern in them, and the wariness. "Alexandria, there is no ghost. No gold."

"There is!" she insisted. He had to believe her.

"Let it be." Mr. Crayne reached out and smoothed her hair back from her head. He winced as though he was fighting wooziness himself. Yes. He had been imbibing. Oh, the desperation of a soul thwarted.

"I can't let it be." Adria's eyes released more tears. "My father— he'll send me to an institution. Mr. Crayne, he'll say that I'm insane!" Adria clawed the front of Mr. Crayne's shirt. "I can't be sent away again. I just want to be free of him. It's why I tried to . . . to meet God face-to-face. I have to find his gold. You have to tell me where it is!"

Mr. Crayne palmed her mouth, shushing her as Lula skidded back into the room. She thrust a bottle and a tumbler at Mr. Crayne.

"Leave us," he ordered.

"But, sir, I—"

"Go."

"Yes, sir." Lula hurried away.

Mr. Crayne poured some whiskey into the glass and helped brace Adria with an arm behind her shoulders. "Drink. Just a small sip. It will burn, but it will soothe as well."

She did. Sputtered. Gagged. The liquid went down and left a hot trail in her throat. "H-how . . . ?"

"One gets used to it." He offered a wry smile. "Unfortunately." Mr. Crayne eyed it and then set the remainder on the bedside table. He grew serious. "Alexandria, I beg you to listen to what I've told you and stop interfering."

Adria looked away.

Mr. Crayne turned her face back to his. "I cannot let you. I cannot let you look for it."

Adria twisted from his grasp. "I have to. You shared your own prison story, but this is mine. You said you would help me fight. Fight for purpose. But how can I find that when I'm shackled to a man who cares nothing for me and only for his own greed?"

The resolve on Mr. Crayne's face wavered.

Adria knew he was questioning whether she meant her father or him. She found her senses clearing, the pain in her chest dulling to a deep ache. "Who are you really, Mr. Crayne? What is Foxglove Manor to you? What is it you guard, and why do you remain here so long after your freedom from prison was attained?"

Mr. Crayne sat back on the bed and raked his hands through his black hair, ruffled already from carrying her to bed and tending to her. He was tormented. She could see it in the way his shoulders were stiff and strained. His jaw was locked with a knotted muscle in it as if he never unclenched his teeth. Mr. Crayne reached for the tumbler of whiskey, but Adria grasped his wrist.

"No." It came out firmer than she'd intended.

Mr. Crayne dropped his gaze to her. There was misery in it. Entrapment. Even a hopelessness that Adria knew all too well.

"No whiskey. Your name, Mr. Crayne. Tell me your name. Who you are. Help me find freedom, and in finding mine, perhaps you will find yours as well?"

Mr. Crayne lowered his hand and rested his palm against her cheek. "My name is Phineas Crayne." He leaned down to whisper in her ear, "I am the guardian of Foxglove Manor. I guard the treasures that pass through its doors. I watch for trespassers. I hold fast to its premises so that the men I owe my escape to can continue to work underground. If I do not do this for them . . ." His voice broke. His breath was hot in her ear. "They will kill me, or worse, my family. I've a sister—if she's still alive—and a mother who for certain must have passed by now. And while you flirt with death, I have yet to experience life, and I will not be cheated of it, nor will I cheat my family of it."

"Who are these men?" Adria whispered back, sensing the weight of Mr. Crayne—Phineas—as he leaned into her.

He turned his head, his blue eyes blazing in the lamplight. "They are dangerous, purposeful, and powerful. Mr. St. John stepped out of place, he is dead, is he not? If your father stole from them and they retrieved it, they will not be intimidated by a small woman trying to steal it again on behalf of her father. Their gold is their gold."

"It *is* gold!" Adria breathed.

"Confederate gold." Phineas glanced over his shoulder as though someone were watching—listening. "The South had to send its riches somewhere. They smuggled them north—who would think to look here? The conspiracy runs deep, Alexandria. Your father got in their way, and now you have as well."

"And where is it? The gold?"

Phineas clenched his jaw again and scowled. "A network that runs through the Great Lakes and into Canada. It started during the war and continues even now. The battle did not end with Gettysburg. The battle did not end at all. In the shadows of that, Alexandria, the precious gold of which you speak becomes minuscule in importance."

31

KAILEY

The stairs creaked beneath their weight as they climbed. Teri hung back at the bottom of the stairs leading to the turret section of Foxglove Manor.

"Watch your step," she called after them.

"We got it." Axel's assurance was confident. Kailey wasn't so sure as she followed him, noting the way the stairs sagged beneath their weight. She lagged and looked down at Teri, who still watched them with wide, interested eyes.

"You said Riley's dad came here sometimes, didn't you?"

Teri nodded. "Sure he did. But it's been quite a while. After we got settled and established as the resident home, he didn't come around as often."

"And Mr. Bascom didn't really have much to do with the running of Foxglove?" Kailey waited as Teri drummed her fingers on the wall. The director of the resident home and the head nurse shook her head.

"There's a board of directors that manages it. I report to them. Mr. Bascom was, for all sakes and purposes, more of an investor. An investor who owned the property."

Axel had stopped on the stairway, his headlamp on, casting a swath of light ahead of them. Now he turned, and for a moment the light blinded Kailey. She held up a hand.

"Sorry," Axel acknowledged, lifting his chin to divert the ray. "I was just going to add that Mr. Bascom came here a few months ago. That was the last time I saw him. In fact, he was here with his brother, Jason."

"I don't remember that," Teri admitted.

"You wouldn't," Axel assured her. "They didn't even come inside. We chatted for a bit, but they were going to go out on the ice and explore the caves."

"Caves?" Kailey didn't particularly like her precarious pose on the antique stairs that provided no reassurance they were stable. But the conversation had thwarted their exploration, and the information at hand seemed potentially important.

"Lake caves," Axel informed her. "They're carved by the lake into the cliff. When you go down on the shore and walk a ways, you can see them. In the spring, when the ice melts, kayakers love to explore them. Sometimes the water is high and the cave ceilings are low enough where you want to be sure you're wearing a helmet. I've seen kayakers bash their heads into the ceiling when a wave pushes their kayak. Helmets are a must."

"But Mr. Bascom and Jason weren't kayaking?" Kailey confirmed.

"Nope." Axel swung his head back toward the top of the stairs. "The lake was pure ice when they were here. You could walk out and explore on foot. It's pretty cool."

Kailey couldn't see any reason to continue the line of conversation. Aside from nature's work of art, the lake caves weren't going to help solve the mystery of Foxglove Manor. Axel took her silence as indication to move forward, so he did, reaching the landing at the top of the stairs.

"You guys have fun," Teri called after them, and then they were alone.

Axel swung his head right and left. There was a small room to the right, a door hanging off its bottom hinge. Another room leading into the turret was to the left.

"Well? Left or right room?" he asked Kailey.

She ran her damp palms down her jeans and then reached back to tighten her low ponytail. "Right." For some reason, the turret room seemed intimidating.

Axel moved right and swiped at a cobweb that hung from the ceiling. "Smells musty up here."

"Mm-hmm," Kailey agreed. Their footsteps echoed in the empty space. Axel disappeared through the doorway, and Kailey followed. He swung his head from left to right, the headlamp helping illuminate the room, even though a window at the far side let in the daylight. It was opposite the lake and looked out into the woods.

Axel neared it and peered out the fogged windowpanes. "So, you said Riley and her dad would hunt for ciphers here in Foxglove Manor?"

"That's what she said." Kailey wandered to the wall on the left that rose and met with the sloping roofline. Old wallpaper had peeled mostly off, but she pushed back a fragile, curled section and noted the smattering of wildflowers on it. Wildflowers in hues of pinks and lavenders and dots of pale yellow made more yellow with age. "Riley said Mr. Bascom believed them to be Confederate ciphers."

Axel rubbed the window with his sleeve, trying to clear it. "And your brother had ciphers written down too?"

Kailey let the wallpaper roll back into itself. "Well, that's what I'm wondering now. I mean, he had lines of letters and numbers. They never made much sense to me. But now—"

"Now you're recalling things?" Axel straightened from his bend to look out the window. He watched her carefully.

Kailey caught Axel's expectant stare, and she turned quickly and exited the room. Axel followed. She hurried toward the turret room and pushed on the door. It opened with all the creepy squeaks of old hinges one would expect in a spooky manor. The room was much brighter than the other. A window spanned the far wall. An old bed frame with no mattress was pushed against a wall, its antique headboard warped and sun-faded. There was a small fireplace in the corner, its firebox empty. The chimney rose to the roofline, which wasn't much more than seven or eight feet from the floor.

"Have you ever wondered why God lets things happen?" She knew her question was a diversion from Axel's.

Axel didn't answer right away. She saw the light from his headlamp dissipate as he clicked it off. They didn't need it in this room. It was bright. The lake outside the window reflected the sunlight and cast its blue hues through the room like a wash of cool color.

"You mean bad things?" Axel assumed correctly.

Kailey nodded, turning to stare out a window. She heard his footsteps behind her as he walked the border of the empty turret room.

"Sure I do. I think anyone would. It's a valid question."

"With no satisfactory answer," Kailey concluded.

"Well, not one people typically respond well to. There's the whole 'you're not a robot and God isn't going to control all circumstances because of free will' argument. And then others say we're predestined for what happens and it's all part of a greater plan. One way, God leaves us free to choose and we screw it up, and the other is equally as hard to reconcile, when you figure God literally allows for the bad things that are coming and moves aside to let them happen."

"And then we're told to have faith." Kailey bit down hard, frustration roiling inside of her. "We're supposed to trust God isn't the cranky old guy in the clouds, but some huggable Jesus we're taught about in Sunday school."

"You sound bitter," Axel observed. He walked toward the small fireplace, allowing Kailey her space.

Kailey followed. "Not bitter. Confused, maybe? Bugged by it?"

He smiled. "It's okay. If we aren't allowed to ask the tough questions, then faith is pretty much voided."

"I guess." She shrugged. It didn't feel good tiptoeing around the memories that were becoming clearer since her conversation with Riley. The window in the turret room revived them even more. Granted, it wasn't this room in which her mother had slammed her arms through the window, yet all the windows of the manor were similar in size and shape.

Axel didn't say anything. He didn't prod or prompt her. Instead, he ran his hand along the molding that split the wall, paying attention to the craftsmanship beneath the layers of dust. The oval firebox of the fireplace was surrounded by a surprisingly ornate trim and mantel for what must have been more of an attic room back in the day.

Kailey watched him and hugged her arms around herself. What they were looking for here was a mystery, as much so as Foxglove Manor itself. Ciphers, ghosts, abductions . . . she looked back out the window. The waves rolled toward her like persistent memories, and the water wasn't gray or murky, but clear. "It was the middle of the night," she admitted softly, even as Axel ran his hand along the fireplace to brush off years of dust and cobwebs. "I woke up to screaming. When I came out of the room, Jude was there, and he took my hand. He never touches me. Never. This was the only time I can ever recall—" Kailey's voice hitched. She swallowed. "Anyway, he tried to pull me back, but . . . I was a curious kid, and my mom was screaming."

Axel's sigh was the only response.

"My dad was dragging my mom back from the window. She'd broken it with her hands or something. She was all cut up and bloody. I started crying. I remember my dad yelling at me to shut up, and Jude tugging on me. Jude was a teenager then, but he was also a kid. I mean, he has autism, so it wasn't like he could reason with me. Jude kept repeating 'Come, Kay-Kay,' but even at five I couldn't run away. Later, my dad said my mom had been sick—it was what he always said when she was strung out. I figured that out when I got older. You know"—Kailey looked over her shoulder and gave Axel an apologetic smile—"a kid doesn't understand her mom was high until she experiences it for herself years later. It's like all the pieces fall into place. An *aha* moment."

She waited for a look of judgment after her sideways admission to having dabbled with narcotics. Axel remained focused on the mantel. Annoyingly so. For a hot minute, Kailey wished he'd cluck his tongue and shake his head. Then she could berate herself for being stupid like her parents, and she could be angry enough at him to shut down completely and walk away. When Axel didn't oblige, Kailey returned her attention to the lake.

"The next morning, my dad packed us up in the minivan and we left Foxglove Manor behind. But when we were in the car on the way home, I remember Jude writing line after line of gobble-dygook."

"The letters and numbers," Axel concluded for her.

Kailey nodded. "Days later, I'd been abducted and returned, and my parents were killed in a car accident my mom caused. At least that's what we assumed it was."

"You don't think it was your mom's fault?" Axel's question was honest.

Kailey played with the buttons on her cotton shirt. "I don't know. I mean, I'm not sure Mr. Bascom committed suicide either. But why go after kids? Me and now Riley? Why not confront the parents right away?"

"Kids are easier. More pliable and chatty."

Kailey could see Axel's point. "Maybe."

"Was there anything else you remember?" Axel knelt in front of the firebox and reached inside and up the chimney as if feeling for something.

"My mom," Kailey answered, "she kept saying *Lucy* over and over again. And then . . ." She lifted her pinky finger to her teeth and started chewing on its fingernail.

"And then what?" Axel urged, his knuckles rapping along the back bricks of the firebox.

Kailey squeezed her eyes shut, against the memory, but doing so made the mental imagery more vivid. She opened them.

"After my dad pulled my mom from the window, she kept trying to crawl back toward it. She was crying for Lucy, and at one point she turned, and her eyes were so wide—so vacant—it was almost like someone was controlling her. I'm sure it was the drugs, it had to be. She'd done stuff like that before at home . . . but . . ." Kailey swallowed. "But my mom just wheezed out the most creepy, eerie phrase I'd ever heard as a kid—and even now."

"What was it?" Axel turned from his crouch at the fireplace to give her his full attention.

"She said, 'We're all going to die. They'll come. They'll kill us. We're trespassers.'"

"Trespassers?" Axel's brows rose.

Kailey could see he was disturbed. She nodded. "It's why we left the next morning. Mom thought Lucy was going to kill us and . . ." Kailey paused, collected herself, then finished through clenched teeth. "The only legible word Jude kept writing that day on the way home was *death*. He wrote *death*, Axel, and then it all came true."

Kailey huddled in the corner of the turret room, her knees pulled up to her chest and her arms wrapped around her legs. Axel was still poking around the fireplace with a weird sort of obsessive commitment. Whatever she'd said in the retelling of her childhood memory, it had plastered a grave look on Axel's face. He seemed more determined than ever to find something, anything, to substantiate the story and the claims that didn't quite intersect.

"Hey, Kailey?" Tracee's voice called up the stairs, and Kailey startled.

"Yeah?" Kailey shouted back.

"Jude wants to come up, I think. He's down here trying to tell me something. Can he come?"

Kailey exchanged looks with Axel, who nodded, and she hollered her permission back. The stairs outside the turret room creaked and moaned as Jude made his way up. He entered the room, eyes wide with curiosity.

"What's up, buddy?" Kailey feigned happiness as she pushed herself off from the floor.

Jude made some motions with his hands.

"Sorry. I thought you were having fun coloring with Maddie." She had left him downstairs, and in Jude's way he was scolding her for abandoning him for so long. He ignored her, focusing instead on Axel. Jude moved toward the fireplace, tipping his head to the side.

"What do you see?" Axel moved aside as Jude approached.

Kailey waited, curious for Jude's reaction and why Axel was even asking.

Jude bent to study the wood surround, and then he too ducked his head into the firebox, as Axel had before.

"Tee." Jude ran his fingers across the scrollwork.

"What does he mean?" Axel questioned.

Kailey approached, doing her own study of the wood scrollwork now. "He's saying *ten*."

"Ten?" Axel frowned.

"Yeah." Kailey concentrated on the carved wood. It was dull, unpolished, but Axel had brushed off the majority of the dust. She ran her fingers across it just as Jude had. He smiled at her. A toothy grin as though she too had discovered whatever it was that he saw.

"Tee." He nodded vehemently.

"Ten what?" Kailey inquired.

Jude dropped to his knees and peered into the firebox. He studied the bricks for a moment, darkened to a coal-black from years of use. "Rrrr," he slurred. Jude looked at Axel as though hoping he might understand. "Rrrr."

"*R*?" Axel bent in and then glanced up at Kailey. "There's an *r* in the brick."

Kailey squeezed in next to them, careful to avoid contact with her brother. "Like a masonry mark?"

"Yeah, but why an *r*?" Axel brushed his hand over the bricks. As he did, his palm blackened from soot. "There's an *e* too."

"And another brick with an *r*," Kailey added. She reached in to brush away creosote from another brick, and it moved beneath her pressure. A grating sound of clay scraping against clay and the brick shifted in its position. "Whoa!"

"Hold up," Axel commanded in urgency. "That one has a *v* on it."

"Tee!" Jude insisted.

"Ten? Why ten?" Kailey was more entranced by the brick that moved. There was a darkness behind it. Like a hollow space. But Jude pushed to his feet and banged his palm on the woodwork again.

"Tee!"

"Ten." Axel stood next to him and leaned into the wood. "Oh, you've got to be kidding me!"

"What?" Kailey wiggled the brick back and forth.

"Your brother has eagle eyes! There are ten scroll folds on the left side of the mantel's top corner."

"So?" Kailey could tell her voice was muffled as she finally got her hand around the brick.

"So, the other three corners, their scrolls only have nine."

"A craftsman's mistake?" Kailey offered.

"Tee." Jude was less agitated now that Axel seemed to identify what he'd been trying to communicate.

"Iiiiiii don't think so." There was excitement in Axel's voice. "What are some of the numbers and letters in the gibberish you said Jude writes—and that you saw in Maddie's notebook?"

Kailey refrained from yanking the brick out with impatient curiosity. She looked up at Axel, then at Jude. "Ummm . . . oh!" She froze as realization dawned. "Axel, there *is* a ten in it. A section of it is ten, *r, e, r, v.*"

"Tee r-e-r-v!" Jude exclaimed and clapped his hands together. That Axel and Kailey had understood finally made him happy. He did a little foot-to-foot hop in a dance.

Kailey smiled but couldn't dispel the regret. She met Axel's confused face. "I don't know what it means."

"But it's code." Axel sounded amazed. "Your brother found the cipher, Kailey. He sees what others don't. It's here, in the house. Literally *in* the house!"

Kailey thrust herself back into the firebox. This time she tugged the brick and it fell out with the force of her pull. She leaned in to peer behind it, balancing her weight with her palm pressed against the remaining bricks at the back of the firebox. There was a scraping sound, and Kailey's weight shifted.

"Axel!" she cried as the back of the firebox moved as if on hinges.

Axel caught her before she fell forward. The opening wasn't large. Not much more than the size of the chimney diameter. But it was large enough to squeeze through.

"Kailey, just wait."

"There's a tunnel!" Her voice echoed into the darkness. She felt Axel's hand gripping the waistband of her jeans as if she were going to fall into an abyss. Holding her arm back behind her, she waggled her fingers. "Your headlamp. I need it!"

"It might not be safe. Let me go." Axel's voice was muffled.

"Oh, heck no!" Kailey laughed and wanted to cry for some strange reason. She felt Axel put the headlamp in her hand and drew it forward, clicking the button. Light flooded the opening and the short tunnel. Kailey stilled. Staring. And then she did the only thing she could think of to do. She screamed.

32

"A rat?" Tracee shivered. "There's a secret tunnel and a rat in the turret room fireplace," she concluded.

Kailey nodded, wiping her hands up and down her jeans, leaving behind traces of black ash.

Axel held his hands up as though the act itself would calm them all. Kailey knew her scream would have awakened the dead. But it had been a rat. A beady-eyed rodent scurrying away a few feet until it disappeared down a chute.

"Where did the tunnel go? It's a turret. The architecture doesn't support the idea of a tunnel jutting out from the fireplace!" Teri sagged onto a sofa in bewilderment.

Kailey regretted screaming to the point of terrifying the entire household. She was lucky Stella hadn't had a stroke. She glanced over at Maddie and Raymond. Maddie seemed checked out, but Raymond's eyes were alive. Judy wasn't far from Stella's side, and she too was leaning forward in elderly anticipation.

"It's a metal ladder," Axel explained cautiously. "It goes down the inside of the turret. A man could barely squeeze down it. I could fit, but—"

"You're claustrophobic?" Raymond barked.

Axel looked irritated. "A little. But the metal is rusted. It may not be safe."

"I'd say this is a legit treasure hunt. But secret ladders to other places in the house"—Tracee stood in the middle of the front room, her arms crossed over her lime-green scrubs—"creeps me out."

Raymond grunted from his wheelchair, and Poe opened an eye from his place on the man's lap and then closed it.

"So, what are we supposed to do?" Teri raised a dark eyebrow, her short hair curling around her ears.

Kailey exchanged glances with Axel, who blew a huge breath from his lips.

"Heck if I know."

Jude was sitting crisscross-applesauce on the floor, sketching. Kailey glanced down. It was the gibberish in minuscule letters and numbers, outlining a perfect replica of the fireplace in the turret room.

Raymond groused again. "Find the treasure, free the ghost, get the girl."

"Get the girl?" Kailey scrunched her face.

Raymond's knowing stare ping-ponged between her and Axel. "Get the girl. As in, he ain't gonna make his move until you get all this other stuff out of the way."

Axel cleared his throat, mimicking Tracee's stance with crossed arms. He looked down at the toes of his work boots.

Kailey frowned. A snicker erupted beside her, and she looked down at Maddie, who sat in her chair, an innocent expression on her face.

"Ghosts and romance mix better than you might think, Raymond." Maddie's eyes twinkled. Kailey would have noticed how tired the old woman appeared, but for the moment, Maddie's night terrors took a back seat to Kailey's need for self-preservation.

"So we're all on the same page, then?" She diverted their attention to the task at hand. "We need to figure this out?"

"Didn't we already?" Teri interrupted. "Jude already has this supposed cipher." She pointed down at his sketching.

Tracee interjected, "How do you know that's the whole of it? And how do you find out what it means?"

Teri nodded in understanding, then recapped like any good director would. "We're going on the assumption that there's hidden ciphers in the manor. We need to see if there's more of them. Assuming they mean something, we then need to crack the code, which hypothetically will lead us to whatever it is that Riley's abductors wanted to find?"

Kailey exchanged a quick look with Axel. They'd not mentioned her own childhood experiences here. The threat of death. Lucy and Kailey's mother.

Axel jammed his hands into his pants pockets and looked away.

"Yes." Kailey nodded. "It's apparent the stories of this place—at least some of them—have merit. But if there *are* more hidden codes around Foxglove than what Jude has, then we need to find them and help put an end to this."

It might flush out the abductors or even expose the reasons for Riley and her own parents' deaths. Kailey didn't add that. Instead, she watched Maddie to see if the elderly soul would even mention the string of strange letters and numbers in her journal. She didn't. Memory loss was an awful thing, and Kailey had the sinking sensation that Alzheimer's was not going to be their friend when trying to uncover where Maddie had even gotten the gibberish that was so much like Jude's from years before.

"Should we get the others involved?" Raymond referred to the other residents not already present and startled into awareness by Kailey's screams. His stubby fingers dove into Poe's white, long fur.

"No," Teri answered before Kailey could. "No, I don't want them upset." She tipped her head toward Maddie. "I wouldn't upset you either, Maddie, except—"

"I know. I inserted myself." Maddie grimaced. "You all think my mind is losing ground faster than a horse in the Kentucky Derby. But those dreams are so real. I *see* her. That girl. I just know that . . ." Her voice wavered, became less confident. "Well, I know that it's not all right."

"'Course not!" Raymond said. "So, we need to figure this out so you can rest easy."

Kailey hid a soft smile. The man was so protective of Maddie. Kailey doubted Maddie had any idea that Raymond was sucker-punched in love with her, and Kailey doubted Raymond would ever do much about it besides just being there.

Being there.

Sometimes being there was the most romantic thing a guy could do.

The thought brought Kailey's head up, and she looked at Axel. He was looking back at her, a steady confidence in his eyes. He raised his brows as if to ask her what was up. Kailey looked away. Raymond's insinuations had gotten into her head.

Tracee clicked her tongue. "Well! I'll take care of the residents, minus you two." She waved her hand at Raymond and Maddie. "They are all yours!" A smile and wink were shot in Kailey's direction. "That should free up you treasure hunters, and I'll see if I can't avoid a run-in with the infamous Lucy while you're all poking noses around here, stirring up dead spirits."

Teri laughed musically and patted Tracee's arm. "Thanks. And I didn't get the evening medications measured out yet either."

"No worries. I've got it." Tracee gave them all a one-handed wave and went off on her responsible way.

Kailey jumped when Raymond clapped his hands. So did Poe, and the cat leapt from Raymond's lap and streaked across the room under a side table.

"Let's get movin'." Raymond pushed himself up out of the chair and reached for his cane. "Codes. Where we gonna look for codes?"

Kailey finally spoke. "I think we should take Jude with us. He's the one who notices the architecture anomalies."

"Architecture?" Maddie's voice quavered. She frowned. "Like the house?"

"Yes. What is it?" Kailey leaned forward.

Maddie curled her hand around her stuffed lion, and a swath of confusion fluttered across her face. "My Jim used to build houses. He was such an artistic boy."

Teri rolled her lips together and gave a quick shake of her head to Kailey. It was a *don't correct her* look. Let the woman believe she had a son named Jim. "I'll stay with Maddie. You all go on and hunt away. We'll start in this room and just see what we see."

Kailey wanted to protest. She'd planned on pairing herself with Maddie and trying to find out more about the pages in her notebook. Maddie wasn't innocent in all of this. Not that she was guilty of something, Kailey quickly reminded herself, but somehow between the gibberish in the book and the night terrors . . . Maddie and Jude both seemed to have some connection to Foxglove Manor in a way that needed to be defined.

"Great," Axel interjected. "Raymond, how about you keep watch over these two ladies, and Kailey, Jude, and I will head to the older section of the house?"

"Maybe the basement," Raymond suggested, raising bushy eyebrows.

"That's what I was thinking." Axel nodded. "In fact, let's leave Jude here. Tracee can watch him for a bit, I'm sure. I want to see if we can figure out where that ladder leads first. Then we can use Jude's sharp eyes to see if we can uncover more in the house."

Kailey bit her tongue and nodded. She could interact with Maddie later, and with fewer people, it would be less chaotic for her. She followed Axel from the front room, catching a glimpse of Maddie as she did so. There was a look in Maddie's eye that snared her, and Kailey tripped, causing Axel to reach for her elbow and steady her. For a moment, she would have sworn Maddie's expression was sharp and knowing. Not bewildered or confused at all. She looked back, and Maddie sat staring out the window toward the lake. Her expression was blank, and her long wrinkled fingers stroked her stuffed lion with shaky, hesitant strokes.

"What is it?" Axel mumbled in Kailey's ear.

"Nothing," Kailey answered.

But she could have sworn she saw Maddie's lips turn upward in a tiny smile.

Axel had outfitted her with a headlamp, and now he handed her a pair of leather work gloves.

"Are there more rats in the basement?" Gloves hardly seemed an appropriate defense.

"Come with me." Axel hiked down the hall but passed the basement stairs, heading for the back door.

"Where are we going?"

Axel looked over her shoulder toward the front room. They could hear Raymond and Teri bantering back and forth. Bringing them into the thrill of the treasure hunt had resolved two major issues. One, an explanation needed to be offered as to why Axel and Kailey were snooping around the manor. Sometimes the truth was the best option. Two, Kailey needed the freedom to leave the residents and, for the moment, shirk her duties as an aide.

"I want to show you something first. Outside. In the back shed."

At least it was an answer. Kailey followed Axel out the door. In the back of Foxglove Manor was a small yard and then thick forest. Nature wasted no time in claiming every spare inch of ground with trees, leaves, and fern foliage. The ferns were mostly brown from winter, but there were sprigs shooting up, promising a green summer.

"Years ago," Axel was saying, "this shed used to be living quarters for the live-in handyman."

She knew Axel had a small mobile home parked on his own acreage a few miles away. She'd just assumed the stone shed that couldn't be more than three hundred square feet housed an assortment of tools and machinery needed for upkeep of the place.

Axel was fumbling around the wooden door's frame until he came upon a key that hung from a small nail. He dangled it from his forefinger and waggled his eyebrows. "I know. Tight security around here."

Kailey offered a small smile.

Axel inserted the key into the old doorknob, and as he did, Kailey took a quick survey of the outside of the shed. It had two small windows on either side of the door, and another window above the door that hinted at a small second level or loft.

The door squeaked open, and Axel hung the key back on the nail. There was an instant whoosh of the smell of oil, earth, wood, and age. He brushed a housefly off the shoulder of his padded, blue flannel shirt and tilted his head.

"Come on."

Kailey followed, ducking a bit since the doorway wasn't particularly tall. Inside, the wood floor was scuffed and worn but swept clean. In the corner of the small room was the remains of an old potbellied stove, but there was no chimney connected to it, and on top of the stove stacked tomato cages were flipped upside down and balanced on it. A push lawn mower was next to the stove. A snowblower. A barrel held all sorts of long-handled tools, including a garden rake, a spade, and a hoe.

Axel ignored it all, acting as though it was all familiar. He reached for a rope that hung about a foot down from the ceiling. Tugging on it, a trapdoor in the ceiling opened, and with it came a cloud of dust and dirt, old leaves, and a mouse nest.

Kailey screamed.

Axel kicked at the nest. "It's empty."

"You've got to be kidding me! What are we doing here?" she snapped. More because she hated mice than she was irritated at Axel.

"I was thinking," Axel said, ignoring her reaction, "you said Riley stated her dad used to bring home little items from the manor. Flea market type stuff. Where'd he get it from?"

"What do you mean?" Kailey felt stupid for asking.

"There's nothing of consequence in the manor anymore." He nodded toward the trapdoor. "But no one ever goes up there. It's a loft packed with all sorts of stuff. So maybe there are clues in the manor, but what if there are clues out here? In the old stuff left behind?"

"Clues about the ciphers?" Kailey kicked at a loose nail in the floorboards.

"Sure. Or what they might be about."

"It's worth a try." She winced as Axel hefted a stepladder from the wall and positioned it beneath the opening.

"Ladies first." He extended his arm.

"Chivalrous," Kailey muttered. She placed a hesitant foot on the first step. Axel moved closer, his hands braced on either side of her. She was a bit self-conscious as she climbed another step. Her rear was practically in his face.

She heard him mumble something. Kailey kept her death grip on the ladder but turned and bent a bit to hear him. Her hair—which she should've tied back—hung wavy and loose and brushed his face.

Axel swiped it away. "I just said to go nice and easy. It's only eight feet."

"Oh." Kailey moved to turn back toward the ladder, but her hair was snagged and yanked. She yelped.

Axel stumbled forward into the ladder, his face hitting the back of her thigh while her head was tilted awkwardly toward his chest.

"Your hair . . ." His voice was muffled. "It's tangled on my button."

"Can you get it free?" Kailey's neck was cranked at an odd angle, and she could tell Axel was doing all he could not to have any inadvertent brushes with her behind.

"Hang on to the ladder," Axel directed.

"I am."

"Okay." He released the ladder and fumbled with the hair wrapped around the button on his shirt. Kailey wobbled as Axel freed her hair, and his hand came up and pushed on the small of her back. Her body was twisted enough to put her off-balance, and without thinking she reached for him and not the ladder.

Kailey's arms encircled his neck even as she was twisted at the waist, her torso trying to maintain balance on the ladder.

"Whoa. I got ya." Axel's hands gripped her waist to steady her, but his eyes had locked with hers.

She stared into his, noted the blue flecks that dotted the irises. She could feel his breath on her face. More so, Kailey could feel the strength in his body. Inner strength that came out into his physical strength and created a powerful pull toward security.

"Kailey." He said her name, which jolted her from her frozen state.

She pushed from him. "Sorry. I'm sorry."

"It's all good." But there was a shiver to his voice that indicated he might have been more affected than he let on.

Kailey made quick work of climbing the remaining few steps on the ladder. She poked her head into the loft. Collecting her wits, she tried to calm the way her heartbeat pitter-pattered, which was how Raymond probably would have described it.

"This place is packed with stuff," she called down to Axel.

"Yep," he responded. "Now, if you can climb up onto the loft, I'll get up there too."

"It's a little crowded." Kailey gave a hesitant sweep of the loft. There were a few old pieces of relatively small furniture that she had no idea how anyone had ever gotten into the loft to begin with. Wooden boxes with old paper labels glued to their sides. A thick blanket of cobwebs and dust, and as she hoisted herself off the ladder onto the floor, her hands scraped over mouse droppings. "Thank God for leather gloves," she stated.

"See?" Axel poked his head through the trapdoor. "God provides for our needs."

Kailey rolled her eyes. There were much larger things she wished He'd make provisions for. Axel grinned, and she noticed for the first time he had long cheek dimples partially hidden by his beard.

"Yay, God," she scoffed, more to get her mind off of Axel's dimples than to mock the Lord.

"Hey." Axel's tone was kind but corrective.

"I know. Sorry," Kailey mumbled and scooted back on the floor to make room for Axel as he pushed himself up. He winked as he landed beside her and brushed his thumb across her cheek.

"Oops. Guess those are freckles. Yep. God provides for our needs—even our desires."

She shivered, and it wasn't because the loft was creepy as heck.

33

ADRIA

"I got nothin' to say." Diggery hiked ahead of her toward the cliff's edge. In his hand, he held a lantern that spread its glow across the blue-darkened earth and rock. The moon hid behind clouds, and the lake aggravated itself against the shoreline. Pestering the sand and the driftwood and the land as though somehow it would give way and let the lake pass.

Adria followed close on Diggery's heels. "I need to know how she died."

"Who died?" he barked, swinging the lantern like he was waving down a ship.

"Lucy Miranda."

"Nope. Nope."

"Diggery."

He swung around, the lantern bobbing. The shadows from the light deepened the wrinkled creases on his face and neck. "Didn't Mr. Crayne tell you to stay out of it?"

Adria cast a surreptitious glance toward the manor. Mr. Crayne—Phineas—didn't know she was here. While he'd seemed to empathize and even sense her urgency for the cause of her father, he was still adamant they leave things be. But she needed to know more. There were pieces to this puzzle that spanned beyond her lifetime.

"Who was Dr. Miranda? What did he do?" she pressed.

Diggery snorted. "He was a doctor. What'dya think?"

"But with Harbor Towne miles away, why would he live *here*? So distant from the people who would need his services?"

"Bah!" Diggery spun back toward the lake and began to swing his arm again. "You're pokin' your nose into places it's gonna get bit off."

"I need to know." Adria stepped up behind him and placed her hand on his shoulder.

"Need to know, eh?" Diggery spit a stream of spit as though he chewed tobacco. Maybe he did. She'd never noticed. "Need to know why? 'Cause you want to know or 'cause your father sent you?"

Adria dropped her hand. Her body weakened at the mention of her father. "How do you know my father?"

Diggery stopped swinging the lantern and squinted into the darkness out over the lake. "Who on the lakes don't know your father? Fontaine. The smuggler. The pirate. He has no respect for no one and no cause but his own."

Adria could attest to that, but even then, and even in spite of her own animosity toward her father, it stung to hear someone else disdain him so. "My father sent me here because—"

"Your father sent you here because St. John owed him. But it ain't St. John he has a beef with. That circle stretches from Michigan to Erie to Huron. Blast, I don't even think your father knows who he is messing with."

"Who then?" Adria asked.

Diggery began swinging the lantern again. Adria looked beyond him to the horizon, where deep blue met navy-blue in a mash of nighttime sky and tempestuous water. She could almost imagine seeing a ship on the horizon.

"Who then." Diggery grumbled. "Who then. You think Michigan is a state of the Union?"

Adria could guess where he was leading. "I always believed so. But apparently, there's Southern influence."

Diggery nodded. "A conspiracy, girlie. Threaded through these lakes like a woven blanket. You can't free a place of the ones who wish to sabotage it. They infest every corner. Banks, theaters, mansions with tunnels that lead underground across towns and to their harbors. Smugglers. Recruiters." He stopped his jabbering and his lantern swinging as though someone had slapped him. Then he added, "But I've already said more than I should."

Not everything Diggery stated was new to Adria. Still, she considered it all in light of her recent conversation with Mr. Crayne.

"Mr. Crayne fought for the Confederacy." The severity of the realization stunned Adria for a moment, along with the fact that it hadn't impressed itself upon her sooner.

Diggery shot her a sharp look through the night. "Told ya, huh? Man was a lad back then. What'd he know but to sign up was heroic. Would've done the same had he lived in the North. Had nothin' to do with allegiance so much as being a cocky young kid."

"Did you fight?"

"Me? I was in my sixties! Figured I'd be dead in a few years anyway, so why hurry it along?"

"But you're here," she stated the obvious.

"And what are you implying?" Diggery set the lantern down by his feet.

Adria hurried forward with an answer. "It seems anyone from Foxglove Manor is for the Confederacy—not the Union—even though they try to appear loyal."

Diggery didn't answer. Instead, he stared out over the water.

Adria followed suit and recognized her eyes hadn't been deceiving her. There was a ship. And a smaller boat rowing its way over the waves toward the cliffs.

"Diggery?" she questioned, not liking but acknowledging the wary shake to her voice.

The old man waved her off. "Best go now, child."

266

"Who are they?" Adria couldn't help but ask.

Diggery cleared his throat, bent, lifted the lantern, and blew through its chimney. The light went out. "They're death," he responded. "Ain't nothin' lives long here at Foxglove Manor."

~

Adria hunkered down as the wind picked up, and she could feel mist off the lake. She couldn't hear the voices, but she knew they were there. After she had left Diggery—the old man believing she'd fled inside as he'd instructed—Adria had watched him as he seemed to walk right off the cliff. Tiptoeing back out on the ledge from which she'd almost thrown herself not long before, Adria lay flat on her belly, ignoring the cold moisture of the rock beneath her. She scooted to the edge and saw that Diggery had traipsed down the side of the cliff, a narrow trail barely visible, his course toward the shore. She peered over now, attempting to make out the shadows in the darkness.

The boat had disappeared from the water, leaving its larger ship floating in the distance. She could make out vague echoes, as if someone were calling from inside the cliff itself, and then three forms appeared on the shore a few yards away from Diggery. Diggery raised his hand in greeting, but his lantern had been snuffed out. Adria strained to hear but could make out nothing but the murmurs of male voices amidst the pounding waves.

Realizing the men were making their way toward the hidden trail to hike topside of the cliff, Adria scurried backward until she felt she could stand hunched over without being seen. Collecting her dress in her fist so she didn't trip, she searched the darkness for a place to take cover. She determined the trees would provide the best shield, so Adria hurried into the grove. Her shoes cracked sticks, and she internally begged them not to alert Diggery and his mysterious visitors.

Their voices became clearer as they neared the top of the cliff.

". . . causing trouble," one said, the first part of his words cut off.

A wave drove into the cliff below.

"Don't worry 'bout him." Diggery was offering some sort of reassurance. "All's right."

"He needs sanctuary for now," the original man stated. Adria strained to see their faces. She could tell they were bearded, but distinct details were shadowed. "When things settle down, hop the Northeastern and make your way to Canada."

She knew the Northeastern meant the railway. Adria drew back behind a poplar tree, its narrow trunk offering little shelter.

The second man spoke now, his voice gruff and deep. "Did during the war, I can do it again."

"Almost got yerself caught during the war too." Diggery slapped the man on the shoulder. They all chuckled, and the third man inserted, "Holbrooke's got a way of slinkin' past."

"Foxlike," acknowledged the second man, Holbrooke, asserting his prowess.

"Crayne still here?" the man who appeared to be the leader of sorts asked Diggery.

Diggery nodded. "Here, but not all here. Not in the mind."

"Drunk son of a—" The wind cut off Holbrooke's declaration.

"Does what needs to be done, though," Diggery reinforced.

"For now," the third man interrupted. "Once Holbrooke is through here, it's time. Changing of the guard."

"You goin' to let Crayne free?" Diggery's tone was carefully controlled, but Adria thought she heard an element of surprise in it.

"Sure. We'll call it that." Holbrooke laughed.

The men walked toward the manor. Diggery followed, then paused. He turned, searching the woods where Adria shrank behind the tree. She could feel his scrutiny burning into her. Then he was distracted as the door to Foxglove Manor opened. The silhouette of Mrs. St. John broke the pattern of light coming from inside the manor.

Holbrooke raised his arm in greeting. The other two men followed suit.

Adria could tell Mrs. St. John didn't respond. The men slipped inside, and she appeared to search the yard before shutting the door. Adria lifted her eyes toward the turret room. Phineas Crayne's window was dark, yet there was movement behind the glass.

A hand came out of nowhere, clamping over Adria's mouth and yanking her backward. Her scream was muffled by a callused hand, and she was jerked into an unfamiliar chest with the scent of lake and fish permeating his body.

"What've we got here?" There was a cackle in Adria's ear.

She struggled against the man's hold, trying to bite at the fleshy hand over her mouth, but it was pressed so tightly she could hardly open her lips. Her attacker spun her around, gripping her upper arms painfully as his fingers dug into her skin. Beady, black eyes burrowed into hers. He had a scruffy beard and a face that Adria was certain she would never forget. He clicked his tongue.

"Ooh la la. I found me a pretty little thing."

Adria struggled, twisting her torso to free herself from his grip. She whimpered as his fingers grew more assertive against her flesh.

"Shut up." He tugged her toward him, and Adria catapulted flat against his chest. She could feel her curves against the stranger, was sickened by his low rumble of a laugh as he too seemed aware of her feminine body, and then she slapped at his hand as he tried to hold her against him, palm splayed across her backside.

"Enough, Clay." Another voice broke the stillness. The man instantly retreated, letting her go with a small shove. Her skin crawled from the feel of him. "Get her to the manor."

She craned her neck to see who was speaking from the shadows. Clay, her attacker, gripped her arm and pushed her toward Foxglove.

"Get goin'." He was irritated, she sensed. Annoyed that his midnight dalliance with a woman had been thwarted by two words from the other man.

Footsteps behind her told Adria they were being followed. The manor door was yanked open from the inside, and Diggery stepped out. Surprise registered on his face as he saw Adria. Concern. Then his bushy brows furrowed, and he hollered, "Ohhhhh no, you don't!" Diggery waved his finger at Clay. "You leave her be!"

"Yes, Clay." The other man's voice rumbled from behind her, reverberated through her with a familiarity that was as bewildering as it was concerning. "Leave the lady be. We can't have her harmed or Fontaine will chase us down for more than his stolen cargo."

Mr. Crayne.

Adria wrenched her arm from Clay and stumbled toward Diggery, whom she didn't particularly feel she could trust anymore and whose familiarity brought little comfort. She stared incredulously at Mr. Crayne—Phineas—who avoided her eyes.

Clay shoved between them, lowering his leering face and holding it inches away from Adria's nose. "You can tell your father that when he steals from the South, the South takes back what's theirs. He'll never find it." The Southern accent grew thicker as the man spoke. He eyed her for a long moment, and Adria held her breath, not daring to speak. "And stay out of our way. Curiosity kills. You know?"

"I said leave her be. She ain't knowin' what you're gabbin' on about anyway." Diggery nudged Clay back with his knuckles.

"No reason to get feisty, old man. You know why we're here. We'll make it quick and be on our way."

Mr. Crayne pushed past them both without a word, and Clay followed, not remotely intimidated by Mr. Crayne. His feet stomped on the polished wood floors, dropping debris of sand and leaves. Diggery turned his frustration on Adria. His expression was undeniably furious.

"You're goin' to just play with fire until it burns you to a crisp?"

"What does Mr. Crayne—what's going on?" Adria tried to ignore the severe pounding of her heart.

"Told ya to stay outta things!" Diggery barked. "Now *do* it."

Diggery marched away from her as fast as the old man could.

His strides were wobbly but purposeful. He steered himself toward the back of the manor, toward the back shed that doubled as his quarters.

Adria slipped inside Foxglove, reaching for the door and shutting it. When she turned, Lula had appeared from nowhere. Her big eyes were wide, which, Adria concluded in between gasping in shock and grabbing for her chest out of fright, was a regular thing with Lula.

"Where've you been, miss?" Lula shook her head as if scolding Adria. "Mrs. St. John has been looking for you for minutes on end! She wanted you to read to her before she retired."

There was such normalcy in Lula's announcement and such complete disregard for the strange men who had tromped into Foxglove Manor, led by Diggery and Mr. Crayne, only minutes prior.

"Where did they go?" Adria tilted her chin up, searching over Lula's shoulder for a glimpse of them.

"Who, miss?" Lula furrowed thin brows.

"Those men!" Adria insisted, urgency making her blood course more fluidly through her veins.

"Men?" Lula questioned.

"Don't be silly!" Adria felt only a tad guilty for snapping at the girl. "They were just here. Just entering Foxglove."

"I didn't see no one, miss." Lula seemed a bit nervous to contradict Adria.

"Three of them were greeted by Mrs. St. John herself!" Adria insisted.

Lula reached out, and her fingertips touched Adria's arm lightly, even as she drew her brows together in concern. "Miss, I think you'd best go to bed. There's not been anyone here tonight. Foxglove Manor has been quiet."

"But Diggery just—"

"Diggery just came and fetched some coffee grounds, miss," Lula stated. "And Mrs. St. John has been in bed waiting on you for the last twenty minutes."

"Impossible!" Adria's arm shot out as dizziness threatened to upset her balance. She caught herself on the wall, blinking to clear her mind.

"Miss?" Lula's voice seemed to come from far away. An echo. "Miss Fontaine?"

And the room went dark.

34

Mrs. St. John was ill too. At least that was what Lula implied as she helped Adria take a sip of cold water and then lay her head back on the pillow to rest. She'd asked again about the men from the night before, and once more she was met with Lula's quizzical response. Now Adria noticed Lula standing by the white desk at the far side of the bedroom, a piece of paper in her hand. She pushed up on her elbows, her hair falling around her shoulders as a surge of anxiety rushed through her.

"Lula, put that away!"

Lula held the letter from Margot. The one where Adria had been threatened with being institutionalized. She'd intended to destroy it—forever—but something had held her back. Now Lula was snooping into business not her own. The girl dropped the letter onto the desk, but it was apparent she'd read much of it.

"I'm not losing my mind." Adria answered the question in Lula's face. She lowered herself back onto the bed.

"Sure, miss." Lula seemed to be piecing together her own summary. Adria seeing strange men. Adria's sister indicating an impending hospitalization. Adria sneaking off and away with Mr. Crayne. None of it appeared as though Adria was in her right frame of mind. Even Adria herself could see how one might question her judgment, if not her sanity. And of course, there was the unspoken of but not difficult fact to deduce. The one that had Adria attempting to meet her Maker at her own hand. That, in and of itself, was worthy of being locked away under careful watch.

Adria vividly recalled Diggery signaling from the cliff. The man—Clay was his name?—who'd manhandled her in the trees. Mr. Crayne. Someone they seemed to be hiding away until he could hop a train into Canada. It screamed of conspiracy. One that no one would believe. Especially if Adria were to lay out an argument that it somehow surrounded remnants of the war from two decades ago.

Mr. Crayne.

The thought of him caused an ache inside her, coupled with confusion. Distrust. A wicked sense of betrayal that collided with a deep hope that there was an explanation. That maybe this was what he'd warned her about.

Lula crossed the room and lifted a cream-colored blanket from the foot of Adria's bed. She waved it over Adria, unfurling it so it lay over her as an extra layer of warmth. "Mrs. St. John took to bed this morning after breakfast. Complaining of chest pains, she is."

"Did you send for a doctor?" Adria inquired, glad to note she was feeling better after her swooning the night before.

Lula nodded. "Diggery went to Harbor Towne to fetch him. Could be hours, though. I'm not overly fond of the missus myself, but she has been a benefactress, you know? Spared me from the poorhouse. I do hope she recovers."

Adria fumbled at the blankets. She should get up. Care for Mrs. St. John herself. Chest pains could be her heart failing. She'd also witnessed the intense disagreement between Mrs. St. John and the unknown visitor from a few days before. And even if Lula was completely ignorant of visitors from the night previous, there *had* been a boat, and men, and Adria *had* seen Mrs. St. John let them into the manor. Perhaps the stress was too much for the older woman. Perhaps it was a ploy to deter attention from the men—wherever they were. Wherever they had gone.

Mr. Crayne would know what to do. But now she severely questioned his authenticity. What if he wasn't as vulnerable as he seemed? Perhaps his broken spirit and penchant toward drink were merely a persona meant to disguise something else—*someone* else. Yet, somewhere, innately inside of her, Adria longed to trust him. It seemed that when she was at her weakest, he was able to summon strength for her, and similarly in return.

"What are you doing, miss?" Lula noticed Adria's intention to rise from the bed. "You need to rest!"

Adria waved her away. "I'm fine. I was just light-headed last night. I feel . . . fine." She didn't. The room was spinning, as if it were tilted to the right and the floor was undulating like the waves of the lake. She squeezed her eyes shut and gripped the mattress before opening them again. The room had stilled, but she noticed her chest felt heavy. Like a weight sat atop it, holding her down until she couldn't fill her lungs with deep breaths.

"You're not fine." Lula pushed gently on her shoulders. "You need to lie back down. I can take care of Mrs. St. John until Diggery comes with the doctor."

"Mr. Crayne?" Adria asked, noting how weak she sounded.

"Yes. Mr. Crayne is here too." Lula nodded. "See? I have help if I need it."

Adria closed her eyes as her head sank into her pillow. She couldn't fathom why she felt so odd. So weak. More sleep would suffice—must suffice, she promised herself. Too many strange visions occurred in Foxglove Manor. The ghost girl, Lucy. Now strange men vanishing into thin air? It was impossible. Implausible. Unless, of course, Adria allowed her mind to think the thought she'd been avoiding so fiercely. Unless she *was* losing a piece of her sanity, and Margot and her father actually *did* know what was best. It would be a lark . . . Adria smiled wryly to herself as she drifted off to sleep, as if she truly *was* crazy, and Foxglove Manor, its ghost, its secrets, and its conspiracies were merely figments of her delusional mind. Stories she'd concocted in her subconscious in order to survive. Because, Adria admitted, she had already proven a failure when it came to dying.

Mrs. St. John thrashed on the bed, her legs twisting the sheets into ropes of material, her nightgown damp with sweat. Adria had risen just after lunch, summoned the strength to go to Mrs. St. John's bedside, but was at a loss as to how to care for her. Lula stood in the doorway, wringing her hands and annoying Adria with her nervous energy.

"I tried smelling salts. I did, miss," Lula stammered.

"Smelling salts are worthless in her condition." Adria reached out to push back loose hair from Mrs. St. John's face, but the woman's arm shot out and batted her away.

Mrs. St. John's eyes were open, staring into corners, shifting this way and that with a look of sheer panic etched into every crevice of her face.

"Theodora!" she cried out.

Adria tried to reach for Mrs. St. John again, only to be clubbed by a flailing fist. This time Adria couldn't hold the abuse against the older woman. She was out of her mind. Curiously so.

"Theodora!" Mrs. St. John attempted to sit up, clutched at her chest, shrieking and pulling her legs up into a fetal position on the bed.

"Go get Mr. Crayne," Adria demanded of Lula, who was paler than the bedsheets. She was at a loss for what else to do. Lula nodded, and Adria had the fleeting question of why Lula hadn't retrieved the turret room recluse sooner. Adria herself was weak and pulled up a chair, lowering onto it to steady her nerves.

Mrs. St. John's legs shot forward, and she went rigid. Her eyes were round as she stared at the ceiling.

"Ma'am?" Adria jumped from the chair and sat on the edge of the bed, closer to Mrs. St. John, whose mouth was moving. Forming words. But she was voiceless. "Mrs. St. John!" Adria leaned over her, almost shouting in the invalid's face to startle her from the frozen stupor. Mrs. St. John didn't respond, only her lips moved as if conversing. Adria heard a slight mumble coming from Mrs. St. John's throat. She could hear whisper-like words forming. Bending, Adria held her ear directly over Mrs. St. John's mouth.

"Theodora. My pet. My precious girl. Theodora. Theodora . . ." Mrs. St. John's faint crooning was strangled by a gargle in her throat.

Adria couldn't stop the cry that ripped from her chest. Her benefactress was dying—*dying*—right before her very eyes.

"Theodora . . ." Mrs. St. John gasped. She slowly turned her eyes on Adria and seemed to look right through her. Adria instinctively turned and looked behind her. The room was empty. Mrs. St. John's fingers clawed at Adria's blouse. Her nails scraped through the material and lined Adria's chest as she pulled Adria forcefully toward her. Mrs. St. John's breath was rancid, but she spat words that Adria struggled to hear.

"Dead girls," she gasped, air wheezing into her lungs and sounding like a punctured bag. "All around us. Dead girls."

Mrs. St. John clawed harder at Adria's blouse as though she felt somehow that Adria was going to pull away. Her eyes were crazed.

"Mrs. St. John," Adria whimpered.

"Cursed place. The fox. Cursed, I tell you. Theodora. Lucy. Be rid of it, Alexandria. Be rid of it!"

"Rid of what?" Adria sensed Mrs. St. John was slipping away. The woman's eyelids closed, then flew open again.

"A new guardian of Foxglove. Not—who—you—" Death gargled in Mrs. St. John's throat. "Dead girlsssssssss . . ." The final word hissed from Mrs. St. John's lips, and her eyes widened, froze, then stayed that way. Her fingers loosened from Adria's blouse, Mrs. St. John's hand falling to the edge of the bed.

She was dead. This time, Mrs. St. John was very, very dead.

35

KAILEY

Two hours of breathing in dust, must, and probably a litany of invisible poisonous, cancer-causing particles. Kailey sat back on her heels in front of an old trunk with piles of its innards stacked around her. Books. Old books.

"If I were a librarian, I'd be excited right now." Kailey wiped her nose with the back of her sleeve, wishing she'd brought tissues to compensate for the allergies that had taken her sinuses by storm. "I sort of wish we were exploring the rat-infested basement or that secret chute with the ladder."

"Hey, I found this!" Axel lifted an old scale, its tin rusted but the increments of weight still legible.

"That's hardly worth anything," Kailey stated.

Axel nodded and set it off to the side. "Probably why Riley's dad never took it from the loft."

"I wonder what all he did take from here. What if he found the key to the ciphers—and took it?"

Axel picked up his phone from where he'd set it on a crate. He checked the screen. "I didn't get the impression that Riley thought her dad had found the ciphers."

Kailey scrunched her face. "True." She picked up one of the

books. It was an old copy of Nathaniel Hawthorne's *The House of the Seven Gables*. "Did you ever read this?" She waved it at Axel, then proceeded to sneeze.

He grinned and gosh darn it if she didn't notice his dimples again. They were getting irritating, they were so attractive, and Kailey was annoyed at herself for ever noticing them today.

Axel sniffed. He must have allergies too. "Nope. I was forced to read *The Scarlet Letter*, though."

"Forced?" Kailey smiled.

Axel shot her a look of boredom. "Not every guy likes to read."

"You don't read at all?" Her voice might have gone up an octave with surprise.

Axel chuckled. "Only if I have to."

She clucked her tongue. "I've lost respect." Setting the Hawthorne novel aside, Kailey picked up another one. *Uncle Tom's Cabin*. Running her thumb over the inset title on its hardcover, Kailey winced. "This book . . . so much pain in history, isn't there?"

"There sure is," Axel agreed. He was fishing through a crate, lifting odds and ends that included a tin can of old screws and a small box of matches advertising a gas station that probably had gone out of business in 1962.

"Why does it still haunt us?" Kailey couldn't help but ask.

"History?" Axel affirmed.

"Yes." Kailey turned the antique hardcover volume in her hand. "Some say this book shouldn't be read any longer. Others argue it's part of history. I mean, think about it. In its time, this book was an exposé in some ways. Showing people the atrocities and grossness of what was happening in the culture. Then the message of the book was twisted and conformed to suit stereotypes that were offensive. Racism still exists like one of man's worst blemishes, and then you have—" she opened the cover of *Uncle Tom's Cabin*—"a nation that went to war once, against themselves, and sometimes I feel like it never truly ended. You know?"

Axel paused, holding a stack of postcards. "I don't think I *can* know. What it was like—during the Civil War—for either side."

"Sure, but . . ." Kailey didn't look at the book in her hand, but instead rested her eyes on Axel, who didn't seem opposed to pausing his own scrounging through dusty items. "Why does life have to be so broken?" She hadn't intended to go deep. Hadn't intended for the tears to spring to her eyes. Kailey swiped at them with her already-snotty sleeve. "My mom was an addict. My dad was—for lack of a better way of saying it—a pansy who figured the best way to deal with my mom was to drink. Then Foxglove Manor had to enter uninvited and ruin our lives. *My* life. Why? Why?" She dropped the open book in her lap and lifted her palms upward in question. "We're still putting together pieces here of something dark that happened during the Civil War. The *Civil War*, Axel. Come on! Lincoln has been dead for over a century and a half, and we're still being touched by it."

"You can't erase history." Axel pressed his lips together. He rubbed his beard with his gloved hand. "No matter how hard we might want to. It follows us. It's embedded in us. In our bones, our DNA. Ancestors and generational sins and habits and memories. It's part of how humankind exists. One generation builds on the next."

"And they all topple," Kailey said absently.

Axel grimaced and lifted a flannel-clad shoulder in a half shrug. "Often. They do."

"People fight too much. Or they hide in their addictions. In the meantime, it's the kids who suffer." Kailey recalled her own childhood. When they'd first arrived, there were two days here at Foxglove when she'd been happy. A carefree little girl and her big brother. Beachcombing, staring at the rock caves carved into the cliff, imagining what it would be like to get on a boat and float on the water.

"So how do we fix it?" Kailey finally asked. She'd asked her therapist. He'd said "more therapy." She'd asked her pastor once, and he'd rattled off some Bible verse. She'd asked a few friends, and some suggested protesting, politics, equal rights, but no one had a good answer for how to make it all actually happen. There wasn't a *fix* to the problem that was humankind. Wounding each other, driven by superiority and greed, manipulating life to best suit oneself . . .

"We can't fix it." Axel's answer was the worst one yet.

Kailey rested her palm on the open pages of *Uncle Tom's Cabin*. "You're such an encouragement," she muttered.

"Seriously." Axel shifted his weight as he sat on the floor and drew his knee up, his elbow resting lazily on top. "I think that's half the issue right there. We *think* we can fix it. That we can somehow dig into the hearts of men and correct them. But we can't. We try. But we can't."

"So then there's really no point at all. We try to survive, and then we die, and hope in the process we can have a somewhat peaceful life. Sucks if you're not white or you're not born into a middle-class, sober family. Odds are stacked against you." Sure, there was bitterness in her voice, and Kailey knew it.

"My gramma used to always say one word, 'stick.' That was her mantra." Axel batted his hand at a fly that dogged his face.

"Stick?" Kailey raised a doubtful brow.

Axel nodded. "Yeah. Stick. Stick to the Creator. *'The world is broken,'* she'd say. *'God can fix it. So, stick to Him and stop trying to do it yourself.'*"

"You know that sounds like a Hallmark card, don't you?" Kailey smiled sardonically and stared up her nose at him.

Axel chuckled. "Yeah. Gramma was a walking Hallmark card. But she was right too, you know. We complicate our purpose in life too much. We try to define it, then build on it, until our ideals become man-made instead of God-directed."

"What's your life purpose?" Kailey challenged him.

Axel stared deep into her eyes. "You really want to know?"

"Yeah. I mean, you're spending your days as a handyman at an old folks' home on the top of a cliff overlooking Lake Superior.

You're smart. You could be in politics or—or be a pastor, or something. Run a homeless shelter. Why here? Why Foxglove Manor?"

Axel ducked his head and picked at something stuck to his shoelace. When he lifted his eyes again, he drew in a deep breath, and there was that steady confidence in his expression that made Kailey ache deep inside. "Because it feels right being here. I can make a difference. In just a few lives. Maybe I can't change the world, Kailey, but God can use me to touch a few."

———

She didn't know why she took the copy of *Uncle Tom's Cabin* with her down the ladder and back to the manor, but she did know she'd made a rather fast and awkward exit after Axel's straightforward purpose statement. It was too simplistic, or maybe idealistic, considering her past. At least it felt that way. Hiking toward the door, Kailey was struck with the desire to avoid people. Avoid Teri and Tracee, Raymond and his mouthy way of things, and Maddie, who—frankly—had given her the creeps when they'd left the manor an hour ago. She diverted toward the path that led down to the shore. Once Kailey reached the shore, she slipped off her shoes. Sure, she was wearing socks, but she wasn't about to strip them off since the sand was quite cold yet. Kailey liked the feel of the cushiony earth beneath her feet. The way the sand shifted and made way for her weight, while not giving way and sucking her into the bowels of the earth.

A huge piece of driftwood—more of a tree, really—stuck up out of the sand like a ready-made perch. Sure enough, a sea gull took off from it as Kailey approached. She checked the smooth, gray-colored wood for bird droppings before hoisting herself up on it. The waves were calm today. Cold, springlike, but calm. Their steady roll in and out was mesmerizing. Sleepy. If the sun were to come out, Kailey might be able to shed her hoodie sweatshirt. As it was, she chose to stay snuggled in it.

For a long moment, Kailey stared out over the water. A few sea gulls swooped and dove toward the water, then rose and took to the sky. Free. It was almost joyous to watch them in their freedom, lifted by the wind. Restful in the presence of creation all around them.

Kailey looked down at the book in her hands. It represented so much pain. So much turmoil and strife. Not unlike her life. Not that she would ever compare her past with the time of slavery; still, didn't so many people have experiences that pointed to the horror and wickedness of humankind itself? There was a need for a saving side. Perhaps the Union had seen themselves as such during the war. Maybe her aunt had thought she played that role for Kailey and Jude. And, really, Kailey knew that in Jude's own way, he tried to be that savior for her as well. Truthfully, they were all failures. Conflict remained, even if it had been lulled into a tempestuous nap, like a beast on the verge of being awakened.

She opened the cover, intent on reading the first few pages of the classic novel. There had to be something to learn from between its musty pages. Something that could teach her . . .

Gnqgy jgq

Kailey stared at the ink script on the title page.

"Maddie's journal. Jude . . ." Kailey's musing was lost over the water. The title of the book was crossed out. Almost angrily. As was the author's name. She thumbed forward another page. Nothing. Another page. No more. There was no more script as she flipped through the pages.

What were the odds? Was this where Jude had first seen the gibberish he sketched repeatedly after they'd left Foxglove Manor? Was it there where Maddie had seen it? But how? Kailey could still see the book on its pile of cohorts she'd lifted from the loft trunk. Maybe twenty years ago, the book had been inside the manor for Jude to find, but there was no way possible that Maddie had urged her arthritic body into the back shed, up a ladder, and through a trapdoor.

She thumbed through the pages more slowly this time. No.

There was nothing more. Kailey caught sight of movement at the top of the cliff. Looking up, she noticed Axel as he walked out toward the edge. Shouting for him, she waved wildly from her perch on the driftwood log. He looked down, caught sight of her, and waved back. Sliding from the log, Kailey held the book close to her, slipped her feet back into her shoes, and climbed back up the trail toward the cliff.

"What's up?" Axel looked cozy as the breeze picked up. His flannel shirt was padded. His brown work pants were heavy and fell over his boots. He'd put on a stocking cap. Heck. He looked delicious.

Kailey waved the book. "There's cipher in here."

"Really?" Axel's voice rose in interest. He stepped toward her to look over her shoulder as she opened it.

"Right here. See?"

"*Gnqgy jgq.* It really is gibberish, Kailey."

"But it means something," she insisted.

Axel took the book from her hands and opened it to the first page. He started skimming it, flinched, and lifted his head. "This book is already disturbing."

"The language?" Kailey acknowledged. "I know. In that first paragraph alone . . ."

Axel shuddered. "Harriet Beecher Stowe sure wanted to expose slavery in all its ugliness."

"Do you think that's what we're dealing with?" Kailey ventured, pointing at the illustration that went with the opening text. "Was Foxglove Manor somehow part of the Underground Railroad?"

"This close to Canada?" Axel seemed to ponder it. "Maybe. But why would anyone today care? Kidnapping Riley? You? It doesn't fit. It seems more like there's something hidden here, like the rumors say."

"Gold?"

"Confederate gold, maybe? Their paper cash is worthless, but gold would still be really valuable." Axel thumbed through a few more pages. "I think we're dealing with remnants of the under-belly of the Southern movement, not so much those who assisted the slaves in their escape." He stopped. The wind ruffled the pages, and Axel smoothed them down with his thumb. "Hey, look at this."

Kailey edged closer, very aware of his body.

Axel pointed. "There are faint circles. Around letters."

"Oh my gosh!" she exclaimed and bent closer to the page. "*P*. Oh, and then down here, an *a*."

Axel turned the page and read, "'He was very much over-dressed, in a gaudy coat of many colors, a blue neckerchief—'"

"There!" Kailey interrupted. She pointed at the *r* in the word *colors*. "It's got a faint circle around it."

Axel trailed his finger down the page. "*L-o-r* . . ." He concentrated as he turned the page.

"Wait!" Kailey grabbed his arm. "*P-a-r-l-o-r*. Parlor. It spells *parlor*."

"Ooooookay."

Kailey gripped Axel's arm tighter, and he looked down at her. She had an involuntary shiver as she glanced at the book in his hand. "What if Jude stumbled on some of the cipher in the architecture because he's, well, he's Jude. He looks at things differently. But think about the rest of us. We don't see things through those eyes that key in on patterns and sequences. We need directions."

"A treasure map?"

Kailey nodded. "Sort of. I think the cipher is the map to the treasure, but this book holds the clue as to where to find the cipher."

"A map to the treasure map?" Axel curled his lip in incredulity.

"Why not?" Kailey pointed at the page. "You're not just going to write a full cipher out on a piece of paper unless you intend to destroy it. This had to last. Someone was going to come back for the treasure, and they needed the cipher, but the cipher itself needed to be hidden."

"So, you're proposing there's more of the cipher in the parlor?"

"It's probably all over the house. Right under our noses. Jude recognized some of it. He wrote it down. When we were kids!"

"If the kidnappers were really looking for something like a treasure—gold or spoils of war—that cipher would be the key. But if they don't have the cipher, or only have part of it . . . then that would be significant enough to kidnap two kids and interrogate them, twenty years apart," Axel concluded.

"And to kill their parents if they were somehow in the way or wouldn't help. Can you imagine how much it'd be worth today if you found smuggled Confederate gold? In the Upper Peninsula of Michigan?" Kailey added. She knew it sounded preposterous, but when Axel gave a short nod, she also knew the plausibility factor had just gotten a whole lot higher.

36

Jason Bascom wasn't returning their calls. Neither was Riley's mom. Axel's arms were crossed over his chest and he looked like a thundercloud ready to burst. Tracee busied herself with putting pills in paper medicine cups and trying to ignore the thick tension between them, as they had a standoff in the kitchen.

"I'm just going to go knock on the door. I did it before and it wasn't an issue." Kailey wasn't keen on the fact Axel was demanding she not go alone. Granted, there was credence—probably more of it than she wanted to admit—but it also meant giving up the freedom to ask more questions. If she had the chance.

"But if—" Axel shot a glance at Tracee, who was, for all sakes and purposes, ignoring them. "Outside." He pointed to the door.

Kailey reared back and stared at him incredulously. "Excuse me?"

"Let's talk outside."

"I don't need you telling me what to do." Kailey winced even as she retorted.

"Don't go all feminist on me." Axel rolled his eyes.

Tracee snorted and dropped some pills into a cup.

Axel tempered the frustration on his face and in his voice. "Just—please. Can we talk outside?"

Kailey dropped her arms from across her chest. "Fine." She caught Tracee's eyebrow waggle as she looked over her shoulder while exiting. Kailey scowled and shut the door behind her and Axel. "I'm just going to try to track down Jason—or Riley and her mom. If we can ask more questions from Riley about where she and her dad looked, we can maybe narrow down where to have Jude start looking." And somehow, in between that long shot, she needed to figure out how to communicate to Jude what she wanted him to look for.

Axel reached for her, but she ducked away. He drew in a steadying breath. "If our theory has even a little bit of credibility—it's dangerous for you to be alone."

"Fine. I'll take Edgar the cat." Kailey tossed Axel a smile to lighten the mood. To prove she really wasn't trying to be mean. "Please, Axel. There's no imminent threat. I'm just driving into town. You trust the Bascoms, right?"

"Well, sure, but—"

"Then I won't be in any danger. I'll stop at the store and grab some eggs and milk like Teri requested, and I'll make sure I'm back by two."

Axel stepped toward her, his eyes drilling into hers. Kailey felt warmth creep up her neck.

"You won't be in any danger," Axel repeated.

Kailey nodded. "Right." She sounded breathless.

Axel put his hands on her shoulders and tilted his head down. She couldn't look away if she'd wanted to. And she wanted to. No, she didn't. It was time to be honest with herself. She didn't want to look away or go away or run away from Axel.

"Two." He nodded.

"Huh?" Kailey was distracted by his mouth. The word *two* had made Axel's lips pucker just a bit. His bottom lip was fuller than his upper, and the scruff around his mouth was neatly trimmed.

"You'll be back by two?" Axel's words were thick.

Kailey drug her gaze from his mouth. "Sure. Two."

This time, the word on her lips must have had a similar impression on Axel. He drew in a deep breath, and it shook a bit.

"Two," he repeated. His mouth had lowered. Kailey could feel his breath on the delicate skin of her lips.

"Two works for me," she mumbled.

"Me too." But his words were muffled as that irresistible cord between them came to its end.

The kiss was gentle, yet Kailey felt it to the tips of her toes. She raised slightly on them, felt Axel's hands at her waist, his right thumb grazing the bare skin where her shirt met the waist of her jeans. Melting into him seemed cliché, but Kailey could understand why women did it. Axel was man. All man. He led the kiss, probing slowly, until Kailey had all but forgotten about the treasure. The cipher. The ghosts of Foxglove Manor or her past.

Axel finished the kiss. Then stole another small one before drawing back. His hands left her waist, and he raked his fingers through his hair. "Two," he concluded, as if the kiss hadn't happened.

"Promise." Kailey nodded. "Two."

It was her new favorite word.

⁓

"What do you mean 'they're gone'?" Kailey stared at the face of the stranger at the door of the Bascom home. The woman opened the screen door and stepped out, wiping her hands on a towel.

"Yep. Packed up and left town. Mrs. Bascom, Riley, and her brother-in-law." Stretching out a hand, the woman finished, "I'm Paula. I'm a friend of the family. Told them I'd clean up so we can get the house on the market and sell it. Riley's mom, she's not a fan of Harbor Towne anymore. Not that she ever really was to begin with."

Kailey's angst had risen with the knowledge that the Bascoms had vanished from Harbor Towne. It made sense, and it didn't make sense. After suffering a loss, many people wanted to make fresh starts. But to leave with your brother-in-law? "Are Riley's mom and Jason a . . ." It wasn't appropriate to finish the question.

"A thing?" Paula supplied with a laugh. "Oh no. Nope. Just been friends, and Jason adores Riley. It'll be good for them all. A new start, you know? After her husband killed himself . . . well, how do you continue to live in the same home?"

"I'd really like to get ahold of them," Kailey pressed.

"'Cause of Foxglove Manor?" Paula assumed and waved the towel in Kailey's direction. "Nah, no need to worry. That place is wrapped up in business legalese. Just 'cause the property is in their name doesn't mean they can just sell it out from under the residents. That's why there's a board, and it's all business-run. Jason assured me they're only selling this house."

That wasn't what had worried Kailey, but maybe it should have. Relieved to know Teri and Tracee, Raymond, Maddie, Stella, Judy, and the other residents didn't have anything to worry about, she tried a different approach.

"Did Riley or her dad ever talk to you about—about Foxglove Manor?"

"Their code hunting?" Paula leaned against the doorframe. "Oh, heck yeah, everyone knows about them by now. Riley is such a cute little writer. The paper put her work right on the front page. People have all sorts of theories about what it could mean."

"Like what?" It was worth exploring.

"I dunno." Paula pursed her lips and shook her head. "There's always rumors and legends."

"Did Riley's article give any details?" Kailey wished she had a copy of the article.

Paula tugged absent-mindedly at her shirtsleeve. "Details? I'm not sure what you mean, but hold on a sec." She disappeared into the house, the screen door banging behind her. A minute later, Paula returned and shoved an old newspaper in Kailey's direction. "Bascoms have about thirty copies of these in a box in the back room." She laughed.

"Riley's article?" Kailey snapped open the very crisp, few-months-old newspaper.

"Yep." Paula crossed her arms over her chest. "Maybe that'll answer your questions."

Kailey skimmed it. Riley's writing was childish, but there it was, her story about treasure hunting with her dad. A mention of rumored ciphers. But other than that, no further details.

"You know, I always suggested they talk to Gary. He has a shop down along the harbor. Small grocery store, really, but he's a lake diver. Always looking for treasure and whatnots since Lake Superior has so many shipwrecks on its bottom. I'm not sure if Riley and her dad ever did. I didn't get the feeling Mr. Bascom and Gary got along very well."

"He's a diver?" Kailey was surprised.

"Oh sure. Divers go out for fun all the time. Sometimes Gary will lead a team, but mostly he just likes to futz around with the town history and artifacts that get donated to the town after some of the dives."

Encouraged, Kailey folded the newspaper. "May I?"

"Oh sure! You keep that!" Paula moved to head back into the house. "You take care, okay?"

"Yes. Thank you." The screen door banged again, but this time Paula closed the inside door as well.

Kailey hesitated, glancing at her phone. It was 1:30. If she were to head to Gary's store on the harbor, there was no way she'd be back at Foxglove Manor by two as promised.

Hurrying to her car, Kailey tossed the newspaper onto the passenger seat and hit Axel's number. It rang a few times and then went to voicemail.

"Hey," Kailey said into the recording. "I've got an extra stop I want to make. A place down on the harbor. I'll be a bit late getting back. But at least I communicated!" she added with a laugh, then hung up. Probably no signal wherever Axel was. Hopefully, he'd get to a spot where his phone would notify him of the message.

~

The store truly was just a little grocery store—and a hardware store too, if Kailey were accurate in describing it to someone. There was a distinct smell of strawberries, which she hadn't expected, followed by a strong whiff of cigarette. A man appeared behind the cash wrap, his large belly barely covered by a navy-blue T-shirt with a logo proudly boasting *Northern Beer Company, Ca, 1942.* He pulled a cigarette from his mouth, smoke puffing from his nose.

"Hello. How can I help you?"

Kailey noticed the rack of Upper Peninsula and Porcupine Mountain postcards to her right. She skirted it and approached the counter. A box of individual packets of mint gum was displayed and next to it a long line of various demo lottery tickets positioned under plexiglass. Kailey introduced herself, and he was indeed Gary. Formalities aside, Kailey explained her mission while being as vague as possible, and Gary's eyes sparked with interest.

"Oh yeah!" He smashed the butt of his cigarette into an ashtray. She watched him and he noticed. "Not supposed to do this indoors," he muttered. "Ah well. So, you're code hunting like Riley and her dad, eh?"

Kailey provided a cautious nod, determined not to share she'd discovered code in an old book or any clues as to where more might be.

Gary waddled his weight across the room toward a bookshelf. "I've got all sorts of books written by local authors. I like this one." He tugged out a blue-covered book with the watermark of an old map across it and the words *Civil War Conspiracy* printed on its front. Gary handed it to her. "Not sure it'll help much with the code hunting, but it'll explain what Riley and her dad were into. Digging up old Confederate history up here ain't what most people expect, but I'll tell ya"—Gary whirled his finger in the air, indicating *crazy*—"people underestimate just how far that war reached."

"There *were* Confederate influences here, then." Kailey paged through the book.

Gary leaned against the shelf. "Mm-hmm. Yep. Frankly, a lot of the history in that book and others is mixed with conjecture. I mean, Confederacy up here was all underground and secretive. Like the Freemasons, you know? Kept it all hush-hush and used codes and secret hideouts. All that fun stuff." Gary grinned like a kid who'd discovered chocolate for the first time. He reached out and took the book from Kailey's hands. She was surprised but watched as he thumbed through it and then stopped on a particular page. Holding it open, Gary handed it toward her. "See there? The Vigenère cipher."

Kailey leaned in toward the page. The mass of letters and numbers looked familiar in their format, if not the actual letters and numbers. She frowned. "What is it?"

Gary pointed a stubby finger at the page heading. "It's a specific type of cipher the Confederates used during the war to get messages out without anyone knowin' how to crack 'em. See?" He sidled up beside her. In spite of the strong smell of cigarettes, Kailey didn't move away. She followed Gary's pointer finger.

"These sequences of letters all match up to a key. If you have the key, you can crack the code. Called a 'polyalphabetic substitution.'"

"You lost me," Kailey admitted.

"Okay." Gary motioned for her to follow him behind the counter to a table just beyond it. "Sit down."

Kailey did.

Gary reached for a pad of paper. "See, you need a keyword or phrase, and then the codes are based on the number shift. So, the alphabet gets written out but keeps getting shifted spaces until you have a table. Then you have a secret keyword. The keyword matches up to the actual message, and then based on the letter shift, you have your code."

At Kailey's blank face, Gary chuckled. "The crux of it is that you need to find the keyword. Then most likely you can just punch it into Google and some sixteen-year-old punk kid with a brain for analysis will have written a decoder script and you can just decrypt it in seconds. Whatever code you find. That's always been my gut. If there *were* a cipher hidden out there at the manor, it'd be Vigenère."

Kailey drew back. "Just like that?"

"Well, it wasn't just like that back in 1864. They didn't have computers. Nope." Gary grabbed the book and turned a few pages to show a black-and-white picture with an inset disk in it. "This is a

Confederate Secret Service disk. See? They could decode messages out on the field, as long as they knew the key."

"So, unless I know the key, it'll be impossible to decode?" Kailey ventured, the sinking feeling growing stronger the more lost she became in the mathematics of code breaking.

Gary pushed back in his chair and reached into his chest pocket, drawing out a pack of cigarettes. "Ehhhhh, yep, unless you're good at that sort of thing. But there's an easy fix."

"Pay someone smart to decode it?" Kailey asked.

Gary gave a guffaw of laughter and slapped his thigh. "Oh man, you crack me up. Heck no. History books, lady, history books. We got them now, you know?" He smiled at her as if waiting for her *aha* moment. When it didn't come, Gary leaned forward and rested his elbows on the table, looking steadily into her eyes. "History already cracked the code and told us the most popular keywords used by the Confederates."

"Oh?" Kailey looked down at the book in front of her as if it would spit the keyword out right then and there.

"Manchester Bluff."

"Where?"

"Not where, *what*." Gary slapped his hand on the table, causing Kailey to jump.

"Huh?" she blurted out, nervous.

Gary leaned even closer, his voice dropping. "Manchester Bluff. *That's* the common keyword for cracking a Confederate Vigenère cipher. They were known for making their universal key 'Manchester Bluff.'"

"Why Manchester Bluff?" Kailey inquired.

"Heck if I know," Gary concluded.

37

ADRIA

"Heart failure." The doctor addressed them all in the front room. Mrs. St. John's dead body lay upstairs in her room.

"She's gettin' stiff already," Lula whispered to Adria under her breath. Adria shot her a warning look.

"Pity," the doctor said as he gripped his bag. "But I doubt had I come any sooner that I could have saved her."

"What caused the heart failure?" Mr. Crayne asked. Adria was very aware that he avoided her gaze. Avoided her.

"We wouldn't know. She may just have had a bad heart, as simple as that."

"I can take you back into town," Diggery offered.

The doctor accepted.

Diggery slipped out the door before any more questions could be posed. The doctor followed, offering a slight bow and some muttering about an undertaker. Once he'd left the room, Adria sensed all strength leaving her knees. She plopped onto a chair, thankful it was right there, and grasped its arms.

Mrs. St. John was dead. *Dead.*

"What do we do now?" Lula stated the very question racing through Adria's mind. Her father would be notified by—well, by someone. Or would he? Perhaps with Mrs. St. John's passing, she was momentarily free of him.

"I sent out a pile of letters," Lula said. "Mrs. St. John gave me strict instructions that in case she ever died, I was to send them out. Don't know who all to, but I saw your father's name, miss, and the name of that congressman what lives in Lansing."

The sinking feeling hit her in the pit of her stomach. So, her father would know soon. Know that Mrs. St. John was dead, that Adria had obviously not acquired what he believed to be his, and that she was now residing very much alone with a recovering drunken recluse, an orphan, and an old man who technically lived in the back shed, not the house.

"You can't stay here, miss," Lula added. "It's a scandal and a half, you being a lone woman."

"There's no one to care," Mr. Crayne interjected sharply, but his demeanor didn't seem to match. He stared out the window, his shoulders rigid.

"I can't go home," Adria was brave enough to announce. "I-I won't go home."

"Well, not tonight, of course not." Lula shook her head.

"No." Adria pushed up from the chair and addressed both Lula and Mr. Crayne. "I cannot go home. You both know why. I've told you, Mr. Crayne, and you"—she directed her ire at Lula—"already snooped and read the letter from my sister. I won't end up in an institution. I refuse."

Mr. Crayne started to clap lazily, yet he didn't tear his gaze from the view outside the front room's window. "Bravo, Alexandria. Now what, pray tell, will you do when the new owners of Foxglove Manor arrive?"

"New owners!" Lula shrieked. "Aren't you the owner?" She gaped at Mr. Crayne, who finally leveled a black look on the girl.

"Why would you assume such a thing?"

"Because—because—I thought that—"

"Even the St. Johns don't own this place, contrary to what Mrs.

St. John was led to believe." He finally turned. With a dark glare, he pointed at Lula. "You. Go. Clean Mrs. St. John as best as you can."

"I can't touch no dead body!" Lula wailed.

"You can, and you will. It will be hours before the undertaker is here."

"But—"

"Go." Mr. Crayne's tone brooked no argument.

The young woman shot Adria a desperate glance, but Adria couldn't respond. She was immobile with her own desperation. As much as she disliked Mrs. St. John, there had been an element of momentary security under her care that wouldn't be afforded now.

She squeaked as Mr. Crayne approached her. "You and I, we must work hastily." His voice had dropped to just above a whisper.

"Pardon me?" Adria drew back. She eyed him warily. "I can't trust you. I can't trust Diggery. Any one of you, really." She was rambling, fear lacing her words.

Mr. Crayne snapped his fingers. "Shush, Alexandria. I know this is all very startling, but you have to trust me."

"Trust you?" Adria scowled. "Trust you? After you smuggle men into the house and then they vanish into thin air? What is going on here at Foxglove that you won't tell me?"

He ignored her question. "It won't be long. Both of our freedoms are threatened. We must fight for them."

"I must fight for my freedom from my father. Now more than ever. I can't be drawn into all this . . . I need to go." Panic welled in her.

Mr. Crayne gripped her shoulders. She tried to wrench herself free, but he held her there, firmly but without inflicting pain. "You're already drawn into this."

"How?" Adria didn't know what he meant, where the pressing timetable came from, and who threatened them.

"Your father's gold. *The* gold. Foxglove hides it, *I* hide it."

"You?" Betrayal knifed through her all over again. He knew? Where her father's stolen gold was hidden?

Mr. Crayne drew back, his eyes holding steady with hers. "I'm the guardian of Foxglove's treasure. Foxglove is the gateway for much secrecy, and men still believe the war can be resurrected. But you and I? We need to escape from this."

"No. Not together," Adria argued weakly.

He drilled her with his dark eyes. "We said we would save each other. God knows we need to."

"You're saying God has placed us together. You a-a drunken Confederate smuggler, and me an unwanted nobody looking for her father's gold?"

"As ludicrous as that sounds?" Mr. Crayne gave a blunt nod. "Yes."

She noticed now that his hands shook on her shoulders. His body quivered. Sweat trailed down the length of his sideburns. There was no smell of liquor on his breath.

"Trust me, Alexandra," he whispered.

"What do we do?" She entertained the notion, allowing her heart to feel what her mind told her to defend against.

"We find the gold."

Adria stumbled behind him as he half dragged her up the stairs toward the turret room. "Mr. Crayne!" she whimpered at his hold.

"Phineas!" he barked over his shoulder.

They reached the top of the stairs and within seconds were in his room. He shut the door and latched it. It seemed she was his prisoner now. The circumstances were changing so swiftly, Adria felt as though she were spinning. Or maybe she was. She lowered herself onto his bed and watched him as he stalked across the room. Uncorking a decanter, he tipped it so the golden liquid fell into the tumbler.

"Mr. Crayne."

He ignored her and set the decanter down.

"Phineas," she stated.

He stopped. Stared at her with wide eyes and then smiled a bit. "It's tea, my dear. I've substituted my preference with tea for some time now, and it's blasted loathsome and utterly miserable."

Her voice squeaked in shock. "How?"

"I may be a stupid man to have stayed in this godforsaken place all these years, but I'm no fool, Alexandria. A man doesn't keep his wits about him stumbling around imbibing on whiskey. That night on the cliff, with you . . . well, you provided me with motivation."

"But I still saw you drink it—smelled it on your breath."

"For all that's holy, woman, I'm not a saint. God knows I've even had the cold sweats. Then Lula kept returning to my room with a full decanter of whiskey, and that was temptation too much at times. Poor girl never realized I'd pour it out later and replace it with tea—it grieved me. Still does. Someday, perhaps, someone will figure out a more civilized way to help a man break free from the demon liquor. Until then, it's sheer self-control and an act of God."

Adria's eyes widened.

"Although stumbling into you when I was, shall we say, tipsy?" Mr. Crayne's eyes twinkled. "That was enough to lend itself toward sobering and helped provide me with motivation."

Adria blushed and looked away. She didn't *want* to like him. She didn't trust him, she reminded herself.

"Now." He approached her and sat down next to her, the bed sagging from both of their weight. He offered her the tumbler. She shook her head. She'd no desire to drink whiskey, or tea, or anything else for that matter. He took a sip and grew serious once again. "There is the matter of our freedom. The gold. My position here at Foxglove is threatened already, which means so is my life. It's been twenty years, and while I've done my due diligence and offered safeguarding for the place and compliance as the Society of the Confederacy smuggles what they will through this house, there's not much left I can do to protect my family—if they're even still alive. And I fear the Society is catching wind that my allegiances are no more for the dead Confederacy than they are for the secret society they still espouse will one day overthrow the government and its good men. My allegiances have only always been toward my own survival and that of my family."

"B-but why must we find the gold?" she dared to question. "Outside of my father, what good will it do? Shouldn't we just *leave*?"

"We can't just *leave* or I would have years ago," he mused. "No. We need collateral against them or they'll come after us."

"How is gold collateral? Wouldn't it be further reason to chase you—us?" she corrected. Adria knew she probably sounded quite addlepated, but all she could do was stare at Mr. Crayne, who sat beside her, his shoulder rubbing against hers, and question everything she had ever known to be true.

"We wouldn't *keep* the gold, my dear, tempting though that would be. It would be evidence against them. Evidence the Society is still alive, the Confederacy still runs thick underground. Those men the other night? They smuggle through here occasionally on their way to Canada. During the war, they recruited men there to fight against the Union. Now the Society continues to try to build up support. If we can supply trustworthy men in leadership with evidence the Society exists, then it may spare us another war— that might be extreme—or perhaps spare us another assassination attempt."

"Evidence?" Adria felt like a colorful parrot she'd once seen in a zoo. She reached for the tumbler, and he relinquished it to her. She took a sip. Tea. Yes, it was tea indeed, although right now she considered wishing that it *was* whiskey.

"Dr. Miranda was the previous guardian of Foxglove Manor. But when Lucy died—well, I arrived shortly after and he had already taken up and left Foxglove Manor."

"And Mr. St. John had taken his place?" Adria inquired.

"Mmmm, not yet. It was empty. They housed me here, in the turret room, and I was directed to stay with Diggery and maintain the place until someone more capable could be had. Mr. St. John eventually came, quite upset and not at all willingly. He owed them—money, a lot of it—for whatever reason, I've no idea. Regardless, they required under threat that I stay on to fulfill my debt to them for being freed from prison and to keep an eye on Mr. St. John. They didn't trust his loyalty."

"It sounds messy," Adria observed. She handed the tumbler back to Mr. Crayne.

"Quite messy, and not always logical, I might add." Mr. Crayne nodded. "Until you arrived. Then I was forced to admit it."

"Admit what?" Adria finally looked at him and wished she hadn't. His blue gaze dove into hers, meshed, and refused to release her.

"That I had cheated myself out of life. As you said"—he lifted his hand and trailed fingers down her cheek—"it's all quite complicated."

"But I still don't understand. Why not just leave? Leave it all behind now? I realize you wish to expose them, and that is noble, yes, but—" Adria shivered.

"Do you remember the night I pulled you back from the cliff?" His fingers continued their path down her neck.

"Yes." Adria could barely catch her breath, let alone understand anything he was telling her.

Mr. Crayne leaned forward, removing his fingers and replacing them at the base of her neck with the warmth of his lips. "We said we would fight together. We're two wretches in need of saving, yes?"

"Yes." Adria's eyes closed.

His lips found her jaw. "I daresay, God brought you here to bring life and renewed hope and dignity into my soul. That you revived in me the will to fight again. I was defeated before you came. The night you burst into my room, I had consumed so much whiskey, even *I* considered death to be a reprieve. Broken people, Adria, have little motivation to better themselves. And if they do, they struggle to find the strength."

"You've—you've considered death before?" Adria's eyes flew open and she drew back.

Mr. Crayne offered her a resigned smile. "Your plight is not unique to you, dear one. It is an ugly one, when the darkness drags you into the depths."

She nodded. She understood. She knew all too well what he spoke of. "But isn't it God who is supposed to save us? Not ourselves?"

"He cannot use another to breathe life back into one's heart?" Mr. Crayne asked, but he was looking at her lips as though he wanted to taste them. He was a man of multiple concentrations and it unnerved her. She could only focus on one. He lifted his eyes and suddenly switched topics.

"Keep in mind, my dear, that if we are to manage this, we must do so quickly. And quietly. There is a small opening in my fireplace. We can sneak through the hatch, and the chute takes us down to the cellar. There's a tunnel there—where we smuggle out men. We can take the gold with us and leave through that route."

Adria was stunned into silence.

Mr. Crayne continued in a hushed voice. "Dr. Miranda's daughter, Lucy, contracted smallpox from some of the prisoners whose escape was manufactured from the camp on Lake Erie. They were smuggled here—much like myself, as well as the men last night. By ship, to the lake caves, under cover of darkness. We've moved as many enemies of the Union through Foxglove Manor as we have gold. Diggery has been deeply immersed in the Society, though he passes blame on to Mr. St. John or Dr. Miranda. He'll pretend he cares for the Union, but he's the worst of the lot. You cannot trust him, Alexandria. The other night is proof of his intentions. And you'll never see the men from that night again. Mrs. St. John led them to the cellar quite efficiently. She was a begrudging accessory to her husband's indebtedness."

"Mrs. St. John!" Adria launched to her feet, suddenly remembering the woman lay dead one floor below them.

"Shush, Alexandria." Mr. Crayne stood and turned her toward him. His expression was now very serious, all playful flirtation and physical affection gone from him. His eyes narrowed. "The point is, after Lucy died, Dr. Miranda went out of his mind. He secreted away any of the gold being kept or moved through Foxglove, and he hid it. He embedded a cipher into Foxglove that tells where he hid the gold, and he created a map of sorts to find that cipher. Layered clues, my dear, in order to protect what he'd siphoned from the Society in vengeance for their bringing smallpox to his daughter. Revenge at its sweetest for Dr. Miranda. The only sweetness he could potentially take from Lucy's death. Your father believes St. John had a part in it. He has no idea he merely scratches the surface."

"Who leads this society?"

Mr. Crayne drew a deep sigh through his nose. "I don't know, Alexandria. I've not been able to untangle it. It is all shrouded in secrecy and immensely frustrating. What I am certain of, however, is that they're moving to clean house at Foxglove. I won't be a part of this any longer, nor will I be wrapped up in the lot of them should they be caught and charged. It would be treason. Besides, they'll do what they must to protect the Society. I don't believe Mrs. St. John suddenly experienced apoplexy and died."

"The other time . . ." Adria breathed.

"Yes. She *was* choked by someone before—and now she suddenly begins to experience hallucinations of her dead daughter and chest pains?"

"Do you think she was . . . ?" Adria couldn't say the words.

Mr. Crayne pulled her toward him, and she didn't struggle against his hold. He was, after all, the only potential safety in a place that danced with darkness. "We're all in danger," he mumbled into her hair. "Which is why we must find the gold and be rid of this place once and for all."

38

KAILEY

The Vigenère cipher. It sounded like something from a movie. A spy movie. Maybe a James Bond or a *Mission Impossible* movie. Kailey gripped her steering wheel with her hands at ten and two, even though typically she used only one hand. There was an intensity in her now. She needed to get back to Foxglove Manor. Needed to unravel the code they'd found so far and see if they could figure out what might be missing and still hidden in the walls and mantels of Foxglove. Apparently, if Manchester Bluff truly was the common key used by the Confederacy, then it would serve to crack the code. She'd already Googled on her phone, and sure enough, Gary was right. There was an easy "enter your key, enter your code" form that would auto-interpret. She didn't even have to figure out the math of it. Praise God or they'd be doomed.

Trees flew by on either side. Her clock read 3:20, so she knew Axel would probably be frigid by the time she returned. Preparing herself for a lecture, Kailey reached for the radio dial for some sort of calming distraction.

She saw the deer in the road the second she lifted her head. Ramming her foot against the brake pedal, Kailey braced herself to jolt forward at the resistance. But she didn't. Instead, the brake pedal hit the carpeted floor. She pumped it. Over and over and—the awful sound of crunching metal was met with the impact of the deer as its body was catapulted onto the hood of the car. Its antlers cracked into the windshield, and the airbag deployed, knocking the wind from Kailey as her body flew into it with force. Kailey could feel the car spin out of control, until another massive thrust sent her sideways into the window of the driver's door.

Dazed, Kailey could hear her own breath in her ears. The dinging of her car, like she'd opened the car door and left the keys in the ignition. She tried to push away the airbag, but her arm connected with something thin and hard that had poked into the bag, deflating much of it already. Antlers. Clawing at the bag, Kailey could hear herself crying as she saw the vacant eyes of the deer, his antlers busted through the windshield. Much farther and she might have been skewered alive. Kailey looked to the passenger side and noted the tree and the branches pushing through broken windows. She wiped at water that dripped down her face and then looked at her hand. Blood.

Her phone. Where was her phone? Kailey spotted it on the floor by her foot. She was able to reach for it, ignoring the sharp pain in her left side. When her hand wrapped around it, Kailey checked for service. There was a signal. She called Foxglove Manor's landline.

"Where the heck are you?" Axel wasted no time answering the phone.

Bewildered, Kailey fumbled for an explanation. "I left a voice-mail."

Silence. Then, "I didn't get it."

"Axel?"

"Yeah?" He still sounded perturbed.

"Um . . ." Kailey winced as a throbbing ache pounded in her head. "I hit a deer."

"Are you okay?"

"I-I don't think . . . well, I'm not dead."

A short laugh void of humor. "Great. Call 911, hon, okay?"

"Hon?" She winced again, feeling another trickle of blood down her cheek.

"I'll call. Never mind. Hang tight. I'm on my way."

Axel disconnected the call. There was only one main highway to town, so at least she wouldn't be hard to find, out here, mashed against the trees in the woods, staring into the dead eyes of a rather monstrous deer.

~~~~~

"Brake line was cut right through."

Kailey heard Axel's quiet announcement, along with the steady beeping of the hospital's heart monitor. "I'm awake and I can hear you," she said a bit crankily.

"Well, praise the Lord!" Teri exclaimed from beside Axel. They both stood over her bed with anxious expressions.

"What did you say, my brake line was cut?" Kailey ignored their obvious concern as she lifted her hand to feel the side of her head. A bandage met her fingertips. "Where's Jude?"

"Jude is safe with Tracee back at the manor. Careful." Axel reached out and pushed her hand away gently. "You just got seven stitches there."

"Am I going to need plastic surgery?" she joked.

"No. They had the plastic surgeon do the stitching," Teri supplied. Then added, "I requested him."

"Thanks." Kailey had been kidding. Now she was more aware of the potential seriousness of her injuries. "Am I okay?" She looked at Axel.

He nodded. "Bruised and scratched. The worst was the laceration on the right side of your head just above your ear. They think the antler grazed you."

"Gored by a deer. I always wanted a creative way to die." Kailey closed her eyes against the pain in her head. "Tell me I at least have a concussion."

Teri's laugh hurt to listen to. "Miraculously no, ma'am. You'll be released, and Tracee and I will take care of you back at Foxglove."

"And the deer is dead?" She couldn't help but ask.

"Very." Axel nodded. He stepped aside as another woman joined them. Her hair was pulled back into a ponytail. She had blond wisps floating around and framing her face and massive blue eyes. Kailey glanced between her and Axel and was stunned by the sudden flood of jealousy that shot through her as fast as adrenaline.

The woman ignored Axel and focused on Kailey. "Miss Gibson, I'm Detective Finnegan."

Detective? Oh. Cut brake line. Kailey tried to collect her thoughts. At least it wasn't that male detective who had first told them about Riley. The one who flirted with Teri. This woman seemed more focused by the way her facial expressions didn't waver from seriousness.

"Can I ask you a few questions?" Detective Finnegan asked politely.

Still, maybe the other guy would have been better. This detective was prettier—obviously—and young. Lithe. Fit. Gosh, Kailey almost felt chunky lying in the bed. What if Axel noticed the attractive detective? What if—?

"Hey. Hon." Axel's hand was on hers.

"When did you ever start calling me that?" She was irritable. Could feel it in every inch of her body. She jerked her hand away from Axel at the same time Kailey wanted to launch herself into him and be held. Just be held.

Detective Finnegan shot Axel a look and then smiled at Kailey. "It's okay. I know you're wiped out and shook up. I just wanted to know if you saw anyone around your vehicle today?"

Kailey shook her head. "No."

"Did you have a run-in with anyone today or recently? Someone who may want to hurt you?"

Kailey searched her memory. "Outside of my kidnappers, I can't think of anyone."

"Your kidnappers?" Detective Finnegan couldn't have disguised the shrill lift of her tone if she'd wanted to. Surprise was etched on her face. Kailey felt a little bit bad. She couldn't reason through her words. Even her thoughts. It was all murky.

"Manchester Bluff," she said. Gosh, she sounded almost drunk.

"What's that, Miss Gibson?"

Kailey waved weakly at the detective. "No, not you. Axel. Manchester Bluff. You can look it up online."

Teri stepped up. "Umm, I don't think Kailey is ready for questions right now."

"I see. That's quite all right." Detective Finnegan moved to leave, and Axel followed.

Well, that wouldn't do.

"Axel!" Kailey half shouted, even though it made her head pound. The room spun. He didn't return. "Hey! *Hon!*" she shouted.

Axel retreated a few steps and leaned over her. There was a twinkle in his eye but a very distinct firmness in his voice. "Rest, Kailey."

"I'm hon, remember?" she insisted. Gosh, had they given her drugs? "*I'm* your hon. Not her—not that blond chick. Me."

"Yes." Axel's smile seemed lopsided to her. Was he laughing? He was laughing. No, he was serious. He was talking to Detective Finnegan. Something about her being taken when she was little. Riley. Riley Bascom. Foxglove Manor.

She met Teri's concerned expression. "I'm his hon," she repeated. "You tell that pretty cop to back off."

Teri bit her bottom lip. "Yes, Kailey. I will."

"Okay." Kailey felt satisfied at Teri's confirmation. Gosh, sleep would feel good right now. It was sure nice not to be gored by that deer.

Foxglove Manor had never been friendly at nighttime, even in the best of nights when she didn't see ghosts. Now, Kailey was propped up with pillows in a dimly lit room, with the shutters wide open expressing a very blue-black view of the lake. She half expected to see the ghost girl. Lucy. But she didn't. Her mind felt fuzzy, her head throbbing. The gash with stitches both burned and ached simultaneously. Jude wasn't on the air mattress. How anyone had convinced him to sleep elsewhere without an ensuing anxiety attack was beyond her. Somehow she had a feeling Axel was behind it.

Kailey squinted at the clock, willing her eyes to clear enough to read the hands. She couldn't see her phone anywhere, which would have been easier.

One in the morning.

Lovely.

The time Lucy started wandering halls, beckoning someone to hide her, and doing that horror movie thing where she hollowed out her eyes and acted more poltergeist than wandering soul.

"Kailey?"

"Gah!" Kailey jumped and yelped, then squeezed her eyes shut against the pain pounding in her head.

Teri padded into the room. She wore beige moccasins with her scrubs so her footsteps didn't disturb sleeping residents. Her dark hair was pinned back on the sides, and she held a small paper medicine cup in her hand.

"How're you feeling?" Teri set the little cup on the bedside table.

"Like I got hit by a deer," Kailey retorted.

Teri set about checking her vitals. Her fingers were gentle and soft as they searched for Kailey's pulse on her wrist. She looked directly into Kailey's eyes when she talked. "I was planning to wake you. I didn't want you to fall too deeply asleep, just in case."

Kailey closed her eyes and smiled. "I woke up on my own. I was half expecting Lucy Miranda to walk through the door."

Teri laughed quietly. "I'm not a ghost. Sorry to disappoint." She held a stethoscope to Kailey's chest.

"Have you ever seen her?" Kailey couldn't help but inquire.

Teri frowned in denial. "No. No, I've walked these halls so many times at night, and not even a shadow. Unless—" she paused and gave Kailey a stern look—"you count Poe. He darted out in front of me the other night on his way to the litter box from Raymond's room. Flash of furry white and I just about peed myself."

Kailey half laughed, half choked at Teri's bluntness. "Sorry about that."

"It's okay." Teri hung the stethoscope around her neck. "That cat has brought Raymond some much-needed comfort. He's spent too many hours worshiping Maddie from afar. I doubt Maddie has a clue Raymond is totally in love with her."

"Do you find it weird?"

"Find what weird?" Teri ran a thermometer across Kailey's forehead.

"Raymond and Maddie. I mean, romance when you're in your eighties . . . why bother?" She didn't mean it to sound so harsh. She tried to soften it with an explanation. "I mean, you're going to die in less than twenty years—at least the odds are high." Somehow that didn't help her sound more sensitive. "Why risk the loss, the ache, the grief for such a short span?"

Teri straightened the blankets around Kailey's feet. "I don't know. Aren't we supposed to live every moment we can to its fullest?"

"What does that even mean?" Kailey asked before she could bite back her words.

Teri's eyes grew soft, and her hand stilled on the blankets. "I think it gives us purpose. To invest in something—someone. We all need someone."

"Do you believe God gives us purpose?"

Teri lifted her shoulders. "Sure? Maybe for some? I think love is purpose enough, don't you?"

Kailey wanted to say yes. Wanted to say that love was the answer to everything. But love died. She knew that firsthand. It also failed. Miserably. She'd no doubt her parents loved her, but had they been adequate parents? Hardly. And Jude. He'd loved to the best of his ability, but that had been thwarted by his disability and . . .

Kailey turned her head away from Teri. She really didn't want the nurse to see the tear that ran down her cheek and wet the pillowcase. How could life have purpose when it was filled with tragedy? Selfish greed that chased down little girls, haunted old homes, and kept life in a chaotic toss and turn? How could life have purpose when you loved only to die, or to break apart, or to . . . Didn't love have a deeper, longer-lasting purpose? Because circumstances didn't necessarily lend themselves very well to love being the all-consuming resolution to life.

"You're thinking way too deep for someone who just sidestepped a head concussion." Teri held out the paper medicine cup. "Take this. Rest. It'll all look better in the morning."

Kailey obliged and took a proffered sip of water to wash down the pill. "I hope so," she muttered, feeling more like a little kid than Teri's adult equal.

Teri patted her shoulder and flicked out the bedside lamp.

"Get some rest."

Kailey heard her feet pad softly out of the room. The door closed. For a moment, Kailey was certain she could see a girl in white, staring at her from the corner. But when she blinked, the girl had disappeared. In her place was a vacancy that was more lonely and more desperate than had Lucy stayed to stare at her with hollow eyes.

39

"I'm not an invalid." Kailey argued the fact that Axel was following her around like a puppy at her heels.

Maddie tapped her fingers on the arm of her wheelchair as they crossed in front of her to sit down. She eyed them both, a tad suspicious, Kailey thought. But then, after that last lucid grin from Maddie, she'd suddenly acquired a nervous energy around the older woman. She couldn't pinpoint why.

"He doesn't want you to keel over." Raymond spoke up from his seat in the corner of the front sitting room. A television in the corner was broadcasting home improvement shows, and Stella and Judy huddled around it even though the volume was high enough to raise the roof. Jude was at the table, a stack of books in front of him. She was relieved to see him in one contented piece.

"I'm not going to keel over." Kailey didn't actually believe her declaration. The accident the day before had left her with a continuous pounding headache, and she wasn't about to admit it out loud, but even her heart this morning would race erratically, then slow, and then give the sensation it was going to pound out of her chest.

Axel pushed a chair into the back of Kailey's legs, forcing her to sit. She didn't argue, though she shot him a perturbed look. She leaned forward, resting her elbows on the buttery softness of her lounge leggings that had tiger faces on them and garish green diamonds.

"Those are lovely." Maddie smiled—a different sort from the other day—and reached out to tap Kailey's leg.

Kailey drew back.

Axel frowned, noticing her withdrawal.

Maddie didn't seem to pay attention. She smiled, increasing the lines around her lips. "My Jim—my son, you know?—he used to love tigers." Maddie tugged on the stuffed animal tucked between her thigh and her chair. She pulled out a raggedy stuffed tiger that was probably older than Moses. "See? This used to be Jim's. He called it Malicious."

"Malicious?" That was it. Maddie was becoming downright creepy.

The old woman stroked the furry forehead of the stuffed tiger. Her eyes appeared unfocused for a moment and then she smiled absently. "Yes. He said Malicious used to talk to him. Tell him things—"

"Maddie," Raymond interrupted, and his wrinkled face was scrunched in concern.

Axel held up a hand to stop him. "What sort of things?"

Maddie continued to pet the stuffed animal. "Ohhh, old stories. About war and gold."

Kailey and Axel exchanged looks.

The TV blared an advertisement for a miracle mattress destined to change the way you sleep.

"Which war?" Axel prodded.

Maddie pulled back as if it was shocking Axel had to ask. "The Civil War. Don't you know that's what he loves? History."

"But—" Raymond was obviously going to argue the nonexistence of Maddie's son.

"Maddie," Axel interrupted and leaned forward. He rested his hands atop the elderly woman's, commanding her attention. "Did Jim write things in your notebook? Codes?" Finally, Axel had broached the topic—the reason why they'd circled around Maddie to begin with. They needed to uncover why she had scribblings similar to what Jude had. How they were both so tied together.

Maddie looked perplexed. She furrowed her brow, and her fingers grew more assertive as they dug into the stuffed tiger. "I don't know what you mean."

"Your notebook," Kailey inserted, scooting forward in her chair. "It has a string of letters and numbers written in it. *Gnqgy*—"

"Stop!" Maddie's testy response caused them all to jump a little. "Don't." She jerked her hands out from under Axel's, clawed at the tiger, and pulled him to her chest. Her expression was intent. Stern. A warning. "You will not ask me anymore. You all know I'm losing my memories. How dare you monopolize on that."

Axel touched her knee. "No, Maddie, we're not. I promise."

"Then what are you doing?"

"We're just asking if you know how the code got in your notebook?" Kailey tried to appease Maddie, whose eyes snapped in irritation. "The day I saw them, you told me *she* had told you about them."

Maddie stiffened and stared down her nose at Kailey. "Fishing. You're fishing."

"Well, we're—"

"Stop tippy-toein'!" Raymond burst out, drawing all the attention except for Stella and Judy, who were arguing over why the interior designers on the television show should have chosen eggplant green instead of meringue for the ultra-mod bathroom reno. Even Jude looked up, startled.

Raymond ignored them. He tossed his arms in the air, sending Poe flying from his lap. "Just ask the woman what you want to know and don't insult her intelligence."

Kailey swallowed her surprise at Raymond's uncustomary outburst.

Maddie seemed rather self-satisfied that Raymond had risen to her defense.

Axel, per usual, rose to the occasion like a gentleman. He dipped his head in acknowledgment. "You're right. Maddie, we're sorry. To be frank, we wanted to ask you about the code that Kailey saw in your notebook a while back."

"Why?" was Maddie's clipped response.

Kailey opted to follow Axel's lead with blunt honesty. "Because my brother and I stayed here at Foxglove Manor when I was little. After we left, he kept writing line after line of almost similar letters and numbers."

"And?" Raymond groused.

Kailey shot him a look. "And Jude also would keep writing the word *death*."

"Death." Maddie grew even more agitated, picking at the stuffed tiger's ear. Her eyes widened, latching on to Kailey. "Did *she* tell you that? Death? If she did . . . then she's *not* okay."

Kailey shook her head. "No one told me that. Jude would just write it."

Maddie shifted her attention to her hands and the tiger. "Death," she muttered. "Death is a part of Foxglove, you know?" She lifted her eyes. "Jim said so."

"I'm so confused," Kailey whispered from the corner of her mouth to Axel.

"So is she," he mumbled back. "Maddie"—his tone was firm—"who gave you the notebook?"

"My notebook?"

"Yes."

"I don't know. It was in my room. I just—use it."

Axel nodded. "And when you say 'she,' who are you talking about?"

"Lucy. Lucy Miranda." Maddie was very confident in her answer.

"When do you talk to Lucy?" Axel placed his hand on Kailey's knee. A cue to not interrupt. She listened to his silent gesture.

Maddie looked desperately at Raymond. The man gave her an encouraging smile. She looked back to Axel. "Sometimes, at night, I-I see her."

"And Jim. Do you see Jim too?" Axel's question made Kailey look at him sharply. Jim wasn't real—was he?

Maddie nodded. "Yes." There was an inflection of hope in her voice. Relief that someone seemed to believe her. "Yes, I see Jim too. He comes more often than Lucy. He is so interested in the war. You know. The Union has never been the same since."

"What does Jim look like?" Axel was grave when he asked, calm and steadying, but with a tension in his shoulders that Kailey could see in his posture.

Maddie's mouth turned up in the corner. She shifted her eyes to Kailey. There was a flicker in them, then a shadow, then her breath caught for a moment, and Maddie seemed to wince in pain before she stopped. Drew a deep breath. "Jim looks like him."

"Who?" Axel pressed.

"The dead man. See? Foxglove is all about death. Lucy said so. She warns us, you know. Jim does too. They're both proof."

"The dead man?" Raymond didn't seem to be able to bite his tongue any further.

"Mr. Bascom," Maddie stated simply, directing her answer toward him. "Mr. Bascom is dead, isn't he? He used to be my son. Before he was dead. Who killed him?" She swung her head to Axel, tears forming in her eyes. "Who killed my son?"

~

Kailey charged from the room. The minute her feet hit the hallway, she was scanning it for Teri. Axel chased after her.

"Hold up, Kailey!"

She swung around. "Mr. Bascom, Riley's dad, was Jim? Maddie's *son*? How did no one know this? I need to ask Teri. She's the director, for Pete's sake."

Axel snagged her hand, linking his fingers with hers. Kailey looked down at their hands. Her skin burned from his touch. Warmth crept up her arm into her cheeks. Axel stepped closer. He surveyed the hallway before leaning toward her. His lips touched her ear.

"Think about this for a second. We've been told Maddie's son was a figment of her imagination. But she's seen him, and she sees the ghost girl. Something's off, Kailey."

"Right." Kailey nodded vehemently. "It's why we need to ask Teri."

"No." Axel tugged her closer. She could tell he wasn't trying to be romantic but was definitely using their closeness as a ploy should someone come upon them. "No. At this point, we need to just work together. If Mr. Bascom—Jim—was Maddie's son, and Riley is her granddaughter, why the secrecy? Who's hiding it?"

"Jason? Riley's uncle?" Kailey closed her eyes to avoid looking into Axel's.

"Maybe. Or Teri."

"Teri?" Kailey drew back. "That makes no sense."

"No. But we also need to seriously consider these ghost-girl sightings. Maddie has seen her. *You've* seen her."

"So?"

"So, do you believe in ghosts?" Axel's question was direct and one that Kailey had never truly come to terms with.

"My mother saw Lucy," Kailey acknowledged.

"Okay. Do you think Lucy is real?"

"She's been dead since the Civil War." Kailey noted Axel's fingers tightening around hers.

"Right."

"What are you trying to say?" Kailey tilted her head. She could see Axel's mind was brewing on an idea. He reached up with his free hand and rubbed his beard. His blue eyes pierced hers.

"I find it strange everyone who sees Lucy has medical issues."

"My mom was bipolar," Kailey stated point-blank.

"She was a drug user," Axel added.

317

Okay. There was that. "I'm not ill." Kailey could play a mean devil's advocate when it was necessary.

"You have been. The headaches. Nausea."

"Chest pains . . ." Kailey nodded.

"Sure. Wait. What?"

"It's stress, Axel. I've struggled with symptoms like this for years."

"Is it stress? Maybe before, but now?"

"Look at what we're dredging up." Kailey yanked her hand from his. "I'm reliving my nightmare, Axel, so of course my stress is through the roof."

"Enough to see hallucinations? Practically sleepwalk off a cliff and end up with hypothermia in the water?"

Kailey stilled. "Is that really what you think happened to me?"

Axel heaved a sigh. "I don't know. I really don't. But what else explains it? Not to mention, we *know* someone cut your brake line. Detective Finnegan was here this morning and they're definitely keeping an investigation open. Neither you nor Maddie have been—well, in a consistent frame of mind. Heck, you were kidnapped and so was Riley. Her dad is dead. Your parents are dead. Jude and Maddie both have parts of an old code we've yet to sit down and decipher, and we know—we *know*—something is still going on here at Foxglove Manor."

"So, let's ask Teri about Jim and then decode what we have and find the stupid legendary treasure and put a stop to it all!" Kailey half shouted. If she hadn't been stressed before, her anxiety was growing by the minute. Kailey reached up to make a pretense of itching her eyes, but it was really to swipe moisture that pinpricked the backs of her eyelids. "I didn't deserve any of this," she whispered.

Axel stepped toward her. "No. But it's our reality."

"Our?" Kailey couldn't help the vulnerable look she gave him. Searching his face, his eyes, his body language.

Axel reached out and ran a finger down her nose. "You are my *hon*, right?" A lopsided smile followed.

Kailey snorted, then half sobbed, then nodded. "Sure. Whatever that means."

"It means you're not alone."

Kailey swallowed the lump in her throat and pressed her lips together. She nodded again. "Okay. That's an awful nickname, by the way."

"Okay, hon." Axel reached out. This time Kailey took his hand.

40

ADRIA

She slipped her arms into her cloak, pulling its hood up over her hair. Adria lifted her sister's letter from her bureau, staring at it for a long moment. Freedom. Escape. It was within reach—wasn't it? She knew, after tonight, if all went as planned, she would have no more contact with her sister or her father. She didn't mourn that, but she did fight reservations of another sort. Placing her life in the hands of Mr. Crayne—a recovering drunk—was perhaps as foolhardy as continuing to pursue her father's missing gold.

"We don't know who we can trust at this time." Mr. Crayne's instruction came back to her. "Too many know of Foxglove and the lake caves. There could be anyone slipping in without my being aware now. Head to your room. Get a warm cloak but leave the rest of your things. Meet me in the study—Mr. St. John's. There's a book there—"

"I've seen it," Adria had interrupted. Mr. Crayne gave her a surprised look. "*Uncle Tom's Cabin*. It has some letters in the front. The title is crossed out."

Mr. Crayne's expression had leveled. He'd given her a short nod. "We need to take that with us."

"Why?"

He didn't answer her, and she'd let it go.

Adria now stared at her reflection in the mirror. She controlled her breaths, even as her image peered back from the mirror. Did she have the strength to do this? Her insides churned. With indecision and the knowledge that regardless of whether she wanted to be, she was enveloped in it all. Mrs. St. John was dead. She herself had not felt well, and though she'd not communicated it to Mr. Crayne, Adria feared that her symptoms might point to something more serious. The dizziness. Her heart pounding. Even the sightings of Lucy Miranda. Could they be hallucinations? The meandering of her subconscious coming to life under the influence of something or *someone* else?

Blast it all. She could ponder that later. Adria left her reflection behind and slipped from her bedroom. It was night, the house eerily silent. Lula had long since retired, still huffing from having to tend to Mrs. St. John's "corpse," as she'd put it. Barring an unexpected intruder, the house would be free for Adria to roam. Stepping down the stairs, she eyed the dark corners, thankful that, for now, she wasn't seeing Lucy. Although perhaps Lucy would lead her to the treasure if she only asked? But hallucinations, or visions, or whatever she was, weren't known for interacting with the living beyond haunting them with the unexplainable.

The study door squeaked as she opened it, and Adria glanced over her shoulder at the empty foyer. The dark paneled walls, the potted ferns in the corner, even the hall tree all created shadows and images that appeared to be living. Just as she'd expected, Mr. St. John's study was empty. Hurrying to the desk, Adria fumbled through the stack of books until she recovered *Uncle Tom's Cabin*. A long look at the sabers gave Adria the fleeting image of their coming undone from the wall, falling, and a gruesome beheading following. It would be sheer irony to die by the end of a Confederate saber. A sense of urgency overwhelmed her as she waited for Mr. Crayne. The darkness was closing in with suffocating force. Why meet here and not back in his room in the turret? There was the passage there, in his fireplace. What purpose did it serve to wait here for him when—

"What're you doing?"

Adria squealed, clutching the book to her chest, the hood of her cloak falling around her shoulders as she whirled toward the voice.

Lula stood in the doorway. She lofted a candle, the light casting unlikely elements of omen about the room. Her hair hung about her shoulders, the hem of her plain cotton nightgown brushing her feet. For a moment, Adria thought Lula appeared to be an older version of Lucy.

Adria searched for an answer, anything that would be a passable explanation to the girl.

Lula stepped into the room. "Are you going somewhere?" She took in Adria's cloak, her shoes, and the book. She felt like a thief, with Lula the authorities.

"N-no," Adria stuttered. "I was—just wandering. I couldn't sleep."

"Wandering in shoes and a cloak?" Lula took another step, her petite frame hesitant. "Are you grieving Mrs. St. John? God rest her soul."

"No," Adria responded. "Yes. I mean, it is a pity she passed."

Lula shared a sympathetic smile. "Mm-hmm. At least you weren't told to dress the corpse in her Sunday best. Alone. Did you know her eyes were still open?"

Adria blanched.

Lula walked to the desk and set the candle on it. "Eyes were open like she wanted to scold me the entire time I dressed her." A little laugh. "Poor old soul. Got her comeuppance in the end, I suppose."

"Lula!" Adria drew back. There was an unexpected edge to Lula's voice.

"It's all right, miss. They're closed now."

They both examined the other. Adria hesitant about what to do next. If Mr. Crayne entered now . . .

"So, what *are* you doing?" Lula asked again.

When Adria didn't answer, Lula crossed her arms over her chest and tipped her head to the side. A small smile touched her lips. "You really are in a spot of trouble, aren't you? What with your sister and father wanting to institutionalize you. And Mr. Crayne making your heart patter at the same time the man can barely stay out of his cups." She padded toward Adria, her bare feet making no sound on the floor. "When I was headed to a future in the poorhouse, I never imagined you would be in the tea leaves for the future of Foxglove Manor."

Adria slipped the book from her chest and stuffed it into the pocket of her cloak. Lula's eyes followed her hand's motion.

"So you found it, eh?"

"Found what?" Adria feigned ignorance.

Lula pointed at the mantel. "I found that a couple of years ago. When they sent me here to live with Mrs. St. John, I proved I'm quite good at things."

Adria could feel her expression fall as small pieces of truth began to seep in. Sent here? "Mrs. St. John took you in."

"Sure she did." Lula gave her a patronizing nod. "And then she balked at everything. Bitter at Mr. St. John for putting her in this predicament. Of course, losing her daughter didn't help her state of being, if you know what I mean."

"Did her daughter die—?" Adria bit off her words.

Lula raised her brows. "Natural? Did Theodora die natural? Sure she did. Just as Mrs. St. John said. Her pet fox tripped her." Lula giggled. "Ain't that funny? Theodora had a pet fox while her father was off and away at Foxglove Manor. Coincidence is no stranger, if you know what I mean."

"Lula?" Adria was starting to put her own theory into place. It wasn't one she invited, as a chill made the bumps rise on her arms.

"What is it, miss?"

"Who tried to strangle Mrs. St. John?"

Lula's hand flew to her chest in a mocking fashion and she gasped. "Why would you think I know that?"

Adria narrowed her eyes. "Be truthful with me, Lula."

Lula glowered at her and then sniffed. "Fine. 'Twas one of the men. They'd snuck in after you were abed. Diggery and I helped— Mr. Crayne wasn't in the know. Mrs. St. John was certain it was business as usual. I suppose Mr. Crayne has told you all that. Men sneakin' in and sneakin' out by way of the basement?"

Adria gave a curt nod.

Lula smiled thinly. "I figured as much. You've wrapped Mr. Crayne around your finger from the first night you stumbled into his room. God knows, I think the man has coveted you from that very moment. It's enough to make me nauseated, but then I ain't much for roses and lusty things, if you understand what I mean?"

"Why did they try to strangle Mrs. St. John?" Adria ignored Lula's coarse insinuation, determined to gain as much info as the nosy little maid knew.

Lula gave a satisfied laugh. "Truly? You have to ask? Mrs. St. John didn't know her place. She kept threatening or making demands and she needed to be gone. When they couldn't do it"— Lula's grin was smug—"I did. Showed all those men how it's done."

Adria reached for the mantel to steady herself. Lula's admission, by this point, was not a complete surprise. But— "You're a child," Adria couldn't help but exclaim.

Lula raised herself straighter. "I'm on my way to bein' a woman. Not much younger than you."

"H-how?" It was the only word Adria could get out.

"Brilliant mind, that's how," Lula stated. "You know that foxglove flowers are quite poisonous?"

Adria shook her head. Wordless.

"Well, they are. Slip them into a drink, crumble them into your soup, all sorts of ways to feed them to you," Lula went on. She walked past Adria and looked out the window toward the lake. "If you give it to someone long enough and strong enough, their heart will just give up. Pitter-patter and then stop. Like a spinning penny. And before that? You get the shakes and the sweats, you're dizzy, and, funny thing I didn't expect, you start seein' things! Mrs. St. John saw Theodora, and you? You see Lucy herself. Poor dead girl. She's so dead, she couldn't haunt this place if the devil himself wanted her to."

"Me?" Adria knew then. It was clear. Admittedly it wasn't something she welcomed, yet Lula's vicious nature was coming out, even though, in the darkness, she still appeared quite innocent, dumb even. "You've been poisoning me?" Adria repeated, sounding a bit dumb herself, she observed.

Lula laughed and turned away from the lake to face Adria once again. "Yeah, well, you're a bit tougher to off than Mrs. St. John. 'Course with Mr. Crayne ever in the way. But he's the real befuddler. I keep givin' him his whiskey, but it's as though the man could dine on a meal of foxglove and not be affected."

The whiskey. Tea. Lula didn't know that Mr. Crayne had been seeking to become sober. The idea that if he hadn't, he too would be on the same road toward death, was startling.

Lula covered the space between them in a swift motion. Adria pressed against the fireplace. Lula slipped her hand into Adria's pocket and tugged out the book. She looked down at it, then back at Adria. "Mr. Crayne, delusional drunk that he is, thinks he's still the guardian of Foxglove Manor. But he's bein' replaced. There's just one small important detail left—'course, if he ain't going to lose his senses or get more tipsy . . . I've been tryin' ever so hard."

"One small detail? Who will guard Foxglove Manor now?" Adria breathed. Scared of the answer. Frightened of the girl. Searching her senses for a feasible plan of escape.

"Who?" Lula patted Adria on the cheek. "Me. I will. I earned it, haven't I? And now I'll just prove my point. I've got the book, but I just don't know what I'm s'posed to do with it." She wagged it in Adria's face. "Still, I'll help the Society find the gold Dr. Miranda so spitefully hid from us, and then you and Mr. Crayne can . . ." Lula chuckled low in her throat. "Well, I'll leave it up to them what's done with you then. I guess you've been spared a full-on foxglove poisonin', although I can't say what's comin' will be any nicer."

41

KAILEY

They spread the book out on the table. Axel read off the circled letters.

Parlor. Study Fireplace Mantel. Hallway. Stairwell.

Now they followed Jude into each room. Waiting. Letting his eyes search for patterns that the average eye was oblivious to. Kailey tried—so did Axel—but there was nothing out of the ordinary with the structure, the molding, the wallpaper, or the . . .

"Kay-Kay!" Jude clapped and smiled. It was becoming less of an anxiety and more of a game to him now. He was heard and he knew it. He raced across the room and tapped the window. Some garbling noises encouraged Kailey and Axel to stare at the window and then compare it to the others.

"I see absolutely nothing." Axel's elbows jutted out as he perched his hands at his waist.

Kailey squinted. It was like trying to solve one of those things on social media that had something random hidden in a picture filled with a gazillion other pictures.

"Uh!" Jude grunted and slapped the window. His index finger tapped a windowpane.

"Wait. Hold up." Axel stepped back a few paces. Understanding dawned on his face. "That's genius."

"What?" Kailey still didn't see what her brother had so easily identified.

"The corners of the windows. There's trim. See? Like lattice in each corner. Only this window . . ." Axel hurried to the window Jude had identified and pointed to its upper right-hand corner. "The lattice makes an *X*."

Kailey sucked in a breath. "So how on earth, if we couldn't see that, would someone else know to look for it? What was Dr. Miranda even hoping for if someone did find his map to the cipher?"

"I think that's our answer." Axel reached to give Jude a congratulatory pat on the shoulder, but he stopped just before his hand connected. Withdrawing, he gave Jude a big smile instead. "People have been looking for this for decades. A century. It takes some wicked observation. I'd bet most people even looked for hidden things like paper or clues in books, something like that. Not in the actual manor itself. Mr. Bascom was on to something. He'd figured that part out, and that's what he and Riley were looking for. Her article mentioned that they were searching for codes in the house itself, right?"

Kailey pursed her lips in realization and nodded. "Yeah. She did."

"So, back when you and Jude were kids, whoever took you somehow knew that Jude had stumbled on some of the cipher. Since then, no one has found any more."

"But Maddie's notebook?" she argued.

Axel grimaced. "Yeah. That I don't get yet."

For the next few hours, they worked with Jude and inspected the rooms the old book steered them toward. More of the letters were found in the woodwork, in the railing at the main stairs, and even carefully inserted into a portion of a stained-glass window. When they were finished with the corresponding rooms from the book and had put the letters in the order in which they'd been found, including the ones Jude already scribbled so often, Kailey practically knew them by memory, the cipher was clear. Maybe not interpreted, but it was clear.

Gnqgy xzx jfw. 12 qlwjx. 10 rerv ksog.

———✢———

Kailey pounded the sequence into the form online that would supposedly interpret it at the click of the submit button.

"That's all we have," Axel said.

Kailey glanced at the book. "And you're sure there's no more rooms we missed?"

"Yep."

"Okay." Kailey typed Manchester Bluff into the key field and paused, her finger hovering over the button.

"Do it." Axel's encouragement fed into her anticipation.

Kailey hit the button. In an instant, words formed in the answer key.

Under the fox. 12 paces. 10 feet down.

Kailey couldn't help the disappointment that flooded her. "That means squat to me. Does it mean anything to you?"

"Not a thing." Axel slumped in his chair.

A creak sounded in the hall outside the study where they sat surrounded by linen-covered furniture and discarded items. They both waited, listening, but no more sound came.

Kailey thought through her conversation with Gary after she'd left the Bascom house. Anything that might trigger a direction in which to move. She snapped her fingers. "Just a second! Gary gave me a brochure about a museum a few hours south of here. He said it's the home of a banker who used to be a part of the Confederate movement. He helped siphon funds through his home and to the lake through a series of underground tunnels. The mansion is actually on Lake Michigan."

Axel nodded patiently. "And this applies how?"

"Well, I'm just thinking . . . tunnels. We know there's one secret tunnel already, in the turret room. What if there are more? Under Foxglove Manor? That would technically be 'under the fox.'" Kailey stood, sliding her laptop away from her. "Let me run to my car and grab the brochure. I'd look it up online, but I can't remember the name of it. It had pictures of the tunnel entrance in that house. Maybe it'll help give us an idea of where to look."

"Go for it."

Kailey moved around Axel, and as she hurried to the door, Axel reached out and snagged the hem of her shirt. He tugged her back before Kailey could prepare herself mentally or emotionally, and his arm slid around her waist as he pulled her against his seated form.

"What are you doing?" His grip was delicious and disturbing simultaneously. Kailey looked down at him over her shoulder.

Axel grinned up at her.

Gosh, she could swim in his eyes.

"You're kind of cute when you're on a mission."

Kailey squirmed. "I'm this close, Axel, *this* close to figuring this out and putting definition into everything that's happened to me, to Jude. Even to Riley."

"And if we actually *find* Confederate gold?"

"I don't care about the gold," Kailey protested. "It'll be proof, though, proof that someone *does*. It'll be something we can take to the police. To your blond detective girl."

His eyes narrowed. "You're jealous."

"Not . . ." she started to say, squirming again as his arm around her waist tightened. "Not in the slightest." She attempted to pry his hand from her side.

"Just be careful, okay?" He leaned into her.

"I'm just going to my car." Kailey dismissed his worry, while inside her stomach flipped as she remembered. Remembered walking alone on the sidewalk. The van. The arms dragging her into the vehicle.

"Want me to come too?" Axel offered.

"Do you really think it's that dangerous to walk outside? I mean . . ."

The phone on the table vibrated. "Bad timing." He reached for it, muttering his surprise it even had enough signal for a call to come through. "I better take this. It's the police." He spoke into the nape of her neck, her hair moving with his breath. "Just be aware. Until we figure this out. Okay?"

"You're being a bit overbearing," Kailey mumbled.

The phone continued to vibrate in his hand. Axel was bold and nuzzled her neck with his nose. "Raymond has emboldened me to stake claim on my woman—*not* Detective Finnegan, I might add."

Kailey pushed herself off his lap and spun around. With an impulsive move, she dipped and planted a kiss on his cheek. "You're a caveman."

He laughed as he answered the phone.

———

Kailey ducked under a branch that overhung the walkway to the gravel drive. Her car was parked facing the lake, its front end still a smashed mess from the accident, the windshield shattered and busted inward. The towing company had brought it here instead of a garage at the request of her insurance company. They wanted to send out an assessor. Kailey wondered if they'd taken into account how far north the poor person would have to come and that someone could assess the car by emailing a picture.

The wind had picked up, and Kailey hunched her shoulders against it as she hoped she could find the brochure where she'd tucked it between the passenger seat and the middle console. Tugging at the passenger door, it gave with a creak and she bent inside, feeling with her hand.

"Bingo," Kailey declared. She pulled out of the car and pushed the door shut. Turning, she almost collided with Tracee. "Whoa! I didn't know you were there!" she laughed.

Tracee smiled, her bag slung over her shoulder and her hands in her pockets. "Didn't mean to scare you."

"I'm naturally jumpy. Especially now." Kailey excused her reaction with the truth.

Tracee nodded, then swung her bag off her shoulder. "Hey, I wanted to show you something."

"Sure." Kailey waited as Tracee dug around in the blue-denim bag. As she waited, a slow unease began to build. Axel's warning echoed in her ear, and her instinctive signal for danger heightened.

Tracee pulled her hand out, and Kailey jumped back. Tracee frowned. "You okay?"

Kailey waited. "Yeah."

Tracee handed her a green hardcover book, its edges worn and unraveling.

"What's this?" Kailey reached for it cautiously.

Tracee shrugged. "I honestly don't know. But . . . well, I know you all were looking for codes and the legendary treasure." Tracee waggled her eyebrows, and her voice held a singsongy tone. "Anyway, when I was in Maddie's room, I found that."

Kailey flipped open the book. A photograph fell out. It was an older picture, but it was obviously Maddie at a younger age—perhaps her sixties—and a young man.

"That's Mr. Bascom—Riley's dad. But he's with Maddie." Concern reflected on Tracee's face. "I was going to ask Teri, but she's been preoccupied with the board trying to restructure now that Mr. Bascom is gone."

"So, you brought it to me?" Kailey was still trying to assess Tracee's motive.

Tracee nodded innocently. "Yeah." She didn't offer more explanation.

"Tracee, what are you trying to say?"

Tracee crossed her arms and looked toward the lake for a long moment. Her chest rose and fell, and finally she met Kailey's eyes. "You know it sucks that I really actually *like* you."

"Huh?" Kailey edged away from Tracee. Her imagination was on overdrive. So was her sense of caution.

Tracee pressed her lips together tightly before speaking. "You know when you ended up in the lake with hypothermia?"

"Yes?" Kailey answered cautiously.

"You saw things, didn't you? Like hallucinations? Maybe the ghost of Lucy?"

Kailey's hand tightened around the now-unimportant brochure.

"It's a symptom of poisoning." Tracee gave a weird laugh, one that sounded both regretful and resigned. "I'm surprised Teri didn't figure it out. Even when I gave her the meds to give you after the accident."

"Poisoning?" Kailey held her hands up as if to ward off Tracee. "You know, if you want to talk, let's go inside." She moved to slip around Tracee, but the nurse stepped back and in her way.

Tracee gave her a sad smile. "Look in the book. On the inside page."

Kailey did. She expected to see another line of the same mysterious cipher code. Instead, her heart stilled for a moment, and she read before lifting her eyes to Tracee.

"'Dr. Miranda, ca. 1864. Phineas Crayne, ca. 1885. Lula B., ca. 1915 . . .'" Then a few more lines of names and dates continually progressing to the present until finally, "'Jim B., ca. 1991. Tracee B., ca. 2018'?"

Tracee seemed to be waiting for Kailey to say more. To connect the dots. But Kailey's heart was in her throat.

"Tracee . . . I don't understand." Kailey tried frantically to put the pieces together.

Tracee tapped the book. "Kailey, it's a journal. We've been keeping records for years. Decades. A century. And see? There?" She put her index finger on one more line on the inner page, written in a script and ink. Guardians of Foxglove Manor.

Kailey looked up. "Please tell me that—"

Tracee's smile was hardly apologetic. "We've been missing one crucial thing as guardians. The full cipher. Once we know the cipher, we would know what the original guardians knew. Where the gold is."

"What are you talking about?" Kailey eyed the manor. Eyed the front door, wishing Axel would come and check on her.

Tracee didn't notice Kailey's shifting gaze. "The guardian of Foxglove Manor was entrusted with guarding the manor's treasure. The map to finding the cipher was in that stupid book. But, God knows, even you had the book, the ciphers were impossible to find! You'd have to know what to look for. Ever since my great-great-grandmother Lula, it's eluded the guardians. And then . . . my uncle Jim. When you were here as a kid, he found out your brother was a genius. Being the landlord, he stopped in to chat with your parents and saw Jude writing some cipher. Cipher we'd spent decades trying to find! And Jude didn't even have the book with the clues to which rooms the ciphers were hidden in!"

It was starting to dawn on Kailey. Slowly. The pieces falling into place. "And then my mom had her breakdown . . ."

Tracee gave a short nod. "Now you're getting it. Uncle Jim was going to befriend them, ask about Jude. But your mom flipped out—about Lucy, about everything, and the next day your family had up and left Foxglove." Tracee offered her a smile that was not genuine, nor was it apologetic. "When the Civil War gold disappeared, my family vowed to retrieve it. And we'll continue until we find it. Thanks to you and Axel, and especially Jude, we're very, very close. Finally."

"You don't know the cipher." Kailey bit her tongue, wishing she hadn't goaded the nurse.

Tracee laughed and rolled her eyes. "I know part of it. When you applied here, I helped persuade Teri you'd be a good hire. What luck! I mean, all these years and you show up again? When you arrived, it was a matter of hours before Jude was sketching. I saw part of the cipher and I knew what it was. I jotted it in Maddie's notebook so I wouldn't forget it. Figures you'd snoop there too, and that loony Maddie would write what I'd noted in her book over and over again, bringing attention to it."

"And you let us all think Maddie was losing her mind by making us all believe she didn't have a son named Jim?" It was all Kailey could do not to slap Tracee.

Tracee blew out a sigh that lifted tendrils of hair from her forehead. Her hazel eyes were glossy, bright, and very pleased with herself. "A little tampering with records, a little classic foxglove in her coffee, and anyone can be erased from an Alzheimer's patient's history to make them sound delusional. She and Jim had a falling out years ago. They barely talked, but he fulfilled his obligations by giving her a place to die in peace, not to mention a grandchild in his later years in life. Of course, Maddie doesn't even recognize Riley."

"But if Jim is your uncle, then Jason is too?" Kailey struggled to keep up.

Tracee's hand lifted from her bag, and in a swift movement Kailey felt a needle plunge into her neck. "Shh . . . it doesn't matter, does it?" Tracee pushed Kailey against the car, shushing her in her ear as she hoisted Kailey's weight up with her arms. "I really wish you weren't so persistent. I actually liked you. When my dad told me to get whatever I could out of you when you arrived, all I could think to do was the age-old proven method. Foxglove poisoning. Make you think you were losing your mind, or sick, and let us in on what Jude knew. But—well, you're tenacious."

"Tracee . . ." Kailey saw the lake going black.

Tracee clicked her tongue. "My dad has waited years for this. When Uncle Jim and Maddie had a falling out, Jim and my dad were on again, off again. It was a race, really. Which son could find it first."

"Your uncle Jim?" Kailey heard footsteps approaching at a rapid pace. She tried to speak, but her tongue felt thick. "Maddie is your grandmother?"

Tracee's smile was lopsided, and her face grew distorted as Kailey tried to focus. "Yeah, well, this place sort of runs in the family, but the gold? It belongs to the guardian, and Uncle Jim was wasting his role. That's why *my* dad tried so hard twenty years ago when Uncle Jim told him about Jude's ciphers. Took you, but you weren't any help. He even tried with your parents before they ran themselves off the road in a panic after he confronted them. They were drunk. It was an accident. My uncle? Not so much. He was going to report my dad once he found out about Riley."

Kailey's head tilted backward. Heavy. It felt so heavy. "Your dad kidnapped Riley?"

"Oh!" Tracee smiled as though welcoming someone at a party. "Kailey, this is my father."

Kailey looked up into the face of Jason Bascom just as the world went dark.

42

ADRIA

"Lula?" Mr. Crayne's voice broke through the study. A draft followed him. Cold air off the lake. He'd left the front door open.

Lula spun, her nightgown slapping at her legs. For a moment, she seemed nonplussed at what to do in the presence of Mr. Crayne, but then she smiled a toothy grin that Adria was quickly coming to despise.

"Ohhhhhh, Mr. Crayne. You knew you were goin' to be replaced, didn't you? Just didn't know it was me!"

His face darkened, his eyes deepened, and his voice lowered. "Lula, listen to me carefully."

"No!" Lula shook her head. "No. I'm done listenin'. The last few years, listenin' to Mrs. St. John nag about this and that, take a switch to me, moan on and on about every wrong her husband committed against her and precious Theodora. No. I'm done listenin'. I've earned my place here. As guardian."

"You're guarding nothing, Lula, nothing." Mr. Crayne stepped toward her. "This place? It's just a station stop for men's greed. They use you to be the face should it ever be discovered. You will take the fall. *I* would take the fall. Their intentions hurt others, their mission is misguided, and worse, it's reprehensible."

"You and your big fancy words." Lula flung her hand toward the door. "Up to the turret room with you. Have a drink. Waste away your life like you have since the day I met you."

Mr. Crayne surged forward and gripped Lula's wrists. "Hey!" Lula cried out, then whimpered as Mr. Crayne's hold tightened. He pulled her toward him and gave her a tiny shake.

"You're a naïve little girl, Lula. Think this through."

She wrestled against him, and her eyes widened. "They're comin', Mr. Crayne. Tonight. Diggery already lit the lanterns in the cave below. He'll be on the cliff's edge in no time, swinging the lamp. And you know what'll happen when they return. I already got my message to them through the last visitors the other night. They know."

"Know what?" Adria looked between Mr. Crayne and Lula.

Lula yanked against her captor's grip even as she laughed. "That Mr. Crayne is so besotted with you, he's going to get the gold and run away. Give me the cipher. I can figure it out for myself."

Mr. Crayne shot a glance at Adria before glowering down at the girl in his grip. "What makes you think I have the cipher?"

She laughed, a bit wildly. "Of *course* you have it! Or know where it's been hidden in this godforsaken place of death. Dr. Miranda entrusted it to you when he left, didn't he? You, the one prisoner that didn't contract the smallpox. You, the one who healed himself by drinking. The sad excuse of a guardian for Dr. Miranda. It's time you give back to the Society what the doctor hid away from us." She spit in Mr. Crayne's direction.

Mr. Crayne shoved Lula backward, and the girl stumbled, grabbing for the mantel. She stared at them and must have read the resolution on their faces.

"You're crazy, you know? If you take the gold, they'll hunt you down till your dyin' day. It doesn't belong to you."

"It never belonged to them," Mr. Crayne shot back. "It was stolen. Cursed. Spoils of war."

"Spoils of war mean it's free for the takin'." Lula ran her finger along the inside collar of her nightgown. "And I watched my ma and pa die with no money and me headin' to the poorhouse. No. No, I won't ever live like that again. I'll die here at Foxglove if I have to, but I'll have my share of the gold. One way or another."

Mr. Crayne backed away a step and tugged on Adria's hand. "Come," he urged, his voice lowering as if to block out Lula. "She's harmless for now."

Adria tugged on his grip. Incredulity filled her as Lula's words began to make sense. "You knew where the gold is? All this time?"

"Alexandria, trust me."

"But you knew?"

"Yes," Mr. Crayne spat, obviously irritated and anxious to finish their escape, especially in light of Lula's proclamation that the Society members were coming. Perhaps even now, Diggery was coming too. To stop them. The dear crochety old man—she couldn't even trust him.

"Why didn't you—?"

"'Cause he swore an oath to the doctor, didn't you?" Lula interrupted. "Guarding his treasure long after he left. The Society thinkin' you guarded the manor, but deep down you were loyal to the man who gave you a place after prison and who spat on the South by taking its own spoils."

"Alexandria." Mr. Crayne gave her as much attention as he could without completely taking his eyes off Lula. "Yes. Dr. Miranda showed me where he hid the cipher in this house. I know its secrets. I've lived his secrets. But that changes nothing. We must go. It's time to end this. All of it."

"But . . ." Adria knew he was right. He hadn't wronged her. Not really. Exposing that he knew where the cipher was and what it meant all along would have only placed her in more danger. The Society would have swooped down on her—on the Fontaines.

"Lula?" Adria hated the look on the girl's face. Smug but a bit frantic. She held the book, clutching it in her hands like the treasure map it was. But it was only one half. The cipher was still unknown to her.

"I need the cipher, Mr. Crayne." Lula hurried toward him, the girlish innocence back in her voice. Pleading. "I can't be a true guardian over Foxglove Manor if I don't know its secrets."

"Come." Mr. Crayne gave a final pull on Adria's hand, and this time she followed him.

"Mr. Crayne, please!" Lula begged after them.

Adria stole a glance over her shoulder as she followed him into the breath of cold lake air, which was saturating the manor as it blew in through the front doors. Lula stood by the mantel, running her hand over the scrollwork. There were a few tears on her face, and her eyes had dimmed.

"Please. I'll never be able to figure it out." Lula reached out a thin arm, *Uncle Tom's Cabin* extended in her grip.

Adria stopped, her halt making Mr. Crayne stumble.

"Alexandria," he warned.

"Please, miss." Lula allowed her lower lip to tremble. "Do it for me. Lula Bascom. I ain't got nothin', and you—you have everythin'."

Adria ducked her head and followed Mr. Crayne's forward motion, hurrying toward the open doors, toward the lake, and the sight of Diggery on the cliff's edge, his lantern waving back and forth.

KAILEY

Kailey's vision came into focus. Jason Bascom flicked a cigarette out of the window of the van as he sat across from her. There were no windows. It was carpeted with no seats. It was very *Criminal Minds*, minus the team from the BAU coming to rescue her. Her head pounded, a hangover from the accident and whatever drug

Tracee had fed her veins. But in the darkness, she began to recognize elements of his voice. Vague ones. Intonations and inflections.

"You abducted me when I was five, didn't you?" Asking the obvious would at least get him talking. Give her time to process it was happening all over again.

Jason leaned back against the inside wall of the van. His graying hair was ruffled, and he wasn't as put together as when she'd last seen him. Tracee was nowhere to be seen. "So you remember?"

"Now I do." Kailey winced as she pushed herself up. "What good does it do to take me again?"

"I need the cipher, Kailey."

Kailey hid her quivering hands under her thighs.

"It's legacy, Kailey." Jason shifted in his seat. "You wouldn't understand. What kind of legacy have you had? Addicts for parents, killing themselves in a drunk-driving accident."

"That you caused when you confronted them!" Kailey recalled Tracee's admission.

Something flickered over his face. "I didn't mean for that to happen."

"No. But it did." Kailey rubbed her eyes. "And what about your niece? Riley? Do you know how you've scarred her for life? Scarred me for life? Is she even alive?"

"Of course she is! I helped her and her mother move." He glared at her. "I'm not an animal."

"Really? You killed your own brother?"

Jason held up a hand. "Technically he killed himself."

"When you held a gun to his head and made him turn on the ignition and suck in carbon dioxide?"

Jason just gave her a blank look. One that indicated he wasn't about to confess the details of his sins. He kneeled and leaned toward her. "Look, give me the cipher. My family has searched for over a century for this gold, and that is too long to just sit back and throw our hands in the air and give up."

"Like your brother did?" Kailey accused.

"Jim was stupid," Jason snapped. "He did the same thing our grandparents and their parents did before them. Searched every room. Recruited his own kid to help like it was some fun treasure hunt. Here I was, older than him, wiser, but he never took me seriously. Ever. He told Mom years ago she'd raised a bad seed in me, and she told him to get out."

"Maddie." Kailey felt an ache in her chest. Did Maddie even remember it? The way she clung to the memory of Jim was unsettling, considering she'd never once mentioned Jason.

Jason's jaw worked back and forth. "Fact of the matter is I'd have taken your brother, but he couldn't put words together."

Kailey stiffened as fury rushed through her in defense of her brother.

"But Jim?" Jason continued. "He was all about Riley. Treasure hunting with his daughter, Riley. But what about Tracee? We've invested our lives into Foxglove Manor. My great-grandmother Lula started here way back at the turn of the century. She was an outcast. A single mother to my grandfather when she was only twenty. Nothing has ever been *easy* at Foxglove Manor."

"So, you finally confronted Jim?" Kailey concluded.

Jason raised his brows and held them there in a look of sheer attempt at innocence. "I gave him a chance. Told him if he didn't include Tracee and me in on this thing once and for all, there'd be more trouble for Riley. By this time you were here and Tracee had already found part of Jude's sketch. The cipher. It was proof it *did* exist. But now I needed that stupid book—*Uncle Tom's Cabin*—so we had the key where to look for the rest of the cipher. But no. Jim wouldn't cough it up, or how he even figured out it was part of the key."

"You threatened your own niece?" Kailey eyed the van door behind Jason. There was no way she could catapult herself forward and get it open to escape without him intervening. She was trapped.

Jason sniffed. "I wouldn't have carried through with it. I don't hurt kids. But I didn't expect Jim to kill himself. Take whatever he knew to the grave? It was spiteful. But then that's how Jim always was. Save his girl and spite me. It's lucky Mom isn't with it enough to figure out what happened."

Little did Jason know . . . Kailey could still hear Maddie asking who had killed her son. How did one say that the war over gold between brothers had claimed their lives? Figuratively and literally.

"So why take me again?" Kailey moved her foot out from under her leg. It was falling asleep and that wouldn't do if she did get a chance to run.

"You have it. The full cipher."

"I don't." Kailey shook her head. She wasn't going to admit she and Axel had just decoded it.

Jason launched himself across the van, his hands wrapping around Kailey's throat. She clawed at them to release, but his grip was iron-clad. She smelled cigarette on his breath. His eyes bulged with intensity. "Don't make me hurt you. What is the cipher?"

"Stop! Fine. I'll tell you!" Kailey gasped as he loosened his grip enough to answer. No gold was worth her life—Jude's life. This ridiculous quest for archaeological treasure had consumed the Bascom family for generations. She would not fall victim to its glow. Kailey rubbed her throat where Jason had choked her. "I'll tell you," she said again.

ADRIA

She hurtled after Mr. Crayne as he hurried her around the corner of the house. Stopping for a moment, he pushed Adria against its stone wall. He spoke low and desperately.

"I'm sorry I left you alone for even a moment. I wanted to gather supplies for our journey."

Adria offered a wobbly smile in the moonlight. "I thought we were escaping through the tunnel. In the cellar?"

"We are. But the gold isn't in the house." He gripped her hand and led her toward the back shed. "Under the fox. Twelve paces. Ten feet down."

"Under the fox?" Adria noticed as they passed by Diggery's cairns. She felt a momentary pang when she realized Diggery was engulfed in this too. The crochety old man who planted foxgloves beneath Mrs. St. John's window.

They reached the shed, where Mr. Crayne motioned for Adria to go around its corner. She obeyed, holding her breath. The lake was beginning to pick up in intensity. She could hear the waves crashing against the cliff. She could taste the cold, icy air on her tongue. Mr. Crayne appeared next to her, and in his hand was a shovel.

"Come."

It was apparent he truly did know where the gold was. His knowledge went beyond the clues to finding the cipher, and beyond the cipher itself. Adria trotted after him until they reached a more barren patch in the back yard. One she'd not seen before.

Adria stilled.

Diggery's fox sat in the middle of it. Staring at her. Unblinking.

Mr. Crayne ignored it and charged toward the barren spot, taking long strides. Twelve of them. He stopped and immediately dug the spade into the earth. The fox startled and slunk into the undergrowth.

"What are you doing?" Adria hissed as the wind picked up and whipped her cloak around her.

"It's here. Under the fox." Mr. Crayne dug again.

"But what about the tunnel, under Foxglove? That the men smuggle through?" Adria would have thought that was a logical place to look. In plain sight, really.

"No. It's here."

"In a patch of lawn?" Adria moved closer. She watched as Mr. Crayne moved dirt.

He waved her off. "Ten feet down."

"You'll never get there in time."

"It's mostly sand." He stabbed the ground with the shovel. "As long as I don't run into a maze of roots."

"But you can't possibly have picked here to dig because Diggery's fox was sitting here! There's no way Dr. Miranda could have foreseen that."

"No. Not that fox. *Her* fox."

"Whose fox?"

"Lucy's fox. Dr. Miranda had given her one for a pet. Just like Mr. St. John gave his daughter Theodora a fox. It's a secret sign for those who need to identify members of the Society. Pet foxes. It's unusual, but nothing anyone would particularly question beyond its mere oddity."

"And?" Adria watched as Mr. Crayne's shoulders flexed. The ground was soft like he'd stated, and he was able to move dirt quickly. He wasn't digging a large square. Just enough to uncover a chest, or a bag, or whatever the gold might be hidden in.

Mr. Crayne jammed his foot against the spade, cutting deeper into the earth. "He buried it out back. Her fox when it died. He made no secret he buried Lucy's fox here."

The hole had grown in width as well.

Now a small pile of bones came with dirt. The skull of a fox.

Adria shuddered and looked toward the lake as she waited. Minutes passed like hours and it was difficult to see, but she could make out the waving shafts of light from Diggery's lamp. "Hurry."

Mr. Crayne gave her a quick look. He increased his pace.

A few more shovelfuls and then there was a *thud.*

"You found it," Adria breathed.

Mr. Crayne dropped to his knees, then his stomach, leaning over into the hold. "Hold my feet," he commanded.

Adria bent, grabbing on to his ankles.

She could hear the breaking of wood as his fist pounded the box. It splintered.

Mr. Crayne cursed.

"Help me out." He spoke as loudly as he dared without drawing attention to their location.

Adria scooted forward and helped him by bracing his torso as he pushed away from the hole. Even in the night's soft glow, she could see how disturbed he was. His face was pale. Ethereal in the moonlight. His mouth was open a bit, his cheek twitching.

"Did you find it? Is the gold there?" Adria reached for him.

"No." He pushed away from her, landing on his backside. He raked his hands through his hair. When he looked at Adria, his blue eyes were wide and troubled. "There is no gold. He buried Lucy. It's Lucy, Adria. Lucy's bones and this."

Mr. Crayne had procured one gold coin that glistened in the light. On it, even in the darkness, Adria could see that Dr. Miranda had defaced its surface with something sharp. Carving into it one word that symbolized his treasure.

Lucy

43

KAILEY

The door to the van burst open. A bright shaft of light poured in, and Kailey saw the barrels of two guns aimed at the inside. At Jason Bascom.

"Jason Bascom?" a woman's voice commanded.

Jason lurched to the side, grabbing Kailey and holding her in front of him.

"Let her go." It was Detective Finnegan from the hospital. "Jason, it's over. Let Kailey go."

"Where's Tracee?" he demanded, his fingers digging into Kailey's arms.

"We apprehended her about fifteen minutes ago."

"How?" His voice cracked.

"A very concerned resident of Foxglove Manor reported seeing Tracee and you carrying Miss Gibson here to a van."

"Raymond?" Kailey knew it had to be the old codger whose protective instincts were as sharp as if he were thirty years old.

Detective Finnegan didn't answer her but continued to address Jason. Her partner held his gun steady, ready if needed. "Jason, it's over."

"No." He stated it plainly. "No. We have to find the gold. I've worked too hard. My entire life."

"Jason." Detective Finnegan slowly lowered her gun while her partner kept his where it was. "Listen to me. There is no gold. There hasn't been for years."

"What are you talking about? There's been a Bascom at Foxglove looking for it since before the turn of the century!"

"Yes." She nodded, holding out her palm. "And there's also been a Crayne in Harbor Towne carrying down the rest of the story. Only your family has always refused to believe it."

"What are you trying to say?" Jason spat. "Gary? Gary Crayne and his stupid lake-diving company? Knows more than I do?"

"He has a coin. It says *Lucy*." She holstered her gun. "It's a family heirloom. Proof the Craynes found the gold years ago—1885, Gary said. He said you knew this. He's told you for years to give it up. He told Jim too." The detective took a careful step up into the van.

Jason tightened his hold on Kailey.

The beautiful detective, whom Kailey was now completely happy to see, offered Jason Bascom a sad smile. "The Civil War gold has long since disappeared. What's left is legacy. Family. Loyalty. The choice between family or greed."

Jason dropped his arm. Kailey scurried past the detective. There was another cop who hurried her off to the side. In the background she heard Jason, his voice clear and strident.

"I swear to God I will find it."

She wondered if he'd ever think to ask what would happen to his daughter—to Tracee. But apparently, that didn't matter.

ADRIA

They had stumbled back into the house and down the basement stairs. Diggery had disappeared from the cliff, a promise that he was greeting whoever had arrived in their boat. Arrived to take care of

Mr. Crayne—to take care of her. She could hear Lula wailing from the second floor. A crazed sort of wail that chased Adria down the stairwell. The basement was dank and humid. Yet pushing aside some boxes made for easy access to a hole in the wall, boarded by a door made to look like a shelf. Mr. Crayne pushed it to the side. He turned and extended his hand.

"Alexandria, let's go."

"But they'll come after us! We don't have any gold to make a case against the Society!" she argued. "They'll believe we've made off with it!"

Mr. Crayne gave her a curt nod. "There's nothing to be done with that. They'll never accept the explanation that Dr. Miranda took it himself."

"Did he?" Adria urged her feet to move, passing by Mr. Crayne and entering the tunnel.

Mr. Crayne didn't pause but moved her forward by sheer force of his presence behind her. "Does it matter? He left one coin. There are no further ciphers. The gold is gone."

The tunnel seemed to go on indefinitely until they reached a dead end, with a ladder that ascended. Adria climbed up, her skirts getting caught under her feet. She reached the top, and Mr. Crayne straddled her from behind, balancing on the ladder as he lifted the trapdoor. It was the middle of the forest, but straight ahead, hidden in the darkness, was a small lean-to.

"Someone will have left a horse in expectation of the ship tonight." Mr. Crayne surged past her and into the darkness.

Adria heard a low whinny, and then Mr. Crayne appeared from the lean-to, leading the saddled animal. He extended his hand. "We'll ride. To Harbor Towne."

"But it's so close—to Foxglove. They'll find us by morning," Adria fretted.

"No, we'll have boarded the *Northeastern*. We'll follow the path they've established and head into Canada."

"Then what?" Adria could feel Mr. Crayne as he moved close to her, his hand holding the horse's reins. He leaned forward, once again speaking with his lips at her temple.

"Then we'll make a new plan. Now hurry."

KAILEY

She hadn't intended to collapse into Axel's arms, burrowing into his flannel shirt. But he was home. He was *her* home, and though it was unspoken, she knew he felt the growing depth between them. He buried his face in her neck.

"You scared about ten years off my life!"

"I'm sorry."

Axel pulled back but didn't release her. "When Raymond saw you and let me know—thank God I was already on the phone with Detective Finnegan."

Kailey mustered a wobbly smile. "I'm fine."

"Right. Sure." He pulled her close again, reassuring himself that she was telling the truth.

"Move over, boy. There are other men here who need a hug." Raymond pushed on Axel's arm. Kailey gave a watery laugh. Axel kept an arm around her shoulders as he turned to the older man.

"Yeah, yeah, you'll have your chance," Axel ribbed. "She's mine, though."

"Well, you ain't the one who was her hero. I saw Tracee and that daddy of hers." Raymond reached out with a stubby finger and tweaked Kailey's nose. "But I guess you'd rather have him over an old codger like me."

Kailey slid from Axel's embrace and moved into the homey arms of Raymond. He was soft and felt more fragile from age than she'd expected. But he smelled like Old Spice, and there was a grandfatherly warmth to him that just made him more endearing.

"Hey, hey, hey!" Axel tugged on Kailey playfully.

Raymond released her and winked. "Ehhh, okay. I'll collect a few more hugs later."

Kailey laughed then. She knew it was more of a joke. She didn't think Raymond was really much of a hugger, so she treasured the one she'd just received even as she returned willingly to Axel's arms.

She noticed Maddie when she looked over Axel's shoulder as he held her. Maddie sat in her chair, holding the stuffed tiger as well as her stuffed lion. Her smile was very aware, that same lucid smile that had touched her lips and unnerved Kailey the other day. It was then Kailey interpreted it. She knew. She knew Kailey would figure it out. Would discover the truth about Jim. It was as though, in Maddie's dissipating mind, Jason had been lost and only Jim remained in her heart. Did she even recall Tracee, her granddaughter? Her *nurse*? Or the motivation that had driven the Bascom family for years?

Kailey pulled away from Axel and moved to Maddie's side. She crouched in front of the lady in her wheelchair. "Your last name, it isn't Bascom, is it?"

Maddie smiled, and Kailey searched her eyes for lucidness. It was there, but also a fogginess seemed to drift over her face. She reached out and grasped Kailey's hand. "Jim is a Bascom."

"I know," Kailey nodded, sensing the others behind her, listening. "So is Jason."

"Jason?" Maddie quirked her lip. "Jason." She was trying to remember.

"Your eldest son," Kailey supplied.

Maddie offered a thin smile. She patted Kailey's hand. "I heard he's a rascal."

Whether Maddie was feigning remembrance or legitimately had distanced herself from Jason, Kailey couldn't tell. "And Tracee, your granddaughter."

"My nurse!" Maddie drew back, shaking her head. She wagged her finger under Kailey's nose. "Don't try to mess with me," she laughed as though Kailey was pulling a fast one. "My mind isn't loopy like a Tilt-A-Whirl all the time."

She really didn't register the relation to Tracee. Kailey could tell that Maddie was genuinely confused and genuinely convinced she was in full control of her memories.

"Why isn't your last name Bascom?" Kailey had to ask. Maddie stared back, this time her expression growing vacant. She increased the rapidity with which she stroked her stuffed animal.

Raymond cleared his throat. "I know the answer to that. And it ain't anything too marvelous, but she was and is an independent woman."

Kailey pushed to her feet, allowing Maddie her space. She turned to the others. Teri. Axel. Raymond. Even Stella and Judy were perched in their sofa chairs, eyes wide at the afternoon's events. But it was Jude that Kailey sought out. Jude.

He sat away from them all, his left hand scribbling rapidly in his sketchbook. The others moved aside as Kailey neared him.

"Buddy?" How did she communicate to him it was over? All of it. The answers to the cipher he'd identified years ago. The fear that gave him such anxiety. Their parents' death—he'd never even referred to it or given any sign to indicate how it had affected him.

Jude didn't respond to her, his pencil continuing to scratch lead onto the paper.

"Jude?" Kailey tried again.

His pencil stilled. His hand froze in its position. Without lifting his eyes, Jude brushed his hand over the sketch before he turned it.

Kailey sucked in a breath. Tears immediately threatened, with that burning sensation that made it almost impossible not to let them spill over. The image of their parents was bold. The lines that emphasized the familiar features were rows of tiny letters. She had to tell him. Somehow, she had to impress upon Jude that after all these years, the cipher was no longer important. He didn't need to associate it with the urgency of their mother's breakdown, with the word *death*, or with anything that caused him anxious fits.

"Jude—" She froze.

Jude's fingertips touched her face. They were warm. Unfamiliar. Tears slipped down her face, and her eyes slid shut. The touch was as impactful as an embrace.

"Kay-Kay." There was depth in her brother's gaze. A sort of release in his eyes. An understanding that came from the talent of his insight. Seeing things that others couldn't. Both inside and out. He lowered his hand and pointed to the lines.

This time, Kailey studied the letters. They were repetitive and tiny, but through her tears she saw them. Clearly. Not the cipher. Not the letters that had dogged them since their first visit to Foxglove Manor so many years ago. It was their parents' names. Over and over. Winding and swirling, creating patterns that grafted their profiles into a lovely remembrance of what could have been. A family. Parents who hadn't been haunted by the vices that sometimes came simply because they were human. Broken.

"La." Jude splayed his palm across their faces. He patted the paper gently. "La."

Love.

Kailey drew in a deep breath, not able to tear her gaze from the portrait her brother had sketched. How was it that he saw through the twisted nature of Foxglove Manor? To the elements of love that intertwined with greed, rebellion, and loss. What other secrets could Foxglove Manor hold? Old secrets, buried in the memories here that perhaps were brighter ones. Ones of people fighting for each other. Family. Maybe even hope shearing its way through the darkness.

Their parents hadn't been there—not really. They might have tried. That they'd brought Jude and Kailey here to Foxglove so long ago for that horrid family vacation was evidence they hadn't completely negated the concept of being a healthy family.

"La," Jude said again. He didn't touch her this time. He didn't have to.

She could feel him. Feel the legacy her parents had left behind in him. He had always been there. In the background. Protecting her. Guarding her. Jude was her guardian. The guardian of Kailey Gibson of Foxglove Manor. Protectors of family—those who treasured their own—they were the true heroes. Quiet and unsung, but never to be underestimated.

44

ADRIA

She stood on the cliff overlooking the lake, the waves rolling toward her, their whitecaps reminiscent of turbulent memories. It was a different cliff, this time. It was Canada. A strange country, a new life.

Mr. Crayne stepped beside her, his impressive form still dark and wary. His hair ruffled in the wind, and the lake stretched and circled around them like a haven that taught them new life. The prospect that maybe Foxglove Manor, its secrets, its wicked intents, would be more of a memory. One that they'd both bear the scars of, but no longer the festering wounds.

Adria looked back over the waters, roiling and slamming into the rocks with a persistence that would never cease. It was the same as the waves of melancholy that still afflicted her. She knew the same still tortured Mr. Crayne. Those days and nights they'd traveled into Canada, she'd seen firsthand the agony of a man without his drink. Even now, his hand tremored as his fingers brushed hers, their hands hanging by their sides as if they wanted to reach for each other but didn't dare. Didn't dare to hope that, somehow, new life really could be found.

"Have you ever considered how little strength we have when you stand by these lakes and feel the power in them?" Adria ventured.

Mr. Crayne didn't answer. The wind plastered his coat against his legs. A fine mist dotted their skin.

"Do you think we'll be safe?" Adria asked.

He smiled. "*Safe* is a relative word, my dear. Is one ever truly safe? From others? From one's self?"

"I don't find much hope in that," she admitted.

His chest rose and fell in a steadying breath. Mr. Crayne pulled the lone gold coin from his pocket. He fingered it for a long moment before responding. "I don't think we were meant to find hope in our circumstances. It's shifting, like the sand on the edge of the water. There's no solid ground there, only inconsistency and question."

"Then what do we do now?" Adria couldn't dispel the shiver that rolled through her. Here she was, beside this man who had been an enigma to her. Weak of spirit at times, and others, the epitome of a confident strength she couldn't understand.

Mr. Crayne's fingers brushed hers again. Her stomach curled as she sensed his smallest finger curl around hers. It was a subtle gesture, but the first time since they'd left Foxglove Manor that he'd reached out to feel her for her. Just her.

"We continue to move forward. That's all there is. That is what God asks of us, I think. To learn from the roads we have walked, and to keep walking them."

"But I get so tired . . ." Her voice trailed as she remembered the night on the edge of a different cliff, when all she'd wanted was to take wing and fly.

Mr. Crayne turned her toward him until they faced each other. He took hold of her chin between his fingers. "There is nothing wrong with being tired."

They were simple words. So simple. But, a lone tear traced down her cheek. There was freedom in the words. An acceptance that she didn't always need to be strong. That her weakness wasn't shameful, wasn't failure, but was part of just being alive.

Mr. Crayne pressed a long kiss to her forehead, then rested his nose against her temple. "Alexandria, we must learn from Lucy—

even if we're not under the poisonous influence of the foxglove. Because Lucy experienced the power of a father. The power that is love. Is purpose. She lived in the heart of her father, as you, my Alexandria, will live in mine. Our gold is not in a coin. Nor is our treasure in a grave, or omened by a ghost, or chased after like one chasing an elusive wind. Our gold is like the power of the lake, an undeniable force, which, long after we're gone, will continue to breathe across our children. We must make our choices wisely. We must build our weak lives on a foundation that does not shift. Like the rock on which we stand. On love. Love that is eternal."

"You won't leave me?" Adria whispered.

A low rumble of laughter was her answer. "I don't believe God ever intends me to be rid of you, my dear."

"Will we ever return?"

"To Foxglove Manor?" He lifted his brows. "Do you wish to?"

"No," was her immediate answer.

Mr. Crayne drew her close then, into his arms, resting his chin on the top of her head. "Maybe one day our children will. Or grandchildren. They can set to rights Lula or her family. Show them the gold is gone. The Society will be dissipated. The Confederacy will become a rotting memory, and our country will be unified. But"—he drew back, and Adria allowed herself to melt into his gaze—"until then, we will build a foundation for our legacy to stand on."

"How?" she asked softly.

Mr. Crayne—Phineas—tightened his hold. "By God's grace. Only by God's grace."

Adria let him hold her. Let the wind brush against her face. And then she closed her eyes and allowed herself to be carried away to freedom in the safe circle of the arms of Mr. Crayne and under the protective guardianship of a God who would create a foundation that didn't shift. A foundation of knowing that life was precious and fragile, but one could fly. One could soar, really. And soaring above the waves with hope was such a lovely thing.

QUESTIONS FOR DISCUSSION

1. Do you believe Kailey's motives in arriving at Foxglove Manor were purely to help Jude? Do you agree with her motives and the actions they led to?

2. Do you find Mrs. St. John's response to Adria's tentative emotional state understandable? What other responses might she have chosen?

3. The primary characters in this story struggle to cope with the trauma in their lives—that is, with the exception of Axel. What do you see in Axel's response to life that provided him with better coping skills?

4. Why do you think Adria's arrival inspired Mr. Crayne to begin the journey to heal from his alcoholism and to right the wrongs he was wallowing in?

5. What historical information did you learn about the Civil War as a result of reading this novel?

6. Once the treasure of Foxglove Manor was discovered, what message did it leave behind for Mr. Crayne and Adria, as well as for future generations?

8. What skills and abilities did Jude display that others didn't possess? What does that say to you about people with autism?

9. What faith takeaways did you find in this story, and how might they affect your outlook on trials in your own life journey?

ACKNOWLEDGMENTS

A massive thanks to my daughter, CoCo, who dreamed up this story with her love of Civil War history and missing Confederate gold. Hours of research done by my own ten-year-old girl in absorbing all the History Channel's episodes of *The Curse of Civil War Gold* led to sincere begging that we write our own treasure-hunting mystery. I hope I've done it justice, baby girl, and who knew the intense history surrounding the Great Lakes and all the many secrets still out there waiting to be solved?

Also, many thanks to my Sunday morning tribe, who let me ramble on about a book I needed to write that had treasure and Lake Superior in it. To Teri, who named Alexandria, and to Tracee, who has begged for some time now to be a villain in my book. You both earned your keep and your place in this novel. To Sara, Jolene, and Christina, for putting up with my conversations about poison, death, ghosts, and justifiable hallucinations.

There's always a litany of people who make these books possible. And, considering this one was written in the middle of a worldwide pandemic and 10- to 12-hour day-job workdays, I also need to thank: Cap'n Hook for holding down the bulk of life while I worked and then wrote and then worked some more. To my kiddos, CoCo and Peter Pan, for putting up with my absenteeism and checking in on me daily to make sure I hadn't succumbed to Covid-19. To my boss, Andy Kamla, for recognizing that working from home is truly an act of faith in a person's integrity, and for trusting that I did *not* spend the bulk of my quarantine writing this novel. Although, I will admit to many thanks for the generous allotment of vacation days that enabled it to actually be written!

To my intrepid publishing team: Raela, Luke, Amy, Noelle, Jenny, and all the others behind the scenes. To my agent-mama, Janet Grant, and the Books & Such Literary Agency. Your faith in my ability to write a story worthy of publication may be quite the risk, but thanks for taking it!

I must also herald Tracie Peterson, Becca Whitham, Kimberley Woodhouse, and Darcie Gudger for bringing Jude back to life to fulfill the most critical of roles in solving the mystery at Foxglove Manor. Originally, Jude was a memory in Kailey's heart. It was wonderful to make him so pivotal.

To my niece Kailey. I'll always see you as the little girl everyone thought was mine. My coffee buddy and my fellow mischief-maker (much to your mother's horror). Thanks for letting me use your name, even though I never asked.

Kara Peck. You all must thank Kara Peck. Otherwise the romance in this novel would be woefully worse than it already is.

To the Sisterchucks. All my love.

Finally, to those of you who have sat in dark moments and considered escaping life through one method or another. You have purpose. I promise. Your Creator designed you with a reason in mind. Though you may not see it now, understand it, or maybe even want it, the value that lays in your existence is beyond explanation. It is a treasure worth far more than gold. Press pause on the contemplation of escaping the darkness through any path other than racing toward your Creator. He's there. With purpose. He'll help you fly.

Jaime Jo Wright is a winner of the Christy, Daphne du Maurier, and INSPY Awards and is a Carol Award finalist. She's also the *Publishers Weekly* and ECPA bestselling author of three novellas. Jaime lives in Wisconsin with her cat named Foo; her husband, Cap'n Hook; and their littles, Peter Pan and CoCo. Visit her at www.jaimewrightbooks.com.

Sign Up for Jaime's Newsletter

Keep up to date with Jaime's news on book releases and events by signing up for her email list at jaimewrightbooks.com.

More from Jaime Jo Wright

In 1928, Bonaventure Circus outcast Pippa Ripley must decide if uncovering her roots is worth putting herself directly in the path of a killer preying on the troupe. Decades later, while determining if an old circus train depot will be torn down or preserved, Chandler Faulk is pulled into a story far darker and more haunting than she imagined.

The Haunting at Bonaventure Circus

◊ BETHANYHOUSE

 Stay up to date on your favorite books and authors with our free e-newsletters. Sign up today at bethanyhouse.com.

[f] facebook.com/bethanyhousepublishers @bethanyhousefiction

OB Free exclusive resources for your book group at bethanyhouseopenbook.com

You May Also Like . . .

Mystery begins to follow Aggie Dunkirk when she exhumes the past's secrets and uncovers a crime her eccentric grandmother has been obsessing over. Decades earlier, after discovering her sister's body in the attic, Imogene Grayson is determined to obtain justice. Two women, separated by time, vow to find answers . . . no matter the cost.

Echoes among the Stones by Jaime Jo Wright
jaimewrightbooks.com

A century apart, two women seek their mothers in Pleasant Valley, Wisconsin. In 1908, Thea's search leads her to an insane asylum with dark secrets. In modern-day Wisconsin, Heidi Lane answers the call of a mother battling dementia. Both confront the legendary curse of Misty Wayfair—and are entangled in a web of danger that entwines them across time.

The Curse of Misty Wayfair by Jaime Jo Wright
jaimewrightbooks.com

In 1929, a spark forms between Eliza, a talented watercolorist, and a young man whose family has a longstanding feud with hers over a missing treasure. Decades later, after inheriting Eliza's house and all its secrets from a mysterious patron, Lucy is determined to preserve the property, not only for history's sake, but also for her own.

Paint and Nectar by Ashley Clark
Heirloom Secrets
ashleyclarkbooks.com